"I'm almost   my wedding night," she whispered.

"No need to be."

He was right, of course. She didn't want to please him or hold his heart or care what he thought.

But as he pulled her away from the window and led her toward the bed, she didn't know if it would be possible to not let any of this matter. Her legs were trembling so badly she didn't think she'd have been able to climb onto the bed if he hadn't lifted her onto it. When she made a motion to scoot back, he halted her.

"Just stay there. Lie back."

"But—"

"Your rules. I'm not going to get into bed with you."

"Oh. I see." As she felt the slide of her hem up her calves, over her knees, she clutched the counterpane. She felt his fingers skimming along the inside of her thighs. Her breathing came in tiny gasps.

She sat up abruptly. "What are you doing?"

"I'm preparing you," he said quietly.

Romances by **Lorraine Heath**

WAKING UP WITH THE DUKE
PLEASURES OF A NOTORIOUS GENTLEMAN
PASSIONS OF A WICKED EARL
MIDNIGHT PLEASURES WITH A SCOUNDREL
SURRENDER TO THE DEVIL
BETWEEN THE DEVIL AND DESIRE
IN BED WITH THE DEVIL
JUST WICKED ENOUGH
A DUKE OF HER OWN
PROMISE ME FOREVER
A MATTER OF TEMPTATION
AS AN EARL DESIRES
AN INVITATION TO SEDUCTION
LOVE WITH A SCANDALOUS LORD
TO MARRY AN HEIRESS
THE OUTLAW AND THE LADY
NEVER MARRY A COWBOY
NEVER LOVE A COWBOY
A ROGUE IN TEXAS

WAKING UP WITH THE DUKE

LORRAINE HEATH

AVON

An Imprint of HarperCollinsPublishers

AVON BOOKS
An Imprint of HarperCollins*Publishers*
10 East 53rd Street
New York, New York 10022-5299

Copyright © 2011 by Jan Nowasky
ISBN 978-0-06-202245-5
www.avonromance.com

First Avon Books digest printing: July 2011
First Avon Books mass market printing: July 2011

Avon Trademark Reg. U.S. Pat. Off. and in Other Countries, Marca Registrada, Hecho en U.S.A.
HarperCollins® is a registered trademark of HarperCollins Publishers.

Printed in the U.S.A.

10 9 8 7 6 5 4 3 2 1

For Franny
When shared with you. . .
Laughter is deeper
Secrets more hushed
Good news more joyous
Sorrows less painful
Moments always, always richer
And New York is way more fun. Totally.
Thank you for including me in your life and offering
me the gift of your friendship. . .
And for always knowing the best wines.

Chapter 1

Herndon Hall, Leicestershire
November, 1860

I'll consider your debt paid in full if you get my wife with child."

Ransom Seymour, the ninth Duke of Ainsley, struggled to concentrate as he sat sprawled in a comfortable armchair in the well-appointed library. He'd been downing excellent whiskey ever since his arrival at the Marquess of Walfort's country estate for his once legendary hunt. After three hours, they were both well into their cups, so surely he'd misunderstood.

"Does your silence indicate your acceptance of the terms?" Walfort asked.

Ainsley scrutinized his cousin and longtime friend, sitting in that damned wheelchair, where he himself had placed the marquess three years earlier. Walfort had aged considerably during that time, his brown hair having gone white at the temples, his brown eyes somber enough to chase off any gaiety in the room. Ainsley released a dark chuckle. "I've had far too much to drink. You would not countenance what I thought you uttered."

"Jayne wants a child. I can't give it to her. You owe me this."

Ainsley pushed himself out of the chair. He'd meant to do so with force. Instead, he staggered and almost lost his balance as he crossed over to the fireplace. He pressed his forearm against the stone mantel to steady himself while he studied the madly dancing flames. Within them he could almost see the night he and Walfort had been barreling wildly through the London streets, the curricle traveling at a dangerous breakneck speed—

He'd wondered but never dared ask the full extent of Walfort's injuries. They'd seen each other seldom in the intervening years, that tragic night a guilty barrier between them. "I owe you your legs. Not my seed."

"You owe me a bloody cock!"

Inwardly, Ainsley flinched, but he allowed none of his rioting emotions to escape his calm façade. Instead, he concentrated more intently on the fire. The flames— red, blue, yellow, orange—swirled in a macabre waltz, no doubt a preview of what his eternity would most assuredly entail. Writhing within them for his sins, his poor judgment. He'd been all of five and twenty. A cursed age for him and his brothers. Westcliffe married at twenty-five and was betrayed. Stephen marched off to war, only to return a lost man. And Ainsley, who was always so damned responsible, managed to destroy a good man's life. And a lovely woman's. And his own, if he was honest about it.

"Are you telling me that you can't . . . that you—" He peered over at Walfort. He owed it to his childhood friend to at least hold his gaze when he asked. "That you can't bed her?"

"I've got no feeling." Walfort pounded his thighs, slammed a fist between his legs with enough force to make Ainsley cringe and the chair creak. "No feeling. She's tried, bless her, she's tried to make it work . . . but all it does is cause her to weep."

Ainsley felt as though his heart had been scored with a thousand daggers. They'd been in London celebrating that Jayne was at long last with child, was possibly carrying Walfort's heir.

"I feel remarkably old at twenty-eight," Walfort, three years Ainsley's senior, remarked. "I want to feel young again."

So they drank and drank and drank. And although Walfort was married, they even visited the beds of a couple of lovelies. Ainsley had never understood Walfort partaking in the latter entertainment. If Jayne were his wife—

"Jayne would never agree to this mad notion of yours. She despises me."

He hardly blamed her for her attitude toward him. In grief over her husband's near death and debilitating injuries, she'd lost the child. Now it seemed she had no hope of ever having another. She was the sort of woman who should never be denied anything her heart desired. It was his second thought upon being introduced to her at the betrothal dinner that had been held in her and Walfort's honor: *If you were mine, you'd never do without.* His first thought had been that he wished he'd met her before Walfort, so certain was he that he'd have been able to charm her into his arms. She was the loveliest woman upon whom he'd ever set eyes. Grace and poise mirrored her every step. When she smiled, she made a man feel as though he were all that mattered.

In no hurry to marry, Ainsley had avoided the soirees of Seasons past whenever possible. Thus he'd missed the opportunity to meet and court Lady Jayne Spencer. Although to hear Walfort tell it, he snagged her heart during their initial dance.

"You have a reputation for charming the ladies. Apply your talents to my wife," Walfort said now, each word biting, clipped, as though forced between clenched teeth.

"You want me to seduce her?"

"I want you to give her what I cannot."

"This is ludicrous." Ainsley shoved himself away from the fireplace, dropped back into the chair, which had suddenly become unbearably uncomfortable, rose and stalked to the window. Unsettled, he refused to acknowledge how often he'd dreamed of Jayne, but he'd never acted upon his interest. He lived his life by a code of chivalry passed down from his ancestors who had fought alongside Richard the Lionheart during the crusades. He did not take women who belonged to others. "Does she consent to this preposterous scheme of yours?"

"I've not yet discussed it with her. I wanted to ensure you were in agreement with it before I did."

He faced a man he no longer knew. Had Walfort's affliction driven him mad? "I can predict her answer with unerring accuracy. She'll laugh, she'll slap my face, and then she'll weep. Not to mention the legal ramifications. If she gives birth to a boy, he will inherit. Even if all of England knows you are not his sire, you will be legally bound—"

"You and I are not only friends, but cousins. We both carry the Seymour blood. It would not be such an offense."

"The cousin who is next in line for your title might disagree."

"Syphilis is causing him to lose his mind. Besides, do you honestly believe that every prince who sat upon the throne and became king was truly his father's son? I doubt it. And I do not care about blood as much as I care about Jayne and seeing that she is happy."

But what of himself? Ainsley wondered. To have a son or daughter whom he could never acknowledge? Did he owe his cousin such a sacrifice? Although his recollections were a blur, he knew he'd been driving the curricle. When it toppled, he was thrown clear, his only souvenir from the incident a thin scar that bisected the left side of his chin. Walfort had somehow managed to get caught up in the rigging. When everything finally came to a thundering halt, he'd been broken. Ghastly. Irrevocably. Broken.

With so much liquor coursing through their veins, neither of them remembered the infinite details. They knew only that Ainsley walked away with one small scratch and Walfort never walked again.

"If I decline your invitation to bed your lovely wife?" Ainsley asked quietly, the abhorrence of being placed in this position tautening his gut. He'd never taken a married woman to his bed. Even the thought was repugnant. He believed in having a jolly good time with any willing woman—as long as she possessed no husband to whom she owed her loyalty. He was a man who honored duty and vows. He held others to his high standard.

"I'll simply ask someone else. And my wife could

very well have a miserable night of it. But you, you've always had a reputation for being a remarkable lover. You could provide her with a night to remember."

"She would not welcome my touch."

"I've no doubt you could change her mind on that score."

"You seem to have discounted the importance of her not fancying me."

"Not at all. I consider it to our advantage that she doesn't think well of you. It would reduce the encounter to a transaction. Unemotional. Detached. But knowing you, you would find a way to give her pleasure—and that would be my gift to her as well. She's had three years of celibacy. She's never complained, bless her, but she was all of twenty-two when joy was brutally stolen from her because of our poor choices. Why should she continue to suffer and pay the price for our sins? A night in the arms of London's most reputed lover? Nine months later a babe suckling at her breast."

"You give my reputation too much credit. Even I cannot guarantee conception with only one encounter."

Walfort shrugged haplessly. Shoulders that had once been sturdy seemed lost within his finely cut jacket. "A month, then. Someplace quiet, discreet."

The answers came much too quickly, without hesitation, as though they'd previously engaged in the argument. "You've given this considerable thought."

"It's all I think about. How to bring happiness to my wife. You owe me this, Ainsley. You owe *her*."

"She'll never agree to it."

"But if she does?"

Before he could respond, the library door opened

and the lady in question strolled in. The first time he saw her, she'd been smiling, her blue eyes alight with joy, her beauty transcendent. Now it was as though a shadow had fallen over her. She was small and delicate, much too delicate for the burdens she presently carried.

She avoided looking at Ainsley as she approached her husband. Her black hair was upswept. Flowing back and tucked neatly into place was the river of white she'd acquired near her temple three years ago as she dealt with the loss of her babe and her husband's mobility. Her violet gown outlined her slender frame to perfection, and Ainsley had an unconscionable—and unforgivable—vision of easing that gown off her shoulders and skimming his mouth over her creamy skin. She would not consent. He knew she would not consent. He was a blackguard to give even a second's thought to how he would carry her into a sensual realm where only pleasure existed.

She was his friend's wife, for God's sake, and Walfort, wallowing in that damned wheelchair, simply was not thinking properly. Jayne would set him straight right quick, and then she would no doubt hold Ainsley responsible for her husband's ludicrous suggestion.

Smiling softly, she bent at the waist and pressed a light kiss to Walfort's cheek. "Hello, darling."

When she straightened, she gazed at Ainsley as though he were a bit of excrement she'd recently scraped off the bottom of her shoe. "Your Grace."

He bowed slightly. "Lady Walfort. May I say that you look lovely?"

"You may say whatever you wish."

For him, she had no smile, no soft eyes, and no gentle tone. Walfort had indeed lost his mind if he thought his wife was going to welcome any sort of intimacy from Ainsley. He suspected she would derive more pleasure from ramming a dagger through his heart than from experiencing his practiced touch.

"Dinner awaits, gentlemen."

"Good. I'm quite famished," Walfort announced. "Ainsley, will you escort my wife into dinner?"

"I don't need an escort," she said quickly. "However, Randall is not presently available, so perhaps His Grace would be kind enough to assist you."

Her eyes as they met Ainsley's held a challenge and more. He knew she wanted to remind him of what his foolishness had wrought—as though he could ever forget it.

"It would be my honor," he responded succinctly, striding toward Walfort.

As he pushed the chair forward, he was surprised to discover how much lighter it was than he remembered. His friend was frailer than he'd realized. Knowing he was responsible, the guilt gnawed at him like a ravenous dog with a bone.

His guilt increased when he found himself enticed by the lure of Jayne's hips gently swaying as she preceded them from the room. He didn't want to contemplate the hell that awaited him if she consented to her husband's insane notion to get her with child.

Sitting at her vanity several hours later, Jayne Seymour, Marchioness of Walfort, brushed her hair, marveling that she'd managed to sit through dinner without making any nasty comments to Ainsley. She'd not been pleased when Walfort told her that he invited the duke to arrive a day earlier than the rest of their guests so they might have some private time together. That he still saw the man at all astounded her. She couldn't forgive Ainsley for the careless disregard with which he lived his life.

Each time she first set eyes upon him, it was like receiving a solid blow to the chest, nearly crippling her with its force. Her stomach cramped with the reminder of what she'd lost due to his selfish actions and his penchant for indulging in all sinful pleasures. Her babe and the man whom her husband had been.

She'd never deluded herself into believing it was anything other than her sizable dowry that had first attracted Walfort to her. His coffers were quite empty when he began to court her, but it had not taken long for him to win her heart as well as her hand in marriage. Theirs had been a comfortable arrangement. She was fortunate. They were compatible. They cared for each other. They enjoyed each other's company. They never argued. She managed his household. He visited his clubs. Life had been calm, pleasant.

Four years into their marriage, she found herself with child. She'd been nearly three months along when she finally told Walfort, who promptly went off to boast about it to his longtime friend and cousin, the Duke of Ainsley. She was unfamiliar with the particulars of what followed. She knew only that both men had celebrated the good news with far too much drink and a dash through the London streets that cost her husband his legs and his ability to sire another child. The grief of his injuries, the strain of caring for him, the emotional turmoil of accepting how their lives were affected, had all been too much. She lost the child. His one hope for an heir. Her one hope to be a mother.

Tonight, with Ainsley sitting at their dining table, so much had come rushing back. Her resentment of the man. The way things had been before that horrendous night when everything went wrong. How any chance for true happiness was now lost. How hard she fought not to let her husband know how dreadfully despondent she was.

Setting aside the brush, she rose from the chair and walked to the door that separated her bedchamber from his, a door he no longer used. He never came to her. Never. Not to say good-night. Not to simply hold her. He needed assistance getting into the high bed that she had to use steps to clamber into. It unmanned him. She knew that. She took such great pains not to make him feel less than what he once had been.

Taking a deep breath, she opened the door and walked through the bathing chamber to the adjacent room. It was dark except for the moonlight spilling in through mullioned windows. She could see the shallow outline of her husband's form resting on the bed, beneath the blankets. Sometimes she feared he would wither away into nothing. She tiptoed over the carpet. "Walfort?" she whispered quietly.

She heard the rustle of the feathered pillow as he turned his head. "Jayne, is everything all right?"

Of course it wasn't. It hadn't been for three long years. "May I lay with you for a while?"

"Sweetheart, you never have to ask anything of me."

She climbed up the steps to the bed, slipped beneath the covers and nestled against him. He wrapped his arm protectively around her, pressing her firmly to his side, her face cradled within the curve of his shoulder. She didn't want to think about all the nights he'd come to her when they were first married. After his accident, when he regained some strength, she'd lain in her lonely bed night after night, waiting for his return. But he never again came, as though if he couldn't make love to her, he saw no point in being with her. But sometimes she just needed to be held, and when those moments came, she slipped into his bed.

She rubbed her feet against his thin calf. "I'm sorry. My feet are cold."

"Doesn't matter. I can't feel them."

He said it without emotion, as though it was more than his lower body that had no sensation, as though his very soul had become paralyzed as well. She couldn't remember the last time she'd heard him laugh. His now rare smiles always contained a hint of sadness. But then she supposed hers did as well.

"You seem rather quiet and melancholy tonight," she said softly. "Shall I cancel the house party?"

"No, no, absolutely not. It will serve us well to have visitors."

He began to absently stroke her arm. She closed her eyes and relished the gentle caress, fighting back the guilt because sometimes it was difficult to be content with only this.

"Jayne?"

"Hmmm?"

"I was talking with Ainsley earlier—"

"Well, I should hope so, since you wanted him to arrive before any of our other guests."

"I appreciate your indulgence." He kissed the top of her head. Her stomach tightened. How she wanted to turn her face up toward him and have him kiss her. Truly kiss her. The way he once had. As though his life had depended on it. But knowing he couldn't finish what they might begin stopped her cold. It was too painful for both of them to be reminded of what they'd never again have, so she pretended she no longer yearned for it.

"Be that as it may," he said after a time, "I was thinking . . . he could get you with child."

She froze, her lungs not even working to draw in air. She was surprised her heart continued to pound. She knew it did because she could hear the blood rushing, roaring between her ears. "Are you . . . you can't be . . . are you suggesting I take him as my lover?"

"For a short time, yes."

She shoved herself to a sitting position and glared at him, for all the good it did with the shadows hiding the details of their features. "Have you gone daft?"

"No, I don't believe so."

"Well, I must wholeheartedly disagree." She quickly scrambled out of the bed, nearly tripping in her haste to escape—as though distance could lessen the abhorrence of the words he'd uttered. "If I wanted a lover, I'd choose him myself, and he certainly wouldn't be Ainsley."

"Be honest here, Jayne. Your unquestionable loyalty will prevent you from ever taking a lover."

"Then why would you even suggest—"

"Because there would be no guilt."

"And how, pray tell, did you deduce that utter nonsense?"

"Because you don't fancy him at all, so it wouldn't be as though you were truly betraying me."

"You have gone daft." She headed for the door—

"Jayne? Please, don't go. Please, hear me out."

Stopping, she glanced over her shoulder to see his arm extended, his hand reaching for her in the shadows of the night. She could win any argument with him by simply leaving the room. It wasn't fair to him, and so they never argued. But this? This was preposterous.

"Please, Jayne."

His voice was rough with his need for her to remain. Unfair. Unfair of him to compel her to stay, knowing guilt would eat at her if she walked away when he couldn't.

She was trembling with anger and disgust at his suggestion regarding Ainsley, yet still she cautiously made her way back to Walfort. She clambered onto the bed, took his hand and held it in her lap, her legs tucked beneath her. She refused to look at him, and instead studied the silhouette of their joined hands.

"The fact that you think so little of him is what makes my plan so brilliant," he said quietly. "It is not as though you will be truly betraying me. Your heart will remain mine."

"And my body his." She couldn't prevent the cutting words from slicing between them. What passed between a man and a woman beneath the sheets was such an intimate act—how could he bear the thought of Ainsley knowing about her what only Walfort had ever known?

"Ainsley has a reputation for being a marvelous lover—" he began.

"I am well aware of that. He is all the ladies talk of."

"So he can make it pleasant for you." He squeezed her hand. "You deserve that at least."

"All of London will know it's not your child. That you've been cuckolded."

"No, they won't. I've never taken out an advert in the *Times* stating my limitations. Oh, there will be speculation, of course, but we can quell that easily enough once people see how thrilled I am that you are with child."

"And if it's a boy?"

"Then I shall have my heir."

"But he will not carry your blood."

"He will carry Seymour blood. As I told Ainsley, it will be close enough."

Her mouth tingled. She thought she was going to be ill. "You've already discussed this madness with him?"

"I had to know he was agreeable."

"Of course he'd be agreeable. It is a skirt to lift."

His low chuckle took her by surprise. "He was not quite so in favor of it as I'd expected. He did not think you would welcome him."

"I will not."

"Jayne, you've been a devoted wife. Why should you not have this?"

She was grateful for the dark, that he couldn't see the blush warming her cheeks or the tears filling her eyes.

"He can give you what I cannot," he said softly. "You are a young woman who has had to lock all her dreams in a musty old trunk, because of your husband's poor judgment."

"In a friend. A friend to whom you would now give me. It's revolting."

"He did not force the drink down my throat. I went willingly into the curricle, encouraged the horses to go faster—"

She brought his hand to her lips, pressed a kiss to the backs of his fingers, knowing he would feel the dampness coating her cheeks, the tears gathering at the corners of her mouth.

"Ah, Jayne."

He wrapped his hand around the nape of her neck and drew her down until her face was buried in the nook of his shoulder.

"Do not ask this of me," she rasped.

"I will not force you. Neither will he, but know that I will understand if you change your mind. You deserve a child. You deserve a man who will not only put your pleasure above his, but will ensure that your enjoyment far exceeds his."

Not Ainsley. Never Ainsley. Sinners would have a need for overcoats in hell before she'd willingly give herself to the man she despised more than any other.

Chapter 2

Jayne slipped out of her husband's bed near dawn, leaving him in the company of his snores. She'd not slept well. Guilt had reared its ugly head, guilt that she'd lost his heir. Not that she knew for certain that the babe had been a boy. But in her heart she couldn't help but think that he had been. Losing the child had been like losing a piece of her soul. And when the full extent of Walfort's injuries had been made clear, all their dreams went astray.

But for him to believe that she would welcome into her bed the man responsible—it was beyond the pale. Reviling. Made her sick at heart. She was grateful that she had far too many other things to occupy her mind today as she prepared for the arrival of her guests. The sooner she got started working on what needed to be done, the sooner she could shove these unsettling thoughts from her mind.

She rang for her maid, Lily. Within the hour, Jayne was dressed in a simple lilac dress so she could move about quickly. At noon she would change into something more appropriate for receiving her guests. Once a yearly event, they'd not hosted a hunt since the accident. She'd feared it would serve as both a distraction from what *might* have been and a reminder of what *had* been. But Walfort insisted it was long past time that they begin to socialize once more. Finally embracing the notion, she had high expectations for uncharacteristic normalcy for a few days.

An expectation that splattered before her when she strode into the breakfast dining room and saw Ainsley already seated at the table. She'd assumed he would sleep in, not be up with the sun.

Ainsley immediately set aside his teacup and rose to his feet. "Lady Walfort."

"Your Grace."

"I hope you're well."

"Your hopes do not concern me, Your Grace."

She thought she noticed a tautening in his jaw. She was not usually a termagant, but for him she was more than willing to make an exception.

"Allow me to express my appreciation for the lovely accommodations," he said laconically.

It seemed they would spar with words this morning. Already she was weary of it.

Walfort would be upset with her if he knew she'd given his exalted guest the smallest bedchamber in the farthest corner of the manor. As a duke, he should have been given a suite of rooms. She suddenly, against her will, felt petty. "We have so many guests arriving—"

"No need to explain. I rather enjoy overlooking the stables."

She wanted the subject changed before she offered him a more accommodating room. "I'd not expected you to be about so early."

"I thought I might be of service."

Had she been eating she would have choked. "Here? Now? You arrogant cad! To think that I would accept anything at all from you, but especially—"

"My help with the hounds?" he interrupted. "Yes, of course. Forgive me. I'm sure your huntsman is quite up to the task of seeing that all is ready tomorrow for the hunt."

She went light-headed and chilled, aware of all the blood draining from her face. He'd been offering to help her prepare for her guests. That was the service to which he alluded. Not bedding her, not getting her with child. Walfort had put these silly notions into her head and she seemed unable to rid herself of them.

"Yes, he is. Quite." She hated that her voice sounded unsteady, that she was unnerved by what she'd interpreted him to be saying. She swept over to the sideboard, striving to stop the trembling in her hands as she selected ham, eggs, and a muffin for her plate.

Drat it! He was waiting to assist her with her chair when she turned around. At least he had the grace to put her at the end of the table farthest from where he was seated. He'd not taken the head of the table, but rather, a chair along the side.

"I desire nothing from you," she whispered as she took the chair he offered.

He leaned in, filling her nostrils with his rich, tangy scent of bergamot and clove. "Then nothing you shall have," he said, his voice low, sensually belying the words he'd spoken, indicating instead that she would have it all. Everything.

The man was indeed a master at seduction, but she would not be seduced. She and Ainsley sat without speaking for several interminable minutes, the only sound the scraping of silver over china.

Finally she dared to peer up at him, only to find his gaze homed in on her as he slowly chewed. He was as handsome as the devil, too beautiful, really. He had one imperfection, and it was presently not visible to her. A scar on his jaw. The wound had still been bleeding when he came to tell her there had been an accident and Walfort was horribly injured. Ainsley had reeked of excesses and indulgences . . . and the coppery scent of blood. Her husband's blood had stained his torn and rumpled clothing.

Ainsley had looked scared that night. And young. It was easy to forget that he was only a little older than she. He had always seemed so mature, in control. Many thought he was the oldest of the three brothers, but in fact he was the youngest. The night she first met him, she was struck by his stylishness and confidence. She knew of his reputation, of course. Women swooned at his feet. Of late there seemed to be an inordinate abundance of spinsters, as women refrained from accepting offers of marriage on the off chance that Ainsley would honor one of them by asking for her hand. With his thick black hair and startling green eyes, he was a god among mere mortals.

Jayne despised him with every breath of her being.

He wiped his mouth with his napkin, elegance in his motions, tempered with masculinity. His large hands held power. His sensual mouth as well. She could imagine him skillfully using both to elicit pleasure. He seemed to hesitate before saying, "Walfort appears . . . more frail since last I saw him."

"He is limited to two activities. Sitting and lying. Neither of which is very active. His muscles atrophy. I fear soon nothing will be left of him." She bit the inside of her cheek. She'd not meant to reveal the last, to give him even a hint of her vulnerability. It terrified her to think of a life without Walfort. Even as he was, she decided, was better than not having him at all. She shored up her resolve, determined to hurt this man who had destroyed so much. "Tell me, Your Grace, does the guilt ever hammer at you enough that you would wish to trade places with him?"

"I would give my soul that he were not crippled. But I must confess to being far too selfish to wish to trade places with him."

Setting down her napkin, she pushed back her chair and rose. "We are very different, you and I. We do not suit at all. I would trade places with him in an instant to spare him all he suffers now—even though I did not cause the suffering that is visited upon him."

Ainsley flinched, the lash of her words hitting home. As she turned and swept from the room, she wondered why she found no satisfaction in the triumph.

Four hours later, Jayne cursed herself for her stubbornness, for not accepting Ainsley's offer to help. She'd forgotten how much was involved in preparing for the hunt and the arrival of guests. Sixty invitations had been sent out. Fifty-eight had been accepted. Including spouses, unmarried sons and daughters, more than a hundred people would soon descend upon her quiet country home. It had been so long, so very long since they'd entertained to this magnitude. An occasional guest for dinner, a relation or two, but not a flock of the curious. In equal measure, she dreaded and welcomed the coming days.

She made her way up the stairs to her husband's bedchamber, hoping he'd been roused already. It took so long for Randall to prepare him for the day. Walfort had lost far too much control over his bodily functions. Four times a year Randall took him to the spa at Harrogate for the healing waters. Although Jayne had always wanted to accompany him, Walfort asked her not to—fearful she would be embarrassed by his limitations. It hurt her that he would think so poorly of her. But she brushed her tender feelings aside, because his challenges were so much more difficult to face. It was only recently—when his physician introduced him to a contraption known as a catheter—that Walfort had begun to regain his confidence and felt any comfort in being around others. He was now spared public embarrassment over what he could no longer control. Such a proud man he was.

Hence the reason Walfort had declared that it was past time for a hunt—even though he'd not be able to participate in what was once his fondest sport. "I shall enjoy listening to the baying of the hounds once again," he'd said.

She admired his optimistic outlook; he never seemed to pity himself. She hoped the entertainments and country party she'd arranged would please him and bring him great joy—and that none of their guests would stare at him with questioning eyes.

How bad is it really, Walfort?

Her heart would break for him if all did not go well.

To her surprise, he was not in his bedchamber. The library, then. Ready and eager to greet those who would soon be arriving. To her consternation, however, the library was empty of his presence as well. Although Randall was sitting in a chair reading.

"Where is his lordship?" Jayne demanded.

Randall shot to his feet and bowed. "My lady. Forgive me. His lordship gave me leave to read one of his books. I thought this one might suffice, and sat for only a moment—"

"I don't give a fig where you sit and read. Where is his lordship?"

He looked decidedly uncomfortable, as though he knew she wouldn't be pleased with his answer. She wasn't.

"His Grace took the marquess fishing."

"Good God, I can't remember the last time I felt such . . . freedom," Walfort announced.

Standing along the bank of the stream, Ainsley glanced over at Walfort. With his back against the tree where he sat, and a pole held loosely between his hands, he appeared to be at peace. Since the accident, whenever Ainsley visited his friend, they'd remained in Walfort's library, drinking, conversing, lamenting their poor choices. Like Ainsley, Walfort was an outdoorsman at heart. Ainsley had been determined that their visit would go differently this time.

It helped immensely that Jayne had been occupied preparing for the arrival of guests and attending to last minute details. Ainsley knew she'd have not approved of his plans. From what he'd witnessed, she was too protective of Walfort, coddled him.

Suddenly, Ainsley wondered if part of Walfort's desire to give his wife a child rested with his need to divert much of her attentions away from him, to give her something else to worry over.

A child would certainly accomplish that. Although most children of the nobility were tended to by nannies and governesses, Ainsley couldn't quite see Jayne relinquishing the reins for any great length of time. She would be involved with the child. It was her nature to protect, to nurture, to ease the way. She would no doubt keep the little pup far away from him—whether or not he was the father. He wondered who was second on Walfort's diabolical list.

He remembered her bright red cheeks during breakfast. He was accustomed to her giving him a cold shoulder, always just shy of a cut direct. But this morning she'd been skittish, more uncomfortable with him than usual. For a moment, when she saw him sitting at the table, it looked as though she intended to march from the room. His accommodations were deplorable. That much he'd anticipated. But her gaze flicking over him and not settling with a glare was unexpected.

He tested his fishing line before testing other waters. "You mentioned your ridiculous notion to Jayne."

He saw no need to further clarify. Only one ridiculous notion had been spouted since his arrival. In truth, it was the only ridiculous notion he could recall that Walfort had ever possessed. When only silence greeted his words, Ainsley gazed back at him once again.

Walfort gave a hapless shrug that unbalanced him. He started to list to one side, released his hold on his pole to straighten himself—

Ainsley looked back at the water, giving his friend the opportunity to grapple with his gracelessness in private. His first inclination was to rush over to assist him, but he knew Walfort would resent the interference, the implication that he couldn't attend to his own needs—even if in many areas he couldn't. Like himself, his friend was a proud man, probably too proud for his own good. He didn't want to consider what it had cost Walfort to ask him to get his wife with child. He wasn't certain he'd be willing to pay the price, no matter how much he loved the woman.

"You had the right of it," Walfort eventually said, sounding winded, as though he'd run a great distance. "She was none too happy with me. Afraid that leaves it up to you, old chum."

Ainsley swung around. "Pardon?"

"You'll need to charm her, wear down her resistance to the idea."

"You have gone mad." His voice held a biting edge. Walfort might find all of this amusing; Ainsley did not. He remembered the chill that entered the breakfast room with her. But more, he remembered the tantalizing scent of her as he assisted her with her chair. Jasmine. Exotic. Enticing. Her flawless skin beguiled him. He'd been so tempted to slide a finger along the column of her throat. He'd wanted to kiss away the firm set of her lips. The last thing he wanted was for Walfort to grant him permission to seduce his wife. He suspected Walfort had no clue regarding how much Ainsley would enjoy doing so. Walfort might view it all as an uncomplicated transaction, but Ainsley viewed it as a quick journey directly into hell.

No matter how short a term he spent with any woman, he shared not only the physical, but the emotional as well. Warmth, caring, concern, enjoyment. Love he held in reserve. He wasn't certain he could withhold that elusive emotion from Jayne. She struck him as a woman who would demand all—even if she came to him expecting naught but his seed. Time with her would not be simple. Complications abounded. He was certain of it.

"You are on the verge of having a hundred guests," he said now, "and you wish me to flirt with your wife?"

"Not openly. I'm not daft. But surely you can arrange moments alone with her. You've done it with other women."

"Your wife is not other women." He was surprised by the roughness in his voice. He turned his attention back to the stream. Leaves were drifting to the ground on the slight breeze. Those killed by the advance of winter. He wondered if Jayne's frigid mien toward him would kill him. Quite possibly.

"Pity both your brothers are married," Walfort said. "I doubt either of them would lack the courage—"

"Courage has nothing to do with it!" Ainsley snapped. Although it did. He feared he could easily lose his heart. But he couldn't confess that to Walfort. "It is simply a bad idea on so many levels, and I believe you and I have already reached our quota for bad ideas."

"I did have a jolly good time of it that night, Ainsley. Until the end, of course. How are my jewels?"

His pet name for the girls he loved. Glancing back, Ainsley met his friend's gaze. "Well taken care of."

"I've thought about telling Jayne—"

"I advise against that course. No good would come of it."

"It might make her appreciate *you* more."

"I see her but once or twice a year. You see her every day. It's a very bad idea, Walfort."

"I suppose— Good God! I've got something here!"

* * *

It was the laughter that drew her to them. It had been a little over three years since she heard it, but she would have recognized Walfort's boisterous, reverberating laugh anywhere.

She'd been following close to the stream when the sound echoed its way through the trees, and then she guided her horse toward it. Now she sat at the edge of the copse of elms and watched as her husband continually lost his balance, righted himself, and tugged on his pole and line. With net in hand, Ainsley waded out into the water and snagged the elusive creature. His laughter mingled with her husband's, and when Ainsley turned back to shore, net held high triumphantly, his smile broad with victory, she wished she could see her husband's face. Surely his held the same joy. She cast a quick glimpse at the groomsman who'd accompanied her. He was wearing a bright smile, and it was only then that she realized her own lips had curved up. And that her eyes misted over with unshed tears. So many in the years since the accident.

"Shall I help them, m'lady?" Chester asked.

"No," she said. "I believe they have it well in hand."

Her voice must have carried on the slight breeze because Ainsley looked up sharply from wrestling the fish free of its hook—

"Damnation!" He shoved his thumb into his mouth at the exact moment the fish plopped free onto the bank.

"Get him, Ainsley, for God's sake!" Walfort yelled.

"Yes, yes. Quite!"

It was a slippery beast, flopping about, evading Ainsley's grasp. Walfort was dragging himself through the mud to assist. It tore at her heart to see him reduced thus, and yet each man acted as though nothing were amiss as they both struggled with equal determination to recapture what had been lost.

Eventually, Jayne couldn't help herself. She slapped her gloved hand over her mouth, refusing to laugh at their antics—quite beneath men with such esteemed titles. "Chester, perhaps you *should* lend a hand."

"Yes, m'lady."

He dismounted and was rushing forward when Ainsley held the fish aloft. "I've got it!"

And promptly lost his balance and landed in the stream. She almost released her laughter then, but refused to be entertained by him—when she didn't even like him.

She watched as he tried to regain his footing while maintaining his hold on the fish. If Chester had not waded in to help, Ainsley would have had to let it go. A shame when Walfort was so frightfully proud of catching the silly thing.

He must not have realized she was there until Chester arrived to help Ainsley, because only then did he twist around to find her. His smile was certain to be causing his jaw to ache. "Do you see, Jayne? Do you see what I caught?"

The tears stinging her eyes moved down to clog her throat. He was lying there, raised up on an elbow, and for the first time in so long, he didn't look pitiful or sad. He appeared triumphant and so very happy. She smiled. "Yes, darling."

"I want him prepared for supper."

Nodding, she realized then as she watched Chester help Ainsley to his feet that the duke would have never released his hold on the fish. Never. He'd have not let

Walfort's small victory escape him. She watched now as Ainsley staggered to the shore and dropped the fish into the wicker basket.

Walfort straightened as best he could. "What are you doing here, Jayne?"

"Searching for you. Our guests will begin arriving at any moment."

"Blast it all! I'd forgotten about that. Wouldn't do for the host to be absent, would it?" She didn't think he was truly expecting an answer, then he added, "Have you seen what Ainsley brought me?"

Only then did she notice the saddle with a high back and sides on the horse the duke led toward Walfort. It looked almost like a chair. She'd never seen anything quite like it. She eased her own horse forward.

"Ainsley's brother raises horses now," Walfort said. "And the saddle."

"His brother raises saddles?" she asked, not certain why she wanted to tease him when she hadn't in so long.

Walfort laughed. "See there, Ainsley? My wife has quite the sense of humor. No, darling. He raises only horses, but he designed the saddle. It holds me in."

Ainsley gave a command and the horse knelt. With some effort, Ainsley and Chester finally got Walfort situated in the saddle. She wondered how they would have managed if she and her groom hadn't happened along. Somehow, she suspected her husband and Ainsley would have persevered. With leather straps and buckles, Ainsley belted him in, and with another command had the horse rise. Her breath backing up into her chest, she waited for her husband to flop over onto the ground just as the fish had, but he stayed seated, his feet latched in the stirrups. When Ainsley patted the beast on the hindquarters, it lumbered toward her, Walfort holding the reins.

Ainsley strode to his horse and mounted with a graceful ease. He joined them quickly enough and surreptitiously reached down, grabbing the tether to her husband's gelding. Chester remained to gather up all they'd left behind, including the fish in the wicker basket.

As the three of them wended their way through the woods, Walfort said, "Did you ever expect to see me riding again, Jayne?"

She glanced over at him. She couldn't remember the last time she'd seen him look so confident. "No."

"I think I could jolly well go on the hunt tomorrow."

"You don't want to rush it," Ainsley said quietly. "You're not completely in charge of the horse, you know."

"Don't think you could keep up with me?"

"I think you and the horse need to grow accustomed to one another before you subject him to a hunt."

"Oh, my overly cautionary friend. I suppose you're right."

If only he'd been overly cautionary three years ago, she thought, and bit back the scathing retort. Ainsley had brought this bit of happiness into Walfort's day, and in so doing, into hers.

"I'm going to name him Second Chances, Jayne. What do you think?" Walfort asked.

"I think it's a lovely name."

"Did you know he'd brought the horse? Blighter didn't say a thing to me yesterday. Marvelous, marvelous surprise. It's going to be a good day. A good few days with friends." He reached over and squeezed her hand. "I'm glad we're doing this."

"As am I."

Her gaze went past her husband to Ainsley. He was watching her solemnly. Perhaps it was the sunlight dappling through the trees or the fact that he was drenched and muddy, but he appeared mournful, regretful. For the first time, it occurred to her that perhaps he'd not escaped from that dreadful night as unscathed as she'd always assumed.

Chapter 3

Jayne had rather dreaded the arrival of their guests, fearing that most were coming out of curiosity regarding her husband. Since his accident, they'd not been to London. She'd expected Walfort to put up a convincing front that all was well. She'd intended to do the same.

She didn't know if it was the result of the fishing excursion or his riding the horse or his being in the company of Ainsley, but he was more relaxed and confident greeting their guests than she'd anticipated. He put people at ease with his limitations. During dinner, when his fish was brought to him, he regaled everyone with his tale of how he'd caught it. Sitting beside her husband at the head of the table and across from Ainsley, she was surprised by the grace with which Ainsley accepted his portrayal as a bungler while attempting to land the fish her husband had so expertly caught. She wasn't certain she'd smile as benignly if the laughter came at her expense.

They were in the grand salon now, listening as Lady Louisa Mercer danced her fingers over the pianoforte with amazing dexterity. She'd had her coming out last

Season, and while she was presently unspoken for, it was rumored that she had at least three suitors vying for her hand. She was a lovely girl, small-boned and delicate. Strange, how watching her Jayne couldn't recall ever being that young. In a single night, a few days, she had aged well beyond her years, which was probably why the more elderly of her guests gravitated toward her while the younger, unmarried ladies tended to keep their distance.

"I cannot tell you how much my husband has been anticipating our visit here," Lady Inwood said quietly. "He has always said there are no finer hunting grounds in all of England than Walfort's estate."

Jayne smiled. "We're very pleased you were both able to join us."

Lady Inwood was nearly fifteen years older than Jayne. She'd provided her husband with an heir and three spares in record time, and with each child, her figure had rounded more and more. Yet she still managed to carry herself with incredible grace.

"The girl is quite talented," Lady Inwood said.

"Quite. Lady Florence will entertain us next."

"I have far more interest in other entertainments."

Jayne snapped her head around and followed Lady Inwood's gaze to where a good many of the bachelors stood on the opposite side of the room, near one of three massive fireplaces. Among them Ainsley, his pose more relaxed than the others. He stood in their midst and yet he seemed apart. While he appeared to be watching Lady Louisa, he was not truly focused on her.

"Who do you suppose Ainsley will entertain while he's here?" Lady Inwood asked slyly.

Jayne shifted her attention back to the woman. "Pardon?"

"It's no secret, my dear, that some fortunate lady always ends up in his bed at these affairs. Many a silly chit has ruined her reputation because she couldn't resist boasting that she'd been with him. My money is on Lady Anna St. Clair."

"Your money?"

"Quite. A few of us married ladies—the older ones especially—always wager. Would you care to place your own wager on whom it shall be?"

She was both intrigued and repelled by the notion. "No."

"Probably to the best. A few have wagered it will be you."

Jayne's jaw dropped, but she recovered quickly enough to snap her mouth shut. If she tried to speak, she'd no doubt be blathering.

"I daresay I think it a fool's wager, however," Lady Inwood continued, as though she'd not just insulted Jayne to her core. "It's well known that Ainsley never takes a married woman to his bed."

As though the ultimate decision rested with him and not her. She almost commented that perhaps married women didn't want him in their bed. Having known their husbands, they were content with that. But she didn't want to prolong this discussion any longer than necessary. "Then why would anyone wager on me?"

"You're young." She lifted a bared shoulder carelessly. "Speculation is that since his accident, your husband—"

"My husband satisfies me in all matters, I assure you." She was pleased that the practiced words had escaped her lips so smoothly. She'd not been certain if the opportunity presented itself that she would be able to successfully protect Walfort's manhood. He considered these people friends, equals, and here they were gossiping about him as though he were little more than gutter garbage. She'd feared it would be the case, hence the hours of practicing the precise words and tone in order to deliver them effectively.

She took satisfaction in Lady Inwood's brown eyes widening. "I meant no insult. It is simply that you have still failed to produce an heir—"

"Did it occur to no one as they were doing all this damn gossiping that my husband and I required time to adjust to the obstacles thrown at us?"

"Yes, of course. As I said, I meant no insult."

"If you'll excuse me, I need to see to my other guests."

Inwardly, she was seething, but had she learned nothing else in the past three years, she'd learned to bury her emotions so far down that even she had a difficult time finding them. She wanted to leave this suffocating room, but she was the hostess, so she smiled and introduced to the assemblage each young lady who had requested an opportunity to perform, hoping that her music would capture some gentleman's fancy.

At one point the hairs on the nape of her neck rose and she turned to find Ainsley's gaze riveted on her. She could see the speculation in his green eyes, the furrowing of his brow. His intense perusal only served to inflame her fury.

She wished this entire affair were over, that she could send all her guests on their merry way. Instead, she smiled and pretended to give a fig about the latest fashions, books, and betrothals. It was all so damned frivolous. She thought her world had stopped falling apart, but she was wrong. It had simply become isolated, her focus narrowed to struggling not to continually grieve for all that had been irrevocably lost.

After the recital, Walfort adjourned to the billiards room with some of the gentlemen. She saw to it that the remaining guests had all they needed to retire for the night. Most had brought their own servants, but hers were still available to help as needed. A few of the guests were sleeping in luxurious tents on the front lawn, but the more prestigious were given rooms. Lady Inwood had been correct: Walfort's estate was known for its hunting grounds, and royalty often visited. Over the centuries, new wings and additions had been added to accommodate them, until the residence resembled a palace.

When the rooms finally settled into quiet, Jayne rapped on her husband's bedchamber door and discovered he was not yet abed. No doubt he remained in the billiards room with his liquor and cigars—and Ainsley. She didn't want to contemplate the direction of their conversation tonight. Who knew what other madness the two of them might conjure together? She should retire and spare herself the irritation of wondering about their conniving. Tomorrow would be another busy day. But she knew sleep would elude her. Instead, she settled her cloak over her shoulders and decided to seek solace in the gardens.

Once outside, she inhaled deeply the brisk night air. The sky was so incredibly clear. A thousand stars and a full moon guided her steps, each one taking her farther away from the residence and her role as gracious hostess. Usually a walk through the grounds relaxed her. Even in winter her gardens abounded with color. Pansies, in particular, nestled in the soil and brought her smiles. But in the moonlight they were little more than silhouettes. A reflection of her life. A mere shadow of what she'd expected it to be.

She gave herself a mental shake. She despised giving in to the morose musings. She had legs, sensations, and a husband who had disappointed her but once in his life. Some women had far less.

She reached a curve in the path and turned onto a less-traveled stretch until she reached a wrought-iron bench. She sank onto it. This isolated section of the gardens was her sanctuary, the place where she'd come to weep copious tears in solitude. She thought she'd succeeded so well in hiding her numerous disappointments and heartaches from Walfort. But then last night when he made his ludicrous suggestion . . . Perhaps he read her far easier than she realized. As much as she fought not to, she did regret not having children. She'd always envisioned herself with several dark-haired sons and daughters.

A twig snapped. She froze, listening intently, not even daring to breathe. She knew she was safe here. It was probably a deer. They often traipsed through the gardens. She heard something brush against the foliage. A looming shadow appeared and stepped into the moonlight.

The very last person she wished to disturb her sanctuary.

"Lady Walfort," Ainsley said, his words accompanied by what she was certain sunlight would have revealed to be a mocking bow.

"Your Grace."

"It's a bit late for you to be out, isn't it?"

"My behavior is none of your concern."

"Are you waiting for someone?"

Had Walfort sent him out to spy on her? She bristled

with the thought, then chastised herself for the lunacy of it. Not to spy on her, but to enchant her, as though Ainsley had any chance at all of succeeding in that regard. She would bed a beggar before she would bed him. A filthy, odorous man in rags would be preferable to the far too handsome and polished lord who stood before her now.

"No."

"Then you won't mind if I join you."

He moved toward her, and she rose. "Of course I mind. If I wanted company, I'd have company."

"It seems we're of like minds. The presence of so many makes me itch after a while."

She shuddered. "I'm not itching."

"But you're bristling."

"I sought solace, which you have destroyed. Good night, Your Grace." She made to brush past him.

He grabbed her arm. "Stay."

She wrenched free of his hold. "I don't believe so."

"Please. I won't speak. I won't even sit. I'll simply stand over here"—he strolled to the other side of the bench—"until the boar leaves."

Her heart lurched. "There's a boar? In my garden?"

His smile flashed in the moonlight. "It's the reason I darted off the path, only to discover another. I think we're quite safe here."

"How will you know when he's left?"

"I'll check in a bit."

She gazed into the blackest shadows through which she'd have to walk in order to return to the house. She didn't hear anything. She glanced back at the bench, at the duke. Reluctantly, she sat and glared at him. "Don't be asinine. Sit."

He did so without uttering a word. Strange, how even with her cloak and his coat, she was aware of his penetrating warmth.

They were silent for several moments before she dared ask, "Were *you* in the gardens to meet with someone?"

She waited, waited, and at last peered over at him. He touched a finger to his lips.

"You may speak," she said curtly, irritated with herself for being somewhat amused by his antics.

"I don't wish to disturb you."

"You've already failed on that account, so answer my question."

"Why do you care?"

"I have my reasons."

"Well, if you must know, I had not arranged any sort of tryst, so no, I was not planning to meet anyone."

"The ladies are wagering, you know. On whom you'll take a fancy to while you're here. If you were to tell me who she is to be, I could place a wager, share the winnings with you."

Again he smiled. "I had no idea you were so devious."

Neither had she. It annoyed her that she was motivated more by curiosity about his affairs than any true desire to win a wager. "So, who is she?"

"I'm not one to seduce and then tell, even when money is involved. If the lady wishes it to be known, that is another matter." He leaned near and she felt the increase in his warmth, smelled the brandy on his breath. "Although if I were you, I'd wager that I'll entertain no lady while I'm here."

"Guilt? Because Walfort can't?"

He straightened slowly. "No. I'm simply not in the

habit of insulting a lady by seducing her in a hovel of a room."

Shame swamped her. It was not in her nature to be so unwelcoming, and yet where he was concerned, she seemed unable to prevent herself from doing what she could to make him aware of her distaste regarding him. She pressed the flat of her hand to her forehead. "My apologies. I had no right . . . I'm sorry. You brought my husband joy today, such as I've not seen him experience in a good long while. And I'm showing my gratitude by acting as a curmudgeon. Forgive me."

"I forgave you before you asked."

She almost released a bitter laugh. He was attempting to charm her. She would not be charmed. Neither did she wish to continue along that path of conversation. She held her tongue, and they sat in silence for several long minutes. She didn't like the comfort of it, as though they were accustomed to each other's presence, as though each could enjoy the company of the other without words. Such ease was reserved for married couples who knew each other well and accepted each other's foibles.

"I do believe there are no finer hunting grounds in all of England than those owned by Walfort," Ainsley said. "The fences and hedgerows are so high that they make for challenging hazards. Sets the heart to racing. The foxes are quick, the hounds quicker. I remember the first hunt after you and Walfort married. I'd never seen a lady partake in the sport before. I thought Walfort was simply indulging you—new husband and all, trying to earn your favor—but you flew over the hazards with the best of us. I was quite enthralled by your performance."

She loved riding over the countryside. Her horse was

a fine fencer. While she didn't want to, she had to agree with his assessment of the joy to be found in the hunt. "There is little that is quite as exhilarating."

"You must be anticipating tomorrow."

She shook her head. "I shan't go on the hunt."

"Why ever not?"

Glaring at him, she said, "I will not leave Walfort to plod back to the residence on his own."

"You love the hunt."

"I love him more."

She could feel his penetrating gaze as he scrutinized her. It made her skin prickle.

"It is rude to stare."

"Why would you not take part in the hunt?"

"I explained my reasoning."

"No, you provided a reason, but not the true one, I wager." As he studied her further, she heard the tapping of his foot, a steady beat—

"You're going to draw the attention of the boar," she muttered.

"You seek to punish him," he said.

"Why should I care about punishing a boar? You're the one who sought to escape him."

"Your husband. You're not joining us in the hunt because he can't."

Irritation swelled. "My purpose is not to punish him."

"Not intentionally perhaps, but the result is the same when you deny yourself pleasure and enjoyment. The guilt adds to his burden."

"I will not throw in his face what he is no longer capable of."

"He may not be able to chase after the fox, but he

brings pleasure to others by inviting them here. Unselfishly he offers them the challenges and victories offered by his land. I think that is far more noble than riding a horse."

She'd never considered that. She had always concentrated on what he'd lost, what he could no longer accomplish, rather than on what he could. She didn't want to contemplate that Ainsley was right or that he was wiser than she. Was she responsible for Walfort's melancholy? Not pleased with these doubts surfacing, she was anxious to change the topic. "I extended invitations to your brothers. They both sent regrets."

"Their wives are . . . in the family way."

She felt a tightening in her womb, an ache for what she would never have. She refused to acknowledge it, to not take joy in another's good fortune. "I fear I'm not quite up on all the family news. How many is this now?"

"It'll be the third for them both. Westcliffe has a son and daughter. Stephen two sons."

"Does Sir Stephen desire a daughter, then?"

"I think he only desires that the child be healthy and that his wife survive the ordeal of birth."

"The ordeal results in such joy." One she was not likely to experience, unless—

Ainsley's gaze clashed with hers, and she knew—*knew*—he was thinking of her husband's silly proposal. She couldn't deny his attractiveness, and his skills in the bedchamber were legendary. But she had little interest in legends. She was the first to look away.

"Do you think he's still about?" she asked. "The boar?"

"Probably. I'm willing to risk having a look, if you like."

She shook her head, not certain why she was suddenly reluctant to leave, to be alone. "I suppose no harm can come from waiting for a few more moments."

"Except that you're getting cold."

Before she could respond, he stood, removed his coat, and draped it over her shoulders. It enveloped her in luxurious warmth and his rich fragrance. She made to remove it. "Now, you'll get chilled," she said.

He closed the coat more securely around her, taking his seat as he did so, suddenly closer than he was before. "My comfort has no bearing here."

"I will not be influenced," she stated succinctly.

"Pardon?"

"I'm well aware that you're attempting to gain favor."

A corner of his mouth hiked up. "Believe me, if that were my intent, I would not be so subtle. I would not speak of my brothers or wagers regarding my possible conquests or my habits when it comes to ladies. No. I would focus on you and you alone." He skimmed his warm fingers—how could they be so warm when the air was so cool?—along her chin, the soft skin beneath it, somehow causing her to face him more directly. "I would tell you how beautiful you looked during dinner. How much I enjoyed the way your eyes sparkled when Walfort ridiculed my attempt to help him land his fish. I would unpin your hair and bury my fingers in it. I would trail my mouth along your throat, your cheek, across your lips, and I would settle in for a kiss that would warm you much more effectively than my woolen coat."

As though he'd actually done all these things to her, her traitorous body heated and yearned for more. She was starving for affection. "Don't," she rasped. "I don't wish to play these games."

"It's not a game to me, Jayne. I take Walfort's request seriously."

"You shouldn't. It's ludicrous. Disgusting. Abhorrent."

"He wants you to be happy."

"Then he shouldn't have been friends with you." She shot to her feet, knowing her words were unfair, but she didn't like his nearness, his sultry voice, his titillating touch. His coat promptly dropped to the ground, and she immediately missed the warmth. But she refused to snatch it back up. Instead, she desperately scanned the shadows. "How will we know when the boar is gone?"

"Considering the time, I suspect by now he's returned to his wife. She never allows him to stay out past midnight. Not even at the clubs."

She swung around. He was sitting negligently on the bench, his long legs outstretched, his tanned breeches hugging his firm thighs. Why did she have to notice every bit of his perfection? "Pardon?"

"I suspect Lord Sheffield has retired to his bedchamber and his wife by now."

"Lord Sheffield? You said there was a boar you were seeking to escape."

"Yes. Quite. Lord Sheffield is a bore. The man's conversations are far less interesting than watching grass grow."

"I thought . . . you led me . . ." She narrowed her eyes. "I thought you meant a creature. A wild hog."

"I daresay that would be far more interesting than Lord Sheffield."

Oh, the man! She wanted to stomp her feet, shake him, make him behave. But she did nothing except express her displeasure with words. "I think you knew what I thought and were content to let me think it so you could work your wiles upon me."

"You are a suspicious wench, Jayne."

"It is Lady Walfort to you. Good night, Your Grace."

With that, she turned on her heel and marched back to the house. The man was insufferable.

And yet for the span of a heartbeat there, as she gazed into his eyes, felt the touch of his fingers, she'd yearned . . . for exactly *what,* she did not wish to acknowledge. But it had been a good long while since she'd yearned for anything that even remotely resembled a dream.

Ainsley sat for the longest time on the bench, allowing the chilled air to seep into his bones, to cool his ardor. It had risen so easily with her nearness, with her fragrance teasing him, with images of kissing her taunting him. She'd been spot on regarding his motives. He'd known what she thought about the boar and had done nothing to correct her assumptions. He'd suspected she'd take her leave otherwise, and he'd been determined to have a few moments alone with her.

He and Walfort had been at the window in the billiards room, enjoying a bit of brandy, waiting their turn at the table, when they spotted Jayne on the garden path.

"You should take advantage of this opportunity to have her alone," Walfort said quietly, his gaze focused on the darkness. "Not many will come your way with all these guests about."

"I'm not going to seduce your wife, Walfort."

"Fine. Then I shall secure another." He twisted around slightly. "Braverton, perhaps."

Ainsley's gut tightened at the mention of a man

whose title opened doors for him that his behavior would not. "He's odious."

"He has sired four offspring on his wife and three on his mistress, so he can certainly deliver the goods."

"It's no secret that he places his own pleasures first."

"That you don't is certainly a benefit Jayne would have enjoyed, but the ultimate goal here is to get her with child."

Ainsley's teeth were on edge as he watched Walfort's gaze sweep over the gentlemen drinking his liquor, smoking his cheroots, discussing the hunt, and waiting their turn to smack some balls around.

"Langford, perhaps."

"I've had the misfortune of seeing him without a shirt. Do you truly want to burden your child with the appearance that one of his ancestors may have mated with an ape?"

Walfort chuckled low. "Who do you suggest, then? If it's not to be you, who? Stratsbury?"

In every endeavor, the man was as stiff as a corpse. "No."

"Fitzhugh? He seems a fine specimen, beautiful actually. No apes in his bloodline. And women adore him."

Because they had similar interests. A taste in men.

"This is a pointless exercise," Ainsley grumbled.

"Then put an end to it and go work your wiles on Jayne."

And so he had. Not that he thought they'd done much good. His heart wasn't truly in the endeavor, because he knew that in order to seduce her, he would have to convince her to betray her husband, her belief in the sanctimony of marriage, and worst of all, herself. For each of those, he suspected she'd never forgive him. But then he'd already given her a good many things regarding him not to forgive. What was adding a few more to the list?

She was so damned beautiful, so gracious, so remarkably strong. Many a woman would not have retained her loyalty to her husband as Jayne had. She was extremely proud and noble.

To give her what she wanted, he feared he might destroy her. In doing so, he could very well destroy himself.

Finally reaching down, he snatched up his coat. Jayne's delicate scent wafted toward him, lingered to be enjoyed with another breath. He imagined her fragrance being held by his pillow.

Like his brothers, he enjoyed women and all the wonders they offered. But with Jayne, he feared he risked something he'd never risked before: his heart.

With a sigh, he shoved himself to his feet and began walking back toward the manor. It was going to require a good deal more than a meeting in a garden to convince her that allowing him to get her with child was as much for Walfort's benefit as hers. His friend harbored a great deal of guilt regarding what had happened that long ago night. And well he should.

They'd both been fools, and Ainsley knew that if he did woo Jayne into his arms, the guilt would only increase. But the truth was—and he suspected Walfort damned well knew it—for Jayne, he would damned well carry any burden.

"I want you in my bed tonight."

Her heart pounding with unbridled excitement and tears stinging her eyes, Jayne stared at her husband, still dressed, sitting proudly in his chair, in *her* bedchamber.

He'd not entered her chamber since he lost the use of his legs. He had certainly not invited her into his bed in all that time. That nothing more than holding and snuggling would occur wasn't the point. He wanted her.

"Ainsley can then have this room."

Her delirious musings came to an abrupt halt, as though she'd been running and smacked straight into a brick wall. Her entire body withered. Her joy crumbled. "Pardon?"

"I went searching for him and discovered he's been given that atrociously small room that was designed to accommodate some king's personal attendant. That simply will not do, Jayne."

He was castigating her? Never had he taken such a tone with her. Straightening her shoulders to toss off the hurt, she informed him coolly, "Our chambers, our suite, are not to be offered to or shared with others. The notion is quite simply beyond the pale."

"But that room—"

"Is sufficient for a bachelor. We have married couples and other guests who required the larger rooms."

"Why not give that room to one of the other bachelors?"

"What does it matter, Walfort? He's probably not sleeping there anyway. I have it on good authority that he will be warming another's bed while he is here." Even though Ainsley had denied it, she was more likely to believe Lady Inwood, who was closer to the gossip than anyone.

Her husband's eyebrows lifted at that. "I daresay you're probably correct." He leaned forward slightly. "And that, Jayne, is precisely why he is such a good choice to get you with child. He has an insatiable appetite where women are concerned, and you'll be but one of a hundred."

Obviously her husband's paralyzed state was extending to his brain. "And that should please me?"

"He has extensive experience. He is sought after. He can make it pleasant for you. And for him it would be simply . . . another night. When he leaves your bed, he would not look back. So there would be no remorse, no regret, no . . . bother."

His words chilled her. As though nothing would be between them except mechanics. She had enjoyed her husband's visits to her bed. Had thought it was more than obligation and duty. Had he considered it a . . . *bother*? "Have you so little care for me that you see me as nothing more than a broodmare? And so little care for your friendship with Ainsley that you view him as nothing more than an adequate stud?"

"It is because I care for you so much that I want you to have this. A child. With no complications."

She shook her head. "I fear you misjudge the ease with which all this will come to pass."

"He's had many women in his life, Jayne, and not a single one ever hated him when he moved on."

"Please cease with this battering, Walfort." Each word was like a blow to her heart. "I am your wife. I took a vow, in sickness and in health, to share your joys as well as your sorrows—"

"And my sorrows would be a good deal fewer if you would do this. Randall!"

His servant stepped into her bedchamber, stopping further conversation.

"Good night, Jayne," Walfort said, just before Randall pushed him from the room.

He left her seething. She wanted to pick something up and throw it at a wall. How could he not fathom what he truly was asking of her? He was the only man who had ever known her body. She couldn't so easily share her most private portions with another man. Especially not with Ainsley.

Joining his body with hers might mean nothing to him, but to her it meant everything.

She rang for her servant, and an hour later she was lying in her bed, in the dark, staring at shadows waltzing over the ceiling. Never in her life had she felt so abandoned and alone.

Chapter 4

It was not so much the actual hunting of the fox that Jayne enjoyed, but the chase. The scramble over hill and dale, the leaping over hedgerows and fences that made the sport so exciting. She couldn't care less about the fox. No, not true, she thought. She'd always been greatly relieved if no foxes were actually killed. She knew that was unlikely today. Without the annual hunt, the foxes were now in abundance. She was quite certain that at least one would lose its life this day.

But she wouldn't be there to witness the brutality of it. She'd strayed off from the main group. It wasn't that she wasn't in the mood for cheer. It was simply that she was having a frightfully difficult time pretending that everything was as it had once been.

It had been particularly grueling to watch Walfort, sitting in that monstrosity of a saddle, his head held high, his smile broad, signaling for the hunt to begin . . . and then to be left behind. She doubted anyone else had noticed that his grin did not reach his eyes. He had so loved the hunt.

She'd been tempted to return to the estate with him. She almost had. But then Ainsley, who also held back, arched a brow at her, and she'd doubted her reasons for wanting to stay. Was he correct in his assessment? Did she add to Walfort's burdens when she refused to partake in activities that he could no longer enjoy? Had he not indicated the same last night when he mentioned how she might lessen his sorrows?

Now she was riding as though the very devil was on her heels. She could even hear him. She glanced back. Blast it! Ainsley was galloping toward her. She'd thought he was going to return to the manor with Walfort, keep him company. She hated thinking of her husband alone. She should turn about. Instead she increased her horse's pace, then settled in as the hedgerow came into view. They flew over it and for that brief moment in time, she was free—

But the landing was ungainly. Cassiopeia lost her footing, screaming as she went down, tossing Jayne off in the process. She hit the ground hard in a graceless sprawl. By the time she shoved herself into a sitting position, Cassie was standing again, but it was obvious all was not right. She favored her right leg. Sorrow filled Jayne because of the suffering she'd caused the poor creature. What in the world had she been attempting to prove?

"Jayne!"

She heard Ainsley's voice before he appeared at the hedgerow, bringing his horse to a halt, taking in the situation on the other side. "Christ! I saw you tumble. Are you injured?"

"I see no reason for blasphemy," she said as she gingerly pushed herself to her feet. Her bottom and hip would no doubt be bruised on the morrow. Not that she intended to reveal that bit of intimacy to Ainsley.

"Stay there," he ordered. "I'm coming over."

Standing as she was on a small rise, she was able to
see him as he trotted away, turned about, and urged his
mount toward the hedgerow. They vaulted over it with
such grace, the horse and man obviously one, it was
quite a breathtaking sight. She didn't wish to be impressed with his horsemanship. But she was. Blast him.

He dismounted with such elegant yet powerful ease.
She could see the corded muscles of his thighs bunching
and rippling. His long, sure strides carried him toward
her. He was magnificent, and she cursed herself for
noticing.

With eyes the green of clover upon which she had
once lain, he scrutinized every aspect of her, causing
flesh bumps to erupt over her. Such a strange reaction
when she was suddenly unbearably warm, her breathing labored as though he clasped her in an unyielding
embrace—when he was touching her not at all.

"Are you injured?" he asked, the concern in his voice
mixed with determination. He was not one to be trifled
with. He would ferret out any untruth. Not that she
cared. He didn't intimidate or frighten her. He quite
simply *irritated* her.

"No."

His eyes narrowed sharply, and she capitulated. "A
bit bruised, but nothing to worry over. It is Cassie for
whom I have concern." She made to march past him
and nearly tumbled again when she brought her full
weight down on her right foot. His hand was immediately beneath her elbow, supporting her with so little
effort.

"You *are* hurt." His curt tone reminded her too
much of the chastisement she'd received from Walfort
the night before.

"It's nothing. A slight sprain, perhaps. Nothing about which to panic. You're quite overreacting."

"Will you be able to dance tonight?"

What an idiotic question. "I don't dance."

He stiffened, his fingers tightening on her arm, his gaze riveted on hers as though she was suddenly a puzzle whose pieces had not been put together properly. "I've had the pleasure of watching you dance. No lady is as elegant upon the dance floor as you."

"I did not mean that I am incapable of dancing. Rather I do not, by choice, dance. You may release me."

He did so, ever so slowly, as though with great reluctance. "Why do you no longer dance?"

"Because Walfort can't."

"I thought since you'd become involved in the hunt, that you agreed with my earlier assessment that to not do what you are capable of doing is merely a punishment for him."

"Your argument might apply to the hunt, but I seriously doubt he would take pleasure in my waltzing in the arms of other men."

"I think he would take pleasure in your smile and the sparkle in your eyes."

An image of being swept along in Ainsley's arms flashed through her mind. They'd never danced. Even before the accident. He'd kept his distance. She'd never thought to wonder why. Not that it signified. "I think you're mistaken. Now I must see to Cassie."

"Allow me to approach her first. If she's in pain, she could strike out."

She didn't like his ordering her about, but neither could she deny the wisdom in his words. The last thing she needed was to be incapacitated when she had so many guests to see after. So she stayed where she was, gingerly testing her own foot. Surely it would be fine by evening.

She watched as Ainsley removed his gloves. To provide more comfort to the horse, she supposed. His fingers were long, elegant, his hands large. He stroked Cassie's withers, murmuring softly, giving all his attention to the horse as though it were the most important creature in the world. She suspected he did the same with the ladies who warmed his bed. She did not want to consider what it might be like to have those capable hands skimming over her flesh. It had been so long, so very long, since she'd been caressed intimately. Walfort seldom touched her without her initiating the contact, and then it was merely a brief joining of their hands or a quick brush of his knuckles over her cheek. She doubted that Ainsley would do anything swiftly. He would linger, entice, stir passion to life. She couldn't hear the words with which he soothed the horse, but the rich timbre of his voice carried toward her, sending shivers of such intense yearning through her that she nearly lost her balance.

Taking a deep shaky breath, she gathered herself up. It was only because of Walfort's stupid proposal and Ainsley's inappropriate words on the bench in the garden last night that her mind was wandering to these dark, forbidden places where she'd long ago buried her desires. Through gritted teeth, she cursed them both soundly.

Unfortunately, at that moment Ainsley crouched, his breeches stretching tightly over his backside and muscular thighs. It was quite obvious that he did not spend his entire day indoors. He did not lollygag about. He was firm and sculpted as though by the hand of a great artist. She imagined how the ladies must have taken such delight in running their own hands over a body that was certain to please.

Good Lord, it was suddenly so remarkably hot. What strange weather they were experiencing this year.

He gingerly examined Cassie's leg, and Jayne lamented that she'd been so quick to brush off his wanting to ascertain the extent of her injury. To have him knead her calf, her foot . . . to simply be touched with tenderness. She longed to have it in her life once more. Perhaps she *should* consider taking a lover. Although Walfort might not be so keen to accept a child who didn't carry Seymour blood.

"How—" Surprised by the strangled sound, she cleared her throat. "How does she fare?"

Still crouched, he twisted around, the front of his breeches much more impressive than the back. She jerked her gaze up to his, expecting to see him mocking her, but if he had any notion regarding where her eyes—and thoughts—had strayed, he gave no indication. A spark of gratitude she didn't want to feel wormed its way through her.

"Fortunately, it's not broken. Just a slight sprain I think. But she'll need to be walked back to the stables. I can do that if you'd like to take my horse."

"A lady does not ride astride."

"I can replace my saddle with yours." He unfolded his body, a study in perfect balance and movement. "Although to be honest, I've always thought the sidesaddle looked like a torture device." She detected a slight challenge in his gaze.

How did he know that she'd long yearned to ride

astride? It seemed a much more pleasant way to travel, but to spread her legs over the horse, in front of Ainsley—it seemed like a rather naughty endeavor. "I'll walk her back."

"Coward." His voice was low, yet teasing.

"I'm not," she insisted. She glanced around for her riding crop, located and retrieved it. If he continued down this path, she might use it on him.

"I'll at least accompany you back to the manor," he said.

"I see no need. I'm quite familiar with our grounds."

"I must insist. The bore might make another appearance."

"I have no fear of Sheffield."

"Well, then, perhaps you'll be kind enough to protect me from him."

Gingerly, careful of her step, she made her way to Cassie and took the reins. "Truly, Ainsley, I see no need for you to give up the hunt."

"Whatever makes you think I've given it up?"

She jerked her head up, only to find him watching her with such intensity that she was unable to hold his gaze. She petted Cassie because the action gave her something to think about other than him. Was he insinuating that she was his quarry? Why did the thought fill her with inappropriate giddiness? He'd not be giving her any attention at all if Walfort hadn't set him on her path. What interest did she have in a man who noticed her only because she belonged to another?

If she were wise, she'd accept his offer to change saddles and allow her to ride his horse. If she had any sense at all, she'd simply straddle his horse now and gallop home. His nearness unsettled her. His masculinity flustered her. It had been so long since she'd done little more than exist. He gazed upon her as though she were lovely, desirable. As though she was once again a woman.

She straightened her spine and forced herself to meet his unrelenting gaze. "I have no interest in your attentions."

"I'm well aware of that."

"Has Walfort instructed you to give them to me regardless of my preference on the matter?"

"I saw you take a tumble. I came to assist. Make no more of it than that."

"You deny following me?"

"Walfort asked me to watch over you."

"I love him."

"I never thought otherwise." His somber voice reflected sadness.

"I miss him," she rasped, blasted tears once again threatening to consume her.

His lips parted and she held up a hand to stay whatever it was he planned to say. She did not want his sympathy, his reassurances, or his flirtations. She shook her head briskly. "Partaking in this hunt was a dreadful idea. I must return to the manor now to see that tonight's ball does not disappoint."

"My horse is spirited, but I'm certain you can manage him. Allow me to change the saddles." He leaned in, his mouth forming a conspiratorial smile. "Or ride astride. It would save time."

Oh, she wasn't half tempted. But that would require assistance, and Ainsley was the only one near enough to assist, which would bring their bodies in much too close proximity. He would either have to boost her up, his hands forming a cradle for her foot, or he would lift her, his hands clasping her waist, her hands folding over his broad shoulders. On the way up, her breasts might brush against his chest. Her nipples puckered painfully with the thought. Perhaps he was right, perhaps she was a coward. She shook her head. "No, I shall walk back."

He grabbed the reins of both horses, leading them, while she strolled beside him.

"Are you certain you can manage with your foot—"

"It was only a momentary discomfort. I shall be fine." And she would. If it killed her.

For the longest time, the most courageous woman Ainsley had ever known was his mother. She'd married young, at sixteen, a man far older than she, the Earl of Westcliffe. She'd given him an heir. When he lost interest in her, she'd taken a lover. She'd given him a son—a carefully guarded secret until recently, with only the immediate family now aware of the truth. When West- cliffe died, he left her destitute, and she promptly mar- ried Ainsley's father. He perished shortly after his heir was born. Ainsley remembered little of the man who sired him. His mother, however, had been a dominant force in his life. As well as a scandalous influence. Ainsley's father had left her well off. She could do as she pleased. What she pleased was to take young lovers.

But now another was threatening to usurp his moth- er's place as the most courageous woman he'd ever known. Jayne.

If he were wise, he'd make excuses rather than an ap- pearance at the ball tonight. No one would question his absence. They would assume he'd found a lovely lady to entertain privately.

But as Ainsley's valet settled the dark green swallow-tailed jacket onto his shoulders, he knew he would attend the ball and that he'd ask Jayne to dance.

Once. He would hold her in his arms and sweep her over the dance floor. Even though doing so seemed cruel because it would remind her of what she'd lost: a husband with whom she could dance.

But she already had reminders aplenty. What was one more?

He'd thought he was well aware of what his night of debauchery with Walfort had cost her. He had failed to consider that she continued to pay the price for their poor judgment. He supposed Walfort lived with the reminder every day. It was no doubt the reason his friend asked of him what he had.

He'd considered it a ludicrous request, was determined not to honor it. And then he'd walked back to the manor with Jayne. She began the journey with such purpose to her stride, but when the manor came into view, she slowed her step as though she dreaded facing what awaited her there. He wasn't even certain she was aware of the change in her demeanor.

For the first time he noticed her loneliness, the deep sadness. She'd been young, filled with hope and dreams and a child, when it was all snatched from her.

What Walfort asked of him suddenly seemed a small price to pay to restore happiness to such a remarkable woman.

She remained loyal to her husband, retained her feelings for him. She saw to his needs, asked nothing for herself. She did not whine or complain. She accepted what their foolishness had wrought; albeit grudgingly when it came to Ainsley. She poured all her anger and hatred into him rather than into her husband. He knew he was not deserving of all of it but understood that she needed someone to blame, and it was much easier to lay the fault at his feet—because at least he could still stand.

Now, in the room he'd been assigned, he rubbed the small scar on his chin. He'd not change places with Walfort, not for the world. But he could not deny that he was partly responsible for the debacle that had led to such unhappiness.

With great difficulty he met his gaze in the mirror. Was he seriously considering fulfilling Walfort's request? Absolutely not. He'd honor Jayne with a dance. Nothing more than that.

As he stepped out of the room he was instantly aware of the liveliness of the manor. He could hear riotous laughter and the din of far too much conversation. Even though people spoke quietly, there were so many voices that they rose in a crescendo. In the hallway, a door opened in front of him and a young lady emerged, her chaperone close on her heels.

The girl's blue eyes widened. "Your Grace."

He bowed slightly. "Lady Louisa. Miss . . ."

"Winters," the chaperone said. An appropriate name considering the chill in her voice.

He extended his arm toward the young lady. "May I have the honor of escorting you downstairs?"

"You risk her reputation, Your Grace," Miss Winters told him sharply.

"Not with you so near," Ainsley responded.

"He's quite right, Miss Winters. I'm perfectly safe." With a small giggle, the girl placed her hand on his arm. "I'm honored, Your Grace, to have you escort me."

She appeared remarkably young. As they strolled

down the hallway, he remembered overhearing one of the gents last night comment on her age while she was playing on the pianoforte. She was not yet nineteen.

He knew he needed to begin seeing about securing a wife and an heir. Of late, his mother had been lamenting his lack of a duchess. "Unconscionable, Ainsley," she'd said. He'd promised her that next Season he would see to the duty. He'd not given much thought to the fact that the majority of the ladies available for marriage would be little more than children. He could not begin to imagine bedding one. No matter how lovely she might be, she would still possess far too much innocence.

"Did you enjoy my performance last night, Your Grace?"

"Indeed. It was marvelous, truly entertaining."

"Will you be seeking a wife soon?"

Why did her eyes suddenly shine with such fervor? And why did she think it was any of her business? These younger girls lacked decorum. Perhaps that was the reason his mother had a young lover. The man couldn't tolerate the silliness of those new to the ballrooms. "If my mother has her way."

She laughed, a high, tinkling, irritating sound. The echo of childhood.

They were nearly to the bottom of the stairs when his gaze fell on Jayne. Now there was a woman. Young, but mature. No silly giggling, no tittering. Her gown was a deep purple, and he knew, without seeing her face, that it would bring out the rich blue of her eyes, that it would make them appear violet.

She must have felt his perusal, because she turned, and the impact of her gaze settling on him nearly brought him to his knees. With her ebony hair and exotic features, she was gorgeous. From this distance, he couldn't see the weariness that often cloaked her. Then her attention shifted to his left and he noted her blatant disapproval. He wanted to announce that nothing untoward had passed between Lady Louisa and himself. The girl's bloody chaperone was near enough to breathe on his neck. Couldn't Jayne see that?

She turned toward someone, saying something he couldn't hear.

"I've not yet accepted anyone's proposal," Lady Louisa said.

It took Ainsley a moment to realize she was talking to him. He smiled as kindly as he could to soften his words as he took her hand and pressed a kiss to her knuckles. "It would be a mistake to wait on me, Lady Louisa."

He saw the disappointment in her eyes as she nodded slightly. Damn it. With that brief exchange, she aged—but still not enough for a man as world weary as he.

More laughter and a few squeals floated toward the stairs as people mingled between the parlor and the entry hallway.

"Your Grace?"

Ainsley glanced over at the footman who was extending a copper bowl toward him. He could see three small slips of paper inside, each carefully folded. "What's this, then?"

"Her ladyship decided to dispense with formal seating arrangements for dinner this evening. Each gentleman draws a number and then seeks out the lady with the matching number. She is to serve as his dinner companion."

"Oh, what fun!" Lady Louisa exclaimed. She squeezed Ainsley's arm. "I shall hope we draw matching numbers."

He would hope for the opposite. She promptly withdrew to find the servant with the bowl containing the ladies' numbers.

"Rather childish," Ainsley muttered.

"But then she is almost a child, isn't she?"

He twisted his head sharply to find Jayne at his side. She'd brought her disapproval of him with her.

"I was referring to this little game you've devised to ensure I'm not sitting in your vicinity during dinner."

"Unfortunately, Walfort insisted you have the chair beside his." She nodded toward the servant. "You may move on."

"Yes, m'lady."

"You seem quite relieved," she said to Ainsley.

"I have little patience for games except for those that take place in the bedchamber." While it was true, he wished he'd held his tongue when her eyes darkened with annoyance. He'd much rather see them filled with passion.

"And what game are you playing with Lady Louisa?" she asked.

"I'm not playing a game at all."

"Is she aware of that?"

"I can only hope. Would it have been better for me to ignore her completely when she stepped out of her room and into my path?"

"She was practically preening as you led her down the stairs. You could have very well ruined her reputation."

"With her chaperone stepping on my heels? I doubt it."

"You will do her no favors if you dance with her tonight."

"I assure you that I intend to dance only once. Whether or not you choose to believe it, I am not in the habit of giving a woman false hope regarding where my affections or interest may lie."

Shaking her head, she averted her gaze. "My apologies. It is not my place to remark on your behavior."

"Quite right. Your time would no doubt be better spent attempting to find the gentleman whose number matches yours."

"Unfortunately, I am already well aware of who the man is."

"Dear God, don't tell me you got saddled with Sheffield. The bore."

"No. I am saddled with the man who has no number." Her unflinching gaze met his, and for some unaccountable reason, his heart sped up. "You."

Chapter 5

Jayne was having a most difficult time remaining annoyed with Ainsley. He was slowly, irrevocably, wearing down her resistance to him, her determination to despise the man for as long as he drew breath. How the bond between he and her husband could remain so strong astounded her. But sitting across from him, with Walfort between them at the head of the table, their devoted relationship was more evident than ever.

"I can't believe Sheffield and his hounds managed to corner more foxes than any others," Walfort had said sotto voce to Ainsley. "He shall surely bore us to death with that tale now."

With only a brief look, Ainsley managed to remind her of every moment she'd spent with him in the garden the evening before. She'd even, to her immense shame, enjoyed strolling back to the manor with him that afternoon. Oddly, they'd barely spoken, and yet she found immeasurable comfort in his presence. Then when she saw him descending the stairs with Lady Louisa, she'd experienced a sense of betrayal. Which was obviously ludicrous, as she wanted nothing to do with him.

Although she'd chastised him for his encounter with

Lady Louisa, it was obvious he held no real interest in the girl. As he claimed, he was being merely polite, but it was equally apparent that the poor girl had fallen for his charms nonetheless.

She hardly blamed her. Ainsley could be quite charming when he wished to be. Although as she considered it, she recognized that she'd never seen him when he wasn't charming. And that realization irritated her.

"I know our guests are leaving on the morrow," Walfort began quietly, "but surely you can stay another day or two."

Ainsley's gaze clashed with hers. She'd so hoped that Walfort had given up this ridiculous notion of his, but obviously he hadn't. She knew it. And so did Ainsley. Why else ask him to lengthen his stay—if not to provide more opportunities to prove the brilliance of his plan to them?

"I'm certain your wife is more than ready to have her household return to normal," Ainsley replied, reaching for his wineglass.

"Our household has not been normal in three years," Walfort said, a cutting edge to his voice that caused Ainsley to wince. While she'd never particularly cared for the man, she did not want old wounds reopened before her guests.

"I thought you would be interested in knowing, Your Grace," she said, "that I spoke with the groomsman before dinner and Cassiopeia will be back to leaping over hedges in no time."

He smiled at her, and she wished he hadn't. It only served to make him more handsome, more appealing. "I appreciate knowing that. It's always sad to have a horse put down."

"What happened with Cassie?" Walfort asked.

"She took a tumble during the hunt," Jayne told him.

Walfort's brows drew together. "Were you hurt?"

"No, not at all."

"Why didn't you say something?"

"I didn't want you to worry."

"You're my wife. It's my place to worry."

The chastisement in his voice embarrassed her. The choice of his words had been a disappointment as well. Not that he would worry, but that he would do so simply because she was his wife. It was her position, and not *she,* that caused him anxiety.

As though sensing the tension, Ainsley asked quietly, "So your foot has recovered enough for dancing?"

Her mouth went as dry as the Sahara that she and Walfort once dreamed of visiting. "It does not bother me." She almost reiterated that she had no desire to dance but refrained, wondering if it would indeed add to Walfort's suffering.

"You knew of the tumble?" he asked Ainsley.

Ainsley sipped his wine, leaving her to confess, "He was kind enough to see after Cassie and to escort me back to the manor."

"Interesting." Her husband toyed with the stem of his wineglass as though he were in deep thought. Perhaps he was not as immune to the notion of her being alone with Ainsley as he pretended.

"How is your mother, the duchess?" he suddenly asked, as though desperate to change the subject.

"She is well," Ainsley said.

Walfort swirled his wine, watching it as though it was the most fascinating display he'd ever seen. "Is she still involved with the painter?"

"The artist? Leo? Yes."

"His mother thrives in scandal," Walfort said to Jayne, as though she were unaware of the Duchess of Ainsley's scandalous behavior.

"She's earned the right to live her life any way she pleases," Ainsley said softly, and yet his voice held the promise of a threat.

He would not have his mother maligned, Jayne realized. She didn't know why she was so touched by his defense of her. She remembered her conversation with Lady Inwood. It was the ladies' boasting that ruined reputations, not Ainsley. He had told her that he did not gossip about his lovers. Suddenly she understood at least one reason why Walfort had suggested Ainsley as a possible short-lived lover: he knew how to keep secrets, and he did what he could to keep a woman's reputation intact. Even his mother's.

"How is Lady Lynnford?" Walfort asked.

"Not so well, I'm afraid," Ainsley said.

Jayne was well aware that the Earl of Lynnford had served as Ainsley's guardian. His wife was very ill. A malignancy of the bone that had been tormenting her for years. Knowing they'd be unable to attend, she had not even bothered to invite them.

"A pity. She was always kind," Walfort said.

"She still is. I say, Walfort, you do know how to go about keeping up one's spirits."

Her husband chuckled low. "My apologies. I did start traveling down a morose path, didn't I? Jayne, please, take us to lighter topics."

"I've been reading *A Tale of Two Cities*."

"Ah, yes," Ainsley said. " 'It was the best of times, it was the worst of times.' "

"That hardly sounds jolly," Walfort said.

"Do you enjoy Dickens, Your Grace?" Jayne asked.

"I do. He has the uncanny ability to capture the reality of life."

"I do not want reality when I'm reading," Walfort said.

The conversation moved on to other writers and other works. Other guests began to join in. Soon arguments, laughter, challenges, and opinions were flowing freely. She watched her husband smile, listened as he laughed, and felt bittersweet happiness.

The balls held at Walfort's estate were almost as famous as the hunts. The previous marchioness, Walfort's mother, had set the standard, and Jayne had picked up the banner and run with it. She couldn't deny the pride that swept through her as she and her husband greeted their guests as they entered the grand salon. She heard sharp intakes of breath and exclamations of awe. The orchestra was seated in the balcony, their music wafting through the room. The crystal chandeliers sparkled as the candle flames flickered. Flowers and greenery adorned the massive room that accommodated several small seating areas.

Now she strolled through, ensuring that their guests knew refreshments were available through the open double doors leading into the next room. She partnered young ladies with eligible gentlemen. As she answered questions and assisted with minor inconveniences—explaining which room held a servant who would repair a torn hem—she wasn't certain she'd ever felt quite so lonely or quite so aged.

"My dear!"

She halted her progress, turned, and greeted her guest. "Lady Inwood."

"You have certainly outdone yourself," she said. The woman leaned forward conspiratorially. "And the previous marchioness as well. You have achieved a comfort and elegance that she could not quite accomplish."

"You give me far too much credit. I daresay, I merely followed her example."

"You are too modest." She glanced around. "Ainsley is in top form tonight. I swear he has the devil's good looks."

Jayne held her tongue, refusing to acknowledge that he was the most handsome man in attendance.

"I don't suppose you know if any of the maids found a bed unmade this morning," Lady Inwood asked, her sharp gaze implying much more. The implication that if Ainsley had slept elsewhere—in a lady's bed—then his would not need tending. Although Jayne suspected the man was clever enough to rumple it before he departed for his rendezvous.

"Not to my knowledge, no."

"We cannot determine who he has selected for a dalliance."

"Perhaps no one."

The older woman scoffed. "Hardly likely." Then her expression turned shrewd. "Although you were seen walking with him this afternoon."

"My horse and I took a tumble. His Grace was kind enough to escort me back to the manor."

"Hmmm. Fortunate for you . . . that you were not injured, I mean."

"Very fortunate."

Lady Inwood squeezed Jayne's hand. "If you do hear anything regarding who has earned Ainsley's favor, you will let me know, won't you?"

Absolutely not! Rather than speak the words, however, Jayne merely smiled. She felt rather out of sorts of a sudden. Turning, she spotted Walfort sitting off to the side, appearing as lonely as she felt. With only a few people stopping her for a quick chat, she managed to make it to his side before the current dance ended. Sitting in a chair beside him, she took his hand. "I think everything is going splendidly."

"You've done a wonderful job of it, Jayne. Even my mother, may she rest in peace, would have been impressed."

"We've been fortunate that the weather has held. I've seen a few go out into the garden." She bit her lower lip. "Is this difficult for you, Walfort? Watching everyone waltzing about?"

"No. I never really fancied dancing."

"But you were so good at it."

"Only when I was with you." His quick smile withered. "Do you miss it, Jayne?"

"How can I when I am right where I wish to be: beside the man I love?"

"You deserve so much better than I've given you."

"Walfort, please, let's not go there."

He nodded. His face brightened. "Ainsley, where have you been, old chap?"

She glanced up as Ainsley came to stand before them. Everything about him was perfect. His cravat appeared as though it had not been touched since his valet secured it. He had not a single dark hair out of place.

With sudden surprise, she realized she was searching for some sign that he'd had an assignation. What did she care what he did with whom?

"I was playing cards," he said.

"He has the devil's own luck at cards," Walfort muttered to her. "Now that you've left the tables, perhaps I'll give it a go. Although I hate to leave Jayne alone."

"She's hardly alone in this mash of people."

"I suppose that's true enough."

She didn't like them talking around her as though she wasn't there. Still, she touched Walfort's wrist, slid her hand over his. "You should go to the card room if that's where you prefer to be. I'll be perfectly all right."

"If you're sure."

"Of course."

"Perhaps to lessen the pain of his parting, you would honor me with a dance," Ainsley said.

She and Walfort both jerked their heads to the duke. Her heart slammed against her ribs and her chest tightened as though her corset had suddenly shrunk. "As we discussed previously," she replied, "I do not dance."

"Of course you dance, Jayne," Walfort said.

"Darling." She shook her head.

"I've made you uncomfortable with Ainsley, have I? With my proposal—"

"No, I—"

"I only want you to be happy. You always smiled so much when you danced. Please, Jayne, I've taken so much from you. Don't let the list include your love of dancing."

Blast Ainsley for putting her on the spot like this, more for being right, that she was punishing Walfort by denying herself the pleasures he could no longer enjoy.

"Oh, all right, then." She forced a smile. "Your Grace, I would be honored to dance with you."

As if on cue, the music faded away, quickly followed by the lilting strains of a waltz. As she rose to her feet and placed her hand on Ainsley's arm, she didn't wish to acknowledge the strength she felt there or the excitement that thrummed through her. She would not anticipate the next few moments. She would simply endure them.

"I do not appreciate the position in which you placed me," she said cuttingly as they moved away from her husband. "You know I did not wish to dance."

"If you truly didn't wish to, you'd have never accepted."

She eyed him sharply. "You do not know me well enough to know what I wish for."

But when he took her in his arms and swept her over the dance floor, a thrill shot through her that she could not deny. She had so loved dancing: the graceful movements, the music inhabiting her soul in ways it could not when she was merely a spectator. And Ainsley, damn him, was particularly talented when it came to leading her. He held her the proper distance away from him, and yet it was as though they were one, without a misstep. His gaze never once strayed from her, as though she were the only one who mattered.

"Do not seek to charm me," she uttered.

"I wouldn't dream of it."

They circled the floor in silence, and she was aware of others watching them. She ignored them.

"Relax, Jayne," he said quietly. "And smile. If not for me, then for Walfort. As I've said before, by not finding pleasure where you can, you punish him, cause him to suffer."

"I suppose you think I should embrace that plan of his."

"On the contrary, I'm having a difficult time understanding it. If you were mine, I would kill any man who touched you. Obviously, he loves you a great deal. So smile for him, sweetheart. Pretend he is holding you now."

"You're nothing at all like him."

"Which is the reason I suggested you pretend. Close your eyes if you like."

Only she didn't want to close her eyes. She wanted to catch sight of the other couples dancing. She wanted to see the glitter of the chandeliers. She wanted to see the flames reflecting off his black hair. As sinful, as awful, as selfish as it was, she wanted to see the appreciation in his green eyes as he waltzed with her.

Perhaps he was pretending as well, but she didn't care. For a few moments she felt young and carefree again. Hope for a bright future soared in her heart. Joy filled her. She wasn't gossiping with the matrons. She wasn't envying the young girls.

She despised the corner of her heart that embraced the prick of jealousy, that knew they had their entire lives filled with promise ahead of them, while she often felt that hers was over.

She was making too much of this, she told herself. It was simply a dance. She could have another if she wanted, yet she suspected that Ainsley had spoiled her for anyone else. Would the same occur if she embraced Walfort's ridiculous plan? If she took Ainsley into her bed—for a single night—would he spoil her for future lovers, make her discontent for whomever she chose? A silly thought, as Walfort was correct: she would never take a lover, would never betray him. Just as, when he'd been able, he'd never betrayed her.

When the final strains of the violins echoed through the room, she bid them farewell with fond remembrance. She would not regret that they left her as so many dreams had.

"Thank you, Your Grace."

"It was most assuredly my pleasure."

She was aware of an odd ache in her jaw and realized that sometime during the waltz she had indeed begun smiling. It was very difficult now to erase the curve of her lips as Ainsley escorted her from the dance floor, back to the corner where they'd left Walfort. Only as they neared, she noticed that he was no longer there.

"He probably went to the game room to play cards," Ainsley said.

"Yes, I'm sure."

He lifted her gloved hand, held her gaze, and pressed his lips against her knuckles. She could feel the warmth of his mouth through her kidskin gloves.

"Rest assured that I will not accept Walfort's invitation to prolong my stay. I will depart in the morning."

"He will be disappointed."

"But you will not. And like your husband, it is only your happiness that concerns me."

He left her there, and she was not willing to acknowledge the twinge of disappointment his parting brought.

It had been a mistake to dance with her. Standing in a darkened corner of the terrace, striving to cool his ardor, he'd known it would be. From the moment he saw her standing in the entry hallway, so beautiful, so poised, he'd known he should not approach her.

Yet he'd been unable to resist. He wanted to see her smile as he'd not seen her smile since his arrival, as he suspected she'd not smiled since the night he brought the news of the accident. But he'd remembered her smile on the night before she married, when she danced with Walfort. Not a single star in the heavens could outshine her eyes.

Tonight it had taken a while, but eventually she succumbed to the lure of the music and the motion of their bodies following where the rhythm led. He could have danced with her all night, but the one dance was scandalous enough.

He knew speculation abounded that she was the woman with whom he'd have a tryst while here. She was the only woman to whom he was giving attention. Quite honestly, no other woman interested him. That *she* did was unfortunate. For in spite of Walfort's insistence that he get his wife with child, Ainsley knew she was too loyal to ever come to him willingly. And he did not take unwilling women to his bed.

He heard the sniffles, the evidence of tears, and realized he was not alone out here. Turning, he spied the shadowy silhouette and immediately recognized the slender form. Even the night couldn't hide her from him. Her back was to him. He could leave with her none the wiser, grant her solitude and privacy, but he suspected she'd had a good deal too much of it over the years. He'd seen her smile wither when she realized that her husband was no longer waiting for her when the dance was over. She'd handled herself with such aplomb. If he'd not felt her fingers flinching on his arm, not seen the flush of pleasure retreat from her cheeks, he might not have known how truly devastated she'd been. So while he knew he should walk back toward the light, toward the doors where people ambled in and out to enjoy the coolness of the gardens, he strolled instead farther into the darkness. "Jayne?"

He heard the hitch in her breathing, a final sniff, before she said quietly, "Your Grace."

"Such formality, Jayne." He slipped his handkerchief into her hand.

"Thank you."

She erased the evidence of her tears with such delicacy. "I shall have it washed and returned to you."

"Keep it. You never know when you might have a need of it."

He was surprised she didn't ask him to leave, and so he contented himself with the opportunity to be near her again.

"It was a mistake to try to pretend that all is as it once was. I forget—no, I don't forget, I just ignore all the things we no longer have." She released a small, pitiful laugh. "I don't mean to burden you. You should return to the festivities."

"I have a reputation to maintain."

She turned then, and somehow the moonlight through the trees managed to limn her face. He could see a trail of tears that she'd overlooked, and the sight of it cut into him with the ferocity of a well-handled rapier.

"Your reputation?" she repeated.

"I'm known for only dancing once and then leaving. If I were to return, what would people think?"

"That perhaps someone has struck your fancy."

She had. But he couldn't tell her that, because she might ask for more of an explanation, and he doubted she would be pleased to know that she fascinated him as no other woman ever had.

He gave her a secretive smile, and Jayne wondered what it meant. She should leave now. She didn't wish to be intrigued by him. "Why have you never married?" she asked.

"My brothers, damn them. They are both madly in love with their wives. Observing them has made me not want to settle for less."

"You are fortunate that your coffers are full and do not require that you marry in order to fill them."

"Walfort would have married you regardless."

She wasn't quite so sure. "I suppose we shall never know." She sighed. "I really should return to my guests."

"You missed some tears." His palm, so warm, cradled her face. She wondered when he'd removed his gloves. Slowly, his thumb stroked the curve of her cheek. "A woman such as you should never be brought to tears. I regret any of my actions that may have led to this moment."

"I could list them for you, if you like, but what would be the point?"

"To punish me. It is what you desire, is it not?"

"I see no point in my desiring anything any longer."

"Nothing at all? What of children?"

"They are not to be had. I will not even entertain Walfort's ridiculous notion."

"But surely there are other things you must desire? When was the last time you were kissed?"

She didn't know why she answered him. Perhaps it was the lull of his voice, the stroke of his thumb, the shadows that offered secrecy. "The night of the accident, before Walfort went out."

"And he's not kissed you since?"

His voice carried a strange undertone—disbelief, anger—she couldn't quite place it. She scoffed. "Why ever would he start what he cannot finish?"

"A kiss need not be the start of anything. It owns itself. It is simply what it is. His hands, his fingers, are not paralyzed. His lips, his tongue . . . are you telling me that in three years he's never once given you so much as this?"

His mouth covered hers, and heat poured through her body. His arm came around her, so strong and sure, her breasts flattening against his solid chest. The hand that had cradled her face continued to stroke her cheek, only lower, near the corner of her mouth until the sensations became part of the kiss.

She knew she should shove him away, should slap him, but it had been so long, so desperately long since she had felt anything beyond the numbness that descended when she realized the full extent of Walfort's injuries. She'd imprisoned her own yearnings as his body imprisoned him. And now those very yearnings were clamoring to escape. She didn't want to acknowledge them.

They terrified her because she so desperately wanted to feel again. Pleasure, hope, possibilities, dreams, passion. It wasn't fair. It wasn't fair to her husband, it wasn't fair to her.

But for the span of several heartbeats, she thought of nothing but the tantalizing touch of his tongue, the richness of his flavor—brandy. His scent filled her nostrils. His warmth wrapped around her. Tears scalded her eyes. It was all so simple, so complex. It awoke sensations that were better left sleeping.

He drew back. The moonlight revealed no mockery on his face. Instead it revealed something intense, something she could not decipher.

"Shame on him," he said so softly that she almost didn't hear it.

And shame on her, she thought, as she scurried across the terrace to the ballroom. Shame on her. Because she'd enjoyed it. She wanted him to kiss her again.

Chapter 6

The ball had come to an end near two. The ladies had withdrawn to their bedchambers. Most of the gentlemen as well, except for a few who continued to play cards or billiards. Walfort was one of the men who had yet to retire. Jayne knew because she was sitting on his bed awaiting his arrival.

Why hadn't he kissed her? Why didn't he simply hold her? He suffered, she knew he did, but what of her, and her needs? So many needs he could no longer fulfill. Yet he was thinking of what she desired when he'd suggested she take Ainsley to her bed. She'd scoffed, grown angry.

She didn't want to betray him, but oh, to feel again. It was cruel and wonderful at the same time. With one kiss Ainsley awoke everything that had been dormant. It terrified her to think of what he could accomplish with more than a kiss.

The clock was near to striking three in the morning when the door to Walfort's bedchamber finally opened and Randall pushed him into the room. Walfort's eyes widened. "Jayne? What in God's name—"

She slid off the bed. "It's urgent that I speak with you."

* * *

He'd been a damned fool to kiss her. What in God's name had possessed him?

She'd tasted so remarkably sweet, had fairly melted against him. He'd been tempted to lift her into his arms and carry her to that tiny bed in that tiny bedchamber he was given and unleash every ounce of passion he possessed. Pleasure her until she set free all the damned yearnings she'd imprisoned.

Instead, he'd made his way to the library, grateful to find it absent of people, so he could indulge in the whiskey and strive to forget the feel, scent, and taste of her. Unfortunately, he was having very little luck there.

He should find a lady to distract him. Only he wanted no other woman. He wanted to gaze into blue eyes and run his fingers through black hair and touch the white streak that so mesmerized him.

He cursed Walfort for putting the notion of bedding his wife into his mind. He'd been able to think of little else since coming here. He would be glad to leave on the morrow.

He glanced at the clock on the mantel. A little past three. "Today," he muttered. "I'll be leaving today."

He finished off the whiskey in his glass, considered opening another bottle, but what was the point? Nothing was going to make him forget the pleasure of that kiss. He shoved himself to his feet just as the door opened.

Randall stepped through. "Your Grace, his lordship instructed me to find you. He wishes to have a word . . . in his bedchamber."

Following the man through the residence that suddenly seemed so ominously quiet, Ainsley wondered why the summons at such an ungodly hour. Perhaps Jayne had confessed about the kiss. Since Walfort had indicated that Ainsley should do a great deal more with his wife, he hardly was in a position to be angry. Mayhap relieved. Mayhap hopeful that Jayne and Ainsley had decided to humor him.

No. Ainsley could not see Jayne agreeing to her husband's plans for getting her with child.

So he was most surprised when he stepped into Walfort's bedchamber and discovered Jayne sitting on a settee before the fireplace, wearing her nightdress and robe, her hair plaited. Walfort sat in a high-backed chair nearby, studying his wife as though afraid she might shatter. Why in the bloody hell wasn't he sitting beside her?

The door closed quietly behind him. Walfort glanced over at him. "Ainsley, good, we wanted to talk with you . . . before either of us lost our nerve."

He immediately sobered. This wasn't good.

"Please join us," Walfort continued.

Ainsley wondered if the vacant spot on the settee had been reserved for him. He strode across the room and stood beside the fireplace, resting his forearm against the mantel. The fire was high, blazing, yet Jayne seemed to be shivering. Her toes peeked out from beneath the nightdress, one foot crossed over the other. She appeared so damned vulnerable. Unlike her husband, she had yet to look at or acknowledge him. Her gaze was riveted on the flames.

"Jayne had a few questions," Walfort began.

"About?" His voice sounded rough, raw. All the damned whiskey burning his throat for the past few hours.

"My plan for seeing that she gains the child she so desperately wants."

Which, judging by the paleness in her features and the bright hue in Walfort's, neither of them was completely comfortable with. "I don't think—"

"Where?" she blurted. "Where would this assignation take place? Would you remain here?"

She was gripping her hands so tightly that the knuckles were turning white. He wanted to kneel before her and hold her, comfort her. He wanted to wrap his hands around hers and rub them until she relaxed. Why was Walfort keeping his distance? He knew that if he were to answer her question, he would reveal that he'd given considerable thought to how he would handle this matter—which would no doubt offend her—but he couldn't leave her wallowing in doubt. He certainly couldn't comfort her in front of her husband. He had no plans to do more than that with Walfort near.

"I have a cottage," he said. "On a lake. To the north. I use it when I seek solitude. It"—is someplace I have shared with few and would welcome sharing with you—"would offer privacy."

"I've been there, Jayne," Walfort said quietly. "It would provide for a lovely month away."

"A month?" She looked at her husband then, and Ainsley could see the disconcertedness in her gaze. Apparently Walfort had failed to provide her with details.

"Yes. From the time your next . . . menses . . . ends until it's time for it to begin again. To be sure."

"A month," she whispered again, returning her gaze to the fire.

Silence stretched between them, the only sound in

the room the crackling within the hearth. Ainsley met Walfort's gaze. You should tell her, he thought. You should tell her all that you did that night. She would not hesitate if she knew everything. Yesterday, he'd thought the confession an awful notion, but tonight he knew it would send her running into his arms. God help him, he wanted her there.

Walfort must have known what Ainsley was thinking, because he gave a slight shake of his head and turned his attention back to his wife. "Jayne, I've long wanted to give you a child," he said quietly. "It is not the way I had imagined it coming about, but it will bring me great joy to see your smile once again dancing in your eyes . . . as it did that afternoon when you told me I would be a father. I've never known such happiness. We can have that again."

Ainsley watched her toes wiggle, her hands loosen. She straightened her spine and took a deep breath. "I have some rules."

"Rules?" Ainsley repeated.

Her gaze captured his. He'd never seen such determination. "You are to never kiss me."

"Jayne—" Walfort began.

"You said this was to be a transaction, without emotion. You said I would not be betraying you because I feel nothing for Ainsley. So be it. He is never to kiss me. I will take no pleasure from the act itself. I realize that he must, of course, in order to—" She latched her gaze back onto his. "But you must do what you can to make our encounters as brief as possible. If you can't abide by the rules, then I see no point in continuing."

He considered storming out and telling her to go to the devil as he went, but beneath her façade, she was frightened by what had occurred on the terrace. He was certain of it. She was afraid he'd hurt her, when it was the last thing he wanted to do. He wanted her to have happiness. He wanted to give her what Walfort could not, regardless of the cost to himself. "I accept your terms."

He might have laughed at the stunned expression on her face if this entire matter weren't so serious. Obviously, she'd expected him to decline, probably *wanted* him to decline.

"But I have a condition of my own," he said somberly.

"What would that be?" she asked.

"You must swear that you will love this child."

"How can you possibly doubt—"

"You despise me, Jayne. My mother, bless her, where Westcliffe was concerned, was never able to separate the father from the child. I'll not have my child suffer a similar fate. Swear—"

"I do. With all my heart. I would never . . . I will love this child."

He shifted his gaze to a man he'd once called friend, although at this moment he was closer to being the devil. "I'll have your word as well."

"Of course. You have it. The child will never doubt my affection."

"Then it seems we've come to terms."

With a jerky nod, she rose to her feet. "My menses began today. I shall see you in a sennight."

She strolled from the room with all the grace of a queen.

When the door closed after her, Walfort said on a rush, "Thank God. I didn't think she'd do it. Pour us a brandy, will you? You may, of course, ignore all her rules—"

"I have no intention of ignoring her rules."

"But it will be little more than—"

"Hell for us all, I've no doubt."

Chapter 7

Blackmoor Cottage
November, 1860

He was not nervous. By God, he was not.

When Ainsley strode through the cottage for the third time, he was simply ensuring that everything was as it should be when his guest arrived at any moment.

Blackmoor was his sanctuary. He never brought women here. The thought of sharing this residence with Jayne—he couldn't deny the pleasure it brought him. It was an odd notion to entertain a lady here. It was a gentleman's retreat. Hunting, fishing, and hiking abounded. The mountains in the distance and the nearby lake provided a magnificent view. He wished it were spring or early summer. He wished he could share much of the area with her, wished she would see it and appreciate it as he did. He wished she were coming here without dread accompanying her, but he suspected she wasn't anticipating her time here at all.

For some reason, she had decided to journey here in hopes of getting with child. His kiss certainly hadn't convinced her that she'd find heaven in his arms. Otherwise she would not have banned him from kissing her again. She'd seemed to enjoy it. So why had she forbidden him from kissing her? Had she enjoyed it too much?

The thought stopped him in his tracks in the hallway. She'd changed her mind about being with him, but put all those silly rules into play. Did she think something this complex could be handled so simply? She was a fool if she thought so, and he'd never judged her to be a fool. Twenty-eight days. Four weeks. The rules wouldn't protect her from his charms, no matter how desperately she wished it. While he intended to honor them as best he could, he also intended to ensure that before she left she found satisfaction in his arms at least one night. It would be a crime to have her and not bring her pleasure.

He heard the clatter of the carriage wheels over the pebbled path. His heart sped up to match the whirring rhythm. Striding down the hallway to the front door, he couldn't remember the last time he'd anticipated a lady's arrival with such eagerness. He stepped out onto the landing and watched as the carriage rounded the bend, stirring the autumn leaves in the abundant trees that grew over his property. The sun was near the horizon, setting for the night, and it turned the burnished leaves a more coppery shade. He was glad she would be here when the days were shorter and the nights longer. Although he couldn't deny that a part of him wished she'd be here in spring. And summer. Even winter.

But he would only have her for this short time in the fall. He intended to make the most of it.

The driver brought the carriage to a rocking stop. A footman leapt down to open the door. Ainsley made his way down the stairs as two footmen emerged from the house to assist with the trunks. He stood impatiently while Jayne's footman handed her down.

She wore a black dress and black hat with a veil. The drab clothing could not disguise her elegance or her beauty.

The footman assisted another lady out of the carriage. Her lady's maid no doubt. He'd not considered that she would bring her own. He approached Jayne. Her fingers were knitted together so tightly that he was certain if she weren't wearing gloves he'd see that her knuckles had turned white. He bowed slightly. "Jayne, welcome to Blackmoor."

"It is hardly a 'cottage.'"

He glanced back at the three levels of structure with the ivy climbing its walls. "Compared with Grantwood Manor it is."

"Nor did I expect servants about."

"They are discreet. They know only that a Lady Jayne has come here for holiday. I thought it important that they realize a *lady* is here, but I saw no need to inform them of titles. They serve only the residence here. You'll never encounter them elsewhere. If danger of discovery lies anywhere, I suspect it is with your servants."

"They're trusted."

"Then all should be well."

"Yes, of course, I'm sorry. I didn't meant to imply—"

"Jayne, this is not the first time I've had an assignation that I wished to keep secret. If my dalliances are known, it is only because the ladies wished it so."

She nodded jerkily and whispered, "I do not wish this one to be known."

"Then it shan't be. Now, come, let me show you to your rooms."

She placed her hand on his arm. In spite of his jacket and her gloves, he could feel her slight trembling.

"It's not too late to climb back into the carriage and return home," he informed her. Although God help him, he hoped she wouldn't.

She glanced up at him, and he hated the veil that prevented him from fully enjoying the rich blue of her eyes. "No, this is important to Walfort."

"To protect your anonymity, perhaps while you're here you should refer to him as Gus rather than by his title."

"Gus?"

"His Christian name."

"Augustus? I never liked it."

"I did call him Wally in school."

"That's even worse. No dignity to it."

"Then perhaps it would be best while we're here not to mention him at all."

"Yes, quite."

He led her up the steps and into the entry hallway. He watched as her lips parted slightly, lips he was forbidden from tasting.

"I was expecting one room, a cot, and a fireplace," she said, glancing around at the portraits, statues, and greenery.

"That sounds like a hovel, not a cottage."

"Is this part of your entailment?"

"No. I was visiting the area when I was eighteen. It simply . . . called to me. I made the owner an offer on the spot. Fortunately, he was agreeable. I always find peace here. It is my hope that you will as well. I've shared it with very few."

"Well, it's lovely."

Not as lovely as you, he almost said, but he doubted she'd appreciate any flirtatious banter. Even if the words were heartfelt and not intended to woo.

The butler stepped into the entryway. Immaculately dressed, he stood tall and proud.

"Manning, be so kind as to show Lady Jayne's maid to her room," Ainsley said.

"Yes, Your Grace." He turned to the woman in question. "Miss?"

"Lily."

"If you'll come with me."

The girl hesitated. Ainsley guessed her to be not much older than Jayne.

"It's all right, Lily," Jayne reassured her. "I'll ring for you when I have need for you."

"Yes, m'lady."

When they'd left, Jayne asked, "How many servants do you have here?"

"A dozen. They are at your beck and call."

"I intend to trouble them as little as possible. Easier to be forgotten that way."

"You are not easily forgotten." He wished he'd held his tongue. He immediately read the discomfort on her face. "This way."

He led her up the stairs. They were not as grand or as sweeping as the ones at Grantwood Manor, but they were wide enough to allow them to walk side by side. Their legs brushed and she nearly stumbled. He was beginning to gain a better understanding of the courage it had taken her to come here. When the initial attraction was strong enough, he'd taken to his bed women with whom he had little more than a passing acquaintance. But he had no doubt that Jayne's experiences were limited to Walfort, that she'd been a virgin on her wedding night. Giving herself to him now was not something she did lightly. Betraying her vows, regardless of the circumstances, could not be very palatable.

At the landing, he guided her to a room next to his. "I have no bathing chamber here," he told her, "but the servants can bring you a tub and hot water whenever you wish it."

She nodded. He opened the door. Her fingers slid off his arm as she wandered into the room. The velvet bed covering, the canopy, and the drapes at the window were blue, matching the shade of her eyes. A week ago everything had been green. The fainting couch near the window, the plush couch and armchairs near the fireplace, were new. Flowers from the greenhouse filled vases. Everything had been arranged with her comfort in mind.

She gave the bed a brief glance in passing. Removing her cloak, she set it on the chaise longue and walked to the window. "What a lovely view of the lake."

"I've always liked it."

He watched as she lifted her veil, exposing the profile of her exotic features to his perusal. His gut tightened as though she'd removed everything, as though she stood before him in total nudity. She pulled out two hat pins, removed her hat, and set it on her cloak. Her gaze shot to the bed again. Straightening, she began tugging on a glove.

"Shall we get to it, then?"

Any ardor he may have felt building plummeted. She

looked as though she was on the verge of being escorted to the gallows. He strode toward the bed. She stiffened, backed up a step, caught herself retreating and angled her chin defiantly. He leaned against the bedpost. "I thought we'd have a relaxing dinner first. Perhaps you'd like to bathe, even nap, after the long journey."

"I wouldn't be able to sleep. A bath might be nice. And dinner. Although I hope your cook didn't go to a great deal of bother, as I doubt I'll be able to eat much."

"Are you afraid?"

"No, I . . ." Her gaze darted to the bed, the window, the seating area, anywhere except to him.

He walked over to her, acutely aware of the tension radiating from her. "Don't think about what's to come, Jayne. Simply leave everything to me. I promise it will not be nearly as awful as you're imagining." He skimmed his fingers over her cheek, taking satisfaction when she finally met his gaze, fighting the urge to take her in his arms because she looked so damned uncertain. "Come to the library when you're ready for dinner. Meanwhile, I'll have the servants bring up bathwater."

He turned and strode from the room. He didn't appreciate at all seeing the apprehension in her eyes. He had his work cut out for him: getting her to relax and enjoy what was to come. Fortunately, it was a task he was greatly anticipating.

Not think about what was to come? Had he gone stark raving mad? It was all she'd been able to think about since the meeting held in the sitting area of Walfort's bedchamber at twenty-two minutes past three in the morning.

As she sank into the warm water in the tub set up

near the fireplace, she wished that they'd simply gotten it over with as she suggested. Instead, the specter of what was to happen later would simply hang over them.

Why had she agreed to this? It wasn't too late to call for the carriage and begin the journey home, before any damage had been done. But Ainsley would correctly judge her a coward, and Walfort, drat him, would be disappointed.

During dinner last night he'd asked her to come to his bed.

"I do wish you'd reconsider your determination to take no pleasure in what is to come," he'd said as she lay in his arms.

"How can you ask that of me?"

"Because I love you, and I want you to be happy."

"What if I don't get with child?"

"Then we shall arrange another time for you to . . . be with him."

If she didn't get with child, then she would find her own lover. Of course, there was the matter of the Seymour blood to consider. Which made Ainsley nearly perfect.

"Will you kiss me?" she asked.

"Pardon?"

She sat up. "Will you kiss me?" She lowered her lips to his. "Please?"

He threaded one hand through her hair, holding her head in place as his mouth nibbled at hers, before settling in with more purpose. Still, her heart very nearly shattered. Where was the passion they'd once shared? Where was the heat? It was as though they were merely going through the motions.

When he finally guided her head back to the nook of

his shoulder, she felt even more lonely, more devastated. They lay in silence with a chasm widening between them that she didn't understand.

"M'lady, are you ready to leave the bath?"

Lily's voice brought Jayne from her reverie. "Yes."

She stood, stepped out, and wrapped the large towel around herself.

"I've prepared the violet gown for this evening," Lily said.

Jayne had brought few clothes, assuming she'd spend most of the time in bed. She'd planned to wear the black again tonight, but supposed she should at least play the part of harlot.

Although Ainsley certainly wasn't treating her as such. He'd been the perfect gentleman upon her arrival. No leering. No sense of victory or conquest. Based on his libertine ways and rumors of his prowess, she'd expected him to take her straightaway to bed. She certainly hadn't expected him to delay the inevitable. She was both grateful and resentful of the reprieve.

By the time Lily had arranged her hair and helped her with the gown, Jayne could barely breathe. She doubted it had anything to do with her corset. She was simply nervous, which irritated her. Many a lady knew no more of her husband on her wedding night than she knew of Ainsley. She would simply pretend they were married and . . .

As though that would ever happen. Never in a million years would she truly entertain the notion of marrying Ainsley. With the man's rumored insatiable appetite, faithfulness would be foreign to him. She wondered how many ladies had frequented his bed between the time he left Walfort's estate and now. Dear God, she did hope he wasn't diseased. Surely he'd have not agreed to this if he were.

With a last glance at her reflection in the mirror, she took a deep breath, walked across the room, opened the door, and released a shriek.

Looking monstrously handsome, Ainsley leaned against the wall, his arms crossed over his black jacket and hunter green waistcoat.

"I thought I was to meet you in the library," she said, fighting desperately to regain her breath.

"You were." He shoved himself away from the wall like some large predatory cat she'd observed in the zoological gardens. "But it occurred to me that since I was an inconsiderate host and didn't take you on a tour of the house, you might not know where to find the library."

"Oh, yes. Quite right."

"You look lovely by the way."

"Thank you. Lily selected the gown."

"Did she put the rose in your cheeks as well?"

Touching them, she felt the warmth there. "Yes, no, I . . ." She shook her head. "I don't know what I was thinking to come here."

"That you'd like to have a child."

"It took Walfort and I four years. We have no guarantee—"

"Except if we don't try, it won't happen at all."

She didn't understand this man. "Why are you willing to do this?"

"To see you happy. If you want a lengthier explanation than that, I will need an abundance of wine."

"Perhaps that is explanation enough." Yet she could not deny the sense that there was more. But did she really want to know it?

He held out his arm. "Come. I have an excellent wine cellar here."

She placed her hand on his arm. "How can you appear so relaxed with what is to come later?"

"I believe in living in the present, not the future. And right now my present involves dining."

She wasn't quite certain that she believed his claim of living in the present. He'd obviously given some thought to their future, because dinner had been designed for seduction. They sat at a small, round, cloth-covered table in a room with a balcony that overlooked the lake, which captured a full moon's reflection. The windowed doors were closed because of the cool night air, but the glass was spotlessly clean and it was as though nothing existed between them and the view. A fire crackled in a nearby fireplace. Candle flames flickered in the center of the table, where orchids released their sweet scent. Moonlight, starlight, firelight, and candlelight provided the only illumination allowed to intrude into the room.

It was cozy and intimate. And very seductive.

The servants would bring in a course and leave, not even a footman remaining behind. She thought she should have been nervous, uncomfortable even, but he made no untoward advances.

"Your servants have this down to an art," she said. "You must often bring ladies here."

He poured more red wine into her goblet. "I've never brought a lady here."

Her gaze clashed with his. She read the truth of his words in the clover green. "Why me?"

"The privacy. The seclusion. These servants are not likely to ever serve at the family estate or in London, so no one will ever identify exactly who you are."

"Do you not give the same consideration to your . . . paramours?"

"I do." He lifted his goblet, swirled the contents. "But my time with them usually involves only a brief interlude, which can be handled in various ways to ensure secrecy. And it's in rather bad form for me to discuss other women. I'm not usually in the habit of doing so."

"I asked, which I suppose was bad form on my part. I apologize. I'm sorry. I don't know how to do this."

"For one thing, stop thinking about what it is we're doing here."

"Much easier said than done."

"Drink some more wine."

"Do you want me snookered?"

"Not particularly, but I do want you more at ease."

She sipped her wine, licked her lips, searched for a safe topic. "Do you fish in your lake?"

"I do. Have you ever gone fishing?"

"No."

"I suspect you would be very good at it."

"Why?"

"It requires patience."

"Are you patient, then?"

"Usually."

She heard in his voice the echo of the one time, the one night, he wasn't. She didn't want to travel there. If she did, she wouldn't be able to carry through on her reason for being here.

"I heard that Westcliffe and his wife had another son."

Ainsley's smile was that of a proud uncle. "Yes, Rafe. As handsome as his father. Takes to crying a good deal of the time, though."

"Your mother must be beside herself with so many grandchildren already."

"I believe they make her feel old."

"Perhaps that is the reason she has such a young lover." Before he could respond, she held up her hand. "My apologies. I do not mean to sit in judgment—"

"My mother enjoys her notoriety. I doubt there is a single person in the aristocracy who doesn't believe Leo is her lover."

"Do her scandals embarrass you?"

"My mother is one of the strongest and most courageous women I've ever known. She's entitled to live as she chooses. Besides, my brothers and I have had our share of scandals. Who are we to judge?"

"You love her."

"Deeply. And Leo makes her happy. I can't fault him for that."

She supposed, considering his own reputation, that she shouldn't have been surprised that he'd be so accepting of inappropriate behavior in others. In a way, it was a bit of a relief, for surely it meant he found no fault with her decision to be here.

But then what did she care what he thought of her? They were not true lovers. They didn't even like each other. They would tolerate each other, make the best of this most uncomfortable and unusual situation.

Each time she emptied her goblet, he refilled it. She

knew she should protest, but her muscles were loosening and a warm lethargy was spooling through her. She thought if she took enough sips, perhaps if she looked at him at just the right angle she might see Walfort, could pretend he was Walfort. While they carried similar blood, shared some of the same ancestors, they favored each other hardly at all. Ainsley was decidedly more handsome, his features more sharply defined.

His eyes were a mesmerizing green, and when he focused them on her, she could almost imagine that he found her beautiful, that he desired her.

But then he desired all women. She was nothing special. He would have her, then easily forget her. He was here out of obligation. A debt owed. A redemption sought.

She should never forget that. If he did manage to get her with child, how would she reconcile the revulsion she felt for him against the gratitude she'd feel? He was the absolute worst choice for this endeavor. She should call for her carriage now.

But she didn't think she could stand the mortification of going to someone else, of asking for this favor. During the past week, she'd allowed herself to dream of holding a child to her breast. To turn back from the dream now when it might be so close to being fulfilled . . .

She drank down another glass of wine. It made everything seem not quite so sinful.

When they were finished eating, he escorted her to her bedchamber. She wondered if she should invite him in now, before the effects of the wine had any chance to fade.

"I'll join you in a few moments," he said quietly,

taking the decision from her. "Remove your wedding ring before I do."

Nodding, she slipped into the room and pressed her back to the closed door. Now the true nightmare would begin.

Unfortunately, she was suddenly far too sober.

Chapter 8

Lily had helped her change into the nightdress. Now, Jayne stood at the window, gazing out on the moon. Terrified. She should have drunk far more wine. She'd placed her wedding ring—which she had vowed never to remove—in a wooden heart-shaped box on the vanity. It was lined with velvet, and she wondered if Ainsley had set it there, specifically for the purpose of holding her ring. She was beginning to realize he was not a man who left much to chance.

The soft rap on her bedchamber door nearly had her flying through the window.

"Enter." To her consternation, her voice mimicked the squeak of a dormouse.

She turned to face the door as it opened and Ainsley strode in. She'd expected him to be wearing a dressing gown. Instead, he wore a billowy white shirt, unbuttoned at the collar and cuffs, and a pair of trousers. After closing the door behind him, he walked over to the vanity and blew out the flame in the lamp.

His steps were eerily silent, and she realized he was barefoot. He wandered over to the table beside the bed and with a brief breath extinguished the flame in that lamp. Two more lamps burned, one on the other side of the bed, one in the sitting area. She didn't know why her maid had left so many burning, or why she hadn't thought to put them out. Perhaps because she saw the darkness as a signal for going to bed.

His long predatory strides took him to one lamp and then the other. She didn't want to acknowledge how graceful and sinewy his movements were. He was obviously in no hurry, completely comfortable in his surroundings. As the shadows followed him, and began to reach for her, she was grateful for the encroaching darkness. At the last lamp, he stilled, held her gaze, and waited—one heartbeat, then two—before sending the final flame to sleep.

Struggling for breath, she watched as his silhouette approached her. When he stepped into the moonlight, she wished she'd drawn the drapes because it was impossible to pretend he was anyone other than who he was. Small tremors cascaded through her and she wasn't certain if they were the result of fear or anticipation.

He wrapped his hand—so warm, so large—around hers, and she was startled by the roughness of his palm.

"I'm almost as nervous as I was on my wedding night," she whispered.

"No need to be."

He was right, of course. She'd worried on her wedding night that she'd disappoint Walfort, but if Ainsley were disappointed . . . what did she care? She didn't want to please him or hold his heart or care what he thought. She wanted everything between them to remain impersonal.

But as he pulled her away from the window and led her toward the bed, she didn't know if it would be possible to not let any of this matter. Her legs were trembling so badly that she didn't think she'd have been able to climb onto the bed if he hadn't lifted her onto it, sitting her on the edge. When she made a motion to scoot back, he halted her.

"Just stay there. Lie back."

"But—"

"Your rules. I'm not going to get into bed with you."

"Oh. I see." He knew how to keep it impersonal. Of course. He had all the experience. He probably knew all sorts of things that she'd not even think to imagine. "All right."

With her legs dangling over the edge of the bed, she lay back and squeezed her eyes shut. She only wanted his seed. Walfort wanted her to have this. It was a transaction. Wasn't that what her husband had called it? Motions. She'd only go through the motions.

As she felt the slide of her hem up her calves, over her knees, she clutched the counterpane. She fought not to squeeze her legs together as her gown was eased up her thighs.

She heard a pop, like the sound of bones creaking when someone knelt. She felt his fingers skimming along the inside of her thighs, spreading—

Her breathing came in tiny gasps. She would do this. For Walfort. Because he wanted this child. She bit her lower lip, mentally preparing herself to receive Ainsley. She felt a slight breeze stirring her curls and then a stroke—

She sat up abruptly. "What are you doing?"

She could make out only the shadows, but it was enough for her to know that he was kneeling between her legs.

"I'm preparing you," he said quietly.

"No. This is . . . this is—" Something Walfort had certainly never done. "It's too intimate."

"You're not ready for me. It's going to hurt and you're likely to bleed. You've made it clear that you want as little intimacy between us as possible. This will hasten things along. Trust me, Jayne."

She wasn't quite certain she could trust herself. She nodded, not sure if he could see her motions, lay back down and dug her head into the mattress. "Make it quick," she commanded, once again squeezing her eyes shut.

He began where he left off, with his tongue stroking her intimately. So intimately. Swirling and dipping, taunting and teasing. Pleasure rippled through her. She wanted to deny it but she couldn't. It felt so marvelous. It had been so long, so very long since sensations had poured through her. She'd locked so much away. When he'd kissed her on the terrace, she discovered he possessed a magical key that would open locks best kept closed. It was the reason she'd forbidden him to kiss her ever again. It was the reason she'd made the rules. When his mouth had molded itself to hers, when it tasted and searched and conquered, she'd known that he was not a man who would settle for a woman remaining immune to his charms.

Now his touch was devastating. She knew she should order him to stop. Order him to cease—and she would. In a moment. Wicked girl that she was, she simply wanted to enjoy the sensations he was arousing for a bit longer. Only a bit.

But he worked his magic until she became completely lost in the sensuality, until it took over and controlled her. It was lovely, so lovely, the pleasure mounting almost beyond endurance.

His mouth continued to play naughty games, to suckle, to lick, to torment. Oh, he was masterful. He knew when to apply pressure, when to go gently. She'd never felt anything so absolutely wicked and incredible. She needed to give it up, she knew she did, but she couldn't, didn't want to let it go.

It had been so long, so long since pleasure had spiraled through her. But she couldn't remember it ever being this intense, this spellbinding. She heard whimpers and cries, realizing too late that they came from her. She shoved her hand against her mouth to hold the sounds at bay. It seemed everything within her needed to be released or she'd die.

The cataclysm that ripped through her then shook her to the core, left her trembling and weak, left her barely coherent. She was vaguely aware of the pressure, then he was pushing into her with such force—

His groan echoed around her, his body jerked over her. She felt his heated seed pouring deeply into her. A last thrust, a low moan that sounded as though it had been ratcheted up from his soul. Breathing deeply, he shuddered above her. Stilled.

"I'd expected . . . a man of your reputation to last much longer."

"Then you are blind to your own allure," he rasped.

He shoved himself away from her, withdrew, and eased her nightdress back into place. Without another word he walked from the room, the door *snicking* softly back into place.

She crawled into the center of the bed, wrapped her arms around a pillow and wept.

* * *

He would never know where he found the strength to walk away from her. He'd wanted to climb onto the bed, take her into his arms and hold her near. Comfort her as she wept. He had no doubt that she would cry. All night she'd tried to appear so uncaring, so unaffected by what was to happen.

But now that it was over, it would hit her. She'd betrayed her vows, her husband, herself.

As Ainsley stood at the window in his bedchamber, sipping whiskey he'd known he would need, he could still smell the scent of her, taste her saltiness on his lips. He'd wanted to skim his fingers over every inch of her, wanted to leave no part of her unknown to his questing tongue, wanted to kiss—

He slammed his eyes closed. He thought he would go mad with wanting before his time with her was done. Yet neither would he give up a single moment that he would have with her.

He tossed back the last of the whiskey in his glass, poured more. It would be some time before he'd be able to go to sleep.

And when he did, he knew he would dream of her.

Chapter 9

He felt like hell when he woke up. The sunlight streaming through the windows caused his eyes to burn and intensified the pounding in his head. He never drank to excess when in the company of a lady, but then, when he finally tumbled into bed, no lady had been present.

Rolling to a sitting position, he realized he'd slept in his clothes. He didn't even remember crawling into bed. He scrubbed his hands up and down his face. He would have a full day with Jayne. A day of politeness, of ignoring their reason for being here—until night fell. Strangely, now that he was coming more fully awake, he was looking forward to being in her company, even if on the surface it would all be platonic.

He rang for his valet, then began stripping off his clothes. A bath was in order, followed by a shave. If he hurried, he could be down to breakfast before Jayne was finished enjoying the meal. It would almost be as though they were married.

Not quite, he thought with a chuckle. If they were married, he'd be greeting her in bed, not at the table. He glanced at the wall that separated their bedchambers.

He wondered if she'd welcome a visit from him this morning. Probably not. She needed a bit more time to adjust to what had transpired between them last night. But tonight, well, he hoped she'd be a bit more relaxed with him.

Even with the aid of his valet, he found himself entering the dining room nearly an hour later. To his utter disappointment, the only ones to greet him were his servants.

"Manning, has Lady Jayne been down to breakfast already, then?" he asked his butler.

"No, Your Grace. Her girl took up a tray nearly a half hour ago."

"I see."

Ainsley strolled over to the sideboard. The offerings were plentiful, but his appetite seemed not to have arrived with him. No doubt the lingering effects of too much whiskey the night before. Nor was he pleased by Jayne's avoiding him—which was her intent by sending down her maid.

Spinning on his heel, he headed for the door.

"Is something amiss with the selections, Your Grace?" Manning asked.

"I'm simply not hungry. Assure the cook that all is well."

"Yes, sir."

Ainsley made his way to the foyer, then ascended the stairs two at a time. His head threatened to return to its miserable aching state, but he endured it and kept up his pace until he reached the landing. His stride long and sure, he crossed over to her door and swung it open without preamble.

Still in her nightdress, her feet curled beneath her,

she was sitting in a chair by the window, gazing out. He had a brief glimpse of her looking forlorn before she popped out of the chair and slammed her hip against the window casing. Her hand was at her throat, her breathing rapid and heavy. On a nearby table was a tray of food that appeared untouched.

"What . . . what do you want?" she demanded, her gaze darting quickly to the bed before coming back to him.

That reaction certainly didn't bode well for tonight. She was having regrets, more than he'd anticipated.

Damn you, Walfort, damn you to hell.

He relaxed his stance, realizing that barging into her room as he had wasn't helping the situation. He was angry that she'd deliberately sought to avoid him at breakfast by having a tray brought to her, and he was angry by her reaction now. But in truth, while he'd hoped for a more pleasant welcome, her reaction was exactly what he'd expected.

"I wanted to make certain you were all right," he said quietly, infusing his voice with a calmness he didn't quite feel. The sight of her in her nightdress brought forth images of him lifting its hem and burying his face between her thighs. Her taste and scent were an aphrodisiac he was anxious to experience again. He was fairly certain she would object to that happening at this moment. He tilted his head toward the tray. "Manning informed me that you had a tray prepared."

"I'm quite well. I simply . . . desired a bit of solitude this morning."

He closed the door. "To deal with your sins?"

She pressed a hand to her forehead. "Is it a sin if I've been given permission?"

"I wouldn't think so."

As though he were approaching a skittish mare, he walked cautiously over to the window. Her apprehension-filled gaze followed his every step. What the deuce did she think he was going to do? Grab her, toss her onto the bed, and have his way with her?

Leaning his shoulder negligently against the wall, he looked out on the glorious morning. "The nearby village hosts a fair this time of year. I thought to ride over, have a look around, enjoy the day."

"It sounds lovely."

He shifted his attention to her. "I was hoping you'd join me."

She shook her head briskly. "No, I . . . I thought to . . ."

He could see her struggling to come up with some responsibility she needed to manage, but she had none, not here, not at his cottage.

"Avoid me?" he asked laconically.

Her blue eyes widened a fraction before she straightened her shoulders. "Of course not. That would defeat my purpose in being here, now wouldn't it?"

"Then come with me."

"Ainsley—"

"You can't possibly intend to spend the greater part of every day hiding out in this room."

"I'm not hiding."

He arched a brow.

"I'm not!" With a mulish expression, she folded her arms over her chest and turned to the window. He wanted to press his thumb to her brow, ease the deep furrow there.

"This time of year, we don't have many days where the sun is so brilliant. We should make the most of it."

He waited a moment, absorbing her silence. "Jayne, it's going to be a very long month. You've established rules to ensure you find no joy in the bedding. At least give yourself leave to find joy in other things while you're here."

"This is so hard, Ainsley," she rasped. "I knew it would be, but I was still not prepared for how blasted difficult it is."

"I know, sweetheart. Hence, the reason that I think attending the fair would be such a welcome reprieve." He shoved himself away from the wall. "I'm going. If you wish to languish here all day dreading the coming of night, so be it."

He'd taken two steps before she said, "I'd welcome the distraction, but it will take me a while to ready myself."

Glancing back over his shoulder, he smiled. "Take all the time you need. Have you a riding habit? I thought we'd take the horses."

"Yes. Yes, that would be lovely."

"Join me in the library when you're ready."

He strode from the room, his step a bit more lively than when he first entered. He felt as though he'd won the battle, but he knew he was still a long way off from winning the war.

As the mare, Lovely Lady, plodded along, Jayne felt her muscles begin to unknot, unwind. With guilt gnawing at her, she'd finally drifted off to sleep in the early morning hours, but upon wakening didn't feel at all rested. And she'd dreaded seeing Ainsley again. She wasn't certain what she expected of him. A triumphant air. A gloating. An arrogance.

After all, she'd succumbed to the talents of his mouth, was unable to refrain from falling into the whirlpool of pleasure he'd created. She almost drowned before he sent her skyward with such speed that she'd been disoriented. And then he'd been inside her, filling her before she even caught her breath.

Yet he'd displayed nothing of the sort. He was quiet, solicitous, almost apologetic. He was also quite right, that leaving the residence would be good for her. She was able to breathe more deeply and relax, knowing they would share no intimacy while they were out.

She regretted the cruel, unkind words she'd flung at him at the end of their encounter the night before. They'd been a defense, because in all honesty, it had felt marvelous to once again experience the nearness of a man—even if it was for far too brief a time. That, too, had prompted her ugliness. Easier to take that route than admit she wished he'd not been quite so hasty in arriving at his own enjoyment. A part of her longed to apologize, knew she should, but she welcomed a few hours of pretending they were here for a reason other than what they were. Perhaps tonight, during dinner, with a bit more wine—

The sounds of revelry reached her ears, cut off her thoughts. The village was up ahead, but it looked as though the fair had spilled out onto the surroundings like fruit from an overturned basket. She glanced over at Ainsley. He seemed at ease and pleased with all he saw. He guided her over to an area where carriages waited and other horses were tethered. The fair seemed to draw quite a crowd. She did hope she wouldn't encounter anyone she knew. How would she explain her presence?

Ainsley dismounted.

"Your Grace!" A young man she guessed to be in his late teens sauntered over and doffed his cap.

"Master Robin," Ainsley said. "How are you, lad?"

"Fine, sir. Need me to watch your horses?"

"Yes, and see that they get some oats." He handed the boy a crown before walking over to assist Jayne. His gloved hands circling her waist, he held her gaze. He had such remarkable green eyes. She briefly wondered how they might sparkle when filled with laughter. She'd heard his laugh, of course, at the river, but had not been near enough to see the mirth filter into his eyes. It unsettled her to be this close to him, knowing that in a few hours she would be much closer again. She forced her fingers to not tremble as she set them on his shoulders.

He lifted her down with as much effort as one might bring down a pillow. She wondered if holding her so near, he would find his thoughts traveling to last night, or had the encounter for him been as Walfort promised her it would be—nothing at all?

Ainsley stepped back and extended his arm. "Shall we?"

She bobbed her head, not trusting her voice. The whole point of this outing was to have a distraction from unruly thoughts. She needed to concentrate on the task at hand. They wandered onto the path that served as the main road into the village.

"Yew Gwace! Yew Gwace!"

Jayne released her hold on him as he spun around. A little girl was running toward him, and Ainsley's smile grew with her approaching nearness. It was a sight that took Jayne's breath.

As the child stumbled to a stop, Ainsley crouched. "Well, if it's not my favorite flower girl."

"See what I've got?" she asked, proudly extending an assortment of scraggly stems and leaves that her tiny hands were choking.

"Very nice indeed."

To Jayne's surprise, he took the offering and gave the girl a crown.

"Fank ye, ye Gwace." With that, she dashed off.

Chuckling, Ainsley stood.

"You paid for weeds," Jayne told him.

"In the spring, they'll have blossoms."

"They'll still be weeds."

"Ah, Jayne, you are cynical."

"Why? Because I believe you wasted a coin?"

"No. Because you see what is instead of what could be." He tucked the gangly plants into his pocket and again offered her his arm. His smile was no longer on display, and she found she missed it. With a bit of flirting, she might be able to entice it back, but flirtation was completely inappropriate under their circumstances. He wasn't her lover; he was simply a means to an end. She didn't want to consider how long it had taken her to get with child the first time. In all likelihood this month would be for naught.

Good Lord, Jayne, when did you become such a pessimist? And a cynic?

Before she knew it, they were in the thick of the crowd. She could see jugglers and acrobats performing off to the side. Ainsley guided her over to a booth where woolen wares were displayed. Mittens, caps, shawls.

"Your Grace," the rotund woman inside the booth said. She gave Jayne a speculative look. Probably not a good idea to be here.

"Mrs. Weatherly." It was apparent that Ainsley knew everyone and they recognized him. But then, he was unforgettable, and she suspected few dukes resided in the area. He patted Jayne's hand. "Tell me, which shawl would you like?"

It took Jayne a moment to realize he'd posed the question to her. "I'm not in need of a shawl."

"You don't have to *need* it. You can simply want it."

"No, I . . ." Didn't want to be any more indebted to him than she already was. She also wanted no reminders of her time here. She was struck with the absurdness of that thought. With luck, he would give her a reminder she would have for the remainder of her life. "They're lovely, but I don't want anything."

"For my mother, then. Which one would she like?"

Why in God's name was he asking her? "Surely, you know your mother's tastes better than I."

"Quite right. Have you something bold, Mrs. Weatherly?"

"Oh, yes, Your Grace. I have a lovely red." She brought forth a crimson piece, a beautiful shade.

"That'll do nicely. How much?"

"A sovereign?"

"Hmm. Seems like robbery to me, Mrs. Weatherly."

Indeed it was, Jayne thought. It was nicely made, but still—

"Let's make it two, shall we? Otherwise, I won't be able to sleep at night."

Jayne stared at Ainsley while Mrs. Weatherly tittered

about and produced a ledger. Ainsley wrote the item and the amount before applying his signature.

"Have it brought around tomorrow. My man will see that you're paid."

"Thank you, Your Grace. Have a lovely day."

The same scenario played out in each booth where they stopped. Ainsley would find an item—a necklace for his sister-by-marriage Claire, lace for his sister-by-marriage Mercy, a pipe for Westcliffe, leather gloves for Stephen—ask the price, then double it.

As they were walking away from the booth where he'd purchased a beaver hat for Leo—who had been his mother's lover for some time now, if rumors were to be believed—Jayne said, "You do know that when you haggle over prices, you are supposed to whittle down the amount."

"For some of these people, what they earn today will get them through the winter. I can afford to be generous."

"Walfort never could." She wanted to bite her tongue, but felt compelled to add, "He had nothing before my dowry. While it was substantial, we certainly couldn't be extravagant. Fortune seems to have smiled on you in many areas."

"Do you expect me to feel guilty because of it?"

She peered up at him. "No. I don't know what I expect. I don't even know why I'm prattling on about it."

"He didn't marry you for your dowry."

She averted her gaze. How had he known it was an area of insecurity for her? "It influenced him."

"I doubt it. I know at least two other ladies to whom marriage would have put far more into his coffers. He gave them nary a look. I suspect it was your eyes that offered him the riches he sought."

She felt a blush warming her cheeks. "You're far kinder than I've ever given you credit for."

"Nothing kind about speaking the truth." As though needing to turn the direction away from him, he added, "I'm famished. Let's see what we can do about that, shall we?"

He purchased a blanket, a wicker basket, and food from different vendors. Before Jayne realized it, she was sitting near a tree enjoying a meat pie. Across from her, Ainsley—stretched out on his side, lifted up on his elbow—was munching on an apple. His gaze took in his surroundings rather than settling on her. She was grateful for that. It was so much easier to relax and think when she didn't have his undivided attention.

He was at home here. She could see it in the ease of his movements, his unhurried manner, as though they had the entire day to lollygag about.

"Do you have work to see to here?" she asked.

His gaze darted to her before wandering off again. "Not really. The land the cottage sits on was not designed to bring in an income. I have no tenants. It's simply a place where I come when I want to escape my responsibilities."

"Do you come here often, then?"

"Once a year, perhaps." He sat up and slung the apple core into the wooded area behind them.

Other people were reclining about, but none looked as noble as he. Some gave the appearance of being upper class, but most seemed to be somewhere between wealthy and poor. In the distance, she saw a roundabout. A menagerie of carved wooden animals hung down from the canopy. Two men, running alongside it, pushed it around. Children laughed and screamed with wild abandon.

She didn't like the hope that fluttered in her chest, a hope that someday soon her child might enjoy a journey on such a contraption. She hadn't wanted to think about what her being here with Ainsley truly signified. A ray of hope in what had become such a desolate life. Perhaps that was the reason she'd been less than kind to him. It was so difficult to think of him giving her what Walfort could not. Yet neither could she deny how desperately she wanted a child. She would sit a boy upon the lion because he would be fearless. A girl she would place upon the rabbit. No, no. Upon the tiger. Or perhaps the lion as well for she, too, would need to be fearless to endure the whisperings that would surely ensue. Regardless of Walfort's claim that no one knew the full extent of his injuries, they would not be spared gossip and speculation. She would be the lioness to protect her child. She suspected even Ainsley would provide a shield. His influence could not be disregarded.

"Have you ever taken a turn on a roundabout?" Ainsley asked, intruding on her thoughts. Thank goodness. She didn't like the direction they were traveling.

"Not since I was a child."

"Well, then, shall we give it a go?"

Shoving himself to his feet, he waved someone over, slipped a coin into the young lady's hand with instructions for seeing that the items were gathered up and delivered to his cottage. Then he was extending a hand toward Jayne. Neither of them had put on their gloves after eating. She didn't want to feel the spark that the touch of his bare skin could ignite. He caused her to feel things with so little effort. Walfort's touch had never affected her so. His was pleasant. Ainsley's was so much more. His was dangerous.

"Come on, Jayne. Before the clouds in the distance catch up to us."

Looking over her shoulder, she saw the darkening skies, suddenly aware of the cooling breeze. It was simply a ride on a roundabout. Ainsley could assist her to her feet and then release his hold. If she were quick, the touch would last no more than a heartbeat. She slipped her hand into his, felt his fingers close around hers, was aware of his other arm anchoring around her waist, bringing her up with so little effort.

Only he didn't release his hold. Instead, he urged her forward with haste, and they were soon tripping lightly across the field.

"Ainsley, we can't run." Even as she protested, she inhaled deeply, filling her lungs, pumping her legs.

"Of course we can. We're doing it."

"It's undignified."

"Who of any importance is here to see? Who cares? Pretend we're young again." The devil was in his eyes and his smile, both challenging her, silently calling her a coward if she didn't keep up.

Blast him! Her hat went flying. He laughed. She realized he'd never put his hat back on. Had this been his plan all along?

Suddenly she didn't care. The wind was in her face, and for this short span of time all that mattered was getting to the roundabout before it started spinning again. She could see the wide-eyed stares of the children, waiting for the motion that would carry away their cares.

Breathless, she didn't know where she found the

strength to step onto the platform. If she'd had any air in her lungs, she might have screeched when Ainsley lifted her up onto the lion. The lion. Had she not just been thinking about it? She grabbed the pole that kept it suspended off the flooring.

Ainsley moved around to stand beside her, one of his hands above hers, the other resting on the back of the animal, as though he thought he needed to be ready in case she were to slip. Then two men, one on either side of the roundabout, grabbed hold of a horizontal spoke and began running. It was spinning around as the scenery around them became blurred.

"Close your eyes," Ainsley ordered. "Let all your troubles go."

If only it were that simple. Still, she lowered her lashes, pretended all was right with the world.

He could watch her now as he'd not been able to since the moment he placed her on the horse outside the stables. Her long dark lashes feathered lightly over cheeks flushed with the effort of her running. His gaze followed the line of her throat, an ivory smoothness he desperately wanted to press his lips against.

Her hair was in danger of spilling over her back. He was tempted to help it along, to reach up and remove the last bastion of pins. How stubbornly they held on. Just like her. Determined to keep a distance between them.

He'd brought her here hoping to bring her some joy. Instead, she'd been constantly, warily, looking around as though fearful that she'd spy someone she knew, that someone would see her with him—and then how the deuce would she explain that?

She didn't want his laughter, his conversation, or his presence. She wanted only his seed, and even that she accepted with reluctance.

He'd never before felt so damned alone and lonely when he was with a woman. He wanted more between them, wanted what he couldn't have, what he had no right to desire. He wanted her to *want* to be with him.

He would spend the month in purgatory if he had nothing more than traipsing into her bedchamber in the dark of night to deposit the fruit of his loins like some lecher who thought of nothing beyond his own release.

But for this moment he had a bit more. He had her slight smile, the wind toying with her hair. He could savor the memory for a few days, and perhaps find a way to obtain another one. He couldn't be business-only with her. That she could be so with him spoke of her dislike of him. He'd known it was there, of course, but now feared he'd underestimated the true extent of it. Would she hold onto it so tightly if he told her every-thing about that night? And the nights that had come before it?

Could he betray Walfort for his own personal gain? What would be the cost to him then? To them all? She'd no doubt despise him even more if she knew the truth. She would take no pity on the messenger.

The roundabout began to slow. He wanted to shout at the men that he'd pay them handsomely to keep run-ning. But it was too late. She opened her eyes, her smile retreated, the discomfort between them reemerged. She slid off the lion, not waiting for his assistance. As the contraption creaked and groaned into stillness, they stood facing each other, separated by an absurd-looking creature.

"Time to grow up again," she said quietly.

When she turned and strolled off the platform and onto the ground, as much as he didn't want to, he followed.

Chapter 10

Her inability to breathe as she stood at the window in her bedchamber had nothing to do with anticipation, for she was not eagerly awaiting his arrival. She was quite simply anxious to get the night done with so she could sleep.

The music had become more lively, the crowd more boisterous, as they'd taken their leave of the fair, and she halfway wished they had remained long enough for a dance. But their nights were to be devoted to other things.

Besides, a light rain had begun to fall just as they arrived at the cottage. The dancing and merrymaking had no doubt come to an abrupt end as people sought shelter. Now, the moon was hiding behind dark clouds and she was lulled by the gentle patter against the window as the moments slowly ticked by.

Where the deuce was he?

She'd bathed before dinner, but tonight they barely spoke a word during the meal. When she wasn't looking at him, she could feel his gaze homing in on her, studying her. Why were things suddenly more awkward?

The worst was over—their first encounter. It should

all be easier now. She knew what to expect of him. Yet as she waited, she wondered if she understood anything at all.

The only light in the room was provided by the lazy fire on the hearth. She wouldn't have to watch him prowling, extinguishing flames. He could come straight to her, lead her to the bed—

Or should she be there already, waiting?

Her nipples tingled with the thought of him kneeling before her, slowly skimming the hem of her nightdress up her calves, over her knees, along her thighs. So leisurely, as though he could see in the dark, could see the tiny scar on her knee—the result of falling from the tree she was forbidden to climb when she was a child.

But at the age of seven, she'd been lured by the forbidden. Now it terrified her.

Suddenly, unbearably warm, she pressed her cheek to the cool glass. Waiting was torment. What was taking him so very long?

It was a mistake to spend the day with her. He'd wanted to stay past nightfall, wanted to stroll through the anonymity offered by the darkness, wanted to dance with her—not the polite, civilized steps in a ballroom, but the gregarious, jolly movements of madness in which the villagers reveled.

He'd found it difficult enough last night to pretend impartiality. Tonight he would descend one step further into hell, not experiencing the pleasure of her touch, knowing she wanted as little contact as possible.

He downed another whiskey and slammed the tumbler on the table beside the window in his bedchamber. The damned rain had stolen the moonlight. He wouldn't see it glistening off her skin, wouldn't have forbidden sights. He would have only the darkness, yet still he knew he'd see the shape of her long, slender legs in his mind, would imagine them wrapped around his waist, urging him on.

Imagination could be a powerful aphrodisiac. Pity he wanted more. Damning the cottage for not having a door between the bedchambers, he crossed the room and went into the hallway. Her door was closed as tightly as her thighs. Could she not open it even a crack in invitation?

Rapping his knuckles once against the wood in warning, he strode in and was hit with her jasmine fragrance. He wondered if it would remain after she left. She was hovering by the damned window again, as though distance would alter the outcome.

At least pretend you want me, he almost shouted.

He should have provided his own list of rules. But then the reality smacked into him. If this was the only way he could have her—he'd take it. At least tonight he had no lamps to douse. The banked fire hardly illuminated the room, but bless the moon, if it didn't choose that moment to peer out from behind the clouds and reveal her wrapped in moonlight.

Her hair was down, loose, and he wanted desperately to comb his fingers through it, bury his face in its softness. He wanted to trail his hand over the strip of white and apologize for his role in creating it, even if he thought it the most beautiful shade he'd ever seen. He wanted to place his palms on either side of her face and plant a kiss on those lush lips that would have her melting into his arms. He didn't want to lead her to the bed. He wanted to carry her. He wanted to lift her hem over her shoulders, over her head. He didn't want to stop the journey at her thighs. He wanted her bared before him.

He wanted her breasts nestled against his palms. He wanted his tongue toying with her nipples, wanted to feel them pearling in his mouth. He wanted the taste of her on his lips.

His errant thoughts had his body in such a state that he could barely cross over to her. No smile greeted him. If at all possible, she was more wary tonight.

He knew he should have been content with taking her hand, with keeping things as impersonal as he had during their first encounter, but surely his patience warranted a little more. Skimming his fingers along her arm, he felt the heat penetrating the gossamer silk, heard her breath hitch, saw her eyes darken. Perhaps she wasn't as immune to him as he'd thought.

He wanted to tell her how beautiful she was, how much he adored her smile, how desperately he wanted to hear her laugh. He wanted to confess that he'd do anything to ensure her happiness. But just as he had last night, he kept the words locked deeply inside, where they could not be mocked, could not bring pain to either of them.

Intertwining their fingers, he led her to the bed, lifted her up, placed her on its edge. She needed no instruction tonight. She simply lay back, offering herself to him.

But he wanted more. Just a small bit more.

Jayne watched as he went down to one knee. The moonlight that had entered the room when he did receded, the clouds no doubt thickening as the rain pounded harder against the panes—as hard as her heart beat within her chest. Her breathing was shallow and ragged. She felt his hands—slender fingers, rough palms, heated skin—wrap around her ankles and glide up her legs, carrying the hem of her nightdress with his journey.

Closing her eyes, she relished the touch she should have abhorred. Wicked of him to give her a little more intimacy, naughty of her not to chastise him for it. Then his mouth followed where his hands had gone and she thought she would melt into the bed coverings. He hadn't shaved before he came to her, and she could feel the tiniest rasp of bristle. She wanted to lock her legs around him, hold him tight. But she had her rules: no pleasure, no pleasure, no pleasure.

She would take none. And yet he was giving it, using his fingers and his tongue, touching her so deeply. She'd thought of this while she waited, hoped for it, knew she was more than ready for him. He had to be aware, and yet he didn't cease his ministrations. He simply carried her higher, higher—

She pressed her fist to her mouth, muffling the cry emerging from her throat as her body erupted with unbridled pleasure. She jerked, spasmed, felt the tears of release trickle from the corners of her eyes. She wanted to be immune, but it all felt so wonderful. She returned from the haven of sensations with the realization that he had yet to penetrate her. She could see his shadow. He was standing. Why wasn't he—

The truth hit her with the force of a battering ram. The reason he'd come to fruition so quickly last night. She was giving nothing. She was simply taking. He was giving everything, all the pleasure, even to himself, so she wouldn't have to endure his nearness any longer than necessary.

Pain ratcheted through her. Did he think she was so selfish?

Lifting up, she reached for him. "Ainsley—"

She'd barely touched him before the hot seed poured over her hand.

"Damnation," he growled. Stepping back, he released more profanity as though he himself were a storm cloud raining down.

"I'm sor—" she began.

"Don't. Simply stay as you are."

He was gone before she could respond. She heard him bump into something, release another harsh curse— under any other circumstances she might have laughed.

He returned to her before she had time to wonder what he might be doing. His trousers were done back up, his billowy shirt gaping open where the buttons were freed. With a damp cloth, he wiped her hands.

"I can see to it—" she began.

"I've got it." When her hands were clean, he said, "I'll need a few moments before . . . we can resume."

With that, he left her. Twisting around on the bed, she watched his shadowy form hurl the cloth into a corner. The fire in the hearth outlined him dropping onto the sofa and burying his face in his hands.

She wondered if he was weeping. She certainly wanted to.

Bloody damned hell!

He hadn't lost control like that since he was sixteen years old and one of the upstairs maids had been toying with him. If he hadn't been fantasizing about Jayne touching him, about her enfolding that soft, warm hand around him . . . If he hadn't been imagining her mouth pressed to his chest, lapping at his skin, trailing over his throat—

Hearing the creak of the bed followed by the padding of bare feet over the floor and carpet, he stiffened. Peering through his fingers, he watched her sit in the stuffed chair beside the fireplace, pull her feet onto the cushion and wrap her arms around her drawn up legs. Legs he'd skimmed his hands along. She wasn't tall, but she was still mostly leg. The flickering firelight danced over her, and he imagined his mouth following the same trails.

With that thought he was rapidly returning back to form.

"You needn't be embarrassed," she said quietly.

"I'm not." He was. Mortified. His curt words came out harsher than he'd intended, two quick slaps that judging by the jerk of her head she'd actually felt. "I simply wasn't expecting . . . I wasn't prepared . . ."

"For my touch. Yes, I know. I figured it out . . . that you were not only . . . pleasuring me." She averted her gaze, stared into the fire. "This is absolutely bloody awful, isn't it?"

Amused by her uncharacteristic use of profanity, he lowered his hands. "As far as bloody awful things go, it's one of the best I've experienced."

She released a sound, possibly a laugh, or perhaps a strangled sob, before covering her mouth. She stared at him for the longest time. "Why are you doing this?"

Her voice was rough, and he realized it had cost her something to ask, and so she deserved at least an inkling of the truth. "Nothing is more important to me than your happiness."

"Why?"

Because I adore you. "I admire you."

"But it's costing you, isn't it?"

"Jayne—"

"Ainsley, women adore you. They fawn over you. They want to be in your bed. And here I am with all my silly rules, and still you destroyed me last night with so little effort."

Her confession pounded painfully into him. "Christ, Jayne, that was not my intent."

"I know." She shook her head brusquely. "I know. But still it happened. It had been so long, *so* very long . . . I didn't want to be reminded of what I was missing. And I wasn't. Instead I discovered what I'd never had. Not like that. Not with that intensity."

What the hell was he to say to that heartfelt admission?

"It's as you say," he told her. "It's because it's been so long."

"I don't think so. Not entirely. You've obviously earned your reputation."

Yet there was no woman he wanted to please more than he wanted to please her. He was not a selfish lover. He knew that. He cared for his paramours, wanted to ensure their enjoyment in his bed because it added to his physical satisfaction. But for Jayne he'd forgo his own pleasure—if he could do it and still get her with child.

"Do you know when I knew this was a terrible notion?" she asked.

"When Walfort first mentioned it, I suspect."

"No. I thought it was a terrible idea at that point. I *knew* it was a terrible idea when you added your condition. You're giving me your child and I'm selfish enough to want to take it."

"I can think of no one I'd rather be the mother of my child."

"But I've treated you so shabbily. I never considered how unfair all this was to you. Walfort's request, my rules—"

"For God's sake, Jayne, you're the one who has had to live with the unfairness of it all. I wish to God I'd not taken the reins that night. I wish we'd have had three fewer drinks, although I'm not at all sure why I believe that's the magic number that would have changed the outcome. I wish I'd convinced him to stay where we were and sleep it off until morning—but he wanted to return to you. Not a single day goes by that I don't relive that night and see all the missteps. If I could unravel the tapestry of events that destroyed dreams, I would. I'd sell my soul to the devil to have everything put back to rights."

She rested her chin on her upraised knees as though she could better see him from that perch—or perhaps see inside him, to the very core of his being, to the secret part of his heart that beat for her.

"I didn't think you suffered," she whispered, so softly that he almost didn't hear the words. "I thought you just went on your merry way. Is being with me punishment?"

Every man should be so fortunate as to have nights with her as punishment. But he held his thoughts, certain she wouldn't appreciate them. Besides, in truth it *was* punishment. To have only a sampling of her but not the whole. But then, he didn't deserve the whole. He didn't deserve even a sampling.

"It is, isn't it? And you're too kind to say. I wanted you to suffer, you know. I wanted you in agony, but what is to be gained by it?" He saw tears well in her eyes. "I do want a child, Ainsley, more than I've ever wanted anything—other than for Walfort to be whole again."

"You can't have the latter, Jayne, but I'll do all in my power to give you the former."

She gnawed on the lower lip that he wanted to nibble on. "Why did you react as you did? Earlier. So forcefully, so quickly. When I touched you?"

Could she be that damned naïve? "Because I'd been in your company all day. Because I wanted nothing more than for you to touch me. I was imagining it, and then it was real . . . and so much better than what I imagined."

"I think that a child will be like that. That no matter how much I imagine it, the reality of that small body nestled within my arms will be the greatest joy I shall ever know. And if I want it that badly, then I can't be selfish in acquiring it."

As well as he knew women's bodies, he still sometimes found their minds, their thoughts, their rationales, difficult to decipher, completely baffling. He didn't know what she was rambling on about.

Releasing a deep, shuddering breath, she unfolded her lithe body and stood. Holding his gaze as the firelight waltzed with the shadows surrounding her, she untied the ribbon at her throat and then slowly gave freedom to the buttons of her nightdress.

The breath backed up painfully in his lungs with his knowledge of where she was going with this. He should stop her. It would be pure torment to have her willingly—and then to have to let her go. But he was in hell anyway. Might as well let the fire burn hotter.

She slipped the gown off her shoulders, and he watched, mesmerized, as it began to slither along her body. Abruptly, her boldness deserted her, and she quickly gathered the silk tightly into a ball at her breasts, stopping the progress of the unveiling as soon as the upper swells were visible. Still his blood boiled.

She held out her hand in invitation. With her actions, she was breaking her own rules. She would find pleasure in his bed. But then they were her rules to break, his to honor, even if he'd had a hand in getting her to break this one.

With his mouth suddenly dry, he reminded himself that she'd not fallen under his spell. She was simply playing the same game as he, making it easier for them both to travel the path they'd set upon. At the end of their time together, she would return to Walfort, hopefully with fewer regrets. But for now, for this moment, she was his.

Pushing himself to his feet, he approached her cautiously. He'd never doubted her courage or her strength, but he suspected she was in uncharted waters. She was not accustomed to playing the role of vixen, even though he thought her well suited to it. She could entice him with nothing more than a smile.

When he reached her, he combed his fingers into her hair and gave them leave to slide through the silken strands.

"I'm sorry I'm so cowardly," she said quietly.

He grazed his knuckles over her cheek. "That is the very last word I'd ever use when describing you." Lifting her into his arms, he began walking toward the bed. "Beautiful, lovely, courageous. Those suit."

Burying her face in the nook of his shoulder, she

wound one arm around his neck while her other hand clung tenaciously to her gown. He regretted that they were moving into the shadows of the bed where the fire was too weak to provide him with the light he desired. He would let her have the darkness tonight, but eventually he would have her in the light. He wanted to know every shade of every color that comprised her.

He laid her on the bed with gentleness, as though she were as fragile as hand-blown glass. Aware of her gaze on him, of her hand still clutching the opening to her nightdress, he drew his shirt over his head and let it fall to the floor. He stretched out beside her, careful not to startle her, not to give her a reason to retreat now. He skimmed his fingers up and down the bare portion of her arm, above the elbow, before pressing his mouth to her shoulder. Against his lips, she shivered.

"I can't see you, you know," he said in a low whisper.

"I know, but while you've known many, I've only known one. Well, two, I suppose now. But last night was so brief. Tonight is a bit unnerving."

"You wouldn't be here if you didn't trust me." He placed his hand over hers. "Trust me completely."

He waited a heartbeat, then two, rubbing his thumb over her knuckles until he felt her fingers unfurl. He slipped his hand beneath hers and brought it up for a kiss, the heat of his mouth coating her skin with dew. Her fingertips skimmed his jaw, reached up to his cheek. Small steps, but steps nonetheless.

He held still while she explored his features, threaded her fingers through his hair. He didn't want to think of Walfort at a moment like this, but he had to wonder what sort of fool would deny her even a hint of pleasure, simply because he was incapable of reaching the summit.

Her palm came to rest against his chest, signaling the end of her exploration. His turn.

He eased her nightdress down past her full breasts, her flat stomach, her narrow hips, along the length of her coltishly long legs. Perhaps this time she'd wrap them around him. Even though she was ensconced in shadows, he had a good idea of what he'd only been able to imagine existed beneath the silk, satin, and lace. She was perfection.

He trailed his hands up her legs, along her sides. "You're perfect."

"I didn't think you could see me clearly."

Not with his eyes, but with his heart. He'd never been much in the way of a poet, but for her he wanted to be. He wanted no false flattery between them. In this impossible situation he wanted whatever honesty they could eke out.

Shoving himself off the bed, before his feet hit the floor, he had his trousers unbuttoned. Quickly, he discarded them and rejoined her on the bed. His patience had reached its limit. It was time to devour her.

With unerring accuracy he cupped her breast, relished the weight of it against his palm. He slid his thumb over the tip, felt it pucker and harden. So quick to respond. She turned her body into him, and he pressed her closer. Heated silk. He licked at her flesh, drawing the taut nipple into his mouth, circling it with his tongue. She released a moan that set his own body on fire with desire.

Her hands took a leisurely sojourn over his shoulders. Her fingers combed through his hair. Her legs became entangled with his, opening her silken haven to him. The fragrance of raw sex teased his nostrils. She was ready for him. Before he ever slid his hand downward and slipped his finger inside her, he knew she was more than prepared to receive him.

His body screamed for him to take her now. To have her. To ride her. But he didn't want a quick coupling. He wanted to explore every inch of her. And he did so. With his hands and his mouth. She writhed and groaned, igniting the tinder of passion. It flared as it never had, burning brightly.

She was unlike any other woman he'd ever known. She possessed an innocence and a wildness. Contradictory and yet complementary. She dug her fingers into his buttocks, urging him closer. Trailing his mouth across the valley between her breasts, he gave the same attention to the other as he had to the first.

He loved the taste of her. Earthy and rich.

"Ainsley, you are driving me to madness," she uttered.

"Then you are where I want you to be." He kissed her shoulder, her throat, her chin. He desperately wanted to blanket her mouth with his, swallow her moans and cries. But it was forbidden. Her damned rule, and he was stubborn enough not to break it.

He would show restraint in that one area, but nowhere else.

He tormented her until she was fevered, crying out for him, urging him to take her. A strangled sob. A tiny squeal.

Positioning himself, he lifted her hips and buried himself in the molten velvet of her core. Heat closed around him as snug as a glove.

Desperately, she clutched him, moved beneath him. She wrapped her legs around his waist and he sank more deeply into her. His groan echoed between them. She was tight, so tight. Snug. She held him as though she would never release him.

Rising up, he pounded into her, feeling her muscles undulating around him. Their breathing became harsh, ragged. Her moans were music to his ears; her writhing was poetry to his soul. She matched his thrusts with a power and an eagerness that surprised and pleased him beyond measure. She was no docile woman, only receiving. She gave all, her body and soul. Perhaps a little of her heart. He would have to content himself with that.

He hovered at the edge of the cliff where passion reigned and pleasure triumphed. When her screams echoed around him, through him, he flung himself into the realm of satiation. Sensations more intense than he'd ever experienced consumed him in a conflagration of fiery release.

When he returned to awareness, her body was limp beneath his, her breathing rapid, her skin slick with dew. He buried his face in the curve of her neck. Kissed her there.

He'd never before felt anything quite this intense. He didn't want to leave her, but he wasn't convinced that she was ready for him to stay.

As gently as possible he eased off her. He pulled the sheets and blankets over her to protect her from the chill that would settle in now that their flesh was no longer joined. He rolled out of the bed, walked to the fireplace, and added more logs to bring warmth into the room for her.

He wanted to tell her that tonight *she* had devastated *him*. Instead, he simply snatched up his clothes and strode from the room.

Chapter 11

She awoke tender, sore, and feeling remarkably lovely. Like a woman who had been well and truly loved. A small part of her pricked with guilt, but she shoved it away. Walfort had encouraged her to come here, to revel in the pleasure that Ainsley could deliver. She couldn't go back now, couldn't return to what had transpired the first night—the cold, calculated callousness of it.

She didn't want to consider what this month would cost her, would cost them all.

Reaching up, she tugged on the bellpull. She clambered out of bed and went to the window. The rain had stopped. She would join Ainsley for breakfast this morning. Perhaps they'd return to the fair. Perhaps they'd stay until nightfall and dance. So many possibilities loomed. For the first time in three years she wanted to embrace the potential of the day.

She recognized the soft rap on the door as belonging to Lily before her servant walked into the room. She was wearing a shawl that Jayne had seen the day before—at a booth at the fair. Ainsley had purchased it and several others.

"How did you come to have that shawl?" she asked.

Stopping, Lily ran her fingers over the lace. "Isn't it lovely? Someone from the village delivered several things this morning. Mr. Manning said the duke told him that I was to have first selection. Apparently it's not uncommon for him to purchase items for his servants. They all love him, you know. Is it all right if I keep it?"

How could they not love him? She was beginning to think he was the most generous man she'd ever known. He gave nothing in half measures, seemed to delight in giving gifts wherever he could.

"Of course you may keep it if that was the duke's wish. See that my red gown is pressed for this evening."

"Yes, m'lady. And for today?"

"The blue, I think."

She was halfway tempted to pen a letter to Walfort, assuring him she was well, but he had specifically forbidden it: "Don't write to me. I don't want you to think about me for a single moment while you're away."

She had expected to think of him every moment. Instead each passing hour brought fewer reflections of him.

If she did write him, what would she say? That last night the duke had awoken portions of her that she'd not even realized had been sleeping? Not just physically, but emotionally as well. The first night she'd wept because sensations sweeping through her body had brought such welcome release and abhorrent guilt. But last night he'd caressed her soul and brought forth a devastating awareness of how cold she had become. She'd built a wall to protect herself so she could never be hurt again, but with hope came the possibility of pain. She was terrified and yet remarkably expectant. A little too much, perhaps, as anticipation thrummed through her when she was dressed and opened the door. It only increased when she spotted him sitting lazily on a bench in the hallway.

She thought that seeing him would quell her excitement, but it only increased as her nervousness asserted itself. Whatever would the day bring and how might it lead them into the night?

He rose in that smooth, confident way he had.

"I expected you to already be at breakfast," she told him.

Smiling, he approached her. "I heard you moving around so I decided to wait." He leaned in, took her hand, pressed a kiss to the place where her cheek met her chin, and she found herself waiting breathlessly for him to slide his mouth over and begin nibbling on her ear. "Good morning. Did you sleep well?"

The words were said in a low, seductive, secretive voice, as though he were asking much more, but she was thrown off by her disappointment that he'd ignored her ear and the sensitive skin below it. Still, she couldn't deny him the truth. "Marvelously, actually. And you?"

He began leading her down the stairs. "Well enough."

She didn't quite know what to make of that, didn't want to consider that perhaps she'd failed him in some way, that he'd not found as much pleasure as she, although his actions the night before certainly indicated that he enjoyed their encounter. "Will we go to the fair again, today?"

"I have something else in mind, if you're up for it."

As they strolled toward the lake, he pondered how earlier he'd thought she'd never get out of that blasted bed. A strange thought considering all his effort to get her into the damned thing. But he'd been anxious to be with her again this morning, contemplated returning to her bed at dawn but decided she wasn't quite ready to spend every hour of every day with him in the boudoir. And so he'd contented himself with prowling through his bedchamber until he finally heard movement on the other side of his wall.

In spite of the fact that he'd been well and truly sated, he had not slept well. His arms felt incredibly empty after holding her. He was chilled lying in his bed without the press of her skin against his. The silence was so disturbing when not filled with her soft breathing.

She'd given him so much more than her body. She'd given him a taste of something he'd never before savored: being with a woman who had the ability to touch his soul. Oddly, he knew she wasn't reaching beyond the physical. And yet there it was. Invisible threads, twining them together, a goal that would create a common bond that he wondered if they'd be able to extricate themselves from when the time came.

It was of no consequence. Her loyalty was to Walfort. As was his own. Duty, love, and honor would see that they parted ways, but he damned well intended to have memories to see him through.

They'd spoken of mundane things during breakfast. The weather. Would the sunshine hold? The fair. The shawl her maid had chosen. Jayne made him confess to purchasing items he didn't need simply to ensure the villagers had a few coins in their pockets. She grew silent for a time after that. As had he. He'd not planned to reveal much of himself to her while she was here, and yet he seemed to be doing exactly that.

He'd never realized what a deep well of emptiness he

possessed, and each moment with her worked toward filling it.

"I imagine it's lovely here in the spring and summer," she said softly now.

"Quite. Although I rather enjoy it in winter."

"I suppose I can see the appeal."

He imagined she looked around and saw the bleakness, but all it did was emphasize her beauty. She was the promise of spring, the kiss of summer. As much as he'd wanted to kiss her properly—or improperly in his case—last night and this morning, he'd refrained, allowing her to hold on to one last unbroken rule. If it was to be broken, like all the ones that came before it, she would have to be the one to break it. He was experiencing enough guilt without adding that final straw.

She pointed toward a white gazebo a short distance from the water's edge. "Is that yours?"

"Yes, it came with the cottage. I believe the previous owner's daughter was married there."

"Not in a church?"

"Scandalous, isn't it?"

"I've never heard of such a thing. Are we going to go fishing?"

He smiled at the abrupt change in topic. "You are impatient, aren't you?"

She peered up at him slyly. "Simply curious."

"Well, then, let's get on with it. Not fishing. Boating."

One of the servants had prepared the rowboat earlier. Ainsley enjoyed the burn in his muscles as he rowed them from shore, but more enjoyed watching her. The tranquility that settled over her upturned face as she sought the sun's warmth. The wind was brisk and chilled as it blew across the water. She'd wrapped her cloak more securely around her, and he regretted that it was not his arms and body warming her. It was no doubt reckless on his part to come out onto the lake when the sky was darkening at the horizon and storms scented the air, but he'd wanted the isolation—to be with her when no one was around to disturb them. Not that his servants had bothered them, but the knowledge was there that they were always present.

Even in her bed he had the sense that they weren't completely alone. Of course, Walfort was no doubt haunting them there. Although Ainsley did think he'd succeeded in erasing the man from her mind for a short time last night. But he'd seen his cousin creeping back into her thoughts during breakfast, so he was grateful he'd planned this little excursion.

She'd not bothered with gloves, and now she trailed her fingers in the frigid waters. "Do you swim?" she asked.

"Yes."

She glanced over at him. "I don't."

"The water's not that deep." A lie. But no sense in alarming her when he would ensure that she not drown. He was a strong swimmer, obsessed with the sensation of slicing through the water. Had swum the lake. Had even considered having an artificial pool—like the ones in London—built at his ancestral estate, Grantwood Manor.

He stopped rowing, brought in the oars and planted his forearms on his thighs. Inhaling deeply, he absorbed the peacefulness of their surroundings—the trees, mountains, and sky so majestic. The silence heavy.

"I believe this to be the most serene place in all of England," he said quietly, loath to disturb the calm.

She sat up. "I feel as though I should be doing something."

"That's the beauty of this place. When I'm here, my troubles do not seem to follow."

She placed an elbow on her knee, her chin on her palm. "What troubles plague you?"

"If I told you, that would be to invite them here."

"You are quite the mysterious one, Ainsley."

She was perturbed but smiling, teasing him, perhaps. Then, as if knowing she'd get nothing from him, she sighed, glanced around, and again dipped her hand in the water. "May I ask you something?"

"You may ask; I might not answer."

She peered over at him. "You mentioned your mother not being able to separate Westcliffe from his father, and yet she seemed to have no trouble where Stephen is concerned. I have seen them together, and there can be no doubt she adores him."

He cursed his loose tongue. When he'd made his stipulation, he should have been content to make it without explanation. He certainly couldn't reveal a dark family secret that had only just become known to the brothers: Stephen and Westcliffe didn't share the same father. Yet neither did he want to lie to her. "Westcliffe very much favors the previous earl—in both looks and temperament. Stephen was spared both attributes, so Mother was able to gaze upon him more favorably."

"Your mother never seemed cruel. I can't imagine her not loving Westcliffe."

"I don't think she didn't love him. She simply wasn't good at showing it." He leaned toward her, skimming his thumb over her cold cheek. "I apologize. I never should have questioned your ability to love any child to whom you gave birth."

She averted her gaze. "I know some ladies who married simply to gain a title. But a title does not warm a woman's heart. You deserve a woman who will love you, Ainsley."

His laughter echoed around them. "I assure you that I will settle for no less."

She gave him an impish grin. "Confess. Is there any woman who has caught your fancy?"

You.

"I do not talk of other ladies when I'm with a woman."

"But you're blushing. There is someone."

He rubbed his cheeks and jaw briskly. "If my face is red, it is because of the cold. If there were someone, I'd not be here with you now. It would be unfair to her."

"I'm glad. Will you be faithful to your wife, then?"

"As long as she is faithful to me."

"If you treat her in bed as you treat me . . . she will be faithful."

"My mother always told me that it was the manner in which a man treated a woman when she was not in his bed that determined how she responded when in his bed."

Her blue eyes widened. "Your mother spoke to you of such things?"

"She is scandalous for a reason, Jayne. Her first husband did not treat her well, and she threatened my brothers and me to within an inch of our lives if she ever learned that we mistreated a woman."

"Westcliffe exiled his wife to his country estate."

He shrugged. She didn't know the entire story and he

wasn't about to tell her. "There was a bit of misbehavior going on there, but all is well now."

"Your mother always frightened me, you know."

"Why ever would you fear her?"

"She is so bold and brash. She does not suffer fools or silly girls lightly."

"You've never been a silly girl."

"You didn't know me when I was younger."

"Tell me one thing you did that was silly." She took on a mulish expression. "Just as I thought. You exhibited no silliness."

"I climbed a tree. Often. I fell once, skinned my knee. I have a scar to prove it."

He narrowed his eyes. "The disadvantage to making love in the dark. Show it to me now."

She glanced around. "No. Someone will see."

" 'Tis my lake. No one is around. Come along, Jayne. Show me your scar; otherwise, tonight I shall leave on all the lamps."

She turned a brilliant hue of red. "One does not engage in . . . intimacy . . . with the lamps on."

Scrutinizing her, he could see the truth of her words etched on her face. Had she and Walfort . . . never . . . except in the dark? He couldn't envision it. He'd doused the lamps and extinguished the candles because he'd wanted to give her the freedom to pretend he was Walfort if she needed that pretense to allow the intimacy between them. But if she'd never—

He thought of last night when she loosened her nightdress and then clutched it close, changing her mind regarding how bold she might be. The light from the fire had been too much. He'd hoped she'd eventually become comfortable enough with him that the light wouldn't bother her, but if she'd only ever made love in the darkness—he didn't understand how Walfort could deny himself the pleasure of gazing on her with candle-light flickering over her skin.

His cousin and his actions baffled him. Walfort took so little from Jayne, gave so little to her. Yet even as Ainsley thought these things, he knew it was not his place to question, to analyze, to wonder. His place was to seduce her, over and over, until he got her with child.

He hefted the oar, then slid the narrow dry end along the bottom of the boat until it encountered the hem of her skirt. "Come along, Jayne, let me see the scar."

She slapped at the oar. "No."

"Then I shan't believe you've been silly."

"I don't care what you believe."

"Then why tell me?"

She was looking around frantically as though seeking the answer. He lifted her skirt so her ankle was visible.

"Ainsley!"

She kicked out, he fell back, the boat rocked, she screeched and grabbed the sides of the boat as though she had the strength and power to calm its motions.

"You're going to cause us to topple over," she chastised.

"No, I won't," he insisted, slowly bringing himself upright and then kneeling. "That's right. Just hold the boat steady."

"What are you doing?"

"I simply want to see the scar."

"Ains—"

"Shh." He lifted her skirt up, up, until he could see her well-defined calves. "Which knee?"

"I shan't tell you."

"Then I shall be forced to examine them both."

"The left."

He grinned. How easily she capitulated. He ran his free hand over the one that led to the knee that bore the scar. Higher went the skirt, until he settled the hem on her thigh. Her knuckles were turning white. Her breathing was shallow, her eyes riveted on him. Slipping both hands along her thighs, he untied the ribbon holding her stocking and slowly, provocatively, rolled the silk down her leg until he could see the tiny bit of puckered flesh.

"If someone sees—"

"No one will see," he interrupted. Even if someone saw, they didn't know who she was, they'd never cross paths again, and he'd come too far to stop now.

"Did it hurt?" he asked.

"I don't recall." She was breathless, struggling to pull in air. He should take pity on her. But he wanted her to want him as much as he wanted her, so that when they returned to the house, they would immediately retire to the bedchamber. He'd draw the curtains if he had to in order to give her the darkness she sought. But he wanted her again with a fierceness that unsettled him. It was as though he couldn't have enough of her.

"It must have," he said. "To scar, it had to be deep. It would have bled."

"Then yes, I suppose, yes, it hurt."

He did not allow his gaze to waver from hers as he leaned down, pressed his lips to the pink flesh, trailed his tongue around it. Her eyes darkened, went limpid. Her mouth softened.

"I didn't cry," she rasped. "I was too stubborn to

cry. My father had forbidden me to climb so he took a
switch to my backside."

His chest ached with that confession. If her father
were still alive, the man might very shortly be feeling the strength in Ainsley's fist as it slammed into his
nose.

"Hmm. Then that lovely backside is in want of attention as well, and I shall have to kiss it later."

She didn't object. She simply watched him as though
she weren't quite sure what to make of him.

"Or I could do it now, I suppose. Hide beneath your
skirt where no one would see me. Nibble my way up
your thigh."

"We would topple over."

"Not if you stayed very still."

"I don't think I could."

"I think you could." He pressed his lips to the inside
of her thigh, just above her knee.

With a groan she dropped her head back. "I think
this is an awful idea."

"I disagree."

He was halfway to where he wanted to be when the
damned skies opened up. Cold rain slashed at the boat.
She screamed, he cursed. He brought down her skirt.
"Don't forget where I was. I shall begin there later."

Her laughter pleased him immensely. He scrambled
back, grabbed the oars, and began rowing as though
their lives depended on it. The last thing he wanted was
for her to get ill or catch her death.

Smiling, shaking her head, she brought her stocking
up and secured it. "You're a very naughty duke."

"I try."

"If it hadn't started raining, would you have really—"

Her words came to an abrupt halt, no doubt because his gaze provided the answer.

He really would have.

"The bank will be particularly muddy," he said. "Stay in the boat when we hit shore. I'll lift you out."

"Ainsley, that's not necessary."

"Jayne, must you argue with me on everything?"

She smiled, then laughed. "You forget, Your Grace, that I have seen you standing at a bank, attempting to lift something from the water. Can you blame me for doubting your ability to deliver me safely to shore?"

As much as he loved her laughter, it arrived with a bit of a sting this time. He groused, "I was acting the buffoon for Walfort's sake."

Her humor fled. "Why would you deliberately make a fool of yourself?"

"To make him laugh, to make him feel that I was not so capable, to give him back a bit of his pride, perhaps."

She scrutinized him as though she didn't understand him. Not that he blamed her. Where she was concerned, he wasn't quite certain he understood himself.

Craning her head back, she welcomed the rain pattering over her face. "We shall probably both catch our death."

God, he hoped not. Not after only two nights. He wanted so many more with her. He wondered if she'd ever seriously consider taking a lover. Then dispensed with the notion. These few nights they would have together were for a purpose. That she had decided to embrace them did not necessarily mean she had decided to embrace *him*. She was working to make the best of an uncomfortable situation. It would behoove him to never forget that fact.

Drenched by the time the boat finally hit the shore, he leapt out, dragged it farther in, and lifted her out. He so enjoyed having her in his arms, even when she more closely resembled a drowned cat. Holding her close, he raced to the gazebo where its roof would protect them from the slashing rain. With regret, he lowered her feet to the flooring. Drawing her near, he enveloped her within his coat, striving to bring some warmth to stop her shivering. It seemed such a natural movement as she nestled back against him, her head fitting securely into the hollow of his shoulder.

"I can't believe the rain caught us so unawares," she said.

"It happens like that here. Now that it's started, it could go on all day. It could stop in a few moments. Unfortunately, I believe our best recourse is to make a dash for the cottage."

"All right."

Yet neither of them moved. He thought if he could get a fire started, he'd be content to remain here with her all day. Simply holding her. Listening to the harsh fall of the rain.

"When we arrive at the house, I'll have a warm bath prepared for you," he said.

"That sounds lovely."

He nibbled on the nape of her neck, capturing the errant raindrops with his tongue. "Perhaps I'll join you."

If he hadn't been holding her, he might have missed how still she became. Was she going to be comfortable, content with intimacy shared only within the shadows of midnight? Did she expect them to go about their business during the day as though they were strangers? Did the night before not show her what could be between them?

"I'm not certain you could behave," she finally said, a slight tremor in her voice that he didn't understand.

"I'm not here to behave. Your presence indicates you're not expecting me to. Besides, the day has turned into one that is best spent in bed."

She turned her head slightly, giving him a view of her profile, her creased brow. "Are you implying . . . during the day?"

He felt as though he'd been kicked by an angry mule. Surely she did not mean what he thought she did. "I've been determined not to mention Walfort while we're here, but are you telling me that he's never . . . that you've never spent a lazy afternoon . . . between the sheets?"

Her cheeks were flaming now and he knew it wasn't from the cold. "It's only proper at bedtime."

Proper? He wanted to tell her that when a man desired a woman, there was no "proper" time. But if he told her the truth, she might begin to doubt Walfort's affection and passion toward her. The very last thing he wanted was to undermine her relationship with her husband, to have her here thinking about Walfort.

"Well, all I can say to that is that my cousin showed remarkable restraint in the past. I seriously doubt I'll be able to manage that."

She twisted her head around and met his gaze. "You want me, even now, when I'm a shivering, sopping mess?"

"I want you every moment of every hour." Realizing

too late that he'd confessed more than he should have, he grabbed her hand. "Come on. Let's get you to the house and warmed up."

Then he would see how receptive she was to his joining her in the bath. Walfort may have only visited her bed in the dead of night, but Ainsley intended to spend the better part of the month there.

He had to keep his stride short so she could keep up. Removing his coat, he held it over her head, trying to offer her some protection from the onslaught of the storm. The rain was slashing them now. Roads would soon be impassable. He was half tempted to sweep her into his arms and carry her to the house.

By the time they entered the kitchen through the back door, they were both well and truly drenched.

"Your Grace," the cook chastised. "You're tracking in mud."

"So we are. Start warming water. The servants are to prepare a bath for Lady Jayne." He hung her cloak and his jacket on a peg by the door. "Not that it will stop us from dripping through the residence."

As he guided her into the hallway, she said, "You should have a bath prepared for yourself as well."

"Ah, Jayne, I thought we'd agreed we would bathe together."

"Too scandalous by half."

"Who's to know?"

"Your servants."

"I've told you. They are the souls of discretion."

"Ainsley, you're seeking to corrupt me." Breaking free of him, laughing lightly, she backed into the entryway, "And I'll not be corrupted."

"Ainsley, whatever mischief are you up to now?" a familiar but unwanted voice asked.

Jerking his gaze from Jayne to the woman emerging through the parlor doorway, he could think only one thing.

Bloody hell. Disaster had arrived.

Chapter 12

After ushering Jayne upstairs to get dry and warm—and with the reassurance that he would take care of this situation—Ainsley joined his mother and Leo in the parlor. It didn't help matters that he was wet and chilled. He poured himself a brandy and downed it, welcoming the warmth it spread through his body.

"You should get into dry clothes and then we'll talk," his mother said.

Easing over to the fireplace, he relished the heat provided by the burning logs. "We'll talk now. What are you doing here?"

"I think the more pressing question is: what is Lady Walfort doing here?"

"She was invited. You were not."

Standing before him, his mother arched a dark brow over remarkable brown eyes that never overlooked anything.

"And while she is here, she is known only as Lady Jayne," he quickly pointed out.

"Why is she here, Ainsley?" she asked with such concern, such worry, that he could hardly stay angry at her.

"She required a bit of a holiday. You can well imagine that there is considerable tension in her current situation."

"Does Walfort know she's with you?"

"It was his idea."

He'd never seen his mother appear quite so flummoxed. "I see."

He hoped to God she didn't. She'd never approve and she certainly didn't need to know that Walfort's child would be her grandchild. He'd not even considered how his mother would be denied knowing her own grandchild. Damnation.

"And your reason for being here?" he prodded, glancing at her and then at Leo, who stood slightly behind her, ever alert, ready to pounce to protect her if need be. He always appeared relaxed, as though nothing ever bothered him. He was easily underestimated. But Ainsley knew Leo would never let anyone harm the duchess.

"We were traveling north to see Lynnford when we got caught in the storm. The roads are presently atrocious so we thought to seek shelter here." His mother studied him with an intensity that in his youth had always made him squirm and confess whatever truth he'd been attempting to hide from her. But he was no longer a callow lad, and he'd protect Jayne from all wagging tongues—even his mother's.

The rain he'd been enjoying so much earlier was now a curse. As thunder rumbled, he realized he couldn't send his mother out in it. The cottage contained six bedchambers. Unfortunately, it did not have wings and they all ran alongside the same hallway.

"I'll have Manning see that two bedchambers are

prepared for you. I would ask that you leave as soon as you are able."

"We'd have not stopped at all if not for the weather. Lady Lynnford is failing. I suspect her end is near. I'm not sure how Lynnford will manage without her."

Ainsley saw something flash over Leo's face—something he couldn't interpret. He wondered if the artist was wondering how long he would retain the duchess's affections once Stephen's father was a widower. Lynnford had been his mother's lover in her youth—something he and his brothers only recently learned. He couldn't imagine how he would feel to discover his father was not the man he'd always thought. Even as the repercussions crossed his mind, he realized he risked passing a similar burden on to his child. Was what he felt for Jayne enough to justify his actions? Was his guilt over what he'd done to Walfort reason for denying his child the truth about his father?

Damn the doubts that were suddenly plaguing him. He'd set on this course and wasn't about to turn his back on Jayne now—not with the knowledge of how desperately she wanted this child.

"With any luck, perhaps the weather will clear off by late afternoon and you won't need to stay the night," he said.

"Oh, I'm certain we should stay the night."

"Then if you'll be kind enough to excuse me, I wish to change into dry clothing."

His mother said nothing more as he quit the room. Thank goodness.

The Duchess of Ainsley was here. Ainsley's mother. Jayne had wanted to die of mortification when the woman stepped out of the parlor. No one of any influence or station was supposed to know she was spending this month with Ainsley. What would the duchess think? What conclusions would she draw?

Jayne was half tempted to remain in the bathwater until she shriveled up into nothing. How in God's name was she going to face the woman? She knew what the duchess had to be thinking—that she was Ainsley's latest paramour. Only she wasn't.

She squeezed her eyes closed. She was, only it wasn't because she desired him. She wanted a babe. What was she doing here? How unfair to him and her and quite possibly a child. Not to mention Walfort. Only he wanted this, so she was here because he wanted it.

Damn damn damn!

Opening her eyes, she saw the tiny scar on her upraised knee. She had yet to dip it below the water, to wash it, so it still held Ainsley's kiss. She imagined she could still feel the softness of his lips, the heat of his mouth. She grew warm thinking about how far he might have taken things if the storm hadn't arrived. The screen around the tub that kept the warmth from the fireplace contained so it didn't spread into the room prevented her from seeing the bed, but she knew it was there. All neat and tidily made. And Ainsley had wanted to spend the afternoon rumpling it—rumpling her.

She pressed her hands to her cheeks. She should have the fire put out. She was so hot that surely the water would begin to boil at any moment.

A rap of knuckles on the bedchamber door sent her heart into a frenzied gallop. Knowing Ainsley, he'd sent his mother away and was now intent on carrying out his promise of spending the remainder of the afternoon in bed. Was she actually anticipating it? Yes, she thought she was. They would draw the drapes, of course, inviting in the shadows.

"It's His Grace, m'lady," Lily said, startling Jayne from her wild musings.

"See what he wants."

She heard the door open, followed by whispered murmurings. The door closed, and she released the breath she'd been holding. She waited for the tap of Lily's shoes as she came to report the duke's message, but all she heard was silence.

Then he appeared around the screen and she sank more deeply into the water, folding her arms over her chest. "What are you doing here?"

"Tormenting myself, obviously. I've only ever seen your hair loose and your shoulders bare in shadow. By God, but you're magnificent."

She didn't need his words to know his thoughts. They were evident in his smoldering gaze.

"Your mother?" she rasped, her throat raw, as though she'd inhaled cinders.

"I'm certain she thinks herself magnificent. I've never given it any thought."

"Ainsley!" she whispered harshly. "Have they departed?"

"No, unfortunately. That cute little scar still requires my attention, doesn't it?"

Yes. "No. Please stay on topic. What are her plans?"

"To stay the night and pray for clear skies on the morrow."

"How did you explain my presence?"

"I told her you were here on holiday."

"And she believed you?"

"Why would she not?"

He prowled toward her, reached down and skimmed his fingers over her knee, sending delicious tingles toward her toes and shoulders. Everything curled.

"Shall I finish what I began earlier?" he asked.

She stared at him in horror. "No! You should not even be in here. Where's Lily?"

"In the hallway. Everything will be all right, Jayne. My mother is not one to gossip."

"I don't know that I can face her."

"If you don't, she'll think that your presence brings you shame. And if it does, then I shall escort you home tomorrow. I'll not have you associate shame with what we're doing here."

He turned away before she could respond. She heard the door close with a quiet snick and realized with increasing sorrow that she'd hurt him. She thought of a time when she wanted to cause him pain, when she would have taken joy in his agony. But no longer. He suffered as they all had. She knew that now. How complicated it all seemed of a sudden.

Her feelings for Ainsley were not what they'd once been. She'd begun to enjoy his company, looked forward to seeing him. But far worse, she wanted a rumpled bed in the afternoon.

Ainsley listened to the slow ticking of the clock, each second an eternity. He had not seen Jayne since he'd left her in the bath—appearing so delectable with the dew coating her exposed skin. He'd wanted to skim soapy hands over her, was prepared to do just that. He shouldn't have taken offense at her embarrassment for being found in his company—and yet he had. He'd always been so careful to protect every other lover, to ensure their relationship was not the fodder of gossip. Why not Jayne?

He wanted her to want to be with him because of him, not because of something with which he might gift her.

"It's not often I see you brood."

Ainsley glared at his mother, sitting on the sofa beside Leo. She wore a burgundy velvet gown that accentuated her dark features. She did not look her age of fifty-two, although he noticed that the salt in her hair was beginning to overshadow the pepper. She and Leo were each sipping wine, waiting for dinner to be served.

Standing beside the fireplace, his elbow resting on the mantel, Ainsley relished the smoothness of the red wine on his tongue. "I'm not brooding."

He was, devil take it, and that irritated him.

"Perhaps I should check on Jayne," his mother said.

"She knows what time dinner is served. It's quite possible she's decided not to join us. The choice is hers. She is here with no expectations or responsibilities. Certainly not to serve as my hostess. She is here to do as she pleases."

"Who are you striving to convince—yourself or me?"

"I simply want to ensure you understand the situation."

His mother's eyes narrowed, and he feared she understood it only too well.

"How is Walfort?" she asked.

"The same as he was three years ago. Crippled."

"And you still feel guilty over it."

"Of course I do. I held the reins and urged the horses into a frenzy. And I believe we've talked this subject to death. Shall we move on to something else?"

"Do you think I should offer Leo's services to Walfort?"

Ainsley felt his gut clench. "For what purpose?"

"I thought he might like to have his portrait painted. He and his wife."

Ainsley downed the remainder of his wine. He'd thought she was offering stud services. What the devil was wrong with him to even have such an absurd thought?

"Is that decision not Leo's?"

"Of course it is, but I'm presently his benefactor, so he paints the portraits I would like to see done."

"How long do you intend to be his benefactor?"

"Until you marry and have a wedding portrait done."

"You do realize that when I marry you will become the *Dowager* Duchess of Ainsley?"

"And it shall make me feel remarkably old, but I shall make that sacrifice for your happiness."

To change the direction of the conversation, Ainsley shifted his gaze to Leo. "Does it not bother you that my mother speaks as though she owns you?"

He smiled, clearly amused. "She owns my heart." He lifted her hand, kissed the back of it. "The rest of me comes with it."

His mother laughed as though she were a young girl, infatuated with her first swain. "Oh, Leo, you are such a charmer. Is it any wonder I adore you?"

"For his sake, I should probably never marry," Ainsley said.

That got his mother's attention directed at him. "You

need an heir. But more important, you need someone so you won't be quite so lonely."

"I'm not lonely."

"You're not brooding. You're not lonely. Are you saying that I don't know how to read my youngest son?"

"I'm saying—" The words died in his throat as Jayne glided into the room wearing a magnificent red gown. The sleeves were long but the square neckline left a delectable amount of skin visible from her throat to the gentle swells of her breasts. Her upswept hair was held in place with a pearl comb that matched the pearls at her throat. She wore her wedding ring—that had been absent since that first night—preparing to play a role of nothing more than guest.

She curtsied before his mother. "Your Grace, forgive me for rushing upstairs earlier without properly greeting you."

"Oh, my dear girl." His mother rose gracefully, embraced Jayne, then put her at arm's length. "Don't be ridiculous. I daresay you were freezing in all those wet clothes. I didn't blame you at all. Ainsley informs me that we're not to use titles here, so you must call me Tess. And of course you know Leo."

The artist was already standing. He took Jayne's hand and pressed a kiss to it. "A pleasure, m'lady."

"Jayne will suffice—since we're not to be formal. I have seen your work. It's truly remarkable."

"It is only as remarkable as my subjects. Perhaps someday you will honor me by allowing me to put you on canvas."

Her gaze jumped to Ainsley. "Perhaps. I must apologize for being late. I took a nap and fell quite asleep. My maid didn't think to wake me."

Ainsley was certain her words were a lie. He had no doubt she'd been fighting with her conscience, trying to determine if she should join them.

"It was no hardship to wait for you," he said. It would, however, be a hardship to be with her all night and not touch her. He, too, would be playing a part: uninterested host. When all he wanted to do was approach her, slip his arm around her and nestle her against his side.

"Shall we go into dinner now?" his mother asked, as though aware that Ainsley was too preoccupied with Jayne to think about anything as mundane as food.

"By all means." Before he could reach Jayne, his mother was escorting her out, murmuring low as though they were sharing secrets. Leaving him with little to do other than glare at Leo.

"I'll have your mother in her carriage and on our way as soon as possible in the morning," the artist said.

"Stay as long as you like. As I said, Jayne is merely here on holiday."

"And I'm a descendent of Rembrandt."

"Are you? Is that the reason you're so secretive regarding your last name?" Leo never discussed his family, his parentage, or his last name.

"Let's join the ladies, shall we?" Leo asked, ignoring Ainsley's inquiry.

As they strolled toward the dining room, Ainsley said, "I know Mother has a tendency to be dramatic. So how bad off is Lady Lynnford?" The earl had served as guardian for him and his brothers after his father died. He'd always felt loved by the earl and his countess.

"Very, I'm afraid. I suspect Lynnford will be a widower before the next Season is upon us."

"I'm very sorry to hear that. Although I have always wondered if he is the reason you've yet to make an honest woman of the duchess."

"Who is to say? She craves her independence."

"I don't see you taking that from her."

"It is not an easy thing to love a woman knowing she belongs to another. But I don't suppose I need to tell you that."

"She is here on holiday," Ainsley repeated.

"And who said I was referring to Jayne?"

Ainsley cut his gaze over to Leo. "I'm beginning to understand why Westcliffe found you irritating when he and Claire were trying to reconcile."

"Why? Because I knew he loved her long before he did?"

Because he was too observant and meddled more than his mother. "I shall have your carriage readied at dawn."

Leo gave him a sympathetic look. "Love is hell, my friend."

Ainsley knew he wasn't in love, but he was damned glad Jayne had decided to join them for dinner, because in truth, he wasn't certain he'd have had the strength to carry through on his threat to return her home on the morrow.

Jayne had expected the evening to be awkward, with the duchess prying and seeking to get to the truth behind her presence, but the woman spoke of her travels, her sons, her grandchildren. It was the talk of her grandchildren that put a pang in Jayne's heart. The duchess would have a grandchild she would never know—although Jayne knew she certainly could find a way to involve her in the child's life. Oh, why had they started down this path? But even as she questioned it, the ache for a child blossomed into something almost unbearable. If she were fortunate to meet with success here, she would find a way to make everything right.

"You know," the duchess began, directing her attention to Jayne, "I thought Ainsley was tossing good money after bad when he set about putting this cottage to rights. It was fairly a hovel when he purchased it. But I find it rather peaceful now. It is as though one can leave one's troubles at the door."

"Quite," Jayne concurred. "It has been a welcome escape."

"I'm sure it has, m'dear. You are so young to carry such burdens. I was not much younger when my first husband passed. Left me destitute. I had not a clue we were in such unfortunate circumstances until the solicitor paid his visit. Westcliffe and I did not converse much at all. I was to provide him with an heir and little else. I did my duty by him, but I must confess they were the longest—and the loneliest—years of my life."

Although the circumstances were different, Jayne had to admit that the past few years were the longest, loneliest, and most nightmarish of her life. "And your second husband?"

Even as she asked, she knew she was being rude, but she wanted to keep the conversation turned away from her.

"Ainsley's father was a dear. I would not go so far as to say we loved each other, but we respected each other, cared for each other, enjoyed each other's company from time to time. He was a good man, your father," the duchess said to Ainsley.

"I barely remember him," Ainsley said.

"He was fit, an excellent horseman, and a good conversationalist." She shifted her gaze to the artist. "But I believe it is only Leo who has ever made me laugh. We underestimate the importance of laughter, I think. It did my heart good to hear yours echoing through these halls this afternoon. You've been too somber of late."

"You shouldn't worry about me, Mother."

"But I do. I worry about all my boys." She glanced over at Jayne. "No matter how old they get, you still think of them as boys." As though realizing that she might have stepped in it, with sympathy in her eyes she reached over and patted Jayne's hand. "No matter. I have heard wonderful things about the fox hunt you hosted. I daresay, you outdid yourself."

"Thank you, Your—Tessa. I believe we shall return to making it an annual event."

"So much effort, though, isn't it?"

"We enjoyed having the company."

"I'm sure."

The topics moved on—to the weather. Would the rain cease by morning? Christmas. Where would the family gather for the holiday? It seemed Westcliffe's ancestral home had become a favorite haunt. His wife, Claire, was apparently an excellent hostess. Jayne thought of all the children who would be there. The squeals, laughter, and pounding of running feet. She wondered if Walfort wanted her to have a child so their home wouldn't be quite so quiet.

She felt the weight of Ainsley's gaze and wondered if he was thinking the same thing—or if he was contemplating all the Christmases he would have without his child.

After dinner, they played cards until the clock chimed ten, then retired to their separate rooms, all saying good-night in the hallway. Closing the door behind her, Jayne pressed her back to it. Ainsley wouldn't come see her tonight. She would be alone.

Wrapping her arms tightly around herself, she wondered how it was that she could *miss* him.

Chapter 13

Before his next visit to the cottage, Ainsley intended to have a door placed between his bedchamber and the one next to it. Meanwhile, he prowled his room, listening to the infernal ticking of the clock, marking away the time he would have with Jayne.

Finally, at midnight, he opened the door, stepped into the hallway, and froze, as Leo was apparently concluding the same actions. They stared at each other for the span of a heartbeat before Leo finally nodded and sauntered into the bedchamber that had been given to Ainsley's mother.

He knew they were lovers, of course. They'd been together for years now. He wasn't naïve, believing his mother kept Leo around simply for his talents with the paintbrush. Still, it was unsettling to have proof of their dalliance. It was time he found out what the man's intentions were regarding his mother. Only he knew his mother well enough to know she'd have none of that, none of his interference. Unfortunate for her, but there was no hope for it. He would talk with Westcliffe and Stephen about this matter when next he saw them.

Leaving behind thoughts of his mother and what

might be transpiring across the hallway, he slipped into Jayne's room. She was perched in a chair beside the window, gazing out. Horror washed over her features.

"You can't be here tonight," she said in a harsh whisper.

He ambled over to the window and pressed his shoulder against it, much as he had that first night. Odd to think how much had changed between them in such a short time.

"What if tonight is the magical night?" he asked.

With a quick shake of her head, she turned her attention back to the rain. "I don't know if we should be doing this."

"Why not? You want a child. I want to give you one. Walfort wants you to have one."

"Your mother will never know he or she is her grandchild."

"Jayne." He knelt in front of her, took her hands. "She'd understand."

"I don't see how she could."

With a sigh, he released her, pressed his back to the wall, raised his knees and draped his wrists over them. "If I tell you a secret, you must swear to never tell a soul."

"I'm slightly insulted you don't realize that all you have to tell me is that it's a secret. I understand the importance with which they are kept."

"We're alike in that regard, yet here I am, considering sharing this one with you."

"I swear." She settled her chin on her upturned knees. "Does it have to do with your mother?"

"Everything has to do with my mother."

"She loves you very much."

"She loves Stephen more . . . because she loved his father."

"But I thought she detested Westcliffe. She even implied so during dinner with veiled mentions of her loneliness."

Ainsley arched a brow, gave her a pointed look. He could almost see the wheels turning through her mind, then her jaw dropped and her eyes opened wide.

"Are you implying Westcliffe isn't his father?"

"I'm implying that my mother would understand— and forgive—your situation."

She was watching the rain again. Her toes curled around the edge of the cushion as though she was thinking so hard she needed the purchase to remain where she was. He wanted to slip his hand beneath the hem of her nightdress, slide it along her calf and find that little scar he'd been giving attention to earlier. Complete the journey that had haunted him all day.

"That's why she loved Stephen," she said on a whispered breath, before jerking her gaze back to him. "She loved her lover. Do you think that's it?"

He shrugged.

"It must be," she insisted. "Who is he?"

"That, I can't tell you."

"Do you know who he is?"

He nodded. "But the man's family never knew. His parents didn't know that Stephen was their grandchild." He couldn't help himself. He reached out and wrapped his hand around her foot. "My whole point in sharing this is that it's something we'll live with, but we needn't feel guilty over it."

"That's what prompted your condition, your rule.

You were afraid if I didn't love you, I couldn't love your child."

"It was a consideration, yes."

"When your mother was talking about her grand-children, all I could think about was how desperately I wanted a child. Am I selfish, do you think?"

"No, I think you give too much of yourself to be selfish."

She gave him a winsome smile. "I'd not expected to like you so much."

"Well, that is a blow to my self-esteem. I thought you liked me the moment you met me."

"I'm not really certain I gave it any thought. Wal-fort occupied all my attention. He was so dashing." She waved her hand in front of her face. "I promised not to talk about him, and yet here I am doing exactly that."

"You can talk to me about anything, Jayne."

"Can I? I've also discovered that I can be quiet around you and not feel awkward about it. That's almost as important as being able to talk. I think your mother loves Leo."

"I don't know if she loves him enough."

"What would be enough?"

"To give up on the promise of love from another."

"Can she not love two men?"

He almost asked Jayne if she could. Could she love two men? Could she love him and Walfort? In all likeli-hood no, so he didn't ask.

Instead he listened to the rain patter and let the si-lence weave around them. He studied her, sitting there contemplating the raindrops. He tried not to imagine her swollen with his child. He might never have the opportunity to gaze upon her in that condition, might never feel the movement of new life growing within her.

But it was too late now for regrets. His seed could have already taken root. If not, the truth was that he wanted her more than he'd ever wanted another woman. Unfolding himself from the floor, he reached down and tugged on her hand. "Come on."

Pulling free, she shook her head vigorously. "No, we can't. Not with your mother down the hall."

He tugged again. "We shall be very quiet."

She again pulled free. "As the past nights have proven, I cannot be quiet with you."

That gave him pause. Had she been quiet with Walfort? Had his cousin not brought her the most exquisite of pleasure? He couldn't contemplate what he might be giving her that Walfort never had, couldn't compare his cousin's prowess against his own. None of it mattered. All that mattered was the moments he had with her now.

This time he leaned in, cupped her elbows and said, "Press your mouth against my chest to muffle your cries."

He brought her to her feet.

"It will be a disaster," she insisted. "I will not be able to relax."

He gave a slight tug and unraveled the ribbon at the front of her nightdress. "I so love a challenge."

"Is that what I am?"

He loosened a button. "Most assuredly. A delightful challenge." Another button.

"The lamp."

An irritating, frustrating challenge.

Moving past her, he bent down and extinguished the flame in the lamp. As he straightened, he felt the press of warm, pliant flesh against his back and smiled. Not so frustrating after all.

Turning, he wound his arms around her. "Oh, you wicked girl."

"We must be quiet," she whispered.

"As two little dormice."

Tumbling her onto the bed, he chuckled low when she released a tiny squeal that she abruptly cut off with a choking sound, trying to swallow the noise. He quickly shed his own clothes and joined her.

Jayne knew this was an awful idea. Where he was concerned, she seemed unable to keep quiet or still. Already her body was writhing over the sheets with the attention he was lavishing on her. His mouth was so incredibly talented.

She remembered their kiss on the terrace. What a fool she'd been to deny herself his questing mouth toying with hers. But it terrified her: the hunger he could elicit so easily. It started with their lips and carried a sensation of pleasure through her that made her want more. So much more.

So she'd been determined to deny herself that much at least. She wanted her encounters with Ainsley to be the unemotional business dealings that Walfort had promised her they would be.

But even now her skin was singing with joy—everywhere he touched. And he had no qualms about touching her everywhere, with his fingers, his mouth, his tongue, his teeth. He nipped and soothed. He caressed so lightly, until she was straining for more pressure, and he would deliver it at the most perfect moment.

It was as though he knew her body, knew what would bring her pleasure better than she did herself.

She found it just as joyous to touch him. To skim her hands over his shoulders, his back, his chest. Her fingers would journey through the light sprinkling of hair on his chest, creating even more sensations for her.

"Shh," he warned, and she realized she was emitting little mewling sounds.

She swallowed down the noises, but trying to hold everything in only made matters worse. The pleasure clawed at her, demanding freedom.

She was more than ready when he slid into her, burying himself deeply, the weight of him welcome and satisfactory. Her low moan was greeted with his deep sigh as he held still. She dug her fingers into his backside, urging him on, but his movements were as slow as honey dripping onto a scone, as measured as the beat of a drum in a regimental parade.

"Ainsley?"

"Shh."

His mouth traveled along her throat, licking, kissing, nibbling. In the darkness nothing except sensation existed. Warm and sultry. Dew coated their skin and they skated over each other. She shoved the sounds deep down, and it served to increase the pleasure, to make her want to cry out.

It was torment to hold so much in. It was ecstatic. He slid out, glided back in. Over and over. With deliberate slowness. Beneath her fingers, his strong body undulated with his controlled actions.

She squeezed her eyes shut tightly. Stars appeared. Dancing, shooting across her vision. Her body curled into itself. She wrapped a hand around his neck, forced him nearer, pressed her open mouth to the juncture of his throat and shoulder. Tasted the saltiness of his skin, inhaled the earthy muskiness of their lovemaking.

Lovemaking. In spite of all Walfort's reassurances that it wouldn't be so, in spite of her insignificant rules, he'd slipped beneath her armor, had leaped over her pitiful hazards, wended his way through a maze of obstacles to establish something magical and wonderful between them. She'd been sitting by the window mourning the fact that he'd not be able to visit her tonight with his mother in attendance, and yet here he was. Solid. Strong. Determined.

What they shared was not what she'd been led to believe they would. No distance separated them. It wasn't casual and cold and stiff. It was warm, hot, and encompassing.

He moved with deliberate purpose and she responded in kind.

Her mouth pressed to his neck muffled her small moans, her tiny squeals as the pleasure built to unbearable proportions, more intense than anything she'd ever known.

When the cataclysm came and she bucked against him, wrapping herself more tightly around him to contain everything, to keep them both earthbound, she was jarred by his shuddering, his final powerful thrusts, the strangled groan deep in his throat as though he were in excruciating agony.

Afterward they both lay still, except for their trembling and shaking. Their harsh breaths echoed between them.

"Christ," he finally whispered, the word sounding as though it were torn from the depths of his soul.

"Were you in pain?"

He laughed low. "No. God, no. But I will confess to never having experienced anything quite so . . . intense. I did think for a moment there that I might expire on the spot." He brushed a kiss over her temple. "You seemed to enjoy things."

"It was . . . yes, I think you have the right of it. Intense." She curled inward and spoke even lower. "I'm not accustomed to talking afterward."

He kissed her throat, her chest, the side of one breast before rolling off her and sprawling out beside her. "Do you prefer the silence?"

"No. I don't think so. But sometimes. It can be nice."

She felt a slight tug on her scalp as he combed his fingers through her hair, and she wondered how it was that he could find her so easily in the dark. It seemed he was aware of every aspect regarding her.

"Will you weep tonight after I leave?" he asked quietly.

"I don't think so. I'm too sated." Then the full impact of his words struck her. "You know I cry?"

"I suspected. *Now* I know."

"It was not very nice of you to trick me like that."

"Sometimes I'm not very nice."

Not true. He was always remarkably nice even when she was a shrew. Nice, kind, and considerate. A gentleman to the core. She wished he wasn't. It would make it so much easier to leave here unscathed.

"She's going to break his heart."

Leo held Tessa against his side and idly stroked her arm. She'd been distracted when he first entered her bedchamber, and it took all his formidable skill to turn her attention to him. Once she'd succumbed to his charms, he ravaged her well and thoroughly. His heart was still pounding with his exertions and he was fighting to draw in breath. No other woman had ever affected him as she did. His joy in her encompassed more than what transpired in the bed. He enjoyed every moment of every day that he was in her presence.

"You're being melodramatic," he said quietly.

"Did you not notice the manner in which he gazed upon her? I think he has already well and truly fallen. I know what it is—the soul-wrenching pain of it—to love someone you can never have."

So did he, but he wasn't going to batter her with it. Nothing was to be gained except to make them both miserable.

"What if she is all he ever wants? He must marry," she said.

"Why?"

She rose up on an elbow, and he ignored the way it dug into his chest. Instead he combed his fingers through her thick, luxurious hair. Only a few short moments ago it had served as a curtain to close them in.

"He must have an heir," she said as though he had experienced a complete leaving of his senses.

"Why?"

"Leo!" She tapped her slender finger on his chin. "You are well aware of how primogeniture works. He must have a male heir to inherit his titles and lands."

"If not, everything would fall to a cousin. What does it matter?"

"It matters. I want him to be happy."

He cradled her face, forced her to meet his gaze.

"You cannot make his happiness for him, my love. He is a grown man now. He'll make his own way."

"But he loves her, and she does not love him."

"She is here for holiday. Make no more of it than that." Even though more was apparently happening. He hadn't told her that he'd crossed paths with Ainsley in the hallway. The knowledge would only add to her worries. He held her still, raised his shoulders from the bed and took her mouth. After ten years, he thought the pleasure of kissing her should have worn off, but it still took his breath, made his heart race and his palms itch to caress every inch of her. He'd had many women before her, but not a single one after her. She was all he wanted, all he desired.

It took everything within him not to ask her once more to marry him. It had nearly devastated him the last time he asked and she refused. It had been two years ago, and he'd been so certain she'd accept his offer of marriage. Instead she'd persisted with her arguments that he was too young, would one day want children, should marry someone closer to his age, as though when he let his arrow fly, Cupid gave one whit regarding the number of years a person had accumulated. Leo had decided then that he'd not ask again—but neither could he leave her. If she wanted to be rid of him, she would have to be the one to turn her back on what they shared and walk away.

As she released that gentle purring in her throat that always initiated a corresponding low growl in his, he rolled her over so he might have his fill of her once again. He was greedy where she was concerned, but he experienced no guilt over it. He suspected that very soon nights would arrive when he would be deprived her solace, her body, her presence. Until that time, he would be a glutton and make her glad of it.

And wonder how it was that she could be so attuned to her sons' hearts and not to his.

Chapter 14

Ainsley awoke the moment the rain stopped. It was the sudden silence that disturbed his slumber. He'd slipped from Jayne's bed as she was drifting off to sleep. He'd wanted nothing more than to remain and watch her ease into slumber, but she'd been fighting to stay awake as though their actually *sleeping* in the same bed was more sinful than what they were doing before she grew so drowsy.

He rose with the sun and dressed. He didn't mean to be a bad host, but he was anxious for his latest company to depart. When only Leo strolled into the breakfast dining room, Ainsley feared his guests might be considering staying for another night.

"Is my mother awake?" he asked.

"Good morning, Your Grace," Leo said laconically as he strolled to the sideboard.

"My apologies, Leo. Good morning to you. I hope you slept well."

"Hardly at all."

The answer didn't please him. It was one thing to see the man sneaking into his mother's bedchamber, another to have their affair tossed in his face. Before he had a chance to contemplate the possible ramifications of his actions, Ainsley was up out of his chair and standing beside Leo. "What are your intentions where my mother is concerned?"

Leo flicked his head, causing the blond curls falling over his forehead to monetarily fly back before returning to where they were before. "More honorable than hers toward me. I'd marry her this afternoon if she'd have me."

"Have you asked her?"

"Too many times to count." He took his plate laden with food to the table and sat.

The man had no respect for Ainsley's position in society. It was one of the reasons he liked him. Leo wasn't easily intimidated. Ainsley returned to his chair and began slicing his ham. "She can be stubborn."

"She thinks our age difference should be a consideration."

"How much younger are you?" He knew the man was younger but had never given it much thought.

"Fifteen years."

"You're only slightly older than Westcliffe."

"I was born not too long after she married his father."

Ainsley studied him. "The difference in your ages doesn't matter to you?"

"Not one whit."

"Do you love her?"

"My heart is not a topic I care to discuss."

"Well, for what it's worth, I think she's a fool not to let you make an honest woman of her."

Leo grinned. "Thank you, Your Grace. I'm certain she wouldn't appreciate your sentiment, but I do." His smile faltered and he poked at his buttered eggs before returning his gaze to Ainsley's. "And what of you? I suspect it is a well-traveled path you were taking last night."

"I will not discuss Jayne."

"Do you love her?"

Setting down his knife, Ainsley narrowed his eyes. "I could have sworn you spoke English, man. Did I mumble my words? She is not a topic for discussion."

"It's a pity we're not staying longer. I should think you'd like a portrait."

He knew Leo wasn't referring to a portrait of Ainsley, but rather, one of Jayne. What would he do with it? Store it in the attic? Take it out to gaze at on melancholy days? Although what would be the harm in hanging it here? He never entertained at the cottage. No one visited—except for his meddling mother and her meddling lover.

After spending time with Jayne here, he wasn't certain he'd ever bring his wife or children here. This cottage was quickly becoming a special place. He wasn't even certain he'd ever return, although neither could he see himself selling it.

"Perhaps when she returns home, you could offer your services. I'm sure she and Walfort would appreciate having an artist of your caliber working on a portrait."

Leo gave a brusque nod. "I shall see to it. In the spring, perhaps, when roads are easier to travel."

"Keep me informed. I may wish to send a missive"— a private one—"along with you."

"Of course. Ah!" Leo rose. "Sunshine has arrived."

Initially, Ainsley thought he was speaking of the sun peering through the clouds, but then his mother strolled into the room. Leo greeted her with a kiss on the cheek.

"Sit. I'll prepare your plate." He guided her into a chair beside Ainsley before wandering back to the sideboard.

"He spoils you," Ainsley murmured.

"I'm most fortunate. And before you annoy me with your next observation—'you should marry him'—he is still young and I am rapidly growing old. It will not be much longer before he tires of me."

"I daresay, you misjudge your appeal."

Reaching out, she squeezed his hand where it rested beside his plate. "You were always the kindest of my sons, the one with the gentlest heart. Westcliffe was harsh because I gave him so little affection. It pains me now to admit it, but it is the truth. I could say I was a child myself when I gave birth to him, but that is no excuse. He also had a hard time of it because his father left him little beyond the title and he was dependent upon your generosity. Stephen resented that he wouldn't inherit a title or property and he rebelled by reveling in naughtiness. And I spoiled him beyond measure. In my eyes, he could do no wrong. You, on the other hand, had a prestigious title, wealth, and a good portion of your mother's love. You have always strived to be the brother they looked up to. And you have always done all in your power to protect each of us."

"Well, I did a bang-up job when it came to Walfort, didn't I?"

She cut a sharp glance his way as Leo set her plate before her and resumed his seat. "I have never understood how he could have come away from the accident so irreparably broken while you"—she slid her thumb over the scar on his chin—"were almost unscathed."

"I wouldn't go quite that far."

"You're like Stephen when he returned from the Crimea. His emotional wounds were far worse than the physical ones. Thank God for Mercy, I say. She put him back to rights." She held his gaze. "Who shall do that for you?"

He was spared from answering as Jayne strolled into the room. He considered extending to her the courtesy Leo had extended his mother—preparing her plate—but he had to give the impression that she was no more than a guest.

Leo, however, had no such qualms or restrictions. He popped out of his chair as though someone had pinched his bottom and approached her. "Good morning, lovely lady. Have a seat and I shall prepare a plate for you."

"No need. I can see to it."

"Surely you will not deny me the pleasure it will bring me by doing such a small favor for you." Taking her arm, he guided her into a chair.

Jayne appeared flummoxed as her gaze darted from Ainsley to his mother. "He's quite charming."

"Yes," his mother said succinctly, causing Ainsley to slide his gaze to her.

He'd assumed Leo had given Jayne the attention to irritate him, to perhaps steer him toward some sort of action—it had certainly pricked his temper, and if he were honest, ignited a spark of jealousy. But he recognized now that it was his mother Leo had been prodding by his attentions to Jayne. "Well, he's not your husband," Ainsley murmured.

He was surprised the scalding glare his mother gave him didn't ignite him. "Leo is always attentive to all ladies. It is part of his charm."

"But I always save the best for you," Leo said smoothly

as he placed Jayne's plate before her. He winked at the duchess and effectively defused her anger or jealousy or whatever the hell it was she'd been expressing.

They read each other so well. Ainsley tried not to ponder how much he yearned for a similar closeness with a woman. He'd never given much thought to the matter of marriage, assuming he'd address the situation when he was ready to produce an heir. He entertained women, they entertained him. He was seldom without company. And yet he was suddenly aware that something powerful and possibly magnificent was missing from his life. Was his reason for being here with Jayne not completely unselfish? He couldn't deny that she filled a void that until recently he'd not even known existed.

His life would be all the more lonely when she left. Perhaps it was time he began to search for a wife. But even that did not seem enough. What he desperately longed for was a love. Such as that shared by Leo and his mother.

He was grateful his mother behaved during the meal. She didn't pepper Jayne with questions or ask her opinion regarding whom he should wed. They spoke of the upcoming Season and how perhaps Jayne and Walfort would finally return to London. He wasn't certain how he would endure it—seeing her there, knowing their paths would cross constantly. Would it be a blessing or a curse? Yet neither could he envision never again seeing her.

It was a relief when they all finished breakfast and his mother announced that it was time she and Leo were off.

They stood on the front lawn, saying their good-byes.

"I'll send word on how Lady Lynnford is progressing," his mother said.

"Give her my love." With Lynnford serving as Ainsley's guardian, Lady Lynnford had been as a second mother to him. She was the gentlest soul he'd ever known. He hated that she was suffering.

His mother wound her arms around him, hugging him tightly and whispering low near his ear, "Please take care. I fear you're treading on dangerous ground here."

When she pulled back, he gave her a reassuring grin. "I am ever careful."

Lovingly, she patted his cheek before moving on to hug Jayne. "It was lovely to see you, my dear. We must keep in touch."

He recognized the signs of Jayne struggling for a response, weighing the awkwardness of a future encounter against the guilt she'd expressed last night. Finally, she simply bobbed her head. "Yes, that would be lovely."

As the carriage drove away, Ainsley leaned toward Jayne and said, "Lovely as hell."

She jerked back. "Whatever do you mean?"

"Keeping in touch with my mother. She's meddling, you know."

"Do you think she knows my true purpose in being here?"

"Not in her wildest imagination would she draw that conclusion."

"I rather like Leo. I do believe he loves your mother."

Last night she'd only mentioned his mother's love of Leo. "I've no doubt you're correct." He skimmed his fingers over her cheek. "What would you like to do today?"

"What I do anytime I've ever entertained and the guests have left. Absolutely nothing."

Jayne borrowed one of the books from Ainsley's library and retreated to her bedchamber. Reclining on the longue near a window, she read for a while. Five minutes to be exact. She rose, walked to the secretary, and sat to pen a letter to Walfort, to let him know she was well. After dipping pen in inkwell, she determined that was an awful idea and would no doubt plague him with the reminder that his wife was with another man.

She walked to the window, leaned on the sill and gazed out for a full two minutes. Then, out of the corner of her eye, she saw Ainsley wandering away from the house. He did love his outdoors. She was surprised by the joy that rippled through her at the sight of him, then decided it was nothing more than a response to being bored. He served as a distraction.

She opened the window and leaned out as far as she was able without losing her balance and toppling to the ground. "Ainsley!"

He spun around. An emotion she didn't recognize ratcheted around her heart, making it difficult to draw in a breath. Still she managed to call out, "Will you wait up for me?"

Even from her precarious perch she could see his broad smile as he yelled, "As long as it takes!"

She released a burst of laughter. "I'll hurry!"

Withdrawing back inside, she closed her window and pressed her forehead to the cool glass. She shouldn't be anticipating joining him as much as she was. It was wrong. Yet at that particular moment nothing had ever felt so incredibly right.

She didn't bother with a hat. She simply grabbed her pelisse, draped it around her shoulders and rushed out. He was waiting exactly where he'd stopped when she called out to him. She didn't know why it pleased her so much. "Where are you going?"

"Nowhere in particular. I just felt the need to stretch my legs."

Before Walfort's accident, she'd loved walking, trudging through forests, over the land. Afterward she felt guilty anytime she partook of an activity that now eluded him. But she didn't have to feel guilty here. Ainsley could easily outdistance her. "Do you mind if I join you?"

"I was hoping you would. I've wandered in sight of your window at least a dozen times now."

She laughed lightly, filled with a joyous ebullience. "You're teasing."

"No."

"Why didn't you knock on my door and ask?"

"I had the sense you wanted to be alone for a bit."

She shook her head. "I thought I did. I was wrong."

"Well, then." He extended his arm and she wrapped hers around it. "Let's see what adventure awaits, shall we?"

They strolled along in silence for several moments before she dared to ask, "So what other secrets do you hold?"

She gave him an impish smile when he gazed down on her. "None I can reveal."

"Do any of them involve Walfort?"

"Why ever would you think that?"

"He's your cousin, but more, he is your friend."

"Because he is my friend, I have locked his secrets

away, and even you do not have the key that will set them free."

She saw the determination in his eyes and wondered at the secrets. They probably all involved naughty things they'd done before she married Walfort. She let her curiosity lapse, for what did they matter?

"I'm not ashamed to be here with you, you know," Jayne said.

"I wasn't certain. It's a very unusual circumstance that has brought us here."

"If I were ashamed, I'd have not come. I'm wary, to be sure, and from time to time plagued with doubts regarding the wisdom of what we're doing, but then I consider what I will gain and am selfish enough to want it and hope that you don't pay too high a price for it."

"If it wasn't a price I was willing to pay, I wouldn't be here."

They had entered a copse of trees. She gazed up at the remaining leaves displaying their abundant colors and listened as they crackled in the slight breeze. The ground beneath their feet was soft, and their steps crushed the leaves that had already fallen. The soil would be richer come spring. Everything circled.

She shook her head. "Do you know what I noticed last night regarding your mother and Leo?"

"That they are not at all discreet regarding their relationship?"

She heard the disapproval in his voice. Considering his reputation, he would be a hypocrite to object too strongly, but from what she knew, he was at least circumspect in his relationships. "That they talk. They communicate. Even when they were giving us a terrible beating at cards, they somehow were able to read each other's minds. Walfort and I seldom talk . . . even before the accident. The night you kissed me on the terrace and you mentioned something about how a kiss owns itself, that it simply is. You were correct. We could have kissed, we could have touched . . . it is as though we placed ourselves in separate cages. I was being a dutiful wife, not a loving one."

"If he never kissed you, Jayne, I can hardly credit him with being a loving husband."

She was caught off guard by the heat in his voice, the temper that accompanied it. Feeling as though the forest was closing in on her, she squeezed his arm. "I'm sorry. I promised not to speak of him while I'm here and yet I'm rambling on. It is simply strange to find myself suddenly discovering aspects to love that I'd never considered. I think your wife will be most fortunate."

She'd nearly stumbled over the word wife, and she didn't know why. Of course, he would marry and have other children. Lots of them, no doubt—based upon his stamina and enthusiasm for lovemaking. She wished him well. She was not feeling anything beyond gratitude toward him, certainly not jealousy. That would be a fool's path.

"*If* I ever marry," he said quietly as they emerged through the trees, giving her a different view of the lake.

"Surely you shall marry."

"As you are well aware, among the aristocracy we marry for various reasons. Political gain. My title brought with it the influence of my ancestors. I have little use for more political swagger." He shrugged. "Financial gain? Again, my ancestors saw me in good stead there. I do not need more wealth. An heir? Unfortunately, ladies do not come with lettering on the forehead to indicate how many sons they may deliver or if they may even deliver a child at all. So what is left to me? Love. *That* is very difficult to find."

"I should think for you that it would be quite easy."

"Why? You don't love me."

"Well, no . . . I love Walfort." It seemed so little to say. "I don't *hate* you."

His laughter echoed around them. "High praise indeed."

"You will find someone to love you, Ainsley. You deserve it." And he did, she realized, more than anyone she knew.

"I thought you *thought* I deserved to rot in hell?"

He was smiling at her, his green eyes twinkling. She imagined he was striving to turn away from a topic he obviously found uncomfortable. "Well, yes, of course, but not until you're old . . . and dead."

He chuckled low. "Ah, Jayne, you have no idea how much I enjoy your company." He changed direction, leading them away from the lake. "I believe I shall take you fishing tomorrow."

She considered asking him what he had planned for tonight, but she knew. For the first time since her arrival, she was anticipating the coming night with astounding excitement.

Chapter 15

Jayne awoke, still lethargic and sated after a less than sedate session of lovemaking. It was still dark so she knew it had been only a few hours since Ainsley had left her and she drifted off to sleep. Strange how she felt as though she were truly waking up for the first time in her life. She couldn't explain it. She'd come here for a purpose, and even if she discovered this morning that she was with child, she would be loath to leave before the allotted time to which they'd all agreed.

Whatever was wrong with her? She should be missing Walfort, and in a way she was, but last night she'd not thought of him at all, not even when Ainsley left her. Instead all she could think about was the duke and the pleasure she found in his arms. His experience made him far more skilled than Walfort, but it was more than his talents. When she was with him, it was as though no one else in the world existed for him. All his attention was focused on her. No doubt it was part of the game at which he excelled: seducing women. Yet it never felt like a game. It seemed he meant every touch, every press of his lips, every caress.

She released a long, lingering sigh, followed by a low moan. Already she—

"Wonderful. You're finally stirring."

With a tiny screech, she scrambled back, sat up against the headboard and stared at the silhouette near the window. "What are you doing here?"

"I live here. 'Tis my cottage."

"I meant in my bedchamber." And she suspected he knew very well what she meant.

"I came to awaken you but couldn't bring myself to do it. I have something to show you, and now that you're awake . . ." He tossed a bundle onto the bed. "I borrowed them from the stable boy. They're clean. I doubt they'll be a perfect fit—he hasn't your lovely curves—but they'll do in a pinch."

"What exactly are they?"

She heard the strike of a match, watched it flare before he lit the lamp. The flickering light revealed him dressed in woolen trousers, a shirt, and a brown jacket—all of which appeared to have come from a beggar.

"Trousers," he answered.

"I can't wear trousers."

"Of course you can. It's still dark. No one will see, but you need to hurry. We must be there before first light."

"And where is it that we must be?"

"Why, where the sprites and faeries play, of course. With any luck, perhaps we'll even capture one."

"Ainsley, what on earth are you on about?"

"It's a secret. Now hurry along."

She was sputtering her refusals when he strode from the room. She should pull up the covers and return to sleep. Instead she drew her nightdress over her head and quickly put on the trousers and shirt. It seemed as though there should be more items than this. They were so light. She felt embarrassed at the thought of leaving the room wearing so little. Wearing only a nightdress to bed was one thing, but to go out into the world without her womanly armor was a bit intimidating. Yet neither could she deny the satisfaction of feeling so unencumbered. It was really quite marvelous not to have all that weight bearing down upon her body.

She dashed to the door, opened it, and found Ainsley standing with his back against the wall. "What should I put on my feet?"

"Riding boots. We'll be taking the horses."

"Then I should put on my riding habit."

"No, you'll be riding astride."

"Ainsley, that's not proper."

He sighed as if she were a burden he wished to cast off. "Jayne, when will you learn that I find proper boring? Come along now. You'll be glad of the trousers when we reach our destination."

She considered arguing further, but an excitement was thrumming through her blood at the mysterious summons. Quickly, she slipped on her boots and buttoned them. Grabbing her cloak, she hurried into the hallway. He wore a rumpled hat now and promptly dropped another on top of her head. Before she could reach up to adjust it, he was doing it for her. When he was satisfied, he studied her with an intensity that made her wish they were going to return to the bed. Was it allowed to make love in the morning?

He leaned in, stopping with his lips merely a hairbreadth from hers. She licked her lower lip, then her upper. Yes, she thought, do kiss me. Forget the silly rule. His gaze seemed to be searching hers as though sifting through her soul. He angled his head slightly. She held her breath. Waiting. Waiting.

He tweaked her nose. "You look adorable."

Before she could respond, he grabbed her hand. "Come along. We're going to miss it if we don't hasten."

They clattered down the stairs, no doubt waking up all the servants. He led her through the front door and down the steps to where the horses waited. With ease, he boosted her onto the saddle. She sat there feeling . . . well, feeling everything between her thighs. How scandalous. A woman's knees should never be so far apart except when her husband was— She cut off the thought. She'd already sent that bit of behavior to perdition when taking a short-term lover. She was beginning to realize that Ainsley was indeed a lover.

"What do you think?" he asked as he mounted his own horse.

"Much more comfortable than a sidesaddle."

"I should think so. Let's give this a go."

Although she was unfamiliar riding in this position, she didn't find it difficult to guide the horse. They were soon loping over the land. The wind brushed over her face. She'd always wanted to ride astride, and here she was doing it. Walfort would no doubt object, but who was she hurting? And who was there to see?

The moon along with the glowing lantern that Ainsley carried guided their way. Even his silhouette cut a fine figure on a horse. Once again, as when he'd vaulted the hedgerow after she took a tumble with Cassie, he was at ease, comfortable, master of the beast. She would enjoy seeing him ride at a full gallop. Perhaps at next year's fox hunt she would ride with him. Even as she thought it she realized that by next year's country party, everything would be different. Would he even come? Would she ever see him again?

They brought their horses to a halt beside a tree almost bare of leaves. It was quite possibly the largest oak she'd ever seen.

"And here we have the best climbing tree in the entire world," he said magnanimously.

"This should interest me because . . ."

"We're going to climb it."

She stared at him, dumbfounded. "You can't be serious. We're not children."

"But we're still young." After dismounting, he hung the lantern from a branch and tethered his horse to a bush. "And it's fairly easy to climb."

"And when was the last time you climbed it?"

He came to stand beside her horse. "Hmm. Let me see. Three days before you arrived."

He slipped her feet out of the stirrups, placed his hands on her waist, and helped her dismount. Then he was pulling her toward the monstrous tree.

"How old do you think it is?" she asked.

"Hundreds of years, I'm sure. It was no doubt used to hang a good many villains. Once you make it to the first branch, you'll find that the others have grown out in such a way as to almost make a natural ladder."

But reaching the first branch was a challenge. He had to lift her, and she had to stretch out. Once she was on it, she clung to the trunk, catching her breath. He scrambled up, then moved past her, guiding her onto the next branch. Higher and higher they went until they were so far up that she dared not look down.

"This is as far as we'll go," he finally said, easing her out onto the branch and helping her to sit down.

She was almost light-headed. "We're fortunate that we didn't have a mishap in the dark. We probably should have waited to do this during the daytime."

"Ah, but then we'd have missed it."

"Missed what, Your Grace?"

He wrapped his hand around hers, brought it to his lips. Although she wore gloves, she could still feel the heat of his mouth. "Just watch."

It began slowly, hidden behind the craggy horizon, revealing itself the way she'd attempted to reveal her body to Ainsley that second night: leisurely, provocatively, almost shyly. She saw the first hint of sunrise as ribbons of dark blue, pink, and orange began to chase away the night sky of black, moon, and stars. She shifted her gaze to Ainsley and recognized reverence in the calmness of his features. It was a look she wanted to see him direct her way.

For all she knew, maybe he did. In the darkness, as he made love to her. Within her bed she could feel, smell, hear, taste so much. But she could see so little. Silhouettes and shadows. She wondered what the light would reveal.

"I am always humbled by the grandeur of nature," he said quietly, as though he didn't want to disturb the beauty unfurling before them.

"I've not climbed a tree since I was seven. I'd forgotten how liberating it was."

He gazed at her. "Is that when you took your tumble?"

She nodded. "After that, I wasn't afraid of the actual climbing, but my father's temper was quite terrifying."

"Pity. I think you were meant to climb trees." He

turned his attention back to the sunrise. "Besides, I rather like your little scar. I think it shows rebelliousness."

Squeezing his hand, she held her silence and watched the sun reign supreme over the land. She wasn't even certain Walfort had ever noticed the scar. But then, he never intruded on her bath, never saw her knee when it was not hidden beneath skirts, a nightdress, or sheets. Now it was a part of her shared with Ainsley and no one else. Their little secret. Her feelings surrounding so trivial a part of her person confused her. Why had she never shared it with Walfort? How had Ainsley known she would love sitting on a tree branch at dawn?

"If I have a little girl, I'm going to encourage her to climb," she said wistfully, then continued with more determination. "I'm going to encourage her to reach for everything, even if she thinks it's beyond her grasp."

"Just as *you're* doing now." His eyes were on hers again, as though the sunrise was suddenly insignificant and she was all important. "I don't underestimate the courage that it took you to come here."

His words touched her heart. She had misjudged this man in so many ways. "I fear I was not as kind to you as I should have been. Nor did I trust your reasons for consenting to Walfort's ludicrous idea. I thought you were interested only in lifting a skirt. I've been here only a few days and already you've given me far more than I expected or in all likelihood deserve."

She didn't notice when he removed his gloves, but his warm fingers were suddenly trailing over her face as though he sought to memorize the sensation of every line and curve.

"You deserve far more than I could ever give you."

I'm falling in love with him.

The thought struck her, knocking the breath out of her. It couldn't be. Her feelings for him were generated by the sharing of their bodies. It was natural to feel love for someone with whom she shared such intimacy. But then she thought of the duchess. She had been intimate with the seventh Earl of Westcliffe yet had not loved him. Did that make her own reasoning invalid?

Was it his smile, his tenderness, his generosity, that was causing these blossoming emotions to burst forth? What she felt for him was so different from what she felt for Walfort. It could not be. It simply could not. It was the situation. Not the man.

When she left here all these confounding feelings would remain behind. He would be no more than an occasional guest when he visited Herndon Hall. She would treat him with politeness and no more.

She would feel the same for any man willing to give her a child.

But even as she thought it, she knew she was lying to herself.

That night, following dinner, they sat in the library, each reading a different tome. Or at least he was. She was simply holding the book open, waiting as each second took an eternity to move on to the next one. What hour was the correct hour for retiring in order to make love?

After their adventure that morning, they returned to the cottage, where she took a nap and then ate an immense breakfast. She'd never been so famished in her life. It had embarrassed her, but amused him that she'd eaten until she was miserable. In the afternoon they rode to the village and enjoyed warm, delicious gingerbread at the bakery. The little girl who had sold him weeds when they attended the fair was on hand to sell him more when they emerged. Ainsley laughed and purchased them for a crown. Only this time, instead of shoving them into his pocket, he offered them to Jayne. She gladly took them. Weeds that meant more to her than any flowers he might have sent her. The moment was something to be shared between them, somehow special.

When they returned to the manor, he made no untoward advances, was the perfect gentleman during dinner. He suggested they adjourn to the library to read before bed. She was left with the sense that his enthusiasm toward her might have waned, while hers toward him seemed only to increase.

It was maddening. She did not want to sit here with Jane Austen. She wanted to be in her bedchamber with Ainsley. She wanted him holding her, touching her, drawing her into the realm of carnal delights. She wanted to massage her fingers over his sculpted muscles. She wanted to hear his moans echoing around her. She wanted to be bolder—

"Is the story boring?"

She jerked her gaze up to meet his. "Pardon?"

"You're fidgeting. I thought perhaps the tale had failed to capture your attention. I have many other books if that one is not to your liking."

She almost told him that she wasn't blind, and could see them lining the shelves. But castigating him would certainly not hasten his journey to her bed.

"I'm simply a bit tired. We had such a busy day that I was thinking of retiring early."

His smile was all-knowing, irritating . . . and the most sensual one she'd ever seen.

"Well, if that be the case . . ." With a fluid movement he set his book aside and stood.

How could he appear so casual when she was practically shivering with anticipation? Placing her book on the table, she rose. When he offered her his arm, she set her hand on it. So annoyingly formal, as though they were once again strangers on the verge of engaging in an unemotional act.

Could he walk any slower? He was very close to standing still.

"My legs are not so short that you must take such small steps," she groused irritably.

Laughing, he scooped her into his arms, apparently relishing her unexpected squeal as she twined her arms around his neck.

"I wondered how long it would take," he said, clearly amused.

"For what?"

"For you to desire me."

"You insufferable lout. It is as I said. I'm rather weary, anxious for sleep."

His long strides began eating up the distance to the bedchamber.

"Put me down, Ainsley. Your servants will know what we're about with such an open display—"

"She's exhausted," he said as they passed the butler. "Can hardly walk."

She buried her face in his shoulder. "You are so cruel."

"If I were cruel"—he began making his way up the stairs—"I'd have waited another hour before putting you out of your misery."

She snapped her head back as they reached the landing. "You knew where my thoughts wandered?"

"Mine were not far behind."

They were in her bedchamber, their clothes scattered on the floor before she realized they'd not doused the lamps.

"The light—"

"Let it stay with us tonight." He wrapped a warm hand around her nape, holding her in place while he trailed his moist mouth over her throat. She closed her eyes on a sigh of pleasure. "Do not deny me any longer the pleasure of gazing on you."

She did not want to consider that the entire day his nearness, complemented by distance, had been a ploy, a way to lure her into yearning for him with such need that she would let all propriety go. No other man had ever seen her standing bared before him, the blush rising from her toes to her hair.

Ainsley leaned back, giving his gaze the freedom to roam over her. She could see the hunger and desire, something the darkness had always denied her. Now that she saw what it had kept from her, how could she welcome it back?

He was athletic and powerful. Long legs and sculpted muscles. She'd felt it all, of course, but to see it was to appreciate it all the more.

"You are so beautiful." He skimmed his thumb over her nipple. "Dark. Dusky. I'd wondered."

His were dusky as well. Turgid. She longed to feel them against her tongue. It wasn't fair that he could have her clamoring for him while he was so unaffected. Well, not completely unaffected. Not unaffected at all.

Every aspect of him stood magnificently proud before her.

He'd been tormenting her all day. She would return the favor. Leaning in, she ran her tongue over his nipple. His chest vibrated with his strangled groan. He threaded his fingers through her hair, held her head, pressed her nearer.

"Vixen."

It sounded as though he'd pushed the word up from the depths of his soul. It made her feel powerful, in control. Brazen.

Taking both his hands, she backed toward the bed, dragging him—quite willingly, judging by the predatory gleam in his eyes—with her. When they reached their destination, he lifted her onto the bed and followed her down.

He didn't resist when she rolled him over, sat up, and took in her fill of him.

"See anything you like?" he asked, his fingers stroking her spine.

With a self-conscious laugh, she peered into his eyes. "You are so comfortable with this."

"I appreciate the marvels and complexities of the human form. Someday we shall have to make love in the afternoon, in the sunshine."

"During the day, you mean?"

He grew still and blinked at her. "Have you never—" He shook his head. "Never mind. I don't wish to know."

But she suspected he already did know. She was being awakened to so many new notions and experiences. To lie with a man with no clothes on at all. With Walfort, her nightdress had gone up but not completely off. Flames never wavered and teased her with glimpses of him. The dark protected their modesty. They would certainly never come together during an inappropriate time such as the afternoon.

"I suppose you don't even limit yourself to bedchambers," she said.

He grinned wickedly. "Another item to add to my list."

"What list?"

"Of new experiences to which to introduce you. A thick blanket in a meadow in the afternoon."

"Outside? I was thinking . . . I don't know. The library."

"The library it is. The next time it rains."

She was scandalized by the notion. And titillated.

"Tonight, however, have your way with me." He shoved his hands behind his head, an expectant look on his face.

"Pardon?"

"You were the one anxious to get me here. Do with me what you will."

She shook her head. "I've not your experience. I will disappoint."

"Jayne, if you do nothing more than straddle me and ride me, you will not disappoint."

Straddle him. She imagined the positioning of their bodies, how it might work, how exposed she would be. He took her hand and wrapped it around his velvet heat.

"At least make me beg," he said with a lowered voice that indicated it would not take much to bring him to that point.

"All right. Yes. You think I can't do it."

"I know you can."

He shouldn't be playful. Walfort came in, saw to business, and left. Inwardly, she shook her head. She needed to stop comparing them. In all matters, Walfort fell short, but then he'd not achieved a reputation as a great lover. Ainsley had.

She did not want to consider how many women had educated him. She would not feel jealous when she was now the benefactor of their lessons. If Walfort had not married so young and limited his conquests to her, he might have been as skilled. Did that mean the fault rested with her?

"You begin by gliding your hand up and down," he said.

"I know how to begin," she snapped.

"Oh, heat. I like that." His eyes smoldered, stoking the fires of her own desires.

He shouldn't be making her comfortable with all this. It was supposed to be quick, to the purpose. She was not supposed to anticipate, to want.

She grew warm with the thoughts of what she could do to Ainsley. Yes, she would very much like to hear him beg. She thought of a cat she'd had as a child and how sensuously it had prowled.

She gave him what she truly hoped was a sultry look—and hoped he wouldn't laugh. If he laughed she would die. "Prepare to beg."

He issued a deep, guttural curse as she stretched out over him. His eyes darkened and he fisted his hands into the sheets, relinquishing all power to her.

And she reveled in it. Touching him, teasing him, taunting him. She used her mouth, her hands, her breasts, every part of herself to torment him. His hands traveled over her with an urgency that surprised her, as though he needed her desperately. His groans echoed through the room. His harsh breathing ignited her desire.

She'd never been so bold, had never known she could be.

But even though she was the one in control, he followed. Touching her, kissing her shoulder, molding her breasts, gently guiding her with murmurs of approval and deep-throated rumbles. She was as fevered as he when he finally growled, "For God's sake, Jayne, end this torment."

She straddled his hips, looked down on him, scored her fingernails up his chest.

He grabbed her hips and bucked. "Woman!"

Feeling victorious, she lifted up, lowered herself, guided him home. With his hands roaming over her, urging her on, she rocked against him. She fanned out her hair until it was a curtain around them. She watched him as his pleasure escalated. Being above him was such a glorious position, gave her such a clear view of him. She was grateful for the light, illuminating the wonder of this moment.

Then the tables turned and all the torment she had been inflicting returned to her full force. She found herself hurtling through star-filled heavens, crying out, felt the power of his release crashing through her as hers erupted. Together. They peaked together. She didn't even know it was possible, was undone by the bond it forged between them.

Something else special that was to be shared between them. A secret bouquet of memories that must remain here when she took her leave.

As limp as a wilted flower, she eased onto his chest and listened to the hard thudding of his heart.

Using only the tips of his fingers, he began to slowly caress her back, and she wondered where he found the energy to move at all. She thought she might never again, that she would simply remain still and silent forever.

"Had I known that with lamplight you'd have transformed into a tigress, I would have insisted the lamps remain burning from the beginning," he murmured.

"Did I disappoint you before?"

"God, no. I like that each time with you is so very different."

"Tonight I felt . . . unencumbered."

"That was quite obvious."

Testing her muscles, she stretched a little. "I don't think I have the strength to move off you."

"Then stay. Your weight is no burden."

"I'm close to falling asleep." His fingers lightly stroking her were luring her into the land of dreams.

"Sleep," he said in a voice as drowsy as hers.

She didn't remember drifting off, but when she awoke, she was alone in the bed, the covers tucked around her, the lamps no longer burning. The fire on the grate provided enough light for her to see his standing silhouette. "Ainsley?"

"My apologies," he whispered. "I didn't mean to wake you."

"What are you doing?"

"I was in the process of returning to my bedchamber. I thought it was what you would want."

It was . . . when she first arrived. Now . . .

"Will you stay with me?"

He didn't answer with words. He simply crawled beneath the covers and wrapped his arms around her.

When she awoke in the morning, he was still with her, holding her.

Chapter 16

As Jayne stood in the gazebo, a cloak and a blanket draped around her, she thought the night sky had never looked more beautiful. Or perhaps it was simply that her life was filled with a richness she'd not expected.

Everything between Ainsley and her had changed. It was as though he could never get enough of being with her. As the minutes of their time together slipped away, so they spent more of those minutes together. They'd completely dispensed with his beginning the night in his bedchamber and then coming into hers. He slept with her throughout the night, and only went to his bedchamber to dress for the day. They would feed each other, laugh, tease, and talk.

They made love in the morning, the afternoon, the evening. Some days they never left the bed. He would have the meals brought to the bedchamber.

They bathed together, read together, ate together, napped together. They trudged over the land. Rode the horses. Took carriage rides. They visited the village. Fished. Climbed in the tree and welcomed dawn. And now he was sharing a bright, though partial, moon and the stars with her.

She watched his shadowy figure as he peered through a telescope he'd placed on a pillar that he'd had built onto the gazebo for just that purpose. Apparently he loved gazing out on the universe. She wished it was summer so she could enjoy it a bit more, but the night was chilled and every so often her teeth clattered, but she wouldn't complain. She wanted to share this moment with him, something special. She was capturing more glimpses into the man, and each one touched her heart.

"There we are," he said. "Now, come here."

She moved beside him and adjusted her position so she was in front of the telescope.

"Are you shaking?" he asked.

"I'm just a little chilled."

"Jayne, you should have said something."

Removing his coat, he draped it over her shoulders. Even with the cloak and blanket, the coat swallowed her and drowned her in delicious warmth. "Now you'll get cold," she told him.

He kissed the nape of her neck. "I believe we've had this conversation before. I'll be fine. Now, peer through the eyepiece and you'll see the moon as few people have."

The bright orange moon filled her vision. She could see strange indentions, circles with ridges. "What are they? It looks as though someone punched it."

"No one knows exactly what they are or how they were created. When Galileo discovered them, he called them craters. Men of learning have been arguing ever since about what they are precisely and what caused them."

"Do you think we'll ever know?"

"I shan't be at all surprised. Look at all the technological advances we've made in so short a time. Railways. The telegraph. All the marvels that were displayed at the Great Exhibition. So many possibilities."

"Do you think there are creatures up there looking down on us?"

"If so, at this moment they would be envious of me and think I'm a very lucky man to be gazing at the stars with such a beautiful woman."

He flattered her with such ease. Sometimes she didn't know how to respond to it so she chose to deflect it. "We're looking at the moon, not the stars."

"We're getting to the stars." He leaned in and she could feel his breath warming her cheek, smell the bergamot scent he favored. "Very slowly and carefully nudge the telescope around until you are no longer seeing the moon but are gazing at the stars."

She did as he instructed. "Oh, they're so much larger and brighter. How many do you think there are?"

"Millions. Too many to count."

"They're so beautiful. Peaceful."

"Hmm. Now, I want you to keep watching them until you see stars of your own."

"What are you—"

"Shh. Trust me."

"Have I not demonstrated that I do?"

"Then trust me a little more." He nibbled on her ear. Closing her eyes, she dropped her head back.

"The stars," he reminded her.

Opening her eyes, she gazed through the telescope, aware of his inching her skirts upward, his hand skimming over her leg until it reached the juncture between her thighs and sought solace there.

"Ainsley—"

"You're so warm there and my hand is cold."

"It's not. How can it be so warm?"

"The wonder of gloves, my sweet. I only just took them off."

The conversation made little sense, but she no longer cared. His mouth was creating delicious tingles along her neck and his fingers were working magic below. Sensations rippled through her, growing stronger with his increased attentions.

With his thumb, he rubbed her sensitive swollen flesh. Her knees weakened. She clutched the railing of the gazebo. She wanted to grab him, but he remained behind her, taunting her. Then he slid one long finger inside her, and she released a tiny cry.

His other hand came around her, slipped inside her cloak and cupped the mound of her breast. Through the cloth, his fingers pinched and pulled, soothed and caressed.

"Ainsley, let's return to the cottage."

"Not yet. Not until you've seen stars."

"I saw stars . . . through the telescope."

"I want you to see stars I created."

Two fingers went inside her, and the pressure built. She pressed herself against the hard ridge of his palm. She was hot now, so hot. Summer had arrived. She no longer needed his coat, but none of it mattered. All that mattered was the rioting pleasure—

And then the stars. Millions of them. Bursting across the heavens, dancing before the moon.

Her cry. His hot kiss against her neck. His fingers stilling. His holding her tight against him as though knowing she was close to collapsing.

"You didn't." She breathed in quick gasps. She had learned so much from him in so short a time. Different positions. Different angles. "Shall I bend over, lay down—"

"Jayne." He pressed her firmly against him, squeezing her tightly, holding her securely as though he were loath to let her go. "Not every moment of pleasure has to result in the depositing of my seed. I wanted you to have this with no expectations."

She was beginning to understand the truth of his reputation as a great lover. It was more than the immense pleasure he brought a woman in his bed. It was the manner in which he treated her when she wasn't in it.

She leaned her head back into the curve of his shoulder and looked up into the heavens. A small part of her wished that from this moment on time would stand still.

But time marched on.

It was raining her last day at the cottage. The sky was filled with thick, heavy clouds that blocked out the sun. The rain beat against the windows with a steady, relentless staccato. It was the type of storm that demanded one stay in bed.

Even without the storm, she thought they would have stayed there.

She was nestled against Ainsley's side after a rather rousing session of lovemaking. He was skimming one finger along her cheek, her chin. Back and forth. Back and forth. Slowly, provocatively.

"I rather like the village," she said quietly. "I'm going to miss it."

"You like the gingerbread."

She smiled wickedly. "Yes, I like the gingerbread."

They'd taken to going to the village nearly every afternoon. They strolled along the street, browsed the shops, and always purchased weeds from Ainsley's favorite flower girl.

"I shall have the baker send your cook the recipe."

She trailed her fingers over his chest. "I shall miss climbing."

"I'm sorry you got another scar."

Climbing down one morning, she slipped, and the rough bark had torn at her knee. "It's not bad. And now my knees match." And it was a souvenir. She would never be able to look at it without remembering how it had come to be.

"I think I shall miss the stars most of all," she said.

"You have stars at Herndon Hall."

"But they're brighter here."

"Perhaps you're only looking at them through different eyes."

She rose up on her elbow. "The way I look at you now. You are so very different than what I thought."

"Are you disappointed?"

"No." How could she be when he had given so much of himself unselfishly. She hoped her child would be like him.

They dressed for dinner and seated themselves at the table in the dining room, but neither of them ate much. Then they returned to the bedchamber and made love through the night. Each time they expected it to be the last coming together, and afterward they would say, "Once more."

Until finally it was the last time. Dawn eased in through the curtains and he pulled her beneath him. As he slid inside her, she could see the farewell in his eyes. This, then, would be their final coming together, the beginning of their parting.

She wanted to run her hands over every inch of him, but he tangled their hands together and raised her arms so they rested on the pillow, leaving her vulnerable to him, but with no fear. She tightened her fingers around his and wound her legs around his waist to hold him near. His movements were slow, deliberate. Long, sure strokes that reached deep inside her, not only to her womb, but to her heart.

She didn't want this moment to end. She'd come here intending to have brief interludes with him, to keep everything impartial. He'd torn down her defenses, touch by touch, smile by smile, laugh by laugh. He'd given her far more than she had expected to receive.

When she was with him she glowed, she welcomed the coming of day, the arrival of night. She tried to convince herself that none of this was real. They'd been here with no responsibilities, no demands, no worries. It had truly been a holiday.

And now it was coming to a close. Reality would soon intrude.

But for this last moment, it was only the two of them, their gazes locked as their joined bodies flowed in a corresponding rhythm. She watched as he clenched his jaw, and she reveled in his deep guttural growls. She responded in kind with sighs and moans.

His hands clamped around hers. She could see him straining to hold back. The dappled sunlight danced over him. She saw him so clearly now. So clearly.

The pleasure built until it exploded in a crashing crescendo. Her back arched and she raised her hips to receive his final deep thrusts. Groans were torn from his throat as he trembled and shook above her. He released his hold on her hands, and she wound her arms around him, held him near, as the lethargy settled in around them.

She heard him swallow as he pressed a kiss to her throat. Why did it make her so sad? He'd just taken her to a glorious place. She usually smiled afterward. But this time she couldn't, because this time she knew it was the last.

Easing off her, he rolled over. Turning her head to the side, she watched as he stared at the canopy. She wondered what he was thinking. She should say something. *Let's stay one more day.* Only she'd want to say the same thing tomorrow. So she said nothing at all.

He sat up, swung his legs off the side of the bed, and waited. She studied his broad back, wanted to run her fingers over it one more time. But it was time to say good-bye. She knew that, knew that she had to let him go. They needed to leave soon. Walfort was waiting for them.

With a heavy sigh, without words, he shoved himself off the bed and left her to begin preparing for the journey. She did what she'd done following the first time they'd come together.

She wept.

Chapter 17

She and Ainsley traveled together in his coach. Her carriage followed, her maid journeying inside. Had anyone asked her four weeks ago how she saw herself escaping from Ainsley's cottage, she'd have said she saw herself racing away, never looking back, leaving him behind with all due haste, staring after her. Sprinting away because she couldn't leave fast enough, wanted to be done with him.

Instead she'd found one excuse after another to delay her parting. Even knowing that Ainsley would be traveling with her, she hadn't wanted to begin the journey home. Their time together had turned into something bittersweet. She'd always believed that Walfort loved her; she still believed that to be true. But she'd never before *felt* loved.

With Ainsley she did.

He held her now, nestled against his side. She rested her hand on his chest and felt the steady, rhythmic pounding of his heart. Beyond the window, she could see the countryside changing, becoming more familiar, more recognizable. She was nearing home. She both welcomed it and dreaded it with all her heart.

The past four weeks had not gone at all as she'd expected. The physical aspects had been far more shattering. The emotional journey was one she regretted ending. She would miss Ainsley so terribly, terribly much.

It would hurt him to know the truth of her feelings toward him, so she intended to keep them to herself, to hold them near, to suffer in silence. Hard to believe that only a few short weeks ago she had wished all manner of torment on him. Now she would do whatever she could to spare him.

She flattened her hand against her stomach. She halfway wished she wasn't with babe. Knowing the man he was, she understood what she hadn't before: it would be a hardship for him to not acknowledge this child. And yet she desperately wanted to be carrying his child—not because it was a child, but because it would be his.

"When will you know?" he asked quietly, and she wondered if his mind traveled along the same path as hers.

"Soon, I should think. I have not always been precise with my . . . menses. A day or two late, a day or two early, it fluctuates. Shall I send word?"

"No."

Squeezing her eyes shut, she fought back the tears. "If I had known then what I know about you now, I would have never agreed to this."

He slid his finger beneath her chin, tilted her head back until he could gaze into her eyes. "Knowing you as I do now, I would have agreed without hesitation. Never doubt that I want you to have this." He threaded his fingers through hers where they rested against her womb. "I hope it happened."

She was not going to weep. She was not. And yet the threat of tears did not abate. "Know that no child in all of England will be loved more."

He gave her a forlorn smile. "I have no doubt."

Past his shoulder she saw the large stone that marked the start of Walfort's property go by in a blur.

"Please have the coach stop. I don't want you . . . we need to part ways here."

He gave the order and the coach rocked to a stop, nearly making her nauseous with the motion. Almost immediately the footman opened the door.

"Give us a few moments," Ainsley barked, and the door was quickly closed.

Easing back so she could see him more clearly, she traced her fingers over the lines on his face, lines too deep for a man his age. "I shall never look upon a star in quite the same way."

He flashed a familiar grin. "Neither shall I, I assure you."

She licked her lips. "In all our time together, you never kissed me on the mouth."

"One of your rules, sweetheart. I was determined not to break a single one. But if you broke—"

With a desperation, a hunger that astounded her, she covered his mouth with hers. He tasted richer than she remembered, and while she may have initiated the kiss, he was not shy about taking it further.

She was barely aware of him moving her onto his lap, securing her against his chest while his mouth plundered hers. She should have insisted upon this sooner, should have sent all her blasted rules to perdition. Their tongues mated and danced, searched and explored, but there wasn't time now, not enough to learn everything.

The first instance when they'd kissed, she was terrified by the feelings he'd brought to the fore. Now she relished in them. She felt so alive. Every nerve sang. Every inch of her skin tingled.

His skilled hands roamed over her, pressed against her. Everywhere he touched, pleasure and desire mingled. She became aware of his fingers massaging her calf, sliding up—

"No, no," she breathed against his mouth, pressed her forehead to his, fought to stave off the tears as long as possible. "Good-bye, Ainsley."

She slid off his lap, reached for the door—

"Jayne?"

She didn't want to look back at him. But he'd given her so much, she owed him at least a final glance. She twisted around. Her heart ached at the raw emotion she saw in his eyes.

"You once asked me if I'd willingly trade places with Walfort."

"And you said no."

"I have since learned that I was mistaken. I would rather be a cripple and have your love for all of a single moment than to live as I am without ever having it."

She couldn't say the words she knew he longed to hear. It would devastate her; in all likelihood devastate him as well. Better to pretend that for them they didn't exist.

Shaking her head, she opened the door, grateful to find the footman at the ready to hand her down. When he closed it, she rushed to her own carriage without looking back.

* * *

Walfort sat in his wheelchair by the window, waiting. He knew she would be returning this afternoon. Strange how he was anticipating and dreading her arrival in equal measure.

He had not loved her when he married her. Had not loved her when he was a complete man. He'd only come to love and appreciate Jayne after so much had been taken from them. Her devotion had astounded him. Her loyalty had humbled him. The sacrifice forced on her—to never have children—had tormented him.

If she knew the truth of that night, of so many nights before it, she'd despise him. He couldn't add her hatred of him as another failure in his life, couldn't burden her with that emotion. Selfishly, neither could he live without her brightening his days.

He saw the carriage rounding the bend in the road leading toward his manor and his heart sped up, pounding with a rhythm that his legs had once used to race over the fields when he was a lad. Damn, but he did miss the mobility he'd taken for granted.

Just as he knew he'd miss the wife he'd taken for granted if she were no longer at his side.

The carriage rolled to a stop. He remained where he was, watching, waiting. Even when he'd had the use of his legs, he never greeted her. Never swept her up into his arms.

He'd give his soul to be able to do either now. Instead he'd given her Ainsley.

The footman opened the door, handed her down. Then she lifted her skirts and rushed toward the house, running up the steps. He heard the door open.

"Walfort!"

"Here, love."

Breathless, she appeared in the doorway, her hair askew. Dear God, but she was beautiful. His heart ached with how much he'd felt her absence.

"Walfort," she rasped, before racing across the room, dropping onto his lap and wrapping her arms around his neck, holding him so tightly as to nearly suffocate him.

Her sobs shook her body, her tears dampened his neck. He drew her nearer, held her securely as his own eyes burned. Deep within him, sadness battled with joy as the truth battered him.

He had no doubt that his greatest fear and his dearest desire had been realized: she'd fallen in love with Ainsley.

Dear God, what had he done?

As the coach neared the cottage, Ainsley felt as though he'd lived through the longest journey of his life. The coach door had closed with a resounding click that Ainsley thought would haunt him for the remainder of his days and nights. He'd dropped back against the plush seating of the coach and waited. Hearing the distant pounding of horses' hooves, he'd glanced out the window as Walfort's carriage rolled by. He'd hoped to catch a last glimpse of Jayne but all he saw was shadows.

Reaching up, he'd pounded on the ceiling. "Return to Blackmoor."

Night had fallen hours ago. He should have stopped somewhere, taken a respite from the traveling and begun again in the morning. Instead, he allowed them to stop only to change horses. Other than that, they pressed on.

When the coach finally came to a halt, he disembarked and headed for the stables. It was long past midnight. Still, he saddled his favorite gelding, mounted up, and sent the horse into a jarring gallop. He was going to grant himself leave to think of her until dawn, and then he would never think of her again. He would move on with his life as though she'd never been part of it. All their days and nights together would be relegated to a distant memory, never to be visited. He'd already made the decision to sell the cottage.

He brought the horse to a halt near the ancient oak tree. Skillfully, purposefully, he clambered up it until he reached *their* branch. He sat astride it with his back pressed to the hard bark of the trunk. Tonight a full moon glimmered in the night sky. His throat was thick with tears but he refused to give them freedom. He'd never wept in his life; he certainly wasn't going to start now.

Even when his father died he'd not cried. But then he'd been only four. He hadn't truly understood what happened. Death was an incomprehensible concept. He thought his father had gone to sleep, no more than that. But he'd never seen him again.

He wondered what his father would have thought of his recent actions, then decided it made no difference. All that mattered was what the principal players thought: Jayne, Walfort, and himself.

As she was leaving the coach, he'd almost told her that he'd fallen in love with her. Deeply. Irrevocably. In love.

Madness. To tell her. To acknowledge it himself. If anything, it would simply make life harder for them all.

In the morning he would return to the cottage and

his inconsequential, boring existence. He would fill his days with work, managing his estates and his finances, and he would fill his evenings with women. Not a single night would go by without a woman in his bed, in his arms, whispering his name.

He would forget her. Jayne Seymour, Marchioness of Walfort. He would never think of her again.

As the moon carried itself toward the horizon, he followed its path and wondered if it was as lonely as he.

Chapter 18

Lyons Place
Christmas Eve, 1860

Sitting in the great room of his brother's ancestral residence, Ainsley welcomed the distraction of Christmas. He enjoyed his older brother's fine liquor—probably a bit too much, if the swaying of the decorated tree standing on the table in the corner was any indication. The family collie, Fennimore, was curled beside the bassinet where the newest addition to the family—Rafe—slept soundly. It was a familiar sight. He had served as sentry for both of the children who'd come before this latest little one.

His mother and Leo were in attendance, but far too somber. They intended to travel once again to Lynnford's estate tomorrow. Lady Lynnford was in rapid decline and the duchess wanted to be there for the woman who had helped her raise three sons. Lady Lynnford never realized that one of them was her husband's. If the duchess had her way, the countess would go to her grave ignorant of that tidbit of information.

Stephen and his family were absent. Mercy had presented Stephen with another son only three days before, so it would be several weeks before she would be out and about.

Thinking of Mercy's situation brought Ainsley's musings careening back to Jayne. He'd had no success in banishing her from his thoughts or memories. Perhaps because he'd only left Blackmoor the day before to journey here. He'd wandered that damned cottage because it still carried her scent, her presence. He'd decided against selling it. When he first spied it, he immediately fell in love with the residence and the land surrounding it. It meant more to him now. Silly to even consider giving it up.

But from Westcliffe's, he would return to his own ancestral estate, Grantwood Manor. He'd neglected it and his other responsibilities far too long. He needed to move forward with his life. He'd decided to take a mistress. One woman. Why exert effort wooing a different woman every night? He would find one who pleased him and set up a house for her. She would see to his needs. He would ensure she was comfortably set. It would be a beneficial arrangement for them both. He should have done it sooner. This flittering about from woman to woman was wearisome. He'd not been with one since Jayne had left, and it was making him antsy. That was the reason for his unease, he told himself; not the damned missive he'd received last week.

Thank you.

The messenger who delivered it had done so with only three words: "For the duke."

He'd promptly departed, as though no reply was warranted or wanted.

Thank you.

Ainsley didn't know if the words had been written by Walfort or Jayne. Walfort in all likelihood. Jayne knew that he wanted no confirmation, had no desire to know if they'd met with success. But how could he not learn of it? It would be all the talk in London during the upcoming Season. Perhaps he'd avoid going into the city. No, it was important that he at least show his face, visit his old haunts, and flirt with the ladies. Restore his reputation. He'd neglected it of late.

Besides, his mistress would be there so he'd be adequately entertained. He was looking forward to it. He should go to town early, find the proper residence for the woman who would occupy his nights, begin arranging—

"Uncle."

He shifted his gaze over and wondered when his brother had acquired a blurred son. He did hope the lad hadn't come to tell him he was needed elsewhere. He wasn't certain his legs would be steady enough to support him. Where were the deuced things anyway? He forced his eyes to focus and arched a single eyebrow. "Nephew."

It was evident by his twitching shoulders that Viscount Waverly, the future Earl of Westcliffe, struggled not to laugh. Somberly greeting each other was a long-honored jest between them. Ainsley couldn't even remember how the tradition had begun.

Waverly wiggled his eyebrows, up, down, up, down. He frowned, scrunched up his five-year-old mouth. Then he touched Ainsley's raised eyebrow as though he expected it to bite.

"How do you do that?"

"Practice, lad." Reaching out, he ruffled the boy's

dark hair, trying not to wonder about the shade of hair that Jayne's child would display. *Jayne's child.* He would not, could not, think of it as his. The pain would be too great. He'd gone into the arrangement knowing the cost. He couldn't regret it now. "You'll learn when you're older. What do you think of your brother?"

"He cries too much."

"So did you at that age."

"No. I never cry. Boys don't."

"He's a boy."

Waverly looked at him as though he thought his uncle should take up residence in Bedlam. Ainsley didn't want to contemplate that if he didn't marry, didn't have an heir, it might be this lad who saw after him in his dotage.

"No, he's not. He's a babe," Waverly insisted.

"Hmm. And what do you think would make him a boy?"

Waverly wrinkled his nose, then glanced down at the crotch of his short pants. "He has one of those. I've seen it."

"Well, there you are, then."

"I think Hope had one, too," he said, referring to his sister, "but hers fell off."

Fortunate for Ainsley, he hadn't taken a swallow of brandy. He'd have unceremoniously spewed it. He fought back his smile. "Did it now?"

He wasn't about to go into an explanation on the unlikelihood of that scenario.

Westcliffe ambled over and laid his hand on his son's head, a possessive but loving gesture. "You're not bothering your uncle, are you?"

"Not at all," Ainsley was quick to answer. "We were

engaged in a philosophical discussion regarding what makes little boys *boys*."

"Snips, snails, and puppy dog tails—something like that, isn't it?" Westcliffe asked.

"Uncle Stephen is going to give me a pony for Christmas," Waverly said, obviously either no longer caring about the discussion or in all likelihood simply having grown bored with it.

When Stephen had married, Ainsley asked him to watch over his property in Hertfordshire. Stephen took an instant dislike to the smell of sheep. Eventually he purchased the land from Ainsley—since it wasn't entailed—and populated it with horses.

"He's a good uncle," Ainsley offered.

Waverly looked at him with big brown button eyes, expectation mirrored in them.

Ainsley grinned. "You'll have to wait to find out what I'm giving you for Christmas." A fishing pole. He thought perhaps in summer he'd take the boy to Blackmoor. That, too, was part of the gift. Still, it wasn't as exciting as a pony.

Westcliffe patted the lad's shoulder. "Run along now. Your mother needs you."

With all the decorum of a future lord, Waverly walked away.

"Come spring, I believe I shall take him tree climbing."

"Not unless you're sober," Westcliffe said as he drew a chair nearer and dropped into it. "You're usually a bit more social."

"A death looms. Being somber seemed to suit."

"Is that all that's troubling you?"

"Little late to be playing the role of older brother."

"I would have played it before but you insisted on usurping it from me. Claire's worried about you. She says you've lost weight."

Ainsley chuckled darkly. "Well, now, if she says it then it must be true. Assure her all is well."

He shook his head. Claire had watched over him when he was younger, which allowed him to play with the others. Hide and seek had been his favorite game. As long as he hid somewhere near Westcliffe, she'd never find him because she was too terrified of her future husband to search any of the hiding areas around him. "My apologies," Ainsley said. "That was curt and rude of me. I appreciate her concern, but all is as it should be."

"I'm not certain that particular wording brings me any comfort. For all I know, you might consider 'as it should be' to be hell."

Ainsley grinned. His brother was far more perceptive than he realized. Anxious to change topics, he said, "We seem to have a preponderance of boys in this family."

"Stephen's wife and mine know their duty." Westcliffe's voice held a teasing lilt. Ainsley suspected Claire's duty was whatever she decided it was. He knew Westcliffe adored her, had years of hurting her for which to atone.

"And if they produced only girls?" Ainsley asked.

"I daresay we'd not love them any less. Have you given any thought to your heir? Claire informs me that several young ladies from the finest families will have their coming out this year."

"So young they'll no doubt appear childish to a man of my experience."

"Are you thinking of someone older?"

"I'm not thinking of anyone at all." Lie. He thought of Jayne. Constantly. It was becoming somewhat irritating.

"Well, then—" Westcliffe slapped Ainsley's knee. "—I shall leave you to it. I've neglected my wife for far too long."

Watching his brother walk away, Ainsley reached for his tumbler.

Thank you.

He lifted the glass slightly and whispered his toast, "Merry Christmas, Jayne."

Chapter 19

Estate of the Earl of Lynnford
Early January, 1861

It was beyond any doubt the worst portrait he'd ever done. Not that anyone who ever gazed upon it would have thought so. It held barely a hint of the reality, but was mostly fantasy. The matriarch appeared hale, hearty, happy, and healthy. Her husband standing behind her, his hands folded over her shoulders, appeared not to have a care in the world beyond those that came with the mantle of his title. Their five children—two sons and three daughters—surrounded them. Leo knew that he'd done them justice. They all looked down on their mother, their love for her evident in their expressions.

"It's beautiful, Leo," she said now, withered and frail on her deathbed, as he held it up for her to view.

"I told you he was marvelous," Tessa cooed, sitting in a chair, squeezing her friend's hand.

"Yes, but I thought you were speaking of other things." Her smile held a shadow of naughtiness, a hint of the vibrant woman she'd once been.

Tessa nodded at Leo. "Thank you."

"If you need me, you know where to find me."

She nodded again. The three weeks since Christmas had been horrendous and draining. But Tessa couldn't leave, refused to go despite the hardship. Lynnford needed her. How often in the last few days had he told her that she was his rock, how often had they held each other and wept?

She watched Leo with his leisurely stride quit the room. How often of late had he provided her with the strength to carry on?

"Will you marry him?" Lady Lynnford asked.

Tessa laughed lightly and adjusted the pillow beneath her friend's head. "Searching for gossip to spread around during the coming Season?"

"I won't be here for the coming Season. You and I both know that."

"Don't talk nonsense." She tugged at the covers until no wrinkle remained.

"I'm ready to go, Tess."

Tessa returned to her chair, took Angela's hand and rubbed it gently, trying to generate some warmth. How could it be so cold? "Then you should feel free to go, my sweet. Heaven awaits."

"You'll see after Lynnie, won't you?"

She pressed a kiss to the frail fingers. "Of course. And I shall be as good a mother as I can to your children. Even though they are all grown. Sometimes I think they need us more when they are grown."

"If you don't marry your artist, then marry Lynnie. He loves you, you know."

Tessa shook her head.

"No need to deny it, m'dear. I know you love him as

well. I also know neither of you acted upon those feelings while I was his wife. But I often saw the longing, especially when we were younger." She closed her eyes, then opened them with renewed energy. "Men are such silly creatures, blind sometimes. I don't think he ever realized Stephen was his until we all thought Stephen had been killed in the Crimea."

Horror swept through Tessa. She'd wanted to spare Angela that pain.

"I love Lynnie," Angela forged on, as though she read all of Tessa's thoughts. "Do you think I would look at Stephen and not see the father in the son?"

"I never told him when we were younger, because I thought the knowledge would be a burden."

"Then it seems you are as silly as he."

It was long past midnight when Tessa came into Leo's bedchamber. He was working on a self-portrait that he thought he might give to her, but when he saw her face, he knew it would go unfinished. He set down his brush, crossed the room in long, unhurried strides and enfolded her in his embrace.

Her tears came hot and heavy, dampening his shirt. No words were spoken. None were needed. It had always been that way between them.

Lifting her into his arms, he carried her to the sofa and sat with Tessa curled on his lap. Her sobs finally gave way to gentle weeping and sniffles.

"Handkerchief?" she croaked.

"I haven't one on me. Simply use my shirt."

"Leo—"

"Use my shirt. I'll put on another."

She did so, then straightened and leaned back. She began toying with his blond locks. "You have the most unruly hair."

"And you have the most glorious." He longed to set it loose, but knew she would welcome no advances from him now. It was too soon, she was too wounded.

"She went quietly. Lynnford and I were both there. He's telling the children now. I must see to making her ready."

He skimmed his thumb over her cheek, a cheek he'd kissed a thousand times. "I know."

"I'm not sure how long we shall stay here."

"Take whatever time you need."

"I do love you, you know." Her voice contained a breadth of sadness that he knew had nothing to do with the loss of her friend.

"I know."

But not enough. She'd never loved him enough.

Tessa's sons and their wives came to Lynnford's estate for the burial of his beloved countess—as did half of London, by the looks of the gathered crowd. She was laid to rest in the family crypt on the estate.

Tessa and Leo had stayed on to relieve the family of the burden of seeing to matters. She felt it was the least she could do for her dear friend. The families—Lynnford's and hers—had returned to the residence following the funeral. They were all gathered in the parlor now, reminiscing about days gone by, before the countess's health had been stricken.

Tessa had been so busy attending to Lynnford's sons and daughters that she didn't see Leo slip away.

He'd been a bit distant, no doubt overwhelmed by all the grief surrounding them. He was so sensitive, so aware of the subtle nuances of others. She decided that they would leave tomorrow. Go to the seaside, perhaps. Stroll along the shore. Listen to the rushing of the wind over the water. It was simply too blasted quiet here.

"I think she would have been pleased to know so many loved her."

Tessa looked up at Lynnford. He was on the other side of fifty-five now, but still devastatingly handsome and dignified. Yes, she had been silly to think anyone would look at Stephen and not see him. Although perhaps people saw only what they wished to see.

"I shall miss her," she said.

"No more than I. I don't know how I shall get on without her."

"One day at a time. It's the best we can do."

"Do you ever think of the future?"

She shook her head slowly. "No, not really." A sensation washed over her, a sense of dread and foreboding. Strange. Although perhaps it was only because death had recently visited here. She needed Leo. She truly did. Where the devil was he?

She touched Lynnford's arm. "If you'll excuse me, I have something to which I must attend."

"By all means . . . and, Tess, thank you for being here."

"It was no trouble, I assure you."

As she passed by them, each of her sons gave her a reassuring hug. Such strong, good men. They were her pride and joy, even if they'd given her graying hair and

Ainsley had yet to wed. He wouldn't like it, but she intended to meddle this Season and begin parading young ladies through his life. She'd been worried about him ever since discovering where his heart wandered. It was a path that would leave him lost and alone. She should know. She'd traveled it long enough in her youth.

She meandered through the hallways until she reached the stairs that led to the bedchamber she was using while in attendance.

She walked in, expecting to find Leo waiting for her. But he was nowhere to be found. In his bedchamber, then. When she turned to retreat back into the hallway, something caught her eye. A folded slip of paper resting on the pillow. The side where she always slept. As she drew nearer, she could make out her name in Leo's elegant script. The man did everything with a touch of elegance.

Unfolding the paper, she read the carefully worded missive.

He is free now, my love, and so must you be as well. Thank you, my dear Tessa, for every smile, every laugh . . . every night you shared with me. May you find your true happiness now with the one who has always held your heart.

I remain your devoted servant,

Leo

Crushing it to her breast, she whispered his name. For more than thirty years she had longed for Lynnford. His freedom now was bittersweet. Hers was unexpected.

Her artist was gone. She'd done a rather poor job of letting him know how very important he was to her. She feared he didn't realize that with him, he had taken her heart.

Chapter 20

Herndon Hall
Late January, 1861

Snow coated the ground but Jayne was not deterred from taking her daily afternoon stroll. Her physician recommended it. To keep her strong, strengthen her endurance for what was to come. The outside air would also make the baby strong. And that mattered most of all.

She kept one hand on her abdomen, rubbing it as she walked. It made her feel closer to the child, although evidence of its existence was sparse. She was not yet rounding, but it was still early. The night she announced her condition to Walfort, he told her that he loved her, and she wept because he'd not said the words since she returned from Blackmoor. He held her through the night as he'd not done in more than three years.

She sent word to Ainsley. Two words actually. They seemed insignificant in retrospect, but then any words would be.

Walfort was effusive with his praise—overly so, she

thought at times, but then she supposed the difficult part for him was now. To see the fruition of his plan, the reality of it. To know they would have a child. He wanted desperately for everyone to believe it was his.

She told him it didn't matter. He would be the child's father. That was what truly counted.

But he would not be deterred. He was making plans for them to go to London for the Season—even though her period of confinement would coincide with those months. She took a deep breath to relax. She would deal with it when the time came. The fact that they might cross paths with Ainsley had nothing to do with her worry over going. A woman great with child simply didn't appear in public. It wasn't done. No matter how much her husband might wish it.

Going to London next Season would suit much better. She would simply have to convince him of that fact. Because she certainly didn't want him to doubt her affections for him or to wonder what her feelings toward Ainsley were.

No. They would not go to London. They would stay here. Their child would stay here. Another deep breath. The decision was made. She simply had to convince Walfort.

Chapter 21

Grantwood Manor, Northhamptonshire
Early February, 1861

Ainsley was sitting at his desk, studying his investments, when his mother barged into the room. He truly needed to explain to her that he required warning when she was going to visit. What if he'd had his mistress at Grantwood Manor, sprawled over his desk with her skirts hiked up to her waist?

It would have been quite the trick, he thought, since he had yet to acquire her.

He came to his feet and delivered an oft-repeated falsehood. "Mother, what a pleasant surprise."

"I returned to London to discover that Leo has packed up all his belongings and gone."

"I'm well. Thank you for asking. And how do you fare?"

"Ainsley, I have no time for trivial matters. Don't you understand? He's gone!"

He arched a brow. "You are flummoxed by this turn of events? I would have thought the note he left you at Lynnford's would have served as notice."

It had certainly taken him and his brothers by surprise. His mother had not shared the words with them, only the gist of the message: her longtime lover had decided to move on to younger pastures. Her words. Ainsley seriously doubted they were Leo's.

"What I am is vexed," she said succinctly now, pacing before his desk as though she wished desperately to lift something from it and smash it against a wall. "All these years I had misled myself into believing he was a man of honor, not a coward. He did not have the decency to face me in person, to say good-bye. He simply assumed I would want to be rid of him."

"How many times did he ask you to marry him?"

She staggered to a stop. He couldn't recall ever seeing his mother this rattled. "I do not see how that signifies."

He moved around the desk and took up a position in front of it, leaning his hip against it, folding his arms over his chest. "By refusing him, you gave the impression that he was merely temporary."

"Temporary until *I* indicated it was time for him to go. When someone of our station takes a lover, that is the way of it. We assume the expenses. We determine when the relationship is over, and I was not yet done with him."

"It has been nearly a month."

"I couldn't leave Lynnford and his children as abruptly as Leo left me. Matters needed to be seen to and their grief was still too raw."

"A month," he repeated.

"Blast you, Ainsley. I know precisely how long it's been. I am well aware of every moment that has been empty of Leo's presence. I have spent the past ten days striving to find him, but I do not even begin to know where to look. He belonged to no clubs. I do not know who his friends are. I know nothing at all about his family." Tears welled in her eyes. He couldn't remember ever seeing his mother weep. The pain of it nearly caused him to double over. "How could I know so little about him when I love him so deeply?"

Uncrossing his arms, Ainsley wrapped his hands around the edge of his desk. "Why are you here, Mother?"

"Because I am well aware that you know a certain unsavory sort. People who spy on others. That's how you handled that awful woman who was causing trouble for Stephen and Mercy. If these *persons* know how to spy, perhaps they know how to find."

"We don't even know his last name. Do you have any notion where he lived before you met him?"

Slowly, she shook her head. "When we were together all that mattered was that we were together."

He nodded. It was quite the dilemma, but he did know someone who could possibly help. "Sir James Swindler is a man I've used in the past. He has a talent for ferreting out information. Let me put a few things together and we shall go to London."

She gave him a grateful smile. "Thank you."

"I should warn you, however, that when Leo is found, I shall be obligated to challenge him to a duel in order to restore your honor."

"Dueling is frowned upon."

"That does not stop people from doing it, and it certainly shall not stop me."

She took a deep breath, straightened her shoulders, and was once again the determined woman who had eased his hurts when he was a lad. "Find him. Then leave it to me to deal with this business between us. Believe me, he shall rue the day he was ever born."

Jolly good for her. At least her tears were gone. He could handle his mother as long as she wasn't weeping.

Inwardly, he smiled. He suspected Leo could handle her as well. Still, God help the man if she found him. A woman scorned and all that.

Leo stood at the edge of the cliff. Below him the sea roared against the shore, but up here there was a certain peace in being above the fray. He'd taken to painting landscapes of late, and he tried now to imbue his current work with this sense of tranquillity that surrounded him. But all he managed were dark strokes and hard edges. He cast the canvas aside and picked up another—to begin afresh, to begin over. It was most difficult, however.

He'd hoped for a new start at this little cottage by the sea. A new direction. People were always disappointing, but the land . . . the land remained steadfast and true. Except for the little bit at the very edge of the cliff that tumbled away beneath the weight of his foot one afternoon and nearly had him losing his balance and toppling onto the rocks below.

He'd have served as food for the fish before anyone found him. This little isolated bit of heaven was quickly turning into hell. He was leasing it for another month, and then he would travel aboard. France, perhaps. Or Italy. Tess had always wanted to visit Italy. He should have taken her.

Better yet, he should have left her years ago instead of pining away for her like a callow lad.

He rubbed an itch on the back of his neck, but that

only seemed to worsen it. Perhaps it was the ghost of the young woman who had flung herself off the cliff. Her story was legend, as was the tale of her sisters. One of them owned this bit of land. When she and her husband were in London, they leased the property. Leo had paid handsomely for the isolation. He needed some time. A man with a wounded heart was not at all pleasant to be around. Of late he was even coming to despise his own company. Avoiding himself, however, was proving most difficult.

The breeze surrounding him took on a sweeter scent, one that reminded him of passion-filled nights. He'd not been with a woman since Tess. Perhaps tonight he would stroll down to the tavern in the village and see what was to be had.

"What do you think of that notion, little ghost? Shall I give it a go?"

"I never knew you spoke to yourself," a familiar voice murmured.

Tessa. He spun around so quickly he threw himself off balance and knocked over his canvas and easel. In spite of the dark circles beneath her eyes and her apparent loss of weight, she was still the most beautiful woman upon whom he'd ever gazed. His breathing was harsh, erratic, his heart having a difficult time keeping up. Inhaling deeply, he regained his composure. He wanted to take her in his arms, kiss her, make love to her on the grass.

Instead he forced out the words, "What are you doing here? How did you find me?"

"Ainsley hired a private investigator. Sir James Swindler."

Leo slammed his eyes closed. In retrospect, when he

paid for his lease, he supposed he should have told the man that he sought a sanctuary and didn't want anyone to know where he was. "I do hope you didn't pay him much. This happens to be his cottage by the sea. His and his wife's. What are the odds?"

"Although it is vulgar to discuss money, we paid him what I thought his information was worth. I would say you're in dire need of having your hair trimmed, but I daresay I think I like it long."

He'd pulled it back and tied it in place with a thin strip of leather. "You didn't answer me. Why are you here?"

"For a proper good-bye. Did you really think I would be content with a letter?"

"It seemed less painful for both of us."

"You assumed I'd choose Lynnford over you."

His harsh laughter echoed around them. "You've loved the man for years. Granted, he'll have a period of mourning, but after so long, that's merely a small inconvenience. Although perhaps he'll forgo mourning. I'm sure he's anxious to be with you again. I certainly wouldn't let etiquette keep me from you."

"He loves me."

"Of course he does. He's not a fool."

"We've had so many nights of talking long past midnight—"

"I don't wish to hear it, Tess. Say whatever you have to say and be gone."

At that moment, Tessa thought her heart would break. To see her beautiful Leo reduced to this, hurting and in so much pain. Even though he was attempting to disguise it with curt words and flat emotion. She'd been with him too long, knew him too well. How could she have been so blind to her true feelings regarding him?

She angled her chin proudly. "Very well. If you insist. I've come to invite you to my wedding."

He shook his head sadly. "That I cannot do, my love."

"But it shall be the talk of London. I want you there. Desperately."

He gazed out to the sea. "I never thought you to be cruel, Tess. I can deny you nothing. But please don't ask this of me."

"But if you're not there, my dear, dear Leo, then however shall I marry you?"

She watched as the shock of her words rippled over his beloved features.

"Me? But you always said no when I asked for your hand."

"I was a foolish woman. Lynnford was the love of my youth. And as we have talked these many weeks as we've not been able to talk in years, so we discovered that neither of us is the person that each of us fell in love with. We were holding onto someone who no longer exists." She took a tentative step toward him. "You love me as I am now. And I shall love you always. Marry me, Leo. For God's sake, marry me."

She didn't recall seeing him move, but suddenly she was in his arms and his mouth was devouring hers. A small part of her questioned the wisdom of this, thought he was still too young for her, but most of her no longer cared.

She loved him, with all her heart and soul. She had for years, but she'd held onto a promise from her youth. Wisdom was supposed to arrive with age, but apparently for her, it had taken a detour.

He lifted her into his arms. "Ask me again."

"Marry me."

"Why, Tess? Why?"

She cradled his cheek, hating that she had given him reason to doubt. "Because I love you more than I have ever loved any man. And I suspect longer. I'm scared, Leo. I will grow old long before you."

He laughed. "Tess, you're old now."

With a screech, she slapped his shoulder. "I'm not *that* old."

He began walking toward the cottage. "I shall always be younger than you, but then I always have been, and what I love about you has nothing to do with your age. You're strong and you're determined and you have raised three fine sons."

"And you have no sons," she reminded him. "What if you decide you want children?"

"For God's sake, I'll borrow one of your grandchildren for a while. You have enough of them running around."

"But they are not yours. They do not carry your blood."

"What does that matter? I love them, Tess, because they are part of you and that makes them mine."

Tears welled in her eyes. "How could I have ever thought I could live without you?"

"It does seem rather ludicrous, doesn't it?"

Laughing, she tightened her hold on him. "Oh, I have missed you."

He carried her into the house and up the stairs to the bedchamber. It was small and simple, but at that moment she would have been happy with a tent.

With a swiftness born of familiarity, he was undoing

her fastenings, removing her clothes as she worked to do the same with his. After all these years, why was it that the anticipation of seeing him naked brought such excitement? Shouldn't she be bored with him by now?

"God, Tess," he said, in awe once she was standing before him unrestrained by clothing. "You are so beautiful."

"I am not so firm as I once was."

"You fit me perfectly. You have aged like a fine wine, and I enjoy very much sipping from you."

He tumbled her onto the bed, and she welcomed the weight of him. He was still firm and well-muscled. She didn't think that he'd ever go to fat. She glided her hands over him, while he buried his face between her breasts, kissing the inside of one and then the other. With his tongue, he drew little stars over her skin.

He caressed and stroked, kissed and plundered. Familiarity made them comfortable with each other, increased the pleasure. Awkwardness never emerged between them. They knew what each other liked, and they delivered.

They became a frenzied tangle of limbs, and when she thought she could stand it no longer, he finally entered her with one sure thrust—

And stilled.

He gazed down on her, and in his golden eyes she could see all the love he held for her. Had she really ever thought she would give this up?

Slowly, he began to rock against her, taking her higher and higher, until they reached the pinnacle of pleasure and flung themselves from it at the same time, their cries echoing around them. Slowly, they returned to reality. She opened her eyes to find him smiling down on her, his golden eyes drowsy. She could hold him here forever.

After several long moments of taking his fill of her, he finally rolled off. Sated and lethargic, she nestled against his side. His arm came around her, holding her near. It took long moments for their breathing to return to normal, for their hearts to stop pounding. Content, she began drifting off to sleep.

"By the way, Tess . . ."

"Hmm?"

"The answer is yes. I'll marry you."

Chapter 22

Ainsley stood in the garden at Grantwood Manor because all the activity in the house was driving him mad.

Tradition dictated that members of the family marry in the chapel on his estate. Westcliffe had married Claire there. Stephen had married Mercy. Ainsley's mother had married his father there. Now she would marry Leo there.

While his sisters-by-marriage saw to all the numerous details, and his overbearing mother made sure every aspect was as she wanted it, Ainsley had merely trudged over the grounds and left them to it. But soon the guests—the elite of London—would be descending on them. Tonight he would hold a dinner and ball in the couple's honor. Tomorrow the ceremony would take place, after which she and Leo would leave for their wedding trip.

At least that's what he'd been told.

He didn't care about the particulars. All he cared about was that Jayne had responded to the invitation and indicated that she and Walfort would be delighted to attend the wedding. She and Walfort.

And the baby she now carried.

He'd known of course that sooner or later their paths would inevitably cross. After all, they moved about in the same circles. Still, he was not as prepared to put on a stoic front as he'd hoped. All his mother's planning—she would not be rushed when she'd waited so long to marry again, and for the last time—had delayed the wedding. Here it was, nearly the end of March. The daffodils as well as several other varieties of flowers that his gardener nurtured were coming into bloom. The house and the chapel were overflowing with flowers from the greenhouse.

But it was not only the flowers that were blossoming. Jayne would be as well. Since she was traveling, it was unlikely that she was showing, but still he would know. He would look at her, and he would know.

He had to pretend it didn't matter. He had to welcome Walfort into his home without revealing how much he had come to care for Jayne. He had to greet Jayne with a cold aloofness that did not give away the fact that he missed her beyond all endurance.

Where was the blasted mistress when he needed her? It would probably help matters if he went about attempting to acquire one. Damn it all. What had his mother been thinking when she invited them?

"Uncle."

He jerked his attention from the blossoms and his troubling musings, arched a brow and looked down. "Nephew."

Waverly stood there with his hands clasped behind his back, a stance very similar to Ainsley's. He wondered if his own son would stand in the same manner. Was it in the blood, or a result of exposure to the family?

"Grandmother sent me to tell you that the first of the guests are arriving. You're to greet them."

"It's her blasted wedding. She can greet them."

"But it's your friend. Lord Walfort."

"Right." Wise of her. Best to get the encounter over with now when there was no one to see. Then everyone could get comfortable before all the other guests arrived. "I shall see to my duty."

He'd taken two steps when Waverly said, "Uncle."

He stopped and turned. "Nephew."

"You need a dog. I don't have one to play with when I'm here."

"Bring yours next time."

"Mother says Fennimore will make a mess in the coach and she will not be happy. Father says we must always make Mother happy."

Ainsley grinned. "Your father is quite right. It is your job to keep your mother happy. I shall have a dog here the next time you come to visit."

Waverly's face broke into a wide smile before he walked sedately toward the door that led into the kitchen. He wondered if his own child would like to have a dog, then shook off the thought. He was years away from having a child. He needed a wife first—and obtaining her would be far more trouble than obtaining a mistress. Here, he had yet to get a mistress.

He strolled around to the front of the house, arriving just as Walfort's carriage and another rocked to a stop. Taking a deep breath, he continued on.

Footmen were scurrying around. Randall stepped out of the second carriage and ordered a footman to remove the wheelchair from the roof. Ainsley had not considered how much trouble would be involved if Walfort traveled. Little wonder they'd arrived hours earlier than needed. Walfort no doubt wanted to be safely ensconced in the residence before the other guests arrived. Ainsley realized he would have to give some thought to transporting him to the chapel with as much dignity as possible.

He reached the first carriage as a footman opened the door and handed Jayne down. Once both her feet were on the ground, she froze, her gaze latched onto his. His memories didn't do her justice and he cursed them for failing him.

She curtsied. "Your Grace, it's so nice to see you again."

He stepped forward, took her gloved hand and pressed a kiss to it. "Lady Walfort, may I say—" His gaze dipped to her waist. He thought he detected a slight rounding. But with the volume of her dress, he couldn't be sure. He wanted to drop to his knees and press a kiss to her belly. "—you look lovely as always."

"You're far too kind."

He hated the formality but would endure it because it was expected.

"Ainsley, old chap, how are you?" Walfort asked. He was still in the carriage, peering out the window.

Ainsley stepped back. Walfort didn't seem at all distressed seeing him for the first time since he'd sent his wife to Blackmoor Cottage. He wondered if he could be as unaffected as Walfort if he found himself gazing upon a man who had known his wife intimately. He didn't think so. As a matter of fact, he knew so. In all likelihood, even if he had no use of his legs, he'd find a way to catapult himself from the carriage and introduce the man to his fists.

"Don't know if you've heard," Walfort continued. "Jayne is with child."

He understood the motivation behind his cousin's announcement. He'd done it for the benefit of the servants. A man thrilled with the realization that his wife would soon give birth. A man letting all know that he was still a man.

Ainsley couldn't help himself. His gaze flickered back to Jayne. "That's wonderful news. Congratulations." He thought his voice could not have carried less excitement if he were already in the grave.

"Thank you," she said softly, and he knew beyond a doubt that she'd been the one to send the missive, even though he'd asked her not to.

He longed to talk with her in private, to find out if she was truly happy now that the dream had become a reality. But they were all on stage, with an audience.

"Come, let's get you settled in the house before the hordes of guests arrive."

While a footman hauled the chair up the steps and into the residence, Randall carried Walfort inside, where he proceeded to settle the marquess in the wheelchair. It was as though someone had sounded a bell. His family swarmed into the entry hallway to welcome the first of their guests.

Well-wishes greeted Walfort's news of his impending fatherhood. He was making quite the production of it. Jayne merely blushed becomingly and avoided gazing directly at Ainsley.

"Come," Claire said. With his mother preoccupied with her wedding, and Ainsley having no mistress of his household, Claire was serving as the hostess, the one arranging things and ensuring that all went as planned.

"We've arranged some rooms in the family wing for you. I believe you'll be most comfortable."

"You go ahead, Jayne," Walfort said. "After that long journey I am more interested in something for my parched throat. What say you, Ainsley? Have you something to offer me?"

"Let's adjourn to the library, shall we?"

His brothers were only too happy to join them. Ainsley suspected they welcomed the excuse to keep themselves from being underfoot—or available to handle tedious tasks—as the ladies worked. Selfishly, Ainsley wished they'd gone elsewhere. Sooner or later he and Walfort would find themselves alone, and then the awkwardness was certain to descend.

"Let's drink a toast to Jayne and hope she delivers an heir, shall we?" Walfort said once everyone had a snifter of brandy.

An heir? A boy who should be duke. The thought hit Ainsley like a punch to the gut. He'd known the risks going in, but surely Walfort wasn't praying for a boy.

If his brothers noticed his less than enthusiastic raising of a glass and "Cheers," they gave no indication. He wondered if they suspected the truth of the matter. Surely not. Why would anyone think he'd do something so incredibly irresponsible?

Ainsley drained his glass and poured another. He ambled over to the window and wondered how he might find a moment alone with Jayne. Then realized the foolishness of trying to achieve that end. What more was there to say?

"So will marriage make your mother less scandalous, do you suppose?" Walfort asked.

"I doubt it," Stephen said, his blue eyes dancing. He

combed his fingers through his dark blond hair. "The Duchess of Ainsley and scandal are rather synonymous. She enjoys a good scandal, especially when she's at the center of it."

"I say, Ainsley, any plans to make your mother a dowager anytime soon?"

He wondered what had prompted Walfort's question and why his cousin should care. Perhaps he was not as unaffected by all that had happened as he appeared.

"This Season, if Ainsley's plan bears fruit," West-cliffe said.

Ainsley jerked his attention to his oldest brother. "I never said anything of the sort."

"At Christmas, when you were into your cups."

He recalled, just barely, mentioning something about the Season.

"Good news, then. It's long past time you married," Walfort said. "And you have some catching up to do with your brothers here."

"Have you become my mother?"

"No, but you have a responsibility to provide an heir."

Ainsley's fingers tightened around his snifter. "What if Jayne delivers a daughter?"

Swirling the brandy, Walfort held his gaze. "Then we shall just have to try again."

He wondered where his cousin intended to find the stud this time. He doubted that he'd have the strength to let her go if he had her for another month, another week, another day, another hour. Just once more.

Gazing out the window, he spied Jayne strolling in the garden. "If you'll excuse me, I forgot about a matter to which I must attend."

He emptied his snifter with one burning gulp, set it aside and strode from the room. He knew it was foolishness to seek her out. Better by far to ignore her, to pretend she didn't exist. But it seemed his head had no control over his legs. Before he knew it, he was in the garden. Then it was only a few long, quick strides and he was beside her.

I missed you. Dreadfully. But he couldn't give the words freedom. They were not his to be spoken. So instead, he asked, "Should you be walking about?"

She studied his shoes as though wondering who had polished them. Finally, she lifted her gaze to his, and he could see that she wasn't quite certain they should be alone in the garden, as though she feared he might seek to ravish her behind the hedges. Not that the thought hadn't occurred to him. The desperation with which he wished to take her in his arms was unsettling.

"Yes," she said softly. "My physician advises it. It's good for me . . . and the babe."

He clasped his hands behind his back to keep them from reaching for her.

"Are you well?"

She nodded, her cheeks blossoming into the color of one of his gardener's prize roses. "I had some nausea in the beginning, but nothing to worry over."

These were not topics usually discussed but he wanted to know everything.

"I feared you'd be angry with me," she said.

"What could you ever do that would make me angry?"

"I sent you the missive after you instructed me not to."

"I was glad you did. Learning of it as Walfort announced it through the carriage window might have given me the vapors."

He could see her fighting back her smile. This was all so bloody awkward. He hated it.

He didn't think it possible, but her cheeks turned even a brighter hue. "He's been so boastful that I've begun to feel rather like a prized broodmare."

"His intentions are honorable. He seeks to spare you from gossip and scandal."

"I simply wish he'd do it a bit more quietly." She glanced around. "Have you climbing trees here?"

"Not good ones. But the stars at night are magnificent."

She held his gaze for a moment before looking down at the ground. "This is terribly awkward. I knew it would be, but . . ."

Her voice trailed off. He slipped his finger beneath her chin and lifted gently until he could look into her eyes. "I've been . . . concerned about you."

He guided her toward a bend in the path that would hide them from view of the house. When he was certain no one could see them, he stopped and simply took his fill of her. He reached out to touch her cheek, caught himself and shoved his errant hand into his pocket. "Are you truly well?"

"I am."

"Is Walfort . . . is he all right with what's happened, now that it's actually happened?"

"Yes, he really is happy. Overly so."

"I'm glad. He treats you well?"

"He treats me as he always has."

No kisses, then. He should have been glad, but it saddened him. He needed to have a talk with Walfort, make sure he understood his duties where his wife was concerned. She deserved—

She released a startled sound of surprise, her lovely blue eyes growing as round as saucers.

"What is it?" he asked, alarmed.

Her smile was one of wonder and delight as she wrapped her fingers around his wrist, tugged his hand from his pocket and flattened it against her stomach. He was surprised by the firmness of her body, the roundness of it. Her dress hid everything, on purpose he was certain.

"Jayne—"

"Shh. Just wait."

Beneath his fingers her body undulated slightly like the tide washing over the shore. The wonder of it nearly dropped him to his knees.

"Did you feel that?" she asked.

"Was that—"

"Your child."

"No." He pulled his hand free and turned away from her. "It's not mine. I gave it to you and Walfort. Meeting you out here was a terrible idea. I knew it was, but still I came. What happened . . . we are not to talk of it. That was the arrangement, the bargain."

"You asked me, now that it happened, if Walfort was all right with everything. Perhaps a better question is: are you?"

Forcing a façade of indifference, he faced her. "I am. It is simply important that we never forget that this is *not* my child."

He saw the pain flash over her lovely features before she shored up her resolve and presented a convincing mask. "Of course, Your Grace. How silly of me to forget. If you'll excuse me, I must complete my turn about the garden. I prefer to be alone. I use the time for quiet reflection and contemplation. It is important that I be calm so I do not have a nervous child."

She didn't wait for his answer, but spun on her heel and walked away from him. Everything in him urged him to call her back, to apologize, to not be such an ass. But feeling the movement of the child—*his* child, no matter what stupidity he had agreed to—had devastated him. He would never hold the child in his arms. He would not see it take its first steps. He would not be there to protect it. He had forfeited the right to be this child's father when he had taken another man's wife.

Now he would exist in a hell of his own creation.

Absence made the heart grow fonder. Or so the old saying went. Jayne had convinced herself that it was true, merely a trick of the mind, memories made sweeter by the passage of time. Until she stepped out of the carriage and looked up to see Ainsley standing there. At that precise moment she realized she'd been deceiving herself.

Absence had not been responsible for the fondness she felt toward him. It was not the reason she carried him into her dreams. It was not the reason she pressed her hand to her abdomen and wondered if she'd see him in the face of her child. It was not the reason that she had written him letters never to be sent.

As she sat beside Walfort in the great hall where an orchestra played and a thousand candles flickered in the chandeliers, she knew Ainsley—not absence—had made her heart yearn for him.

To see him again had been a blessing and a curse.

He remained devastatingly handsome. His patrician features were perfection—except for the one tiny scar. But even it no longer offended her. Upon first seeing her, he'd given his green gaze leave to wander over her with the familiarity of a long-ago lover. She'd grown warm beneath his perusal. She'd wanted to step into his embrace and kiss him in order to make up for all the kisses she'd denied them when they were together. But all the opportunities lost could not now be regained.

During dinner she'd been like a miser. Collecting and hoarding every glimpse of him, every word he uttered. She was pathetic and pitiful and racked with guilt.

She'd not realized how very lonely she was at Herndon Hall until she returned from her time at Blackmoor. The child would fill the emptiness. She wished only that Walfort would make more of an effort to do so as well.

"Are you well?"

Smiling at Walfort, she took his hand and squeezed it. "Of course."

"Is it difficult for you being here, seeing him again?"

Her throat knotted, yet still she managed to force through the lie. "No, of course not." Did he not realize it was entirely inappropriate to be discussing something so personal and intimate in this venue, a room crowded with people celebrating the upcoming marriage of the Duchess of Ainsley?

"Gentlemen have been effusive with their congratulations. I'm not sure anyone suspects that I didn't have a hand in your current situation," Walfort said.

She saw the doubt in his eyes then, the discomfort at the reminder of how he had come to be in this position. She leaned near, as though they were two lovers sharing a wicked secret that no one else was to overhear. "But you did have a hand in it, didn't you? I believe it would be best if we didn't discuss it here."

"I daresay, you're absolutely correct."

He was nervous, she realized. Worried that someone would doubt his manhood. How difficult this was for them, how difficult for them all.

"I was just admiring the flowers," she said, to change the topic, to get them onto safer ground.

"Yes, they're lovely. I say, I think I'm going to the card room for a bit. You don't mind, do you? It'll give you a chance to visit with the ladies."

He didn't wait for her response, but signaled to Randall, who was always at the ready to be of service. She watched until he disappeared from the ballroom. Rising, she opened her fan and waved it briskly to create a small breeze. It was so terribly warm in here. The press of people, she supposed.

She smiled as Ainsley's sister-by-marriage approached. "Lady Westcliffe, you've done a marvelous job here."

Lady Westcliffe's eyes twinkled. "Mercy and I did what we could. If Ainsley would see to securing a wife, it would have fallen to her, of course."

Jayne felt a pang of remorse at the mention of Ainsley with a wife. How would the woman feel if she ever discovered—

She must never know. No one must ever know.

"Congratulations to you on providing your husband with another son," Jayne said.

"I must confess that I despise the way we make it sound as though it is an obligation rather than a joy. I do believe he'd have been just as happy with another daughter. And what of you? A miracle has occurred, has it not?"

Jayne couldn't help herself. She pressed her hand to her stomach. "Yes, it was quite unexpected but very welcomed." *Why was it unexpected, you dolt, if your husband was visiting your bed?*

"Well, not completely unexpected, of course. We had all but given up hope, but . . . well . . . I'm sure you understand what I'm blabbering about." A twinge. Not the baby moving. She was hungry. She'd been too nervous to eat much during dinner. Not willing to risk upsetting her digestion. "I believe I'm going to have a bit of refreshment."

"Please do. When I am with child I am hungry all the time, especially when it's a boy. They eat in the womb as they will eat through life—voraciously."

Lady Westcliffe was escorting her to the refreshment area when she excused herself after someone caught her attention. Jayne continued on.

"Oh my dear, there you are. I've been searching for you."

Turning, Jayne forced herself to smile. She wondered if the usual wagers were going on here. "Lady Inwood."

The woman squeezed Jayne's hand. "I have heard the most delicious gossip." She pulled Jayne back behind a towering frond. "Ainsley is in love."

Jayne felt a stab of . . . jealousy? No, it could not be jealousy. Disappointment? No, she had no right to feel that emotion either. "With whom?"

Her voice sounded as though she was strangling, but Lady Inwood seemed not to notice as she glanced around, and Jayne was certain she was on the verge of pointing out the fortunate lady.

"That's the mystery," Lady Inwood said, sotto voce, putting her hand beside her mouth as though fearing someone would decipher her words by reading her lips.

"Then how do you know he's in love?"

"As you're well aware, when we were at your residence for the fox hunt, our wagering was for naught. We were unable to determine who occupied his bed. So it has been ever since. No rumors. Nary a one regarding who has caught his fancy for an evening of delight."

"Perhaps it is simply because we are not all in London. Gossip is a bit more difficult over distance."

"I daresay it has never mattered before, where the duchess's sons are concerned. We have always been able to ferret out their latest conquests, when there were conquests. It is as though Ainsley has gone into hiding."

"I'm sure he's been busy with his mother's upcoming nuptials."

"A man of his virility?" She shook her head. "Balderdash. Only one explanation makes any sense. He is in love. Now we are wagering who the lady is who has managed to rein him in. What will you wager?"

Stupefied, Jayne shook her head. "I would not even know where to be—"

"Ladies."

Jayne swung around to find the object of their discussion presenting them with a devilish smile, as though he knew what they were whispering over.

"Your Grace," Lady Inwood purred. "You must be so delighted that your mother is marrying, but it does increase the pressure, does it not? It leaves you the only one unmarried."

"Not true. My nephews and niece are as yet unwed,

so I have quite a bit more time before I'll feel the need to tie the knot." He turned to Jayne. "Lady Walfort, I promised your husband that I would ask you to honor me with a dance. I hope you will not deny me so simple a pleasure."

"Yes, no, of course. I would be delighted."

"Lady Inwood, if you'll excuse us . . ." Ainsley said.

The older woman shifted her gaze between Jayne and Ainsley as though she feared she'd missed out on something. "By all means. Enjoy yourselves, especially as Walfort wishes it."

Very smoothly, Ainsley escorted Jayne to the dance area.

"It seems you've come to my rescue yet once again," Jayne said as he took her into his arms for the waltz.

He grinned wickedly, teasingly. "And what gossip was she whispering in your ear?"

"Rumor has it that you're in love."

His smile vanished like snow touched by sunlight. "The basis for such gossip?"

"You've not been seen with a woman since before the fox hunt at Herndon Hall. And there have been no whisperings about you entertaining a lady."

"So they are assuming love is the root of my sudden abstinence."

"It would seem so, yes."

"Such romantics filled with such silliness."

She glanced around. So many people. She felt them pressing in on her. Air. There seemed to be no air. It was stifling and warm. She should ask him to take her out to the garden. No, that would be inappropriate. She would go when the dance was finished. Alone. Just to take a couple of deep breaths.

"I wanted to apologize for my temper in the garden," Ainsley said, drawing her attention back to him.

"It is I who should apologize. It was wrong of me. Cruel even."

He smiled wryly. "Jayne, you could not be cruel if you had a torture chamber within easy reach."

"It is only that it was the first time . . . that I felt it. It was suddenly . . . real, and I didn't want to be alone with . . . the joy. And I'm being cruel again." The words seem to be coming from far away, from someone else.

"Jayne—"

She thought he stopped dancing, but people swirled around them in a blur. Darkness hovered at the edge of her vision and began closing in.

She was vaguely aware of Ainsley sweeping her up into his arms. "Salisbury!"

The urgency in his voice silenced the orchestra. Or so she thought. She couldn't be sure. She was in some sort of strange fog. His stride faltered not at all as he issued orders to his butler.

"Send for my physician immediately. I want him here before I've reached the stairs. And for God's sake, find Walfort."

It was only as he laid her on softness and moved back that she realized he'd brought her to a bedchamber, but not the one she shared with Walfort. This one was larger, grander. It had to be Ainsley's.

She was hot, cloying with dampness, and trembling. Holding her hand, he sat on the edge of the bed and stroked the stray strands of her hair off her brow. "Your maid will be here any moment."

"What happened?" she forced out through a thick tongue.

"You swooned."

"I don't swoon."

His mouth twitched. "Trust me, Jayne, I have dealt with enough swooning women to know a swoon when I see one."

In a panic, she pressed her hand to her stomach. "Am I going to lose this baby? What if my losing the other had nothing at all to do with the accident but was some flaw in me? What if I'm incapable of carrying a child until it's born?"

"Look at me, Jayne. Look at me."

His voice was calm, firm, demanding. She gazed into his beautiful green eyes.

"You will not lose this child. Do you understand?" he asked. "You will not. I will not allow it."

She drew comfort from his confidence. Did he ever have any doubts at all about anything?

"What's going on here?" Walfort asked.

She saw the battle work itself out over Ainsley's features. He did not want to leave her, but it was not his place to be here.

Stoically, he released her, stepped back and faced her husband. "She swooned. I've sent for my physician. As soon as he— No. We need not wait. Mercy. Mercy was a nurse in the Crimea." He spun around. "Mercy!"

He staggered to a stop. "How long have you been standing there?"

"Not long," Mercy said, marching into the room. "I thought I might be needed."

She came around to the other side of the bed and took Jayne's hand. "Everything will be all right."

"I don't want to lose this child."

"Of course you don't." She turned her attention to the men. "Out now. Both of you."

"I need a quiet moment with my wife first," Walfort said.

Mercy nodded, stepped away and began issuing orders to the servants. With obvious reluctance, Ainsley walked from the room.

Walfort rolled forward. He peeled the glove from her hand before closing his fingers around it, skin against skin. He studied their clasped hands as though he'd never seen them before. "Ainsley is right, you know." He lifted dark eyes to hers. "You won't lose this child. We won't allow it."

She placed his hand against her side. "I felt it move today. I should have told you. I want you to be able to feel it, too."

"And I will. As soon as— Oh."

She could barely see him through her tears as she said, "That was it. That was the baby."

"He's a strong bugger."

"I think he will be, yes. Or she. He could be a girl."

She watched his throat work as he swallowed. He nodded. His eyes grew damp. He placed his head near her hip and wept. As though all the repercussions of what they'd done had finally hit him.

But she didn't know if they were tears of sorrow or joy.

Chapter 23

They waited in the library. He and Walfort. Drinking whiskey, each lost in his own thoughts. The excitement in the ballroom had dissipated with his rapid departure, Jayne in his arms. Claire, with her usual aplomb, had promptly ended that portion of the night's festivities. A late night repast had been prepared and the guests summarily retired to their respective chambers.

Or so Westcliffe had reported to Ainsley. He knew he should give a fig that he had a residence filled with guests and that on the morrow his mother would marry, but at the moment he cared only about Jayne.

The physician arrived, nearly an hour ago. With each passing moment, Ainsley's worries increased. He'd promised her that she'd not lose the child. He didn't have a clue regarding how to keep the promise.

"You fell in love with her, didn't you?"

He glanced over at Walfort before returning his attention to his whiskey.

"I'll assume your silence is a yes," Walfort said.

"Assume whatever you damned well please." He shoved himself out of his chair. "Did you honestly think

I wouldn't?" He stormed to the fireplace, tempted to toss his glass into the flames. He wanted a conflagration that equaled the one inside him. He pressed his forearm to the mantel. "You're married to her. You had her in your bed every night. You had her at your table every morning."

He spun around. "Whatever possessed you to keep your mistress? What possible purpose could she have served except to ensure you didn't honor your vows? By God, Jayne deserved a man who would keep the vows he made to her."

"I loved her. My mistress. I still do. Maybe that's the reason I drank so much that night. I wanted to forget I had a wife waiting for me at home. A wife with child. Maybe I wanted to wash away the guilt. I was betraying two women at the same time. I didn't feel good about it, Ainsley, but duty—"

"Duty be damned. Jayne deserved your faithfulness."

"With your reputation, with all the thighs you've parted, do you think you'd have had better luck at it, at not straying?"

"I know I would have."

"You self-righteous prig. You were as drunk as I that night. From what were you trying to escape? Your bachelorhood, your wealth, your title? You had it all. Everything. You still do! Including your damn legs!"

"I don't have Jayne." As soon as the words were spoken, he regretted them. Damnation. He slammed his hand against the mantel and cursed again.

Walfort, as though he recognized that Ainsley's temper was close to boiling, returned to his brooding silence, sipping his whiskey. Ainsley stared at the fire.

That was how the physician found them a few moments later. One sitting, one standing, both staring. Ainsley fought not to grab Dr. Roberts, shake him and ask after Jayne. He was not her husband. He could not overstep his bounds here without causing speculation, so he bit back all the questions that plagued him.

Dr. Roberts nodded at Ainsley—"Your Grace"—before approaching Walfort. "M'lord."

"How does my wife fare?"

"Quite well. Too much excitement I'd say. What with the dancing and all. Not uncommon for a woman in her condition. Let her rest for a day or two and she should be right as rain."

Ainsley felt such relief that he dropped into a nearby chair. What an idiot. He'd overreacted. It wasn't like him to do so. Dr. Roberts offered more assurances before taking his leave.

Ainsley got up and poured himself more whiskey. "You should go see her."

"I don't need you to tell me what I should do with my wife."

Biting back his temper, Ainsley downed his whiskey before pouring more.

Walfort said quietly, with an apologetic mien, "I hadn't expected it to be so hard."

Ainsley glanced back at him. "It isn't as long as you remember for whom we do it."

He sat in the library long after Walfort had gone to see Jayne. He heard the door open. He expected to see one of his brothers strolling in to check on him. Instead it was his mother, who came to stand before him.

"Jayne will be fine. She needs only rest," he told

her, as though she'd asked. Why else would she be here except to discern the health of Jayne?

"Yes, I know. Mercy told me."

He nodded. He'd forgotten Mercy had been there to assist the doctor. His attention was so focused on Jayne that it was a wonder he remembered his name.

"I've been thinking about things since Walfort announced that Jayne was with child."

"Shouldn't you be concentrating on your wedding?"

"Don't make light of this, Ainsley. I'm most disappointed in you. You were instrumental in that accident with Walfort, then you cuckolded him—which I suspected at Blackmoor—but still to have not taken care with the girl, to ensure that she did not get with child—"

"It was done a-purpose, Mother, with Walfort's full consent and blessing."

It was not often he took his mother by surprise, but still he took no satisfaction in her wide rounded eyes.

He continued, "Jayne wanted a child more than anything in the world, and we owed her that. Because of our selfish stupidity, she lost the one she was carrying."

"Oh, my dear son." She sank into the chair opposite his. "What in God's name have you done? What if it is a boy?"

"Then Walfort will have his heir."

"An heir who should have been yours."

"I wanted to see Jayne happy more than I wanted an heir. He shall not suffer because of it, Mother. He may not inherit as prestigious a title as mine, but I shall see to it that Walfort's estate flourishes, even if I must do it in secret, behind his back. This child shall have more wealth than he would have had otherwise. And he shall have Jayne as his mother. There is no greater gift that I could have given him than Jayne as his mother."

"You love her."

The words came out as a statement, not a question, yet still he answered.

"With all my heart." He plowed his hand through his hair, lowering the drawbridge to his soul for a brief instance. "The past few months have been pure hell."

"Oh, Ainsley."

At the sight of despair on her face, he abruptly closed the fortress, took a deep breath and straightened. "It is done. I shall simply have to live with it and its consequences."

She squared her shoulders and gave him that steely, no-nonsense resolve. "We must set our course on finding you a wife."

As though a solution to his heartache were so easily achieved.

"There is no other woman for me, Mother. I've not been with another since I left her. I have no interest in another." Which was the reason he'd yet to acquire a mistress. It sounded like such a good idea until he thought about actually being with her. She could not replace Jayne.

"Well, I can tell you from experience," she said, "that with enough lonely nights behind you, you'll seek out another. And who knows? Perhaps you'll be as fortunate with her as I've been with Leo."

He did not share her optimism. Perhaps because he knew there was only one woman for him, and she would never be his wife.

"I'm sorry if any of this has reduced the joy you'd thought to find tomorrow," he said.

"My heart aches for you, m'dear, but as long as Leo stands beside me tomorrow, nothing will diminish my joy of becoming his wife."

"Why do you think he made such a secret of his last name?" he asked, to lighten the mood.

"He's an artist. He's eccentric."

"Still, it seems that you should have known you'd become Mrs. Pinchot before you agreed to marry him."

"His last name could have been Dunghill and I'd have not changed my mind. Such is love. Besides, I rather like it. Although many have told me that I shall always be 'Duchess.' I suppose I've held the title long enough to go by it if I so desire."

"Do you desire?"

She shook her head. "Mrs. Pinchot suits me just fine."

She rose, leaned over and kissed him on the cheek. "You were so terribly well behaved when you were a child. I worried about you. I suppose you had to be naughty sometime. But you rather outdid yourself here. Outdid your brothers as well."

"I believe Stephen held his own as far as bad behavior."

"Be that as it may, do try to start behaving again, won't you?"

As she walked from the room, he downed the last of his whiskey. Perhaps he needed a wife. He'd once thought he'd marry only for love. Perhaps it was enough to marry in order to forget.

It was late the following morning when Jayne opened her eyes to find Ainsley leaning against the post at the foot of the bed. He was devilishly handsome in his black jacket and trousers. His cravat was perfect, just like the rest of him.

"Mother and Leo wanted me to give you their good-byes."

"They've left? Is the wedding over, then?"

He grinned. "Hours ago. The guests have all been fed and are on their merry way. At least a dozen ladies wanted to speak with you, but Walfort and I decided you didn't need to be disturbed. They were no doubt just looking for fodder for gossip anyway."

"I'm sorry that I made such a spectacle of myself last night."

"I fear I rather outdid you in that regard. I'm glad it turned out to be nothing."

"As am I. Was the wedding nice?" she asked.

His grin broadened. "My mother was as giddy as a young girl."

"Leo makes her happy."

"He does indeed."

"I'm sorry I missed it."

"I'm sorry as well. The doctor thinks a few days of rest and you'll be fine."

"Yes, I think perhaps he's right. I feel rather silly simply lying here."

"I shall bring you some books from the library."

"I would like that."

"You should know that in the next hour or so I shall be leaving for London. Important matters require my attention."

She nodded. "Yes, of course."

"I have something to give you before I leave." From behind his back he brought forward a long, slender wooden box. She knew what it was, of course, and her heart contracted into a painful ball that had difficulty beating. He placed the box on the bed beside her. "When the child is old enough, I'd like you to give him this. It was my father's. I'm not sure I ever told you that. He used it to spy on Napoleon. Or so I'm told. I don't remember his ever saying that, though. He and I used it to spy on the stars. It's the only vivid memory I have of him. I want your child to have it. Whether it be a boy or a girl."

Her heart was breaking. Damn him for this. "*You* should give it to him when he's older."

"No, I don't see myself visiting Herndon Hall any longer. I've acquired a distaste for fox hunting of late."

"Don't do this, Ainsley," she rasped, tears stinging her eyes.

Shaking his head, he gathered the droplets with his thumb. "I have no choice. Do you remember that first night when you told me that you didn't expect it to be so blasted difficult? I am now where you were then."

"Walfort will be lost without you. You are his dearest friend." *And I will be lost as well.*

"Walfort will be too busy raising his child to give much thought to my absence. You are to stay here until you feel well enough to travel, and you are not to leave a moment sooner." Leaning over, he pressed a kiss to her forehead. "Good-bye, Jayne."

She watched as he strode from the room. She wondered if any of them had truly understood the cost of what they were asking of each other.

Chapter 24

Ainsley sat at the desk in the library of his London residence and studied the names that had been presented to him. He intended to make the most of the coming Season. Next year Jayne and Walfort would no doubt decide it was time to return to London. He wanted to have a wife in hand before then, one who would be content to live in the country and never again set foot in a ballroom.

Fortunate for him, Claire was well ensconced in Society and knew which ladies would have their coming out and who, from Seasons past, still remained available. She'd prepared a list of candidates to assume the mantle of his duchess. He'd encountered a couple of the ladies at Walfort's when he was there for the fox hunt. He immediately scratched them from the list. Those who were ten and seven went next. What did he need with a child?

Ten and eight? Ten and nine? Still too young.

Twenty. Heading for the shelf. Risky. But then so were those who remained, as they were older. What was wrong with them that they did not appeal to suitors?

Within the hour, he had scratched off every name

without having met most of the women. With a sigh, he leaned back in his chair. His heart wasn't in the hunt.

It had been two months since he'd arrived in London. He knew Jayne and Walfort had returned to Herndon Hall. They'd even hosted a hunt late in April. He'd received an invitation, which he respectfully declined. He'd heard from those who attended that it was a smashing success. He found comfort in knowing that Jayne was doing well and up to the task of hosting the affair. He knew he should have made an appearance, but he simply hadn't been able to bring himself to do it.

He'd not expected to miss his old friend and cousin so much. Knowing that he had no plans to visit anytime in the near or distant future made matters all the harder. More than once he'd almost readied his coach to go for a visit.

But he knew things between them would be more awkward than before, would never again be as they were. It was inconceivable all the things he'd not considered when he accepted the terms of that ludicrous proposal.

A knock on the door brought him from his reverie. His butler entered, quietly crossed the room and extended a silver salver. "A missive from Herndon Hall has arrived, Your Grace. The man who brought it assures me it is quite urgent."

Ainsley's stomach clenched. It was too soon for Jayne to have given birth. *Dear God in heaven, don't let her have lost the child.*

Opening the message, he stared at the words that seemed to have no meaning.

It is with the heaviest of hearts that I inform you that Walfort is dying. He asks that you bring his jewels.

The coach traveled down the road, the horses galloping as fast as the coachman could drive them.

Without truly being aware of his surroundings, Ainsley stared out the window as the trees and sloping land flashed by. The jewels were safe. He had them in hand. But delivering them seemed like such a terribly bad idea.

Walfort is dying.

He had hosted a fox hunt a few short weeks ago and all was well. How the devil could he be dying? It didn't signify.

Ainsley caught sight of the large boulder that marked the beginning of Walfort's property. He remembered how Jayne had ordered him to stop when she saw it. He wanted to call up for the driver to stop now. He didn't want to continue on to Herndon Hall; he didn't want to see his friend diminished by death. Why had he stopped his visits? Fish needed to be caught, foxes chased, and horses ridden. Conversations over whiskey needed to be had.

He'd thought himself unselfish to leave them in peace, but now he wanted every moment back. Death had come with no warning.

Only three years separated them. What would he do if he had only three years to live? What if it was something they'd done together that resulted in this decline? What if he could have prevented it? Had he failed his cousin once again?

The recriminations swirled through him as the

coach turned onto the road leading through the estate. The trees were heavy with leaves awaiting the first breath of summer. Gorgeous. He saw a fox peer out through the brush and then dash away. It would still be here for this year's hunt, but Walfort wouldn't. It was impossible to contemplate. Herndon Hall without Walfort . . .

The coach slowed—"Stay here"—and he leaped out before it stopped. Although he dashed up the steps, it seemed he wasn't moving at all. He barged through the door.

The butler came to attention. "Your Grace."

"Is he in his bedchamber?"

"Yes, Your Grace."

"The marchioness?"

"She's not left his side."

He raced up the stairs, taking them two at a time, his heart pounding to an erratic rhythm. At least he wasn't too late.

He hesitated for a moment outside the bedchamber in order to gather himself, regain a calm façade. Then he shoved the door open and strode in.

Although the windows were open, the room smelled of sickness and death. The sunlight was doing a poor job of battling the shadows. His gaze fell on the frail figure lying in the bed, then it shifted to the woman sitting in a chair beside it.

"Ainsley."

His name was only a whisper upon her lips, hers a shout within his heart. She rose and walked around the bed. His gaze immediately dropped to her belly. Was it slightly more rounded than it had been before? Impossible to tell. She touched it self-consciously. Tears brimmed in her eyes. She was a woman who should never have cause to weep.

"Thank you so much for coming," she said.

"How could you think I wouldn't?" As ill-advised as it was, he stepped forward and cradled her face between his hands. He could see the toll Walfort's illness had taken on her, yet still she was the most beautiful woman he'd ever seen. Her courage, her strength, were all too visible. She was battered but not defeated.

"How could this have happened?" he asked.

Looking momentarily lost, she shook her head. "I don't know. His body is poisoned."

"Someone is trying to kill him?"

"No, no. His physician says that Walfort's body has turned on him. It has stopped functioning properly. He is inflicted with a deadly fever. There is no hope."

He slid his hands down her arms and took her hands into his. "I've brought my physician, Dr. Roberts. He's excellent. We'll see what he has to say."

More tears welled in her eyes. "I'm so glad you're here. I didn't know whether to send for you—"

"Of course you should have."

"He would have it no other way. I don't know why he was so insistent that you bring him his jewels. I don't know what he expects to do with them."

"He hasn't told you about them, then?"

"No. I don't even know what kind they are. Rubies. Emeralds. Diamonds. What does it matter?"

It mattered.

"Ainsley?" Walfort croaked. "Is that you, old man?"

Ainsley gave Jayne's hands a final squeeze of reassurance before he strode over to the bed. Jayne followed, her footfalls soft until she was standing at its foot, one hand wrapped around a post as though she required the support to remain upright. How difficult this had to be for her. Walfort looked bloody awful. His skin had an unnatural pallor to it. His eyes held no life at all. "Always in want of attention, aren't you, Walfort?"

His cousin released a weak laugh. "I was always the more interesting of us."

"Still are."

"Did you bring them? Did you bring my jewels?"

"They're here. I left them in the coach."

"I need to see them."

He glanced quickly to the side, to Jayne, before turning his attention back to Walfort. "You haven't told Jayne about them."

"No. You do . . . that. You owe me . . . that." His breathing rattled, each breath labored. "It's your fault, you know. Your fault I'm here."

"Walfort, no," Jayne pleaded. "Don't say these things."

"It's all right, Jayne," Ainsley said. "Let him have his say." He deserved the verbal lashing. So he stoically held his friend and cousin's gaze.

"See? He knows it's true. Just as I've been telling you. It's his fault." Walfort struggled to push himself up, and Ainsley stepped forward to help him, to settle him back against the pillows. "If only you'd given me the bloody reins, I wouldn't have been forced to take them from you."

Ainsley froze, everything within him stilling. Walfort seemed to sink farther into the feather pillows. "You wouldn't give me the bloody reins," he went on. "You weren't going fast enough. I wanted to go faster. I told you to give me the bloody reins. But no. You had to always be so damned responsible. You said we'd kill ourselves." Walfort released a strangled sob. "It seems I bloody well have."

Staring at him, Ainsley shook his head. "I was driving us—"

"Not fast enough to suit me. I grabbed the reins . . . shoved you off."

Ainsley fought to remember, but it was all a blur, the events encased in a fog of liquor.

"I lost my balance," Walfort continued. "Fell forward. I still remember the terror of it, the agony . . . and then nothing. I was so grateful for the nothing."

Ainsley felt as though he'd been bludgeoned. He thought he should have felt immense relief but all he felt was betrayed. "All these years, I was shackled to the guilt."

"As well you should be. If only you'd gone faster."

"Walfort, surely this is your fever talking," Jayne said softly. "None of this can be true. You could not be that cruel."

"I am on fire, but I am lucid. He would not give me the reins, so I snatched them away."

He sounded like a petulant child who was being denied his favorite sweet.

His shoulders shook as he began coughing. Jayne hurried over, put her arm around him and lifted him until the spasms stopped. Then she gave him a drink of water and gently lay him back down.

He rolled his head to look at Ainsley again. "Please. My jewels. Bring them to me."

Jayne patted a damp cloth over his brow. "What sort of jewels are they that they are so important to you?"

"They are my children."

* * *

Standing at the window, unconsciously rubbing her hand over her swollen abdomen, Jayne gazed out on the drive where Ainsley's coach waited. Still stunned by Walfort's revelation, she watched in a sort of detached manner as Ainsley assisted a woman to the ground. From this distance, she appeared close to Jayne's own age. She was fair. Blond beneath the hat, Jayne thought.

Her heart constricted painfully as Ainsley lifted out a young girl, and then another even smaller. She didn't know why she expected them to be older, so much older. Born years before she and Walfort married. Surely it was only the distance separating her from them that made them look so small and young.

Dr. Roberts exited next. The one who had seen to her after she fainted at Ainsley's ball. Perhaps he could save Walfort. They were due a miracle. But then she thought of the child she now carried. Another miracle. How many was one family allowed?

She moved to stand by the foot of the bed, her shoulders back, her hands clasped tightly and perched on her stomach, her chin held high. She knew her duty. She would be an accommodating hostess.

"Do you hate me?" Walfort asked.

With her eyes on the door, she ignored his question and asked one of her own, "They are quite young. The girls. What are their names?"

"Mary and Elizabeth. I named them after Henry the VIII's daughters. When I married you, you became Jayne Seymour, his only true love, if history is to be believed."

His words made no sense. They were little more than gibberish.

"When did you name them?" she asked.

His chuckle was brief, too much effort. "When they were born. When do you think?"

"When were they born?" It sounded like another woman's voice asking the question with no emotion whatsoever. A steady cadence.

The patter of footsteps in the hallway kept him silent. Or perhaps he'd never intended to answer at all. Jayne took a deep breath to steady her nerves and wondered distractedly if this was how Anne Boleyn dreaded the coming moments as she was led to her execution. She felt as though the ax were coming down on all she'd ever believed about her marriage.

Her first thought upon gazing on the woman who came through the door with Ainsley was that her features were quite plain. She was the sort who would be unnoticed in a group of ladies. Then Jayne chastised herself for so ungracious a thought. Obviously on some level she appealed to Walfort. Her dark blue traveling dress indicated that she was either of a high station or she had a benefactor who paid a pretty penny for her clothing. If that benefactor remained Walfort, Jayne did not wish to know it.

Ainsley guided the woman to Jayne. "Lady Walfort, allow me to introduce Miss Madeline Brown."

The woman took a deep curtsy. "My lady." Her voice was soft, cultured.

"Miss Brown, I believe my husband wishes to have a moment with you. I will leave you in privacy."

She was almost to the door when the woman exclaimed, "Oh, Wally!" and the girls—brown-haired, brown-eyed, his eyes—were racing past her crying, "Papa! Papa!"

She stepped into the hallway, well aware of Ainsley behind her. She greeted the physician, forcing words through a throat that refused to work properly. "We shall give them a few moments," she said to the doctor, "and then you may examine the marquess. If you'll be so kind as to excuse me, I'm in dire need of some air."

"Of course, my lady."

She could barely see the stairs through the tears that had gathered. She felt Ainsley wrap his hand around her arm.

"Careful," he cautioned.

She gave him leave to guide her down the stairs and escort her into the garden. She broke free of his hold as soon as she was on a familiar path. "How long have you known about his 'jewels'?"

He hesitated before saying somberly, "As long as they have been with him."

She refused to ask exactly how long that was, but it seemed she was not yet ready to stop tormenting herself completely. "The smallest girl. How old is she?"

"Jayne—"

"I can guess but I'd rather know for sure."

"She recently turned three."

"If I had not lost my first child, he—or she—would be a little over three now. So he was seeing that woman while I was with child."

"Jayne, don't torment yourself."

"Was he with Miss Brown the night of the accident?"

"Jayne, nothing is to be gained—"

She spun around to confront him. She could see the agony of the truth on his face, in his eyes. But she had to hear the words. "Was . . . he?"

He hesitated and the muscle in his cheek ticked before he replied, "Yes."

She dug her fingernails into her palms, needing the discomfort so she could force back the tears. "So you were both not only drinking and gambling—as you told me—but fornicating as well."

"Yes."

"I thought he loved me. Or at least had a care for me." She wound her arms around her chest. "Oh, it hurts so bad."

He reached for her, and she stepped back.

"Do not touch me. You knew. You knew he did not honor his vows. Why did you not tell me?"

"No good would have come of you knowing the truth. It would have only made you miserable." He shrugged. "And he could no longer be unfaithful. He does love you, Jayne."

"But not enough. And you, by holding silent, you condoned his actions. My God, with your reputation with the ladies, you no doubt celebrated his poor behavior. Women are nothing to you."

"That's not true. You—"

"I don't wish to hear it. Your excuses, your poetic words, your sweet gestures. They are all designed with one goal in mind. I fell for them. I allowed you and my husband to convince me that a situation existed where vows mattered not at all. Everything, everything was a lie."

She walked away from him, needing time alone. He must have sensed what she required, because he did not follow. She retreated to the bench where she'd wept so often after Walfort's accident. Before she wept for all he lost, all the dreams shattered by the accident. Now she wept because he had betrayed her and their vows. With Ainsley's help, he convinced her to betray herself and *her* vows. Vows that she now understood had only ever meant anything to her.

It hurt. It hurt so terribly badly. More so, because Ainsley had been complicit in the deceptions. She had trusted him with her body, her dreams, and a portion of her heart. And he had known, always known, that everything she treasured was a lie.

Dr. Roberts had examined Walfort and declared him beyond help. Ainsley had arranged for him to return home then. Walfort's own physician would be seeing to his remaining needs.

In spite of Walfort's revelations that afternoon, Ainsley's chest ached as he leaned against the bedpost and studied his sleeping friend. He'd told Jayne that he could keep vigil for a while to give her a bit of a reprieve. Miss Brown was putting the girls to bed.

Jayne had strolled through the garden for more than an hour. Ainsley had wanted to stay with her but he sensed that she wanted to be as far from him as possible. Discovering that Walfort had a mistress was a horrible blow. He'd seen the devastation on her face when he revealed what the jewels were. Then he'd seen the stoicism with which she greeted the woman. Her courage, her strength, her determination—never in his life had he admired a woman more.

Jayne was correct. With his silence, he had condoned Walfort's actions all those years ago. Why had he not beaten him to a pulp back then? Why had he not fought to make him realize that his greatest treasure was his wife?

Walfort's eyes fluttered open, and Ainsley said, "You lied."

Walfort stared at him.

"About the reins. Taking them from me."

"No."

"Why would you let me believe all these years that my reckless handling of the horses resulted in the accident?"

"Because, my friend, guilt is a very valuable currency, and I needed to ensure you watched over my jewels."

"I would have watched over them regardless," he said.

"I had to ensure it, old boy."

He didn't want to broach the subject, it was none of his concern, but suspicions lurked and he was disappointed enough with Walfort at that moment to pry. "The girls knew who you were."

"Naturally."

"How? When did you see them?"

Walfort rolled his head to the side, gazed toward the windows, and Ainsley wondered if he sought to escape.

"When, Walfort?"

"When I would go to Harrogate for the waters. Maddie and the girls would meet me there."

"Jayne deserved much better."

"And now she will have it. I will not be in the way."

Ainsley felt as though he'd been bludgeoned. All the fury dissipated. He moved closer so his friend could see the earnestness in his eyes. "Dammit, Walfort, I don't want her, not like this. For all your faults, I have always loved you as a brother."

"You were always the better man. I thought if I were in your company often enough that you'd rub off on me. I pray to God that I did not rub off on you."

"Fight this thing, blast you. You can defeat it."

Walfort shook his head. "No, I can't." He motioned Ainsley nearer. "See after Jayne and the child. It will be difficult for them. And promise me that you will take care of my jewels. See that they are provided for. Find them suitable husbands."

"You are a manipulator to the end, aren't you?"

Walfort gave him a weary smile. "I shall take that as your assent."

At that moment Walfort appeared at peace as he drifted off to sleep. Ainsley cursed him to perdition, but he knew he would fulfill these latest requests.

Jayne sat in a chair beside the bed, her hand curled around one of Walfort's. He was fevered, muttering in his sleep. Every now and then he would mumble "Maddie." Or Elizabeth. Or Mary.

She despised the way that she waited for him to utter her name. It was only one syllable, for Christ's sake. It required only one movement of his jaw. She couldn't help but believe that her entire marriage had been a farce. Perhaps her entire life. She wanted to rail against him, pound her fists into his chest; she wanted him to live so she could reconcile her emotions, so she could discover why she'd not been enough.

In spite of it all, she didn't wish death upon him. She knew now that he wasn't hers. He never had been. How could she have been such a fool?

The babe rolled from one side of her stomach to another, as though sensing her stress and striving to bring her comfort. He was such an active bugger. He would be active, like his father. Now he would grow up knowing no father. Not the one who had intended to claim him or the one who had given him life.

"I want to thank you for your kindness to me and my girls," Miss Brown said.

Jayne glanced over to the other side of the bed, where the woman was sitting on its edge, gently mopping Walfort's brow.

"Not all wives would be as accepting of a mistress," she continued.

"He asked for you," Jayne said with as little emotion as she could muster. "I must assume he cares for you."

"I met him in a bookshop. The book I wanted was on a shelf I could not reach, so he retrieved it for me. Our hands touched, and it fostered a spark between us that I cannot explain. We walked to a nearby park and talked for hours."

Jayne didn't want to hear this, she didn't care, and yet she was morbidly interested. Why not dig the knife more deeply into her heart? "What did you talk of?" she asked.

Miss Brown released a small laugh. "I can't remember now. We always had something to talk about. I probably should not say, but . . . I visited here while you were away on holiday. The girls and I."

Jayne didn't want to contemplate that he'd arranged her leaving for Blackmoor so as to provide an opportunity to be with Miss Brown. But all of his actions were suspect now. Still, she heard herself say, "I'm glad."

Miss Brown looked at her, her eyes blinking in confusion.

"I would not have wanted him to be lonely while I was gone," Jayne explained. "Especially as now it seems he hasn't much more time to be here."

"He always spoke so highly of you. I thought I should have been jealous that he had such deep feelings for you as well. But he would not have tolerated that. The jealousy. I knew I would like you before I met you. Under other circumstances perhaps we'd have been friends. Or not. My father was a clergyman. He did not approve of my choices. I've not seen him in years. He doesn't even know he has granddaughters."

So many choices that led to such sadness. Jayne wondered if they were all worth it. Walfort had been an adulterer, and he made an adulterer of her. Yet as the babe kicked once more, she knew she could not regret her sins. She'd made the decision expecting Walfort to live to a ripe old age. He'd made his proposal expecting the same.

Walfort opened his eyes and smiled softly at her. "Jayne."

At last, her name on his lips. She squeezed his hand. "Would you like some water?"

"No." He rolled his head to the side and smiled lovingly at Miss Brown. With so little effort, he communicated so much, and Jayne wondered if she'd ever really known him. "I need a private moment with my wife."

"Of course, my darling." Miss Brown kissed him on the cheek before leaving the room.

"Do you hate me so very much?" he asked when she was gone.

Slowly, she shook her head, knowing she should fight back the tears but suspecting they were more honest than any words she could speak. "Why, Walfort, why?"

"We cannot control our hearts, Jayne."

"But we can control our actions." She gave her head a brisk shake. "My apologies. I do not wish to torment you."

"Strange," he rasped. "I felt so guilty because I had children and you did not. I thought if I could arrange for you to have a child, then . . . the guilt would ease. Yet instead I leave you to raise it on your own. Even when I strive to be thoughtful, I'm a complete cad."

She had no response.

"I was an unfaithful bastard," he continued. "I love Madeline, but she is a commoner. I needed your dowry and I enjoyed your company. It shames me to say it . . . but I did not begin to love you until after the accident. Your loyalty and faith humbled me. You made me a better man than I was, made me wish I had been a better man before. Ainsley is that better man. He always has been."

She wrapped both her hands around his and held his gaze. "In spite of all the revelations that have come about today . . . I still love you."

He closed his eyes on a sigh. "Then I shall die a most fortunate man."

Chapter 25

Death came in the hushed stillness of dawn.

With hardly a word spoken, they journeyed to London where Walfort was to be laid to rest. While Ainsley had a servant escort Miss Brown and her girls to their London home, he accompanied Jayne to Walfort's residence. Once there, mourning cards were sent out, and soon the ladies of society descended like ravenous ravens to flutter around Jayne. He knew they sought only to comfort her, but it was a task he would have preferred had been reserved for himself.

But since their encounter in the garden, she'd not spoken to him except when necessary. She was incredibly formal, unnaturally stoic. He'd heard Miss Brown sobbing uncontrollably after Walfort's passing but had yet to see Jayne shed a tear. And that worried him.

Still, Ainsley admired Jayne's dedication to ensuring that Walfort's funeral was one befitting his title and station. The glass-sided hearse and four, carrying the mahogany casket, traveled slowly through the people-lined streets on its way to St. Paul's, where Walfort would be entombed. Walfort's riderless horse plodded along behind it. With shutters drawn, a dozen black carriages that housed the male members of the family and close friends followed. Black ostrich plumes fluttered in the slight breeze.

Following the interment, the gentlemen returned to the residence. Adhering to the custom that ladies not attend funerals, the society matrons waited with Jayne in the front parlor. As Ainsley passed by on his way to taking the gentlemen to the library for libations, he caught sight of Jayne with women sitting around her, his mother holding her hand. Her pale pallor concerned him. He wanted to lift her into his arms and carry her upstairs to her bedchamber, away from the madness.

Instead he pushed forth to the library, where footmen had already begun pouring drinks for the guests. When all had a glass in hand, Ainsley lifted his and an expectant hush filled the room.

"To Walfort. He was courageous in all things, met all of life's challenges head on. You will be missed, old friend."

"Hear! Hear!"

As Ainsley downed the whiskey, Lord Sheffield said, "At least we can all be assured that there will be fox hunting when we join him. I daresay, he'll see to it that all is put to rights in that regard."

Another toast followed, more whiskey was swallowed, and quiet conversation and laughter ensued as the gentlemen began to reminisce about Walfort. Ainsley wandered over to where Westcliffe and Stephen were talking. Now that he knew the truth of their parentage, it amazed him that he'd not suspected before. Westcliffe was dark-haired, like his sire, and Stephen was blond, fair as a summer afternoon. Westcliffe's eyes were brown, almost black, and Stephen's were blue.

"The arrangements for Walfort were nicely done," Stephen said quietly.

Ainsley nodded, distracted by the gentleman he'd spotted nearby talking with Lord Sheffield. "Do my eyes deceive me or is that my cousin Ralph Seymour talking with Sheffield?"

Both his brothers looked discreetly in the direction Ainsley had indicated. "I'd say so, yes," Westcliffe murmured. "He's next in line for Walfort's title, isn't he?"

"Quite. Does he look to be a man going mad with syphilis?"

Westcliffe and Stephen both looked at him as though he were the one going mad. Had Walfort lied about that as well? Damn him! The man was turning out to be a master manipulator.

"Think I'll have a word." But getting there meant running the gauntlet of those who wished to offer their condolences. It was no secret that he and Walfort had been close. So he graciously acknowledged the kind words that were spoken as he wended his way toward his target. He wasn't quite there when he heard Sheffield say, " . . . bated breath to discover if Lady Walfort will deliver a son."

"I don't know if the courts will care one way or the other. My cousin was paralyzed. If he got her with child I'll eat my hat."

"Shall I fetch it for you?" Ainsley asked.

Ralph jerked around so quickly that the whiskey in his glass nearly sloshed over the sides. "Cousin. You're not on the branch of the tree that's in line for the title so perhaps you've not given it any thought."

"But it's obvious you have. If you're wise, you'll hold your tongue on the matter."

"Is that a threat?"

"It's a promise. Lady Walfort has suffered enough during the past few years and she deeply mourns the passing of her husband."

"That does not mean he got her with a child. I've heard rumors that you danced with her, that you were seen walking alone with her in the garden."

"As a favor to Walfort, I attended her where he could not."

"Does that include her bed?"

His fist shot up so fast that the pain was ricocheting from his knuckles to his shoulder before he even realized he'd delivered the blow to Ralph's chin. His cousin dropped to the floor with an unceremonious thud. Completely out. He wasn't going to get up any time soon.

Westcliffe and Stephen were instantly at Ainsley's side.

"Looks as though Cousin Ralph has had a bit too much to drink," Westcliffe said, signaling for two footmen. "Get him to his carriage."

Ainsley looked over to see Sheffield grinning like a loon.

"At long last, I'll have a nonboring tale to tell," he said triumphantly.

"I'd keep it to yourself, Sheffield," Ainsley warned.

"Of course, old boy." But he was fairly bouncing on the balls of his feet as he shouldered his way through the men who'd gathered around at the commotion.

"Apologies," he said to the gentlemen. "I could not let an insult to Walfort go unchallenged. Drink up."

Westcliffe took Ainsley's arm and led him to a distant corner of the room, Stephen following in their wake.

"What the devil was that all about?" Westcliffe asked once they were away from prying ears.

"He questioned the legitimacy of Jayne's child."

"You must know everyone's questioning it."

"It doesn't matter. She was with child when Walfort died. The courts will recognize it as his."

His words were spoken with too much vehemence. Both of his brothers were studying him as though only seeing him for the first time.

"It's none of my concern—" Westcliffe began.

"No, it's not," Ainsley assured him.

"Good Christ, is it yours?" Westcliffe asked, his lips barely moving.

"It's Jayne's."

He left his brothers staring after him. In the length of a single heartbeat everything had changed.

"You are so fortunate to be with child," Lady Inwood said. "You should pray for a son. Then you will not be dependent upon Ralph Seymour's mercies."

Sitting in a corner of the parlor, surrounded by ladies, Jayne felt as though there was absolutely no air to breathe.

"Ainsley has certainly been a godsend, hasn't he?" Lady Sheffield asked. "He's handled so many of the arrangements."

Was it her imagination that she heard insinuations in their voices? Why could they not leave her in peace?

"Will you return to Herndon Hall now?" someone asked, a voice she didn't recognize.

"No, no, you must remain in London," Lady Inwood insisted. "To be a widow and with child? You need us to see you through it."

Jayne was somewhat relieved to see the Duchess of Ainsley step forward. Although she had relinquished the title when she married Leo, she was still addressed as such and shown the deference that came with holding the title for so long. "I believe," the duchess said, "that what Lady Walfort needs is to do what is best for her. She also requires rest. Surely it is past time for all you dear ladies to take your leave."

She began ushering them from the room, but each circled back to give Jayne one last message of condolence and reassurance that they could be called upon if needed. In the entry hallway they were soon joined by their husbands. Then finally, at last, silence.

Jayne saw the shoes first, black and polished to a shine. Slowly, her gaze traveled over the black trousers, the black waistcoat and jacket, until it settled on green eyes.

"A bloody awful day," Ainsley said.

She drew comfort from the words, words she'd wanted to say. "Yes."

"My mother, Leo, and I will stay here through the night in case there is anything you need."

"That's not necessary. I shall be alone in all the days to come. I might as well begin getting used to it."

"Not tonight. You need to eat, Jayne."

"I have no appetite."

"The babe does."

She placed her hand against her side. "I think people are gossiping. They don't believe it's his. And now he's not here to convince them. Rather bad timing, that."

"It doesn't matter what others think or believe. It only matters what you want."

Only she didn't know.

He had food brought to her on a tray. While she ate, he told her about the grandeur of the funeral procession, all the people lining the streets. Walfort had gone out in style. She thought he would have been pleased. In spite of all the revelations at the end of his life, she had cared for him too long not to do right by him in the end.

After she'd eaten as much as she could stomach, she allowed the duchess to escort her to her bedchamber, where a bath was prepared. She wanted to be alone, but the duchess remained, talking constantly of nonsensical things as though she felt a need to fill the hovering silence.

Once she was in her nightdress, Jayne strolled to the nursery that she'd begun furnishing for the first time she was with child. Sitting in the rocker, she was finally, at long last, alone with her sorrow.

In the library, Ainsley looked up as his mother walked into the room and went to the table holding several decanters. She poured herself a brandy and sat in a chair across from him, one beside Leo, who was keeping Ainsley company—even if it entailed little more than drinking with him.

"How is she?" he asked.

"I'm most worried about her. She's presently sitting in the nursery and rocking. But all afternoon and evening, she does not weep nor wail. It's not natural. It cannot be healthy for the child."

His stomach clenched. He couldn't bear the thought of Jayne going through another loss such as that. Would she even survive it? He stood. "I'll speak with her."

He took two steps before his mother spoke up again. "Ainsley?"

Stopping, he glanced back at her. He knew the sorrow on her face had nothing to do with the mourning of Walfort.

"Have you considered, my son, that you should marry the girl?"

Far too many times to count.

"It's customary for a wife to mourn for two years," he reminded her.

"A year would suffice, but in this instance . . . she carries your child, Ainsley. Marry her and claim it."

"The terms of our arrangement were that this child would be Jayne's and Walfort's."

"Forgive my indelicacy but he is dead."

"It does not change the fact that he boasted to all of London that he sired this child. His passing complicated matters. I cannot deny that. But it does not relieve me of my promise not to claim this child."

"Must you be so blasted noble? It grows wearisome."

"I took everything from him, Mother. I will not take what was to be his child. Besides I doubt Jayne would have me."

"She never struck me as a fool."

He almost smiled at the clipped edge that accompanied her words. In her eyes, her sons could do no wrong. He wondered if Jayne would feel the same about hers. He suspected she would. With only a nod, he left his mother then, knowing she would not follow.

It was strange to walk through the somber residence, to compare it with the joviality that abounded at Herndon Hall the last time he was there for the fox hunt. Death brought a pall over everything. It didn't help matters that none of the clocks released a single tick or tock—having been stopped at the hour of Walfort's passing—and all the mirrors were draped in black crepe. He made his way up the stairs to the nursery.

At the door, he hesitated. It was closed. He should knock, but if he announced himself, she might not invite him in. With a deep sigh, he opened the door. The room was dark, save for a single lamp that burned low. He heard the heartrending weeping, and it took him a moment to locate her. She was sitting on the floor, pressed in a distant corner, her face buried in her hands, her rounded shoulders shaking with the force of her sobs. His courageous Jayne, alone with her sorrow. She would not succumb in front of his mother. But at least she was able to grieve in private.

He considered leaving, but he could no more abandon her now than he could cease to breathe. Quietly, he moved over to her and crouched, his knees popping to announce his arrival.

As though only just noticing his presence, she began to roughly swipe at her cheeks. "Please go away, Ainsley."

He grabbed her wrists to still her actions, and she jerked free. "Please leave me in peace."

"Are you in peace, Jayne? It hardly sounds like it. I know you mourn him—"

"I mourn so much more than his passing. It was all a lie. He made a mockery of our life here. He loved someone else."

"He loved you."

"He did not! And you knew!" She slammed her balled fist into his shoulder. "You knew! I thought . . . I thought you had a care for me."

"I do have a care for you." *I love you*, but now was not the time to tell her the truth of those words.

"No, you don't. You would not have kept his secrets from me. The guilt over what we did gnawed at me. As much as I wanted this child, I betrayed everything I held dear. It was so easy for the two of you because you place no value on loyalty, on vows. I thought I knew you, but the man I knew would not have condoned what Walfort did. You are cut of the same cloth. Please leave me."

"I am not like him. I would never betray you."

"You already have." She hit him again. And again.

His heart died a bit with each blow. He had never meant to bring her this pain—even as he'd known when the proposition was first made that she would have to betray herself to embrace it.

He wrapped his arms around her to stop her flailing and rocked her. "Easy, Jayne, easy, sweetheart. You don't want to hurt the child."

Her sobs broke free, racking her body. "I wish I'd said no, Jayne. I swear to you, I wish I had."

"I hurt so bad, Ainsley."

"I know."

"Why did he have to leave me now?"

And he knew in spite of the betrayals, she still loved Walfort.

"It's all right, Jayne. It'll be all right."

He didn't know how the bloody hell it would be, but he would find a way.

Chapter 26

Two weeks had passed and Jayne's lethargy seemed to worsen. She couldn't seem to decipher her feelings regarding Walfort or Ainsley. The only feelings she truly trusted were those she felt for the babe. She knew she should return to Herndon Hall, but she seemed unable to work up the energy required to order the servants about.

With her elbow resting on the sill, and her chin propped in her hand, she sat at the window in her bedchamber gazing out on what she could see of London at night. Which wasn't much. Trees blocked her view of the street. She saw the lighted drive but knew it would remain empty. The Duchess of Greystone was hosting a ball this evening. It was always well attended, so Jayne knew no one would call this evening.

From time to time since the funeral a few of the ladies made a morning call, but it was always awkward, and they were all so incredibly boring. Except for Lady Inwood, who had no qualms whatsoever about spreading gossip. She'd even offered to let Jayne join in the wagering surrounding Ainsley. It seemed he'd made it

known early on that he intended to select a wife this
Season, and while he had yet to attend a ball, speculation was high that he had already made his selection.
Jayne did not want to acknowledge how it unsettled her
to know that he was searching for a wife.

She certainly had no desire to marry him, doubted
she would ever marry again. She heard the clatter of
horses' hooves and the whir of wheels on the cobble-
stone. A coach approached. As it drew near, she recognized the crest on the door. Ainsley.

Her heart leaped, and she fought to calm it. But it
increased its tempo as he stepped out, obviously on an
outing, dressed in a swallow-tailed jacket. In one hand
he held his top hat and walking stick.

He disappeared from sight, and she refrained from
opening the window to lean out and strive to catch another glimpse of him. He'd not visited since the night of
the funeral, the night he held her while she wept. The
night, to her immense embarrassment now, she lashed
out at him. A thousand times she considered sending a
note of apology for her outburst, because she missed
him. As much as she didn't want to acknowledge it,
she did. Often since leaving Blackmoor she thought
of him—always with guilt. All of her thoughts should
have been on Walfort, although she now knew most of
his were not on her.

The knock on her bedchamber door had her coming
to her feet. "Yes."

Lily stepped inside. "His Grace, the Duke of Ainsley
would like a word."

She felt so drab and dour, already in her nightdress.
But for her this Season there would be no balls. "Tell
him I'm not at home. No." She shook her head. That

wouldn't stop him. "Tell him I'm already abed . . . no." Drat him! "Send him up."

"Yes, m'lady."

Jayne moved over to the sitting area, positioning herself so a sofa was between her and the door, would be between her and Ainsley. She didn't want to give the impression that she was extremely glad of his presence. It was inappropriate. A woman in mourning was supposed to be sedate, not anxious for her caller to arrive.

When he strode in, she thought she'd never seen a more handsome man. Based on his expression of horror, however, he'd never seen a more disheveled woman.

"Your Grace, how good of you to call."

"For God's sake, Jayne, after all we've been through don't be so damned formal."

"It's late and this is my bedchamber. Formality is required. You appear to be on your way to a ball."

"I was, but I changed my mind when I saw all the carriages lined up. I wasn't in the mood for a tedious night." He set his hat and stick on a chair near the door before prowling toward her.

"You're near enough," she said when it became obvious the sofa would not serve as an obstacle for him.

Thankfully, he did stop, but his gaze wandered over her and she felt it almost like a touch.

"You're not eating," he said.

"I am . . . just not very much. I suppose your mother told you that." She dropped by each afternoon for a few moments.

"I don't need her to tell me what is quite obvious. I daresay, you're not sleeping either."

"Some . . . I—" She sank down into the chair. "I don't know what's wrong with me."

"You're grieving."

"I don't know if that's it, Ainsley. I feel nothing."

He studied her for a moment before saying, "I've come to invite you to have dinner with me tomorrow evening at my residence."

"I'm in mourning. It would be entirely inappropriate."

"Jayne, you need a few hours away from all this. Wear your widow's weeds. I'll bring my carriage 'round at half past seven. I'll carry you out if I must."

"Ainsley—"

"Jayne."

She wanted to shriek. She didn't know if she'd ever known a more obstinate man. Yet neither could she deny how lovely it would be to be with someone who didn't treat her as though she might break at any moment.

"Very well," she said petulantly. He must be given the impression she wasn't giving in too easily.

"Good." He removed his jacket and laid it over the arm of the sofa.

She sat up straighter. "What are you doing?"

"Going to ensure that you sleep well tonight."

"Ainsley—"

"Jayne." Reaching into his waistcoat pocket, he removed a small vile.

"What is it?"

"Oils. I'm going to rub your feet. It'll help you relax."

"No." She tucked her feet beneath the chair. "You'll start with my feet and then you'll journey upward and . . . it would be entirely inappropriate."

"I promise I will not venture higher than your ankles."

She shook her head. "My ankles are swollen. You don't need to see them."

"Move to the sofa. Or better yet, the bed."

"Do you not listen to a thing I say?"

"What are you afraid of, Jayne?"

That I'm swollen and miserable and that you'll be repulsed by me.

"I'm so sorry," she blurted.

He furrowed his brow. "For what, pray tell?"

"For lashing out at you . . . the last time you were here."

"I didn't take your words to heart. I know how difficult all of this has been for you."

"Unbearable sometimes."

"So tonight I'll give you something pleasant to take into your dreams."

He held out his hand, enticing her with those long, strong fingers. "Come along, Jayne. Move to the sofa."

Against her better judgment she did as he bade. When she was settled in the corner, pillows at her back, he sat at the opposite end and lifted her bare feet to his lap. Mesmerized, she watched as he poured several drops of oil onto his palm before setting the bottle aside. Then his palm kneaded her sole.

"Oh, dear God."

"Nice?" he asked.

"Wickedly wonderful. You've done this before."

"I once knew a lady who knew a great deal about the sensuous arts."

"And you did not keep her?"

"She was not mine to keep. Close your eyes."

She did, as his fingers worked their magic over the balls of her feet. "Tell me a story, something from your youth."

"My youth. Well, I was a very clever lad."

His melodious voice droned on as he told her about playing a game of hiding with Claire. The deep timbre and his constant massaging of her feet lured her away to a place of no troubles, no grief, no sorrow.

She awoke from a deep sleep with only a bit of sunlight dancing into the room. She didn't remember climbing into bed, nor could she remember the last time she felt so rested. She was beneath the covers but aware of a weight on her hip. Ainsley's hand cupped over her. He lay on top of the covers, his waistcoat gone but his shirt and trousers still in place. He must have carried her to bed. How tired she must have been not to stir when he moved her.

His long dark eyelashes rested on his cheeks. She did hope her child would inherit those. In truth, there was nothing about him that she didn't want to see in the child. She had missed him so. She hadn't wanted to admit it, but the truth mocked her now because it was so lovely to wake up with him in her bed.

Slowly he opened his eyes. "Good morning."

His voice was rough from sleep, stirring her in ways she should not be stirred, reminding her of other mornings.

"Lady Inwood told me that you had intended to find a wife this Season."

"Hmm. Yes, I'd considered it. I still might." He gave her a devilish smile.

"The ladies are wagering, you know . . . on whom it will be."

"So are the gents, from what I hear. Even my brothers, blast them."

"Who do they think it will be?"

"They've both chosen different ladies. They are both wrong. One lady talks so quietly that I must always bend over in order to get near enough to hear what she is saying. Marriage to her would give me an aching back before too long."

Jayne laughed lightly. "And the other?"

"The opposite problem. When she begins to speak, I must pull back in order not to go deaf from her cater-wauling. Makes me appear to have some sort of twitch."

"I had no idea that the wife hunt was so troublesome."

"It is quite the bother. Perhaps you should marry me to spare me the horror of it."

He was teasing, surely. Still, she shook her head. "I think I shall be like your mother. A woman of means who can do as she pleases."

"I would always allow you to do as you please."

"Oh, Ainsley, you don't half tempt me." She rolled into a sitting position and saw the time on the clock on the mantel. "Good God! It's half past ten! If someone sees that your coach—"

"I sent my driver on."

She glanced back at him, and he gave her an innocent shrug. "I never leave my coach outside a lady's residence."

"And if I'd not admitted you?"

"I'd have walked, caught a hansom. I'm resourceful." He pushed himself up, leaned in and kissed her cheek before she could stop him. Then he was out of the bed and crossing the room to retrieve his waistcoat, neck-cloth, and jacket. "Let's have some breakfast, shall we?"

It was the oddest thing, but she was suddenly quite ravenous. "You must leave immediately afterward."

"You have my word."

"You may borrow one of the rooms if you wish to freshen up."

After bowing, he took his leave. When she reached for the bellpull, she realized she was smiling.

She looked better, much better, this morning. The circles were still there, but not as dark. He would see to it that she slept well tonight, so perhaps tomorrow they would be gone completely. And she was eating. It was ridiculous the pleasure that realization brought him.

She wore black. He wanted to see her in red.

"How long do you intend to stay in London?" he asked.

Her brow furrowed, she glanced up at him. "I'm not sure. Another week or so I suppose. Not much longer. I rather dread returning to Herndon Hall."

"Come to Grantwood."

With a sigh, she shook her head. "Ainsley—"

"You have few memories there."

"You do know it is quite rude to interrupt."

"My apologies. But I can decipher the objection written on your face. Hear me out."

"Extend to you a courtesy you do not extend to me? Why ever should I?"

"You are irascible when you are with child."

"You are stubborn," she said.

"Quite."

"Perhaps we'll discuss it during dinner this evening."

"So you will join me?"

"Did you ever doubt it?"

His answer to her was merely a grin. He'd not been

teasing when he suggested she marry him, but based on her expression and response, she was still too fragile to consider such a proposal. He had won her over once before. He could do it again. It required only a bit of patience.

Chapter 27

Jayne could hardly believe the excitement that thrummed through her as she waited for Ainsley to arrive. A night away from the oppressive house. She needed it. She knew that she did.

She rather wished she didn't have to wear black, but it helped to remind her to remain somber. Tonight was simply a break from the mourning. It did not remove it all together.

She was sitting in the parlor attempting not to appear anxious when she heard the rap on the front door. Her butler was soon standing in the doorway. "His Grace, the Duke of Ainsley."

He bowed out and Ainsley strode in, so dashing in his swallow-tailed coat that it very nearly took her breath. He'd worn similar clothing last night, but for some reason he appeared even more handsome now. Lest he decide to try to kiss her on the cheek, she lowered her veil.

"I daresay, you didn't have to go to so much bother for dinner with me," she said as she walked over to him.

He extended his arm. "No bother."

She placed her hand on his arm and allowed him to

escort her from the house. "I've actually been looking forward to this," she confessed.

"As have I."

He handed her up into the coach. As she settled onto her seat, he took his place opposite her. The coach lantern was lit, allowing her to see him clearly. She was surprised that he'd not chosen to sit beside her. The last time they journeyed alone in his coach, they'd been so close that a shadow could not have squeezed between them.

As the coach rattled over the cobblestones, she felt compelled to fill the silence. "The air seems to be less cloying tonight."

"It's better in the country."

"Do you not like the city, then?"

"It serves a purpose, but I must confess that when I'm married I shall come to London as little as possible. I prefer the outdoor activities offered by the countryside."

It was no doubt the reason he was so fit and that his skin was so bronzed.

"What is your favorite sport?" she asked.

"Swimming. I recently had a small pool built at Grantwood. If you come to visit, I shall teach you how to swim."

She imagined the slickness of their wet bodies, gliding over each other. "Right now, I would no doubt sink straightaway to the bottom."

He grinned. "I doubt it."

Although the curtains were drawn on the coach and she couldn't see the passing buildings, it did seem that they'd been traveling for some time now. "I didn't think your residence was so far."

"We'll dine at my residence, but I have a little surprise planned first."

She'd had far too many surprises of late. "And what would that be?"

"If I tell you, it won't be a surprise."

"This was not what we agreed to."

"Trust me, Jayne. I believe you'll enjoy what I have in mind."

She became aware of the clatter of more vehicles and Ainsley's coach slowing. "We're in the thick of it."

"You may peer out if you like," he said.

She considered it. "I shall wait."

Eventually the coach rolled to a stop. A footman opened the door and Ainsley disembarked before handing her down. They were in an alleyway, but still she recognized the building.

"Covent Garden? Are you mad?"

"It's closed to the public tonight."

"Then why are we here?"

He smiled broadly. "Because it's open to us."

"I'm in mourning. I can't be entertained."

"You shan't be. The actors are atrocious, from what I hear." Taking her hand, he led her toward the steps and a back door, where he knocked.

It opened and a wizened man peered out. "Your Grace!"

"Mr. Smith."

"This way, sir."

They went through back hallways and up two flights of stairs to a private box. Mr. Smith immediately left them. Jayne eased down to a plush chair. "Is this the royal box?"

"No, it's mine," Ainsley said as he joined her.

"How did you manage this?"

"Fairly easily."

"It can't have been easy."

"Let's just say that I'm a man of influence and leave it at that, shall we?"

A man of influence, of wealth, of generosity. A modest man. She'd been so afraid to trust the feelings she had developed for him during the month they were at Blackmoor. Could it be that she had seen the real man there?

Lights lit the stage.

The curtains were drawn back. Jayne leaned forward and allowed the actors to transport her to fair Verona.

He'd considered paying the actors to perform a comedy. He was certain she needed some laughter, but in the end he'd decided that she needed to shed some tears. He'd had a devil of a time leaving her this morning.

He focused on her now. She was giving rapt attention to the performance, almost as though she was on stage with them. Her eyes had been filled with excitement when he arrived at the residence. It had done his heart good. The exorbitant amount he was paying for private use of the theater was money well spent.

Theirs had been an unusual courtship, which began last November—even though he'd not realized it was courtship at the time. Courting her now was a bit more difficult because of all the social mores that insisted she be in seclusion.

As the star-crossed lovers were mourned, he saw the tears begin to trickle down her cheeks. He wanted to wipe them away himself, but tonight he intended to be only a friend. So he handed her his handkerchief and watched as she delicately patted her face.

And then a heart-wrenching sob broke free. He moved in, wrapping his arms around her, turning her into his chest, holding her near. He knew her sorrow had nothing to do with the performance. She was weeping now for all she'd lost and all that faced her.

"I hate this," she said. "I hate that I'm all weepy."

"You've earned the right to cry."

Straightening, she eased back. "It makes me feel weak."

"You're hardly weak."

He could see her studying his features, and he wondered where her thoughts wandered.

Taking a last swipe at her tears, she squared her shoulders. "I suppose we should be off."

"Are you ready for dinner, then?"

"I'm actually quite famished."

Dinner took place in Ainsley's garden, with candles flickering on the small round table, while the gas lamps sent out a soft glow. She could smell the roses, and from time to time she caught a hint of his fragrance.

"You've gone to a great deal of bother," she said.

"Not I. My servants. And I pay them well enough to do it."

These were not the servants at Blackmoor. They had no notion that she'd spent an illicit month with Ainsley, that they'd shared dinners aplenty.

"Do you wonder what they're thinking?" she asked.

"Whatever it is, they'll keep it to themselves."

"You trust so easily."

"And you no longer do."

He was right. She'd thought she understood the state

of her life, only to discover that much was not as she'd thought. "I'm trying."

She realized her words were true. She didn't want to view him through a veil of distrust.

"Have you seen Miss Brown of late?" she asked.

"Yesterday. She and the girls are well."

"I don't understand her. I don't believe I could settle for so little."

"Sometimes little is better than nothing at all."

She studied him for a moment, remembering his heartfelt declaration as she was exiting the coach after leaving the cottage. She could not deny that their time together had created an intimate bond between them, but she was at a loss regarding how to characterize what she felt toward him. She wondered if his words had been merely spurred by the moment, or if they had burst forth from the depths of his soul. She said, "You felt that way at Blackmoor."

"I was grateful for the days we had together. And the nights, of course."

Sometimes it was difficult to separate the days from the nights. Near the end, they'd all simply run together.

"I wonder if she'll ever marry."

"If she does, it'll be by choice. Unlike my mother after her first marriage, Miss Brown is well cared for. Will you ever marry?"

She gave a start at his question and decided a topic change was in order. "I don't know. I hear from the ladies that Lady Louisa Mercer is betrothed."

"It seems walking down the stairs with her did not harm her reputation in the least."

She smiled at the memory. "She was smitten with you."

"But I was not with her. She was far too young. I prefer my women seasoned."

She widened her eyes. "You make them sound like a course during the meal."

"It's not that far off. I like them with a bit of spice to them. I always liked that you were not afraid to speak your mind."

"I was rather tart with you on occasion, as I recall."

"You can be so again, Jayne. Never fear telling me what you are thinking or feeling."

"At this moment, Ainsley, I'm little more than confused. I've enjoyed tonight. And yet I feel guilty about it."

"You shouldn't. You've been a perfect lady and I've been a boring gentleman."

"You're never dull." Realizing that her plate was now empty, she settled back. "I don't believe I can eat another bite. You have a marvelous cook. I can't remember the last time I ate so much. Rather vulgar of me."

He didn't respond. Merely watched her over his wineglass, a satisfied smile on his face.

"Next Season, I shall be able to attend balls. Will you dance with me then?"

"I can dance with you tonight." He stood up and was pulling out her chair before she knew what he was about.

She considered objecting, but who was to see?

Taking her in his arms, he began to hum "Greensleeves" as he swept her over the grass. She heard the laughter, startled to realize it was hers. She felt young again, the way she'd felt on the carousel. How was it that he could make her feel without care and with so little effort?

A fog had begun to roll in and very little moonlight outlined him. But the light from the gas lamps lining the path wove around them. Shadow and light. Shadow and light. Always he was watching her, his gaze never wavering. He held her securely, as though he would never let her go.

Within his arms, she didn't feel ungainly. She didn't feel that she wore widow weeds. It was as though she wore the most lavish of ball gowns. He did that to her. Allowed her to imagine a life other than one she led. When she was with him, she felt as though she lived in a fantasy. It wasn't real; it couldn't last, no matter how much they wished otherwise.

Still, for tonight, she could almost forget all the troubles that waited outside her door.

Chapter 28

"I fear I may have done something very bad."

Studying Miss Brown as she sat in a chair in front of his desk, wringing her hands with such ferocity that he was surprised her skin didn't peel away, Ainsley might have reminded her that it wasn't the first time she'd engaged in naughty behavior—but then he was hardly in a position to cast stones. "Miss Brown, it is not my intention to serve as your conscience, but rather to simply ensure that you and your daughters do not go without."

She gnawed on her lower lip until he feared that she'd draw blood. Obviously she wished to unburden her soul.

"Would you like me to fetch a man of the cloth, so you might confess your sins?"

With tears welling in her eyes, she shook her head. "You've been so good me, Your Grace. I simply wasn't thinking is all."

"I assure you, my dear woman, that you are not the first to have done something without thought and then to later regret it. I daresay I've regretted things that I've done with a great deal of thought."

She almost smiled at that. He saw it in the twitch of her mouth.

"It's just that Mr. Seymour took me off guard with his questions. I wasn't expecting something so personal."

Everything within Ainsley stilled. "Mr. Ralph Seymour?"

"Yes, Your Grace. Wally's cousin. The one who would inherit if . . . well, if Lady Walfort wasn't with child."

"And what, pray tell, did he ask of you?"

"If Lord Walfort had"—more hand wringing, more lip worrying—"bedded me since his accident."

"To which you replied?"

"I said he hadn't." She leaned forward to emphasize the truth of her words. "Because he hadn't."

Of course he hadn't.

"But then, well, my pride spoke up. I didn't want him thinking the fault rested with me so I told him that Wally couldn't . . . that he was broken. I told him how he cried. I shouldn't have done that. I know that now. Mr. Seymour looked so triumphant, so pleased, and I wondered why he would care. And then I thought to myself, 'Silly girl, he wants the titles,' and so I thought I should come tell you straightaway."

It had been a week since he'd danced in the garden with Jayne. Sometimes he thought about asking for her hand in marriage before the babe was born. He did not want his child to have to fight for his place in society, a place that was not rightfully his. This latest news certainly didn't help the situation. "When was this?"

"Two days ago."

Not so straightaway.

He rose to his feet. "Thank you, Miss Brown, for coming forward with the information. I shall have a word with Mr. Seymour and see that he doesn't bother you again."

"He asked if I'd be willing to say it in the courts. I don't want to do that, Your Grace. I don't want to stand in the dock and tell everyone about my life with his lordship. But he said I might have to. I might be forced to."

"I wouldn't worry about it overmuch. Gentlemen often say a lot of things that don't come to pass."

"Wally did," she said wistfully. "Said he'd marry me one day. But then he married someone else, and it was too late for me. By then I loved him. And then there were my girls to consider. Who would favor a woman with two bastard children?"

"Walfort did, and you shall continue to be provided for. You mustn't worry over it, and you must always come to me when matters such as this arise."

"I will, I promise. I'm just so grateful for all you do for me."

She began to wax on poetically, but he didn't have time to let her ramble. He escorted her to the hallway, then turned her over to the footman to see her out. Closing the door behind him, he walked to the window and stared out.

Action needed to be taken and it needed to be taken quickly. For all their sakes.

As much as Ainsley disliked the way Cousin Ralph was going about things, he had to admit that he'd certainly managed to put the color back into Jayne's cheeks. She was pacing her parlor when he arrived. His intent had been to merely ensure that Ralph hadn't come to call. And he hadn't.

But Lady Inwood, an overflowing fountain of gossip, had.

"He's apparently questioning whether this child could be Walfort's and he's making no secret of the fact that he doesn't believe it could be."

"It isn't," Ainsley reminded her.

She stuttered to a stop. Sank into a chair. "This is just bloody awful."

In long strides he crossed the room, knelt before her and took her hands. "The best way for me to protect you and the child is with my name. Marry me, Jayne. Let me claim the child as mine."

"This is not how things were supposed to be."

"No, but they are the way that they are. Walfort is not here to dispute Ralph's claims. You and I know the truth of the situation . . . as does Miss Brown."

Her eyes widened slightly. "He's spoken to her, hasn't he?"

"Yes. He's going to make a stink of things. If we knew this was a girl, the entire matter would be moot. But if it's a boy . . ." He stood up, moved over to the fireplace. No fire burned; he wasn't cold. But he needed the distance. "Everything changed with Walfort's passing. Everything. I want to claim this child as mine—whether it is a boy or a girl. If you set your course on insisting this babe is Walfort's, you will place Miss Brown in a difficult position. Her word against yours."

"I would be believed."

Jayne's station in life, her position as Walfort's widow, gave her some currency, but would it be enough?

"In all likelihood, but why set yourself on this path when there is no need? Marry me, Jayne. Let me provide you with a safe haven from gossip and recognize this child as mine."

She rose from the chair and began to pace. "This is absurd. Walfort is barely gone. Tongues will wag if we marry straightaway without a period of mourning. If you recognize this child, people will have confirmation that I was not faithful. The last remaining vestiges of my reputation will become tattered."

"Better tongues wag now than when this child is born. As for your mourning period, I understand that you need this time. We will have a chaste marriage while you grieve."

She stopped her pacing and rubbed her brow. "I feel as though I'm jumping from the pan into the fire."

Tears welled in her eyes, and he cursed Walfort.

"You are known far and wide as a remarkable lover," she said, "and you are extremely talented at being discreet. I do not want another marriage as I had before."

"I know that his actions hurt you . . . dreadfully. I understand that you view me as guilty by association. But I swear to you that if you marry me, I will never take another woman to my bed."

"Walfort gave the same vows before God."

Damnation but he'd had enough. "I am not Walfort," he ground out through clenched teeth. "And that child is not his. I'll be damned if I'm going to allow it to be brought into this world and have to fight for what is not even rightfully his."

"Allow?" Unfortunately, he could see in her eyes that he'd sparked her anger. "How dare you! You went into this arrangement perfectly willing to give up your child—"

"No! I was never willing, Jayne. It has always torn

at me that this child would not know I was his father. But I shoved my own needs and desires aside because of guilt. Guilt as it turns out that I might not have even deserved."

He stopped, trying to rein in his temper. Too soon. It was too soon to tell her everything. He seriously doubted that she would return his feelings in full measure.

"Jayne, this child should not suffer because of wrongs I was striving to make right."

She lifted her chin in stubbornness. "And it won't. Walfort claimed this child as his in his will. Mr. Ralph Seymour can rant all he wants. It will not change what will be recognized by law."

"What is recognized by law is not always what is recognized by Society."

"Walfort . . . before he died, I promised him this child would be known as his. While he was far from perfect in life, I do not wish to make a fool of him in death. You will stand behind that claim, won't you?"

Never in his life had he ever betrayed a woman's trust in him. He never spoke of his lovers. When he took a woman into his arms, she became his to protect: her reputation and her heart. He could do no less for Jayne. But what she asked of him, he hated with every fiber of his being. Still he nodded. "Yes."

Blast her for being so damned stubborn!

Sitting before the fireplace in his library, Ainsley drank his whiskey and cursed Walfort for actions he'd taken that caused Jayne to doubt her appeal, her judgment, her desires. He felt as though he was engaged in a war he had no idea if he could win. She was mourning the loss of so much—more than her husband. All she'd believed about her marriage had been torn asunder. Why would she trust him now when he'd known it was all a farce and held the truth from her?

He should have told her, but then she'd have thought he did it to achieve his own ends.

Now he wanted her more than he'd ever wanted anything, and he wasn't quite certain how to acquire her.

It didn't help matters that she was struggling with her loyalty to Walfort. Yes, they'd all made promises, but they could not have foreseen that everything would unravel with Walfort's passing.

"Ainsley's worried about you," Tessa said, sipping tea in Jayne's parlor. She'd arrived only a few minutes earlier, and Jayne knew immediately by her mien that the purpose to her visit had little to do with simple kindness. "He can be quite protective of those he cares for. Irritated Westcliffe no end when he was a lad because Ainsley was so much younger, but he was always seeing to things, making sure all was well."

"He has no need to worry about me. I'm not his responsibility."

"Perhaps not. But a small part of you—the part that grows inside you—is, is it not?"

Jayne felt her stomach drop. "I suppose I should not be surprised that you know everything."

Tessa gave her a gentle smile. "Not everything, but enough."

"Does everyone know, do you think?"

"By everyone I assume you mean within the family. No. Leo knows, of course, but then Leo knows everything. You would think that an artist would only look at the shell, but he has the ability to search much deeper.

I believe that's the reason his portraits are so magnificent. Of course, I'm also biased. Be that as it may,
others may begin to believe Ralph Seymour's claims in
time. Who is to say? But if I have raised my sons to be
anything, it is to be accepting. Westcliffe and Stephen
both chose their wives well, and they share the same
willingness not to judge. However, my dear, I must be
very honest with you."

She set her teacup aside and held Jayne's gaze. "I
know what it is to have a son and to keep from him
the truth about who truly sired him. It is an unbearable
burden. I also know that Ainsley is a man of honor,
whose loyalties are now torn. It will only worsen for
him once this child is born. Mourning be damned, I say.
Give this child its true father."

"You assume much, Your Grace."

"I know, m'dear. But know you will have the houses
of Westcliffe, Lyons, and Ainsley behind you. They are
a formidable trio, my sons. Few in London are willing
to incur their disfavor. Or mine, for that matter."

"It is barely a month since Walfort's passing. People
will gossip—"

"They gossip anyway."

Long after she left, Jayne sat in the parlor and stared
at nothing, her thoughts drifting back to a night when
she'd traded all she believed in for a chance to hold
something she treasured.

As though sensing its mother's distress, the child
within her kicked. Once. Twice. Thrice. It did not carry
Walfort's blood. In her selfishness to want a child, she'd
accepted Walfort's excuses and justifications in the
event this child was a boy, but now they were not so
easy to live with. If this child was a boy, would it be

fair to deny him a dukedom? Would it be fair to expose him to Ralph's accusations? What had seemed so simple then seemed so complicated now. Doors had closed and opportunities had opened. She felt lost, at a crossroads, not knowing which path to take.

Chapter 29

Please inform the marchioness that the Duke of Ainsley has come to call."

Standing in the entry hallway, Ainsley tugged off his gloves. More rumors were floating about. If ladies were calling, Jayne was certain to have heard of them. He wanted to judge for himself how much they were upsetting her.

"I fear she is not at home, Your Grace," the butler said.

Ainsley stilled. "Not at home to me, you mean? I will see her if I have to find her myself."

The butler cleared his throat. "She left for Herndon Hall this afternoon."

With a sound curse, Ainsley headed out the door.

The carriage had come to a halt some time earlier. Jayne didn't know the exact hour. She knew only that darkness had fallen, rain poured down, and a footman stood ready with an umbrella should she decide to disembark. She sent her maid in as soon as they arrived. Yet in spite of the dampness and chill seeping into her bones, she couldn't bring herself to leave the confines of the carriage.

The door clicked open. She didn't know why she wasn't surprised to see Ainsley climb inside and take the bench opposite her.

"What the bloody hell are you doing, Jayne?"

"How did you know I was here?"

"I made a call at your residence. Fairly killed my horse to catch up to you. Did you think I would let you run off without coming after you?"

"I wasn't running off. I—" She had been running away. She looked out the window toward the residence. "I can't bring myself to go in. It wasn't quite as difficult in London because we hadn't been there in so long, not since the accident. But here, for more than three years, it was everything. And everything was a lie."

"Jayne—"

"I had to leave London, Ainsley. I feel as though I'm suffocating there. You, your mother, the ladies, Cousin Ralph—I have no peace. I can't think, I can't breathe. I know so many people mean well." She released a wry laugh. "Some do not. I thought if I came here, I could at least breathe. But I can't seem to leave the carriage. I don't know what I was thinking."

"It was not my intent to suffocate you, Jayne. But I promised Walfort that I would . . . care for you. Come to Grantwood Manor, Jayne. You will be away from the madness that is London. You can heal in spirit. Give birth to your child. Return here when you are ready."

She felt the tears sting her eyes. He was not going to pressure her to marry him. It was both a relief and a disappointment. "Yes. I think I should like that very much."

* * *

It was late when they arrived at Grantwood Manor the following night. Here the only black crepe to be seen was what she wore. Here the clocks *tick-tocked*. She felt a lifting of her spirits that astounded her. She'd not realized how much she needed to get away from the oppressiveness of both the London residence and Herndon Hall.

Ainsley had been the perfect gentleman on the journey here. He'd regaled her with tales of his youth, the history of his ancestors. They'd spoken of nothing intimate. Yet there was a sense of intimacy. It was simply his way—with his silken voice and his gaze never straying from her. She told herself it was because he was always in the mode of seducer. A habit formed during years of frequenting bedchambers. His reputation surpassed that of his brothers. Did he truly believe he could give it all up for her? Did she?

She wanted to as Ainsley led her up the stairs, but then the reality of the situation came crashing around her as he opened the door to the bedchamber beside his. She was certain it had never occurred to him that she would sleep anywhere except within easy reach.

"I should sleep at the end of the hall," she said.

He shrugged. "Select whichever room you want."

She didn't want the room she'd had before. She didn't want the room where Walfort had slept. To move to another wing would be ludicrous. Strolling down the hallway, she looked into every other room. None was as big as the one he offered her. None was as inviting. She would be here until she gave birth. Her back had begun to ache on the journey, and she'd been quite miserable. She reached the end of the hallway, pivoted, and returned to the door he'd first opened for her. "I suppose this one shall do. But you are not to use the door between the bedchambers."

"I would not dream of it."

"That is a lie. I suspect you were dreaming of it on the way here."

"A small lie. Is it my fault that I find you irresistible?"

He was such a charmer, always knew the right thing to say. She wished she could trust his words. "Ainsley, do not woo me with false flattery."

"One day, Jayne, I shall convince you that I've never given you false words."

She opened her mouth to remind him—

"Omission is not false words."

"It is still a falsehood."

He shook his head.

"Would you care for a late night repast before bed?" he asked.

"Yes, thank you."

While the servants hauled up her trunks and put away her belongings, she joined Ainsley in the smaller dining room at a table with only four chairs. She sat across from him while simple fare was laid out before them. She popped a square of cheese into her mouth and followed it with a grape.

"I suspect many mothers will be disappointed that you're not in London for the Season," she said.

"They would be more disappointed if I were there and not paying attention to their daughters."

"You might be surprised. Someone might catch your fancy."

He lifted his wineglass. "Someone already has. As you well know."

"I am in mourning," she reminded him exasperatingly.

She watched his jaw clench just before he gulped down more wine. "I'm well aware of that. Just don't expect me to be too jolly about it."

She wanted to change the subject. "You and your brothers grew up here, didn't you?"

"Yes. Mother preferred Glenwood Manor to Lyons Place. Of late, however, we've been gathering for Christmas at Lyons Place. Claire has made it a true home for Westcliffe."

"Your residence already feels like a home."

"Not when I'm here alone. It's too blasted quiet."

The prospect of silence was what had driven her away from London and Herndon Hall. She didn't want to be alone with her thoughts.

He'd been devoted to her during their month at Blackmoor, but then she'd given him everything. They'd lived in a bubble, but now the bubble had burst. She had no doubt that in time he would grow weary of her. Then she would face the challenges of raising her child alone.

Following dinner, Ainsley tried to convince her to join him in the library for a bit of reading, but she retired to her room. He went to the library, but rather than grab a book, he grabbed the bottle of whiskey and headed for the garden.

Trekking beyond the house, beyond the lighted path, he reached an area blanketed in darkness except for the glow of stars and moon. He sat on the grass, opened the whiskey, and took a long draught, relishing the burning and the penetrating warmth.

Jayne was correct, blast her. He'd gone into this situation knowing he could never recognize this child. It did not stop him from wanting to nor did it prevent him from wanting her, but his desires were ill-timed. She needed to heal. This child would be born. Walfort would be recorded as its father. Ainsley would do all that he could to protect it.

Stretching out on his back on the cool ground, he stared at the stars. Their distance made them all the more appealing. Jayne said she was suffocating. He brought her here to breathe. By God, he would give her room to breathe.

Sitting by the window in her bedchamber, Jayne did not want to admit that she had enjoyed sharing dinner with Ainsley. Even when they did not speak, it was a comfort to have him near. But was that enough?

She nearly leapt out of her skin when he came bursting into the room.

"Come along. I have something marvelous to show you," he announced.

"But I'm in my bedclothes."

"Doesn't matter. There's no one to see."

He ducked into a bedchamber across the hallway and emerged with an arm filled with blankets. His excitement was contagious.

"What is it, Ainsley?"

"You have to see it to believe it."

He led her through the manor. Once outside, he said, "Grab my arm. Don't let go."

She curled her fingers around his arm and allowed him to lead her through the garden, away from the house, the lights. "We should have the torches lit."

"No, they'll interfere."

He came to a stop. She watched as his silhouette, limned by moonlight, arranged the blankets on the ground. Then he took her hand, drew her down until she was lying on the blanket, gazing at the stars. She saw one sweeping across the sky, followed quickly by another, then another.

She released a small laugh. "What's happening?"

"I don't know, but I've seen it before. It's as though the stars are racing across the sky."

"Do you think we're only allowed one wish?"

"I think you can have as many as you want."

She studied the sky. So many things to wish for. That she would have met Ainsley before Walfort. But what guarantee did she have that he'd be any more faithful? That she'd not had a month with Ainsley that caused her to doubt her affections for Walfort. But then she would not have a child.

"Is it wrong that I'm glad to be here?" she asked, not certain why the words burst forth.

"Is it wrong that I'm glad you're here?"

It was so much easier talking to the stars.

"I was not such a good wife." She'd thought saying the words would ease the burden of the guilt. It had been with her ever since she left Blackmoor. Her greatest fear was that somehow Walfort had known how she'd felt, that somehow the knowledge led to his decline.

"You were an exceptional wife."

"You were a much better friend to him than I."

"Not such a good friend. I fell in love with his wife."

He rose onto his elbow and cradled her face. "I fell in love with you while we were at Blackmoor," he admitted.

With a sad smile, she shook her head. "It was lovely

while we were there, but it was only fantasy. We had no responsibilities. It wasn't real."

"For me it was extremely real."

"Because it mostly involved the bedchamber, and that is where you spend a great deal of your life."

"Not so much as you might think. I've been with no woman since you."

She hardly knew what to say.

"I was going to take a mistress," he confessed. "But I could never work up any sort of enthusiasm for the search. Then I decided to take a wife, but no woman appealed to me. I finally realized why. None of them were you. I love you, Jayne."

This time, the words spoken with such intensity, resonated through her heart and soul.

"I have from the moment I met you," he continued. "Not deeply of course, at first. But there was a spark, a twisting of my heart, and I regretted that I'd not met you before Walfort. I thought if I had . . . that you would have become mine."

"Ainsley, please don't do this."

"I know the timing could not be worse. You are far along with child—my child. A child I want to recognize as mine. Marry me, Jayne."

He'd asked before, but she'd not taken it seriously. Now his declarations and insistence terrified her. "It would be scandalous."

"We've been scandalous before. It did not turn out so poorly." He splayed his fingers across her belly. "I want to claim this child as mine. That is what I wish whenever I see a star fall. That you and this child will be mine, and all of London will know it."

She skimmed her fingers up through his thick hair.

"You ask so much of me," she said.

He pressed a kiss to her temple, to her forehead, to her other temple. "Just consider the possibility. Truly consider it. That's all I ask."

He settled his mouth firmly over hers, taking possession as though he owned it. She let him. She welcomed him. It was more than she remembered. Perhaps because this time it wasn't the forbidden taking place in the shadows of a terrace or a good-bye that nearly tore her heart from her chest.

It was a tentative beginning, a starting over. Something they'd truly never had. Always before the scepter of scandal and the whisper of betrayal had loomed over them like black thunderclouds rolling over the lake on a winter evening.

She knew that tonight it would go no further than this: an exploring of heated mouths, soft groans, and low moans. She was not ready for more than this. Her emotions were too raw. But she took what he offered, allowed it to fill a well that had gone dry. She had longed for so much more than what Walfort could give her. And what he withheld from her had nothing to do with his paralyzed body. She knew that now.

He had always given the better part of himself to Madeline Brown, while she received the crumbs. She deserved more. She deserved everything.

From the first Ainsley had given it to her, had never held back, had always taken her needs into consideration and placed them above his own. But it wasn't the real world. It was a secluded place where they had frolicked.

Drawing back, Ainsley sipped at the corner of her mouth, then pressed his forehead against hers. "Jayne, let me sleep with you tonight. To hold you. Nothing more."

"Yes," she whispered.

Lifting his head, he gazed down on her. "Wishing upon stars seems to work."

"I want to come to know the real Duke of Ainsley."

His smile flashed in the moonlight. "You already do, sweetheart."

Over his shoulder she saw a star shoot through the sky and made a wish.

Forgive me, Walfort.

Chapter 30

When they returned to the house, he followed her into her bedchamber. She clambered onto the bed, then watched, mesmerized, as he removed his jacket and waistcoat. He didn't even bother to look in the direction that he tossed them, but they landed with unerring accuracy on the chair anyway, and she wondered how often he'd followed those same motions. His movements were fluid, confident. He sauntered over to the bed, sat on the edge, and placed her bare feet on his lap. Slowly, he kneaded the ball of one foot and then the other.

"You're so very skilled at this," she said.

He rubbed his hands over the arch of both feet. "I'm skilled at many things." His gaze holding hers, he moved his fingers in ever widening circles up to her ankles. His eyes darkened into a challenge. "But there is one thing I've never done."

His hands moved higher, carrying her nightdress with it, reminding her of their first night together. She clamped her knees together. "Ainsley, we can't."

"I'm well aware of that, but what I want now . . . I want to see your belly. I want to see where the child grows."

"Ainsley—"

How could she refuse such a heartfelt plea? Licking her lips, she nodded.

Ever so slowly, as though he were unwrapping a precious gift, he moved her nightdress up over her knees, past her hips, up to her chest. He placed his hands on either side of her waist and studied her increasing girth.

"So beautiful," he whispered. He lifted his gaze to hers, and she could see the wonder in the green. "You're so beautiful, Jayne."

Lowering his head, he placed a kiss on the spot where their child—for this moment in time it was *theirs*—grew. Straightening, he drew her nightdress back down to her ankles.

"I'm glad you're here. I'm glad the child will be born here."

He joined her that night, beneath the sheets. His body warm and familiar. Comforting. He didn't tempt them with passionate kisses or sensual caresses, but he held her near, stroked her back, her arm, her hip. They lay on their sides, facing each other, talking quietly. About his brothers and their families. About his mother and Leo. Her parents were deceased and she found a mercy in that for they would not know the questionable things she'd done.

When she fell asleep, his arms were around her, and she felt safe, protected, and, for the first time since Blackmoor, she was not lonely.

Jayne awoke alone to thunder booming and rain slashing against the windows.

After ringing for Lily, she climbed out of bed and walked to the window. It was a gray, gray day. No walks in the garden, but she could stroll through the manor. She was unfamiliar with a good bit of it. She'd only been here for the duchess's wedding. Then she'd done no exploring. Surely, he'd not mind if she did so today. She would ask him over breakfast.

But after she was dressed and went downstairs to the breakfast dining room, she discovered that he wasn't there.

"He's already eaten, my lady," the butler told her. "He's in his study now, working. Would you like me to escort you there?"

"No, that's quite all right. I shall just have something to eat and then I believe I shall stroll through the residence, if there are no objections."

"None at all. He informed me that you have leave to treat the house as though it were your own. If there is anything you want seen to, you have but to ask."

Nodding, she turned away and went to the sideboard where an abundance of food waited. She'd been unable to eat in the early months, and lost her appetite after Walfort passed, but now she was famished. She ate so much that she thought she might burst. When she was finished, she strolled through the residence, imagining herself as mistress here.

At the top of the landing, in one of the wings, was a portrait gallery. The windows stretched the length of the room. She sat in a chair and watched the storm rolling over the land. It was beautiful, yet powerful. It rivaled all the emotions roiling through her. All the feelings for Ainsley that she'd squashed were rising to the fore—so quickly, so forcefully. She loved being in his presence. Loved the way he made her feel treasured. He would do the same for the child. She couldn't imagine this child growing up and not walking within his shadow.

"Stephen proposed to Mercy there."

With a start, she smiled and glanced back over her shoulder. He looked so relaxed, so at home. To spend all her days and nights with him . . . if only this child would wait a year to be born.

Leaning down, he pressed a kiss to her forehead before sitting in the chair beside hers. "Did you eat this morning?"

"Like someone with no manners. Two plates' worth. You have a wonderful cook."

"I'll let her know."

"I could do that. See to your menus."

"You're not here to tend to my needs."

"I shall go stark raving mad if I have nothing to do, because then all I have are my thoughts for distraction. I don't like the directions they go."

"Do they want to take you away from here?"

Slowly she shook her head. "No, they consider staying."

The pleasure reflected in his eyes warmed her, and she gave her attention back to the rain. "You have no fox hunting here."

"No."

"What do you do when you entertain?"

"Shooting. Have lots of birds."

"Are you skilled with a rifle, then?"

"I'm somewhat of a marksman, yes. Considered demonstrating for Cousin Ralph."

"I don't really blame him, you know. He has so much to gain."

"But he could have gone about it differently. Should have spoken to you instead of the gossips."

"Is that what you would have done?"

"I suspect I'd have done nothing—or at the very least, I'd have given you time to mourn. Inconsiderate lout."

She smiled at his disgust with Cousin Ralph. "You take his accusations personally."

"He's threatening to make my child's life miserable. I won't stand for it, Jayne. If you don't marry me, I shall bring the full weight of my title to bear against him."

"Even if he's right?"

"It is a dilemma."

He didn't remind her that it could all go away if she married him. Cousin Ralph might not care about making her unhappy. Ainsley obviously did. She wanted to erase the furrow between his brows. She nodded toward the outdoors. "What is that building over there?"

It was brick and stone. Long. A short distance from the residence.

"My pool. I should show it to you when we go on a walk."

By afternoon the rain had stopped and they strolled through the garden. Then he took her to the pool.

It was long and narrow, the water still, except for the steam rising from the surface. Steps led down into it.

"So you just swim across it?" she asked.

"Yes. Back and forth. It's not very deep. Even if you don't swim, you could go into it."

"It would be like taking a bath in a huge tub."

He laughed. "Not exactly."

"I should like to watch you swim sometime."

"I suspect I'll be doing a good bit of it at night."

She stared at him. "Really? Why ever would you swim at night?"

He cupped her face. "You really don't understand how irresistible you are, do you?"

Tilting her head back, he lowered his mouth to hers. The kiss was gentle. An exploring, a communicating. Before him, she'd never realized that kisses could take a variety of shapes and forms. Softly, provocatively, he teased her senses. She found herself leaning into him, wrapping her arms around his waist. He undid no buttons, lifted no hems, and yet she felt as though he were making love to her.

He could convey so much with his lips, with his fingers lightly touching her cheeks, his thumbs slowly circling at the corners of her mouth. She wanted to fall into him, against him. She wanted him to lie her down and kiss all of her.

All thoughts of anything beyond the two of them disappeared when he gave her such undivided attention. Would he still be kissing her like this when they were old? Was it only the newness or perhaps the lure of the forbidden that spurred him on now?

He drew back and held her gaze. "I'll swim at night so I'll be too tired to do the wicked things I'd dearly love to do to you."

"What is the longest you've ever stayed with one woman?"

"Never compare yourself to other women."

"What if I appeal to you only because I am a challenge? If I am yours, you may very well grow tired of me."

"Never."

"You can't know that for sure."

"What I know is that I have never felt for any woman what I have felt for you. I don't know how many different ways I can say it or show you. Sometimes, Jayne, you must simply have faith."

Have faith. Have faith that he would not hurt her. Have faith that he would not cast her aside once he had her. Have faith that he truly loved her.

She hated the doubts that plagued her as the days and nights slipped by.

Every afternoon, he joined her in the garden for a walk. Sometimes they would stroll for more than an hour, talking, enjoying the flowers.

Often he would read to her in the garden. At night they would watch the stars.

She had the opportunity to observe him as he tended to the business of his estate and other properties. He was firm when he needed to be. It was obvious that those with whom he dealt respected him and valued his opinion.

She'd always heard that he'd inherited his wealth. While that was no doubt true, it was quite obvious to her that he took great pains to look after what had been entrusted to him. When troubles arose, he would discuss them with her, as though her opinion had value. He made her feel appreciated in so many ways.

And always, always, he slept with her, held her through the night.

So she was surprised one night when she awoke to find herself alone. She stroked her hand over the indentation where he'd been sleeping. The sheet was cool to her touch. He'd been gone a while, then.

She rolled out of bed, stretched to one side, then the other. Oh, her back was hurting. She needed Ainsley to rub it. Strange, how she knew she had but to ask and he would comply. He gave her so much attention, more than she'd had in her entire life. It was as though he lived for moments with her.

She padded out of the room and into the hallway. The door to his bedchamber was open, but he wasn't there. Perhaps he'd grown hungry and was enjoying a late night repast. But when she went to the kitchen, she found it empty. Then she remembered him saying that he often swam at night.

The grass was cool beneath her feet as she made her way to the building at the far side of the garden. She could barely believe that August was already here. The Season would be coming to an end. She wondered who had become betrothed. It had been so long since she was in London to enjoy the Season that she didn't even miss it. Much better to spend the warmer months here, where the air was so fresh and she could move about so easily.

When she reached her destination, she hesitated. Would he dislike being disturbed? Or would he welcome her? Welcome her, no doubt.

Opening the door, she stepped through it. The sultry warmth greeted her, coating her in dew. The light from lanterns battled the shadows, causing them to dance mysteriously between the walls. She stood there, watching his powerful muscles bunching and stretching as he sliced through the water. He was quite simply beautiful.

While she would be content whether this child was a girl or a boy, suddenly she very much wanted to have a child that resembled Ainsley. Something in her heart twisted and turned. She'd been so afraid to acknowledge her feelings for this man. They filled her with guilt. They had ever since Blackmoor.

She'd told herself that he called to only the physical in her, but they had been remarkably chaste since coming here, and still he stirred within her dreams that she'd long denied herself.

He reached the edge of the pool, turned—

And stopped, his gaze falling on her. He breathed heavily, the water lapping at his chest. Flicking his hair back, he began plowing through the water, walking toward her. "Interested in a midnight swim?"

She laughed. "No, I just woke up and you were gone. I don't know. My back was hurting. I just . . . wanted to find you."

God, she was rambling. Whatever was wrong with her?

"Come. Get in the water."

"No, I . . . I don't think it would be wise in my condition."

He started up the steps. Her eyes widened at the sight of him. "Oh, my."

She turned away.

"You've seen me without clothes before," he said, and she heard the humor laced in his voice.

"Yes, but it's been a while." He wore trousers to bed. At least here. With her.

He took her hand. "Join me in the pool, Jayne."

"I really don't think—"

"Good. I don't want you to think. I just want you to feel."

She laughed. "Ainsley, you must stop interrupting me."

"You can even keep your nightdress on."

"It'll weight me down."

"Then take it off."

She couldn't, but she didn't resist when he pulled her to the water's edge.

"Come into the water and I'll rub your back."

"Oh, you don't half tempt me."

He drew her into the curve of his body. "What would it take to tempt you all the way?"

She stared up at him. "How can you desire me?"

"How can I not? You're the mother of my child, the center of my heart."

Before she could comment, as though expecting her refutation, he was guiding her toward the steps. Her bare toes touched the water first, and she nearly groaned with the thought of how wonderful it would be to completely submerge herself in the warmth. As she went deeper into the water, her nightdress billowed out around her, then sucked in close to her body.

The water was lapping at her breasts when Ainsley began to lift her hem.

"You said I could remain clothed," she chastised him.

"I can't see anything, and you'll be more comfortable if you shed the weight."

She didn't argue. The shadows in the water did prevent him from getting a good look at how cumbersome she'd become. Once she was divested of her nightdress, he moved around behind her and began to gently knead her back.

"Oh, that's nice," she said, settling her head into the crook of his shoulder.

"There's something about the water that's very healing." Slowly, he turned her around and lowered his mouth to hers while his hands continued to roam over her.

Everywhere. Everywhere.

And she returned the favor, skimming her fingers over him, wrapping them around him.

He groaned low. "Oh, you wicked woman."

"How is it that you make me so comfortable with all this?"

"Because nothing between us should be forbidden."

Reaching up, she kissed him. She wanted him as she'd never wanted anything. She wanted—

"Oh. Oh." She pressed a hand to her side while pain swept through her.

He backed away. "What is it?"

"I'm not sure. I think . . . I think I should return to the house."

"Why?"

"I think it's time, Ainsley. The baby. I think it's time."

He grabbed her hand. "Jayne, marry me. Now. I'll send for the clergyman."

"Ainsley, I can't. Not like this."

He studied her for all of a heartbeat, and she felt something shift between them. Something unwanted. Regretfully, she realized that she finally accomplished what she had so long ago desired: to hurt him beyond imagining. But rather than solace, it yielded only pain.

He helped her out of the pool, but no warmth accompanied his touch. She found herself grieving once again.

Chapter 31

Every time Jayne screamed, Ainsley downed a glass of whiskey. It wasn't fair that he had the means to dull his pain while she didn't. What she'd felt in the pool was only the beginning. It took another day before her labor began in earnest. He'd immediately sent for the physician and his mother. He didn't know why he thought she needed to be there. Leo now sat with him in the library to wait.

Ainsley wasn't even certain why he remained. He'd given everything to Jayne. Everything. And it had not been enough.

Her screams sounded through the residence. Why did he have to feel them in the core of his being? Why couldn't he just ignore them?

"Why is it taking so damned long?" he asked.

"It's the way of it, my friend," Leo replied. "I must confess to being extremely grateful that I don't have to listen to your mother going through this."

"She's happy with you, Leo. I'm grateful for that. And that you made an honest woman of her."

"I would have long ago, but . . . past loves, like mange, are sometimes hard to be rid of."

In spite of the circumstances, Ainsley smiled.

"I'd have thought you'd be married to Jayne by now," Leo said.

"It is not my choice that I'm not." He wanted to claim this child as his with a furiousness that astounded him. But she wanted him to walk away, to honor a ridiculous agreement. He wanted the woman and the child—both as his. Openly, publicly. Mourning be damned. Etiquette be—

As her scream once more echoed through the hallways, Ainsley gripped the mantel in order to prevent himself from slamming his fist into it. What if he lost her?

Lost her? he thought. What a fool he was. He never possessed her.

"Something must be wrong," he said, gazing at the open door. Why wasn't his mother bringing him news? Didn't she realize he'd sent for her so she would keep him informed?

Women died giving birth. He couldn't imagine the world without Jayne in it. Even if she no longer resided here after the babe was born, at least she existed elsewhere. That would be enough. Just to know she was somewhere. Happy. Walking through fields with her child in tow. Surely a dark-haired child, with her blue eyes.

He heard the patter of running feet and was halfway across the library when Lily dashed through the doorway. She gave a quick curtsy. "Your Grace, her ladyship is calling for you."

"What the deuce is wrong?" He was in the hallway before he'd finished asking the question, racing through the manor, up the stairs. He burst through the door into his bedchamber.

Jayne was still abed, a mound visible beneath the sheets. She was bathed in sweat, gasping. She held out her hand to him. "Ainsley, I'm so sorry."

Rushing over, he took it, squeezed it, touched her brow. He would willingly die to take this suffering from her. "Jayne—"

"I was wrong, so terribly, terribly wrong. I hurt you. I know I did."

"It doesn't matter. I'll stand by you and the child. Just get this matter, this birth, over with. Be done with it."

"I will, but first marry me."

Stunned by her words, the last he'd expected, he stared at her. "Pardon?"

"Marry me."

"I believe I'm supposed to ask you."

"You've already asked . . . and I said no. Such a silly thing to do. I fell in love with you at Blackmoor. I think Walfort knew. I struggled with the guilt. Then when he died, I thought I didn't deserve happiness. I didn't deserve you."

"Jayne, sweetheart, I don't know anyone who deserves happiness more than you."

"Marry me then."

"I will." He smiled, brushed the hair off her brow. "As soon as—"

"Now. Before the babe is born."

He glanced at her stomach, at the physician, at the midwife, at his mother, who merely nodded.

Releasing a strangled groan, Jayne squeezed his hand. "Please. I want him to carry your name. I want him to be yours. Or her. I don't care if it's a girl or a boy. I just want there to be no doubt that it's yours. That I'm yours. That we're yours."

"Right. Mother, get Leo and send a servant for the clergyman. Hurry."

"Yes, of course." His mother dashed from the room with all the vigor of a woman a third her age.

"With all due respect, Your Grace, you'll need a special license," Dr. Roberts said.

"I have it."

Jayne smiled at him then. "I knew you would. You never leave anything to chance."

"Not when it comes to you, Jayne Seymour." Kneeling beside the bed, Ainsley pressed a kiss to her hand. "Still, you couldn't have decided this a bit sooner?"

"Guilt. It's a bloody awful— Oh, oh, oh!" She gripped his hand so tightly that he almost yelled as well.

Leaning up, he brushed his lips over hers. "I love you, Jayne Seymour, future Duchess of Ainsley, with all my heart and soul."

"Will I be enough for you?"

"You've been enough for me for a good ten months now, and a good part of that time was without all the benefits I shall enjoy as your husband. Fifty years should be no trouble at all."

"Do I look too awful . . . for my wedding?"

Her face was damp, her hair plastered to her head. She appeared so incredibly tired. To say she looked awful would be a kindness, because it was much worse. "To me, you are always beautiful."

A commotion at the door drew his attention. His mother, Leo, and the clergyman entered the room.

"You'd best make this quick," the physician said. "The babe's almost here."

It was quick. They exchanged vows, and when it came time for a ring, his mother pressed one against his palm.

"Your father gave it to me on the day we married," she said, with tears in her eyes. "It was always to be yours when you found your duchess."

And she no longer had a need for it.

Ainsley slipped it onto Jayne's finger. "With this ring, I thee wed."

"I pronounce you man and wi—"

Jayne screamed.

"Out," the physician ordered. "All the men are to leave this instant!"

The clergyman finished the words to the ceremony as he was scrambling for the door, Leo following quickly on his heels.

Only Ainsley stood his ground, still holding Jayne's hand. "You're stuck with me now."

So he was there, by Jayne's side, when his son made his entrance into the world, squalling at the top of his lungs, a thick thatch of black hair covering his head.

The tears scalded Ainsley's eyes and he blinked them back. It was done. His heart hammered out an unsteady tattoo. He felt the same sort of exhilaration he experienced during a hunt—only it was grander, more humbling. He was swirling through a riot of emotions: joy, worry, the weight of burdens, the lightness of bliss.

His heir. He had his heir. More, he had his son. And Jayne. He had Jayne.

Leaning down, he kissed her brow. "Thank you. Thank you from the bottom of my heart."

It would have tormented him to know that his child would not be entitled to his rightful legacy. Blood did matter, and this boy had Ainsley's blood pumping through him. One day he would be the Duke of Ainsley. But for now, he was the Marquess of Bellehaven.

* * *

Jayne could see it was with a great deal of reluctance that Ainsley left so the physician could finish tending to her. The babe was bathed, then so was she. The bedding was changed. She slipped into a fresh nightdress. Then she sat in bed and held the baby. She'd been so weary that she thought she would immediately fall asleep and not wake up for days. But suddenly she had a burst of energy and excitement and she wondered if she'd ever sleep again.

As the door opened, she glanced over to see her husband prowling toward her. Her husband. Why had she ever resisted the inevitable? She loved him, knew beyond a doubt that he loved her. She could see the depth of his feelings in his eyes. His gaze warmed her. She'd been content with what she had, because she'd never known anything grander.

Sitting on the edge of the bed, he leaned in to kiss her. Not brief this time. They had no audience. His mouth moved over hers with a promise for passion, a vow for pleasure.

He drew back and she saw within the green depths of his eyes that even now he still found her desirable.

"I suppose we shall have to delay the wedding trip," he said with a wicked smile.

"At least a month."

"Decide where you want to go—"

"Blackmoor," she answered without giving him time to finish.

"Blackmoor it shall be."

His gaze shifted to their son then. Their son. She could not fathom what it would have cost him to give up the child, to not acknowledge it. His depth of love, even for a friend, knew no bounds. He was quite simply the most remarkable man she'd ever known. And he was hers. As was his child.

"He's so beautiful," she whispered.

"Almost as beautiful as his mother."

She glanced up at him, wanting to judge his reaction to her next words. "I should like to call him Tristan. Tristan Augustus Seymour. If that's all right with you."

"I like it very much."

She saw the honesty of his response in his eyes. He'd never be dishonest with her.

Tristan's eyes blinked open and his little brow furrowed, his mouth puckered. Ainsley leaned in. "He has your eyes." A deep, deep blue.

"For now. The color could change. It often does with babes."

"Was it excruciatingly awful? It certainly sounded as though it was."

"At the time, but the memory is already fading. And it was very much worth it to hold this little one in my arms. Thank you, Ainsley."

"You're welcome, my duchess."

Reaching up, she skimmed her fingers over his unshaven jaw. "I did fall in love with you at Blackmoor," she said. "I should have told you then, when I was stepping out of the carriage, but I feared it wasn't real. I thought coming here would prove me right. But all it did was make me love you more." She glanced down. "I fear he will suffer for our indiscretions."

"He would have been the subject of gossip either way. But people have short memories, and more titillating gossip will shove us from minds. Soon, no one will remember that we weren't married when he was conceived. All they will see is how very much I adore you."

"And you don't really give a fig what people think."

"I don't. Besides, his is a very powerful family."

Jayne was in the nursery, putting Tristan back in the crib after a late night feeding, when Ainsley returned home from a journey to London. It had been six weeks since they were married, and she thought she would never grow tired of seeing him walk into a room. He strode over to her with purpose in every step.

When he was near enough, he drew her into his arms and kissed her as though his very life depended on it. Six weeks, and every kiss was accompanied by an urgency. Through all the nights when they could not yet make love, he had kissed her and held her and slept with her.

It was marvelous, so absolutely marvelous. He'd once told her that a kiss was simply what it was: a kiss. But with him it was everything. It need not start something more, and yet it was powerful enough to stand on its own.

It was only when they came up for air that she was finally able to ask, "Did all go well?"

"It did. There is no whisper of doubt that Tristan is my rightful heir. Unfortunately, you, however, are now as scandalous as my mother."

"I've come to rather like scandal."

He arched a brow. "There shall be no more of it."

"Only in your bedchamber." She rose up on her toes, nibbled on his wicked mouth. "Perhaps we should begin tonight."

"Are you well enough?"

She gave him a saucy smile and nodded. "I saw the physician today. I may begin my wifely 'duties.' "

"May you *never* consider it a duty." As he lifted her into his arms, his green eyes held a predatory gleam that caused her to grow warm.

She snuggled into his shoulder as he strode from the room. "I thought it was so romantic the first time you carried me to bed."

"Do you not think it romantic now?"

"I think it more so. Promise me that you'll never grow tired of me."

"I promise."

He carried her into his bedchamber and she flattened her hands against his chest. "Ainsley, I want you to kiss me."

He grinned. "With pleasure."

"No. I mean, when we're making love. I want you to kiss me and kiss me and kiss me. To make up for all the times when we didn't before."

"Ah, Jayne, here you are with rules again."

"But don't you like this one?"

"Let's just see how it goes."

How it went was wonderful.

He began by kissing her deeply and thoroughly. Slowly, provocatively. No rush, no hurry. As though they had all night. She supposed they did.

He curled one hand around her neck, holding her in place, while his mouth continued to plunder and the talented fingers of his other hand began to loosen the pearl buttons on her nightdress. She worked off his jacket and unfastened the buttons of his waistcoat.

He peeled back her nightdress and his burning mouth trailed down her throat, over her shoulder, along the swell of one breast and then the other. Wherever he went, he coated her skin in dew.

"I have missed the taste and feel of you," he said, his voice raw with desire.

"You shall never have to do without again."

Straightening, he grinned down on her. "What a vixen you have become."

"I was taught by an exceedingly talented lover."

"How fortunate for me."

He returned his mouth to hers. She could not fathom that she had been so silly to deny them before the simple pleasure of a kiss. It increased the intimacy and stoked the fires of passion. He slid the gown off her shoulders completely and it slithered to the floor. He only removed his lips from hers when he needed to. Otherwise, he was there conquering what he had already won.

Then she was standing before him naked and proud. She saw the appreciation in his smoldering gaze. He bracketed her hips.

"Your hips are wider."

"To accommodate the birth of your son."

He went down on one knee and pressed a kiss just below her navel. "I do like the changes to your body."

Unfolding his own, he took her into his arms and carried her to the bed. He shed the remainder of his clothes and stretched out beside her, once more his mouth blanketing hers.

She scraped her fingers up into his hair, holding him near, kissing him deeply. Her hands explored the familiar contours of his body. He was exactly as he'd been before. Still firm. Still sculpted. Lean and muscled. A great sinewy cat moving over her.

She would have him for the rest of her life.

His talented hands roamed over every dip, peak, and valley. His mouth left hers, to journey along her flesh, trailing across her neck, teasing the delicate underside of her chin. Lower, to her shoulders. A nip here. A love bite there. Lower still to her breasts, heavy in his palms. His tongue circled her nipple, his breath coating it in dew.

With her thighs, she squeezed his waist. With her fingers, she rubbed his shoulders. She felt the deep rumble in his chest vibrating against her stomach. There was no purpose in their coming together tonight, no pressure to get her with child.

Just like his kiss, their lovemaking owned itself. It was pleasure simply for the sake of pleasure. It was giving and receiving in equal measure. It was what it should have been all along, and she suspected that for him, it was what it had always been: a generous gifting of passion.

His mouth whispered a path to her other breast, giving it the same ministrations as it had the other. She lifted her hips, imploring him to hurry, but he would not be swayed from his quest to reexplore all that he'd once known.

"Ainsley, you're driving me to madness."

He chuckled low. "Good."

Lower he went, kissing her intimately. A swirling of his tongue, a tug on her sensitive flesh. She whimpered, moaned, dug her fingers into his arms. She wanted to fly, but not without him.

Every touch ignited sensations, and she was soon writhing beneath him, crying out for him, urging him nearer.

Rising above her, powerful and determined, he plunged into her and went still. A soft moan from him, a deep sigh from her.

It had been so long, and yet everything was so familiar, as though they were two pieces of a puzzle that had been misplaced and were suddenly found and snapped back together. This was where she belonged, she realized. Beneath him, beside him, near his heart.

"I love you, Jayne," he said in a raw voice before returning his mouth to hers.

As his body rocked against hers, as the passion built into a fervor, he kissed her hungrily. Each powerful thrust carried her higher. His kisses elevated her even higher than that.

Until there was nothing except the sensations, nothing beyond them. Just them. Moving in a fluid, familiar rhythm, his mouth latched to hers.

When the crescendo came, he captured her screams and she swallowed his groans.

Afterward, she lay snuggled against his side. "I like when you kiss me during . . ."

"I like when I kiss you. I enjoy kissing very much. Even when it's not . . . during . . ."

Laughing, she rubbed his chest. "You told me on the terrace that long ago night that a kiss need not be the start of anything, that it owns itself." Lifting herself up, she met and held his gaze. "I think the kiss that night was the start of us, Ainsley. You woke things in me that had long been asleep."

"Then why forbid me from kissing you?"

"Because it terrified me. What you made me feel. I thought as long as you didn't kiss me, I'd be able to keep my distance from you. But each moment with you only drew me nearer. The feelings I have for you still terrify me. They are so grand, so intense."

"That's good, because the love I have for you terrifies me as well. I've never loved anyone, Jayne, not like this. There is nothing I will not do for you."

"Will you kiss me again?"

"I shall always kiss you again."

And he did.

Epilogue

Grantwood Manor
Christmas Eve, 1865

Ainsley had invited his family to spend Christmas at his estate this year. Jayne had seen that everything was done to perfection: the tree, the trimmings, the meals. She was a gracious hostess, and he couldn't deny the pride he felt at her accomplishments. Holding his soon to be two-year-old daughter, Annie, on his lap while his son, nieces, nephews, and recently acquired dog played around him, he thought he'd never known such contentment.

When they went to London for the Season, they always hosted a ball. In the beginning, they had been the talk of the Town. Their hasty marriage had been the fodder for gossip. His claiming Tristan as his son sparked further rumors. But as he'd predicted, everything eventually died down, and now he and Jayne were discussed as though they were the characters of some fairy tale who lived happily ever after—if they were spoken of at all.

Other gossip reigned. Miss Brown married a viscount

who made it clear that he would see her daughters properly situated in society. Ainsley and Jayne had attended the wedding. He could say with absolute certainty that Miss Brown had chosen well. She was happy and loved.

His mother alighted gracefully in the chair beside his. "I'm not certain when you boys were growing up that Christmas was ever quite so jolly. My sons seem to have a gift for bringing joy to others."

"It's easy enough to do when one is happy in oneself."

"I would be much happier if someone were to tell me what Leo is giving me for Christmas. Obviously the size and shape tells me that it is a painting, but a painting of what exactly?"

Of the entire family circled around his mother. Leo had done it bit by bit with such skill that it was impossible to tell that the family had not all been gathered in one place but had their individual portions done within their own homes.

"Surprises are good, Mother. They keep you young."

"Leo keeps me young." She glanced around the room. "I had no idea, at the age of sixteen, when I was so terrified at the thought of marrying Westcliffe's father that I would take such a wondrous journey and acquire so much for which to be thankful."

"It wasn't always easy."

"No, but then it makes everything that much better when we acquire all that we want. And right this minute, Lady Annie, I need a curious child to come look at the tree with me." With that his mother was up and snatching his daughter from his arms. Annie squealed with delight.

"Do *not* have her unwrap your gift," Ainsley commanded.

"I cannot control where small children's fingers go." Before he could issue another order, she was strolling away.

Rising to his feet, he chuckled when he saw Leo halt her progress. Her husband knew her too well. Ainsley suspected the gift would be peered at later tonight after everyone had gone to bed. Leo would be with her when she first saw it. Ainsley had no doubt she would cry, and Leo would hold her. His mother was a fortunate woman to have in her life a man who loved her so much.

"Was she trying to get you to reveal what the portrait is?" Stephen asked as he and Westcliffe came to stand beside him.

"Indeed."

"Mother's never been good with secrets," Westcliffe said.

"With having them kept from her," Stephen clarified. "She's damned good at holding them herself."

"She told me she's writing her memoirs," Ainsley said.

"Good God," Stephen uttered. "Not sure I want to read those."

"I don't believe they're for us. I believe they're for her grandchildren."

"No," Westcliffe insisted. "My children do not need to know about their grandmother's exploits."

"I don't know. Sometimes I think maybe it's a good thing not to take everything to the grave." He would be forever grateful that Walfort had confessed his role in causing the accident. Although he still wasn't certain he believed him. But that night no longer haunted him. Although there were times when he did miss Walfort terribly. He knew Jayne had similar moments because a faraway look would come into her eyes. Then she would smile at him and everything would be all right again.

"Well, hopefully, it'll be some time before Mother's making that trip to the grave," Stephen said.

His brothers strolled away to join their wives.

Glancing around, Ainsley spotted Jayne. She was difficult to miss in her vibrant red. He loved the way she looked in that shade. But then he loved the way she looked in anything. Or nothing at all.

Catching his eye, she smiled at him and walked over. "What mischief were you and your brothers up to?"

Leaning down, he bussed a quick kiss over her lips. "None whatsoever."

"Why don't I believe you?"

"We were discussing Mother and hoping she lives to a ripe old age."

"I don't think she'd allow any other outcome to her life. She used to terrify me, you know. She was always so strong and bold. Not afraid of anything."

"Very much like you."

"You make me strong," she said, sidling up against him and slipping her arm through his. "I like celebrating the holidays here."

"I enjoy the noise of the place when everyone is underfoot, but I must confess to looking forward to getting you alone later."

She gave him a saucy look that boded well for what would transpire later.

"Claire informs me that Ralph Seymour has announced his betrothal," Jayne said.

"Jolly good for him." Since acquiring the titles, he'd proven himself to be a worthy marquess—much to Ainsley's surprise.

"I find I rather like him," Jayne said with a sigh.

"You sound disappointed."

"Not really. It's just that sometimes I remember how I almost denied him what was rightfully his—and in so doing, I would have denied our son his rightful titles. What a stubborn wench I was."

"Still stubborn."

Playfully she slapped his arm.

"Uncle."

Ainsley glanced down, not as far as he once had. "Nephew."

Viscount Waverly expertly arched a brow at him. He'd mastered the gesture only a few months earlier. "I believe we should all be allowed to unwrap one gift before going to bed."

"Do you now?"

"I discussed the matter with my brother and sister, as well as my cousins, and they are all in agreement."

"We do not run a democracy here, Nephew."

"No, but you are outnumbered."

"Thinking of going into the military, are you?"

"No, but Rafe probably will. He likes to play with his soldiers. Is that what you got him? More soldiers?"

"No." He'd purchased telescopes for each of the children. Small ones that would fit in their hands. The one he had inherited from his father he would give to Tristan someday. But not yet. "Tell you what, Waverly. If I am allowed to select the gift to be unwrapped, then one gift shall be opened tonight."

The lad narrowed his eyes and then nodded.

"Then let's get to it. You may open the gift from your aunt Jayne and myself."

* * *

An hour later, each child had unwrapped his or her telescope. Bundled in their coats, with their parents guiding them, they were now gazing at the heavens in wonder, searching for falling stars. Nearby his mother—still holding Annie—stood with Leo, all of them with smiles as bright as the moon.

Ainsley knelt beside Tristan and helped him peer through his telescope. "Do you see the moon?"

"I could touch it."

"Not quite, but almost. Now search for the stars."

Standing, he smiled as Jayne wandered over to him.

"I believe the gifts are a success," she said.

"Hopefully they'll learn that there is so much they can reach for."

He glanced around at Westcliffe holding Claire, Stephen with his arm around Mercy, and his mother snuggled against Leo's side. They'd all taken different journeys to arrive here, but here they were. And he was glad of it.

"Uncle?"

"Yes, Nephew."

"I spied one. A falling star. What do I do now?"

"Why, lad, now you think about what your heart desires and you wish for it."

"Will it come true, Papa?" Tristan asked.

"Absolutely."

"You sound quite sure of yourself," Jayne said.

Wrapping his arm around her, he drew her in against his side, where she belonged. Where she would always belong. "I have proof. The first time that we gazed at the stars at Blackmoor, I wished that you would love me."

"Oh, I think that would have happened without any wishes. I love you so much, Ainsley."

While the children gazed at the heavens, he sought his own heaven, lowering his mouth to Jayne's and kissing her deeply. He no longer had a need for wishes, because he already possessed everything his heart would forever desire.

Benjamin Franklin is credited with creating the first catheter, and its use had increased by the Victorian era. However, physicians still didn't know about the importance of sterilization. So a device that gave Walfort more freedom would eventually lead to his demise, by introducing bacteria into his system. Today we would know his illness was septicemia, but his doctors would have only known he had a deadly fever.

I wish to acknowledge Suzanne Welsh, R.N., for helping me understand how Walfort might have died, the symptoms he would have exhibited, what the physicians might have deduced, and how quickly he would have declined. Any misrepresentations of the medical aspects of this story are mine. In addition, I suspect, in reality he would have been delirious with fever. I hope, dear reader, you will forgive me for keeping him lucid, but he had much to account for and strive to make right.

I have long been fascinated by stories of women discovering that their husbands have another family they knew nothing about, and that fascination served as the basis for this story. At his core, Walfort was not a bad man. He was simply terribly flawed. I hope you're as happy as I am that Jayne and Ainsley found each other.

Next month, don't miss these exciting new love stories only from Avon Books

Wicked In Your Arms by Sophie Jordan
Though she's the illegitimate daughter of London's most despicable lowlife, Grier Hadley possesses the allure of an elite. And though he's a proper prince expected to marry someone of similar breeding, Sevastian Maksimi can't seem to keep his eyes off of the wild vixen. All it takes for these two is one kiss to blur the lines of class, desire and love.

His Darkest Salvation by Juliana Stone
Returning from a stint in hell, shapeshifter Julian Castille has one thing on his mind: to win back his soul. So when past flame and fellow shifter Jaden DaCosta reignites their passion, Julian's initial reserve melts under the heat. But with their souls on the line, this infatuation may prove fatal as they fight for their immortality.

The Amorous Education of Celia Seaton by Miranda Neville
Seeking revenge on the man who ruined her London season, Celia Seaton takes advantage of Tarquin Compton's amnesia by pretending to be his fiancée. As time passes by, the two fall helplessly in love and—repeatedly—in bed! Then his memory returns. Can the two overcome the lies of the past while embracing the truths of the future?

A Scoundrel's Surrender by Jenna Petersen
Years ago, overcome with a secret too scandalous to share, Caleb Talbot abandons his lover without explanation. Now, years later, the two unexpectedly reunite in London, and Caleb knows he's made a terrible mistake. As he tries to win Marah Farnsworth back, will Caleb be caught up in his painful secret or will true love prevail?

At Avon Books, we know your passion for romance—once you finish one of our novels, you find yourself wanting more.

May we tempt you with . . .

- **Excerpts** from our upcoming releases.

- Entertaining **extras**, including authors' personal photo albums and book lists.

- Behind-the-scenes **scoop** on your favorite characters and series.

- **Sweepstakes** for the chance to win free books, romantic getaways, and other fun prizes.

- Writing **tips** from our authors and editors.

- **Blog** with our authors and find out why they love to write romance.

- **Exclusive content** that's not contained within the pages of our novels.

Join us at
www.avonbooks.com

AVON *An Imprint of* HarperCollins*Publishers*
www.avonromance.com

FTH 0708